THE
WITCH'S BOY

Also by KELLY BARNHILL

The Mostly True Story of Jack
Iron Hearted Violet
The Girl Who Drank the Moon

Praise for THE WITCH'S BOY

"With its family secrets, dark and enchanted forest and resourceful children, *The Witch's Boy* echoes the spirit and tone of old Grimm's fairy tales . . . This spellbinding fantasy begs for a cozy chair, a stash of Halloween candy and several hours of uninterrupted reading time."

—*The Washington Post*

"Barnhill creates an absorbing world of kingdoms and prophecies in which transformation comes through language, and through courage and self-awareness as well . . . [*The Witch's Boy*] should open young readers' eyes to something that is all around them in the very world we live in: the magic of words."

—*The New York Times*

★ "Warring nations, mysterious stone figures, and the running thread that magic is alive and dangerous all add to the gripping core narrative of two children who find wells of strength and ingenuity from being pushed out of their comfort zones . . . Offer [*The Witch's Boy*] to Gaiman and Wynne-Jones fans, and to realistic fiction buffs who are open to brilliant coming-of-age stories sharing space with touches of magic."

—*The Bulletin of the Center for Children's Books*, starred review

★ "The classic fantasy elements are all there, richly reimagined, with a vivid setting, a page-turning adventure of a plot, and compelling, timeless themes."

—*Kirkus Reviews*, starred review

★ "A classic origin-quest tale . . . brimming with a well-drawn, colorful supporting cast, a strong sense of place, and an enchanted forest with a personality to rival some of the best depictions of magical woods."

—*School Library Journal*, starred review

THE
WITCH'S
BOY

KELLY BARNHILL

ALGONQUIN YOUNG READERS 2015

Published by
Algonquin Young Readers
an imprint of Algonquin Books of Chapel Hill
Post Office Box 2225
Chapel Hill, North Carolina 27515-2225

a division of
Workman Publishing
225 Varick Street
New York, New York 10014

First paperback edition, Algonquin Young Readers, September 2015.
Originally published in hardcover by Algonquin Young Readers, September 2014.
Printed in the United States of America.
Published simultaneously in Canada by Thomas Allen & Son Limited.
Design by Neil Swaab.

LIBRARY OF CONGRESS CATALOGING-IN-PUBLICATION DATA
Barnhill, Kelly Regan.
The witch's boy / Kelly Barnhill.—First edition.
pages cm
Summary: When a Bandit King comes to take the magic that
Ned's mother, a witch, is meant to protect, the stuttering, weak boy
villagers think should have drowned rather than his twin summons
the strength to protect his family and community, while in the woods,
the bandit's daughter puzzles over a mystery that ties her to Ned.
ISBN 978-1-61620-351-1 (HC)
[1. Fantasy. 2. Magic—Fiction. 3. Witches—Fiction. 4. Robbers
and outlaws—Fiction. 5. Twins—Fiction. 6. Brothers—Fiction.
7. Friendship—Fiction.] I. Title.
PZ7.B26663Wit 2014
[Fic]—dc23   2014014704

ISBN 978-1-61620-548-5 (PB)

10 9 8 7 6 5

To Jake Sandberg—
cousin, co-adventurer, associate schemer,
and my first best friend—
this book is lovingly dedicated.

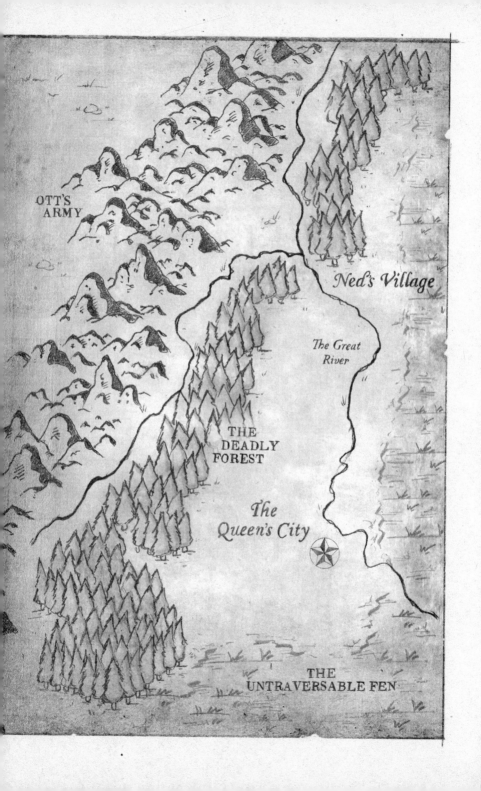

1

———

THE TWINS

ONCE UPON A TIME there were two brothers, as alike to one another as you are to your own reflection. They had the same eyes, the same hands, the same voice, the same insatiable curiosity. And though it was generally agreed that one was slightly quicker, slightly cleverer, slightly more wonderful than the other, no one could tell the boys apart. And even when they thought they could, they were usually wrong.

"Which one has the scar on his nose?" people would ask. "Which is the one with the saucy grin? Is Ned the smart one, or is it Tam?"

Ned, some said.

Tam, said others. They couldn't decide. But surely, one was better. It stood to reason.

"For god's sakes, boys," their exasperated neighbors would sigh, "will you stand still so we may look at you properly?"

The boys would not stand still. They were a whirlwind of shrieks and schemes and wicked grins. They would not be pinned down. And so the question of which one was the quick one, the clever one, the more wonderful one, remained a subject of some debate.

One day, the boys decided it was high time that they built a raft. Working in secret, and with great attention to detail, they constructed it using scraps of lumber and bits of rope and cast-off pieces of broken furniture and sticks, careful to hide their work from their mother. Once they felt the vessel was seaworthy, they slid it into the Great River and climbed aboard, hoping to make it to the sea.

They were mistaken. The vessel was not seaworthy. Very quickly, the rushing currents pulled the raft apart, and the boys were thrown into the water, fighting for their lives.

Their father, a broad, strong man, dove into the water, and though he could barely swim, struggled through the current toward his children.

A crowd gathered at the edge of the water. They were afraid of the river—afraid of the spirits that lived in the water who might snatch a man if he wasn't careful and pull him toward the dark muck at the bottom. They did not dive in to assist the man or his drowning children. Instead, they called out helpful comments to the terrified father.

"Mind you keep their heads above the water when you drag them back," one woman yelled.

"And if you can only save one," a man added, "make sure you save the *right* one."

The current separated the boys. The father couldn't save them both. He kicked and swore, but as he reached one boy—the closer boy—his twin had been swept far down the length of the river and out of sight. His body washed ashore later that day, swollen and aghast. The people gathered around the small, dead child and shook their heads.

"We should have known he'd bungle it," they said.

"He saved the wrong one. The wrong boy lived."

2

A SHARP NEEDLE AND
A BIT OF THREAD

THE WRONG BOY WAS barely alive. He had swallowed so much of the murky river that his small belly swelled. His lungs sagged under the weight of water—they slurped and wheezed and wouldn't hold air. His father gently laid the boy on the ground and tipped back his chin. He pressed his lips to the boy's lips and blew his own breath into the boy's mouth, again and again and again.

"Don't be scared," the father whispered. "Don't be scared." But if he was talking to the boy or to himself, no one could tell.

The boy didn't breathe.

"Come on, Neddy," the father said. "My little, little Ned. Come now and wake for Papa. Open your eyes."

But the boy didn't open his eyes. Finally, after several breaths forced into his mouth, Ned gasped. He coughed and coughed again, as river water cascaded in great gushes from his mouth. He breathed, though not very well. His lips were blue and his skin was as pale as bone. The father removed his coat and wrapped it around his son.

Ned coughed violently, his small body rattling from his eyebrows to his toes.

"The sea, Tam," he sighed. "Th-th-the s-s-sea..." He shuddered. His teeth clattered and clacked. His father gathered him into his arms and carried him home.

By the time they arrived, Ned was insensible with fever, and his father could not wake him.

Back at the river, a handful of men and women from the village walked quietly down the long, lonely shore to retrieve the body of the drowned twin. The boys' mother waited, seated on a rock, straight backed, her fingers shirring the fabric of her dress, gathering fistfuls of skirt and letting it slip through her open hands, over and over again. Her eyes gazed at nothing. She had a name, but no one used it. Her children called her Mother, her husband called her Wife, and everyone else called her Sister Witch. She was a woman of power, both loved and resented, and she was listened to—*always*.

"All that magic," the people muttered among themselves as they cradled the dead boy in their arms and carried him back, "and for nothing. She cannot save her own children. What on earth was the point?"

Sister Witch was the keeper of a small store of magic—one so ancient and so powerful that everyone knew it would kill a man if he touched it—but it did her no good. Her magic could only be used in the service of others. (This is what people believed, and Sister Witch allowed it. They were only wrong by one word. *Should*. It only *should* be used for others. It was a dangerous thing, her magic. With consequences.)

"Stupid," people said. "A waste."

But some, who remembered the help they had received from the magic worker—their sicknesses erased, their crops rescued, their lost children miraculously found—who were still grateful, pressed their hands to their mouths to stop their grief. "Poor Sister Witch," they said. "The poor, poor thing." And their hearts broke, just a little.

The boys' mother heard the muttering, but did not respond. People would think what they liked, and would likely think wrong. This was nothing new.

Finally, as the light of the day began to slant and thin, the dead child was brought to his mother. She sank to her knees.

"Sister Witch," an older woman said. Her name was Madame Thuane and she was the youngest member of the Council of Elders. Though she was normally imperious and stuffy, not to mention suspicious of the witch, the presence of the dead child seemed to break her. Her eyes flowed and her voice cracked. "Let me bring you a cloth to wrap him in. And we shall lay him out as tender as can be."

"No, thank you," Sister Witch said. No one could help her. Not this time. She ignored the eyes of her neighbors on her back as she

6

laid the boy's head on her shoulder and wound her arms around his body and carried him home for the last time.

The house, when she arrived back, was quiet and sad. Her husband lay on the floor next to the bed, fast asleep, utterly exhausted by worry and grief.

Ned, her living child, struggled for breath. His lungs were dank and muddy. The Great River boiled inside him, its fever claiming the victim who should have drowned. There was little chance the boy would survive the night. Not without help.

"Oh no," Sister Witch whispered. "That will not do at all. My little Ned will live."

She went to her sewing basket and retrieved a spool of strong, black thread. She pulled out her sharpest needle and, running the tip of it along the edge of a whetstone again and again, made it so sharp that the merest touch on her finger produced a tiny bloom of red, red blood.

She paused, brought her wounded finger to her lips and sucked the blood away. She closed her eyes and looked, for a moment, as though she was coming to a decision.

Should not. Not could not.

The house's beams creaked and the rafters rattled and a foul smoke leaked through the floorboards.

The house stank of magic—sulfur, then ash, then a blistered sweetness.

The magic, she knew, was awake, and listening and hungry.

It wanted *out*.

"You stay where you are," Sister Witch chided. "I'll not be needing you." The magic—an ancient, foul-tempered thing—said nothing at first. It was trapped inside its clay pot and secured in Sister Witch's workshop—a dry, sandy room dug out under the house, accessible only by the trapdoor hiding under the rug. It rocked on its shelf, knocking its pot against the wall.

You can't do it without us. The magic did not say this aloud, but Sister Witch could feel it all the same. *Come now, you bossy old meanie. Let us out. We want to help.*

"I mean it," she said, though her voice had much less conviction than before. "I'll be fine on my own. And you'll just muck it up."

The magic muttered a rude word, but Sister Witch ignored it.

Fuming and fussing, it rattled its pot against the shelf, and then was silent. A tight, dry, listening sort of silence, as though it was holding its breath.

"There's a dear," Sister Witch said out loud, as though praising a petulant child. Then she set to work.

She rummaged in her linen chest until she found a bit of white cloth—not as clean as she hoped, but clean enough.

It is not enough, the magic whispered.

"I'm not listening to you," Sister Witch said as she attempted to scratch off the spots with her thumbnail.

Come now, the magic urged. *Death is not for the powerful and it certainly is not for the clever. The boy need not die. Do you even know where the dead go? Neither do we, and we do not intend to. Let us help, Witchy Dearest. Please.*

She would not let the magic help. This is what she told herself

8

as she kicked the rug away from the trapdoor. She would not use the magic for personal gain. This is what she told herself as she crept down the ladder and faced the clay pot on the shelf.

"This isn't magic," she said, as she set the skein of thread on top of the pot. The clay pot shuddered and smoked. The thread glowed orange, then yellow, then blue, then white. It shimmered.

Ah! The magic sighed. *Ah, ah! We knew—*

"SILENCE," she ordered, and the magic obeyed. She wrapped the thread in the cloth, and scurried up the ladder, as though burned.

The thread was terribly heavy.

It hurt her hands to hold it.

"It isn't magic," she said out loud, as though she could will it true.

And it wasn't magic after all. Not really. The thread never actually touched the power inside the clay pot. It was only *near* it. There's a big difference between *almost* and *actually*. Just as there was a difference between *should* and—

She shook the thought away.

Tam's body lay on the kitchen table—cold, swollen, and horribly still. Sister Witch sat next to him, running her hand along his cheeks and his brow, letting her fingers twist in those dark, damp curls. And she waited for the sun to set.

When someone dies, the soul stays trapped inside the body until nightfall. And then it emerges and goes . . . elsewhere. No one knew where. Sister Witch had seen this, many times. But she had never interfered.

Until now.

The sun hovered over the edge of the sky, lurid and fat as an overripe peach, before slumping toward night. The light oozed overhead in garish colors; it was a sky that announced itself.

Ned coughed and sighed. "T-t-tam," he whispered through his dreaming.

"Soon," his mother said to her living son across the room. She leaned in and kissed each eyelid of the dead twin. "Very soon."

The sun widened, rippled, and disappeared under the lip of the land. Tam's body shuddered slightly, and she watched as his soul uncurled from his mouth, just as she knew it would. And, oh! It was beautiful! The soul sprouted slowly, unfolded petal by petal, before opening like a flower and hovering before her. Sister Witch felt her breath catch. My child! She thought. My little, little child. She threw the white cloth over the soul and swaddled it like an infant. She clutched it to her chest, crooning all the while.

The soul fluttered and wiggled in its wrapping. It shuddered and squirmed under the white cloth, desperate to get away.

"I know, darling," she whispered to the soul. "I know my sweet, sweet boy. I'm sorry. But I won't lose both of you. Not at once. Indeed, I cannot bear it."

She kept her voice even and light. But her heart was breaking in her body. It shattered to pieces. And it would never heal. She brought the soul to her lips, kissing it gently.

"Stay with your brother," she said as she pressed the soul to the dying boy's chest. "Keep him alive," she said as she readied the needle. "Keep him safe," she said as she untangled the thread, slicing off a section with her teeth.

And, as she pierced both soul and boy, as she stitched the two together, she said this:

"Mother loves you. Don't forget it."

And, in the darkness, and in that grieving house, the soul opened its throat and screamed.

And the scream became a sigh.

And the sigh became a cough.

And Ned began to heal. And he lived.

3

THE STONES

I T WAS EVENING, AND the shadow of the trees cut across the smallest and youngest of the Nine Stones.

If she had eyes, she would have opened them.

If she had a mouth, she would have yawned. Or even smiled.

"I'm awake," she said, astonished. *Something* had woken her, though she had no idea what.

"We all are," another Stone said. The Sixth, she thought. It had been so long—so very long—since she had heard any of their voices. Indeed, she had quite forgotten them.

"Does that mean—" she stopped. She couldn't even *say* it.

"Perhaps," the other voice said. The one that may or may not have belonged to the Sixth. "We can hope. Or we can despair and go back to sleep. It doesn't matter either way."

"I'll hope," the youngest Stone said. Her voice was small and thin and brittle. It crinkled at the edges.

"*Don't*." The Eldest. She'd know his voice anywhere. It rumbled under the earth and buzzed against the sky. It sent rocks rolling and pebbles spilling out of the riverbeds. It was a voice that mattered. "The last time we hoped, there was war. And loss. And pain. And there's more coming. I can *feel* it."

The eldest Stone was silent for a long time. Minutes. Hours. Days. What is time to a Stone? The Youngest started to wonder if he had forgotten about her.

Then: "*Wait*. Don't hope. Don't wish. Don't despair. Just wait. Our prison was our fault, and our redemption will come in a flash—or not at all. It is not ours for the choosing."

And so they waited, the Nine Stones together. They waited and waited and waited.

4

THE WRONG BOY

NED'S FEVER FINALLY SUBSIDED, but he wasn't the same. His step slowed, his eyes no longer glittered, and his laugh left him completely. He sat in the corner in a stupor, making small dolls from scraps of fabric, and hugging them to himself. His eyes were tight; his mouth was set. He wouldn't speak.

"He'll come 'round," his mother said firmly, as if just saying the words would make it so. "Just you wait."

But he didn't. Not for ages.

The stitches on Ned's chest, so cruel they looked at the time, had melted into his skin just moments after she made them—they could not be undone. An unforeseen consequence. One of many. When she pressed her hand to his chest, she felt the beating of his heart—and the flutter of something else. She closed her eyes. She imagined that beautiful soul. She told herself it was for the best.

"You are simply yourself," she said to Ned, though she knew it was a lie.

"And you are loved," she added. Which was true.

But did he believe her? Sister Witch had no idea.

Her husband, meanwhile, had taken to spending all day and most of the night at the mill, or in the forest, or chopping wood for the woodpile. There was enough wood towering behind the barn to build another house. Or construct an enormous raft to sail the sea or to save a boy from drowning. *It's not your fault,* she told him over and over. But it didn't help. She watched him, that gray skin, those leaden eyes, his mouth frozen in a frown. He was not a tall man, but he had ox-broad shoulders and limbs as thick as tree trunks. Still, each day he bent under the weight of his guilt and his sadness, a great millstone around his neck. He couldn't look at Ned.

Well, it stood to reason. Ned had his brother's face.

(And more than just his face, Sister Witch thought grimly.)

And still, Ned said nothing. *The fever,* Sister Witch told herself. *The grief.* But as the years passed, Ned's silence grew and grew. It pressed upon his face and his body. It leaked into the house and spread outward into the yard. His silence had weight. It had substance and presence and teeth. And people noticed.

The longer he said nothing, the more people whispered *wrong boy,* and the less power Sister Witch had to combat it. The phrase, it seemed, had stuck.

And so Ned grew.

The wrong boy, the village said.

The wrong boy, the world said. Year after year after year.

And Ned believed it.

5

ÁINE

FAR AWAY, ON THE other side of the world, a girl named Áine lived with her mother and father, whom she loved very much. When Áine was very small, her mother was a fisherman—the most skilled and honored of any along the coast. Her skills at navigating were legendary, and it was said that she had journeyed farther into the uncharted portions of the sea than anyone ever before had. From her mother, Áine learned to manage a craft, to read the water, to chart a course, and to wrestle a fish and ride out a storm. Everyone said that she'd be as good as her mother someday.

But then her mother's vision suddenly went dark.

And then the shaking started. And the fits that lasted for hours.

Soon the beloved fishing boat had to be sold to buy medicines to keep the illness at bay. And the maps were sold. And the tools were sold. Heirlooms. Rings. Winter boots. A wedding dress. Even her mother's spyglass. Everything that could be traded for coins was brought to the marketplace—anything to make her improve. And the medicines worked. Until they did not.

And when Áine was only ten years old, her mother began to die.

During those last moments, Áine sat at the sickbed, still trying to coax broth into those blistered lips, still trying to dab the fever away with a cool, wet cloth, still trying to save her. By now her mother's eyes were bloodshot and sightless, with a thick yellow slick creeping across the whites. She licked her lips and gasped, grabbing Áine's hand.

"The wrong boy," her mother whispered, her voice as rough and dry as a mouthful of sand. She coughed. "The wrong boy will save your life, and you will save his. And the wolf—" She choked and shuddered.

But what a wolf had to do with boys (right, wrong, or otherwise) Áine's mother didn't say. Instead, she pressed her hand against Áine's heart one last time, before letting it drift back down to the bed. And soon her shallow breathing stopped, and she was gone.

Now Áine, being a practical girl, an industrious girl, and not prone to sentimentality or grief, didn't waste time weeping. She loved her mother and missed her terribly, but crying couldn't get the washing done or the bread made or soup cooked, and it certainly couldn't bring her mother back from the dead. Besides, Áine's father wept enough for the two of them.

Áine's mother had taught her well. She knew how to keep a

house clean and warm and safe. She knew how to tie nets by hand and use them to snatch a fish from the city sloughs and preserve them with smoke and salt. She could stretch a roast from dinner to breakfast to a stew that would last a week or more. She knew how to drive a hard bargain at the marketplace—which was handy because her father had locked himself in his room with a jug of wine and his howling sadness. He stopped going to the shop where he worked. He stopped speaking. His tears flowed like swollen rivers and threatened to drown the both of them. Áine waded through the swamp of her father's grief.

Meanwhile, the coins in the jar grew fewer and fewer, until they disappeared altogether. Meanwhile, the oil jug grew lighter and the pantry thinned and the bean pot was as empty as Áine's heart. Even the fish deserted them.

Eventually, the shopkeeper came to the house and said that her father need not return. Shortly after that, their landlord told them to pack up their things and find a new place to live. Áine was finally at a loss. She went into her father's room and woke him up.

"Father," she said. "The shopkeeper says that you needn't come back, and the landlord says that we must move, and there are no more coins in the jar, so I cannot buy flour, so I cannot bake bread. And there is no soup on the stove because we ran out of meat." Potatoes, too, Áine thought. And lentils. And fish. And salt. And any other bit of food that might have been sliced into the pot. In her mind, she calculated how much was needed to keep them fed through the week. Through the month. Through the year. *Where would the money come from?* She had no idea.

Her father dried his eyes and sat up. He was a big man. A giant. His red hair blazed as though his mind was on fire, and his face had the cunning look of a bandit—for that was what he was, before Áine was born, though she did not know it. Not yet. He ran his hand over his red beard, pulling it to a sharp point, and tilted his head at his daughter. His face softened. He pressed his lips together as though he was coming to a decision. "So, my flower," he said slowly, laying his great, broad hand on her cheek, and leaning over to kiss her forehead. "You're saying we have nothing, then?"

Looking back on it, Áine wished she had taken greater notice of the strange gleam that appeared in her father's eye at the mention of the word *nothing*. As though the word itself, or the fact of *nothing*, was a magic thing. A talisman of power, or doom.

"Nothing at all?" he pressed. The gleam deepened.

"No father," she said carefully. "I would never say we have *nothing*." (Again! That gleam! Why had she not noticed it?) "We have our hands and our heads and strong backs. That's always *something*. Mother always said that sharp wits are more valuable than a castle full of gold." The girl swallowed and closed her eyes. She missed her mother so much she thought she might break in half. "And she was always right."

Her father's green eyes crinkled at the edges, and each crease held a slick of a tear. He tilted his head back and let out a cry that sounded at first like a wail but turned into a huge, booming laugh. His voice was brittle and bright and sharp—as though his sadness had shattered suddenly, spangling the dusty floor with glittering shards. He stood, grabbed his daughter by the waist, and swung her around as though she weighed no more than a measure of wheat. He sat her on his shoulder like a bird.

"Indeed, my daughter, my treasure, my hope," he sang. "The world is large and nimble and rich! And this village is too tiny for people as clever as us. Pack our things, my angel, and let us be off!" He set her lightly on the ground, grabbed his hood and his boots and an empty leather sack, and set off into the night. "I'm off to gather supplies, my flower!" he called from outside. "Assemble your possessions. We leave before moonrise!"

There was little to pack. So much of what they owned had already been sold. What little they had fit easily into a small rucksack—with room to spare. What was left of her mother's things—papers, a couple of sensible dresses, bundles of journals and Áine didn't know what else—remained sealed in their leather-lined box. That she would *not* leave behind. She sat on the box and waited for her father.

She didn't know how he would purchase what they needed with no money, but her father astonished her by coming home with a full purse hanging from his belt and the once-empty sack, now very full and very heavy, slung over his shoulder.

"Father—" she began.

"No questions," he said. His eyes were bright and feral, his cheeks flushed. His gaze darted this way and that, as though they were, already, beset by enemies. "Come! To our horses!"

"We have no horses!" Áine protested.

"We do now," her father said with a wild, wicked grin. He grabbed her arm with one hand and their possessions with the

21

other and pulled what was left of their life in that house into the darkness outside.

They traveled east over desert, over grassland, over swamp, and through the mountains, until they came to a deep, dark wood. The largest forest in the world, people said.

Áine pressed her hand to her mouth and tried not to scream. "We cannot go in there," she gasped. The forest was an enemy, made long ago by the magic of the wicked Speaking Stones. It destroyed cities and farms and murdered untold numbers of people. And even now it was cursed, its trails wandered and shifted and its trees were foul-tempered and malicious. Everyone knew that. Áine had known the story for as long as she could remember.

"Do not be frightened, my love," her father said. He reached out and laid his hand on the first tree. Áine watched in astonishment as the tree straightened itself, just a bit. And before her eyes, a trail emerged, broadening as she gazed.

"Father . . ."

"Not every story is true," her father said. "And sometimes the things that were wicked become the things that save us, and the things that were good doom us to misery and pain. We lift our eyes to the heavens, but we live on the ground. Come. Let me show you."

Her father wasn't afraid, so neither was Áine. They made their way down the shadowed trail.

He had grown up in this wood, he told her, and was a young man in this wood, and would have lived there forever had it not been for the love of a good woman who wanted a simple, honest life in the village. But then she died. He told Áine that the wood meant her no harm, and would provide a life for them.

Not, by any means, an honest life. *Banditry.* She did not say the word out loud, and her father didn't explain, but the fact of it remained. The word hovered between the two of them, like a cloud.

It's what he was. *Before.* She understood it now.

He found the house he grew up in—a tiny thing made of stones and timbers, with a mossy roof, hidden in a thicket of trees next to a waterfall and a deep pool. (*No fish,* Áine noticed at once. They were too far upstream. Pity.) There was even a dilapidated barn. He made her wait outside, and he rummaged through the house for a moment or two. Finally, she heard her father let out a whoop of joy, and he came out the front door looking somehow taller, stronger, and more wild than when he went in. He wore something around his neck—a bit of stone that looked very much like an eye tied up with a thin strap of leather.

"Father," Áine began, "what's that around your—"

"No questions," her father barked, his face suddenly stormy, the eye around his neck flashing bright. Áine recoiled, but relaxed when the stormy look was replaced by an expression of such gentleness, such grace, that she convinced herself that she must have imagined that anything was amiss. "We have no time for questions, my flower. Look! Our new home!"

It was a mess, but Áine loved it. Within the week it was as tidy and clean and homey as any merchant's house in their old city. Áine's father rebuilt the barn, and taught her how to hunt with a bow, how to coax food from the ground, and which mushrooms and berries and roots and mosses were safe to eat. He snatched milking goats and laying hens, and every once in a while, a barrel of wine.

He warned her about the wolves. "Mind you shoot them before they rip out your throat," he said darkly. "Never trust a wolf."

Every time he said this, she felt the outline of her mother's hand, pressing over her heart.

After that, they always had enough to eat. And Áine was happy. Mostly. She loved the wood, and she loved her father, and both loved her in return. And though sometimes, when she lay in bed, the wind in the trees sounded so very much like the ocean that she felt a sob pierce her chest like a needle, she knew it was for the best.

The river by her house flowed to the sea, after all. And that would have to be enough.

And it *was* enough. Until it wasn't.

6

————

A VISIT FROM THE QUEEN

NED WOKE, AS ALWAYS, before the sun rose. He pulled on his tunic, and then, noticing the chill in the air, pulled on another one. His father, in the other room, snored prodigiously, rattling the floorboards and the windows, and jittering the dishes. His parents would wake soon, and he preferred to be out of sight when they did. Sliding his feet into a pair of goatskin boots, each as soft and worn as slippers, he padded silently out into the yard. His house, like most houses he had ever seen, was built of river stones and mortar with a timber framed roof. It was a pleasure to climb.

Ned greeted every morning from the roof beam of the house, regardless of the weather. He liked to watch the world *start*. The sky was deep purple and soft gray. Mist clung to the fields, obscuring the view and blurring the world.

He reached into his tunic pocket and pulled out a bit of wood and a very sharp knife, and began to carve out a figure. This he also did every morning. It was a thing he was good at—not that anyone knew. How could they? Each evening, he took his carving to the shore of the Great River and placed it in a paper boat, launching it into the current. He showed his figures to no one, and he never saw them again.

He hoped they made it to the sea.

The sky lightened by inches as Ned worked, his two legs splayed down the mossy slopes of the roof. He could hear his mother and father begin to rouse themselves inside the house. He heard their low murmurs and their hurried ministrations. He heard his name being spoken with a heaviness in their voices, as though it were a great burden. They were getting ready to go to the village for the Queen's Jubilee—a countrywide celebration of her seventy years of benevolent rule. The queen had spent the previous months travelling from village to village to mark the occasion, and now, at last, she made it to Ned's own. His was the farthest out, the most remote, and the most unfashionable village in the whole kingdom.

Next to Ned's village was the forest.

No one went into the forest. Not soldiers. Not warriors. No one. Except for Ned's father, the woodsman. Only he was brave enough.

Still, there would be crowds and food and singing and merry-making. And people attempting to look their best. And sidelong glances that Ned could *feel*. He could always feel them. His parents intended for him to join them at the festivities. They had made themselves very clear.

But he wouldn't go, he told himself. He wouldn't.

He focused on the carving. The knife he held was small and clever—a bone handle and a blade made from polished steel. It responded to the slightest touch. Ned gave his figure a three-buttoned coat and the high boots of a woodsman. He carved curly hair, bright eyes, and a sideways smile. There was, of course, a resemblance to Ned himself, save one key distinction: Ned never smiled.

Nearly an hour after his parents woke, his mother and father walked into the yard. His father wore the same coat and boots that he always did, but she was wearing her second-best dress and her twice-dyed purple cloak. Usually, she only went out in simple browns, but today was special. It was not enough, apparently, to *be* a woman of power: She needed to look like it too. "Ned," his mother called from the vegetable garden in front of their house. "It's time to go. The procession will be here soon. Come down now, please."

Ned shook his head. He did not call back to his mother, nor did she expect him to. No one expected him to say a word. He rarely spoke, and when he did, his words came out in a stuttering mess. He would sweat, he would shake, he would feel as though he had a boulder strapped to his chest. Words were his enemies. They rattled in his mouth like broken teeth, or tumbled off the page like scattered dust after a sneeze.

He held up his bit of wood and his carving knife in hopes that she would notice that he was terribly busy and need not accompany his parents. The whole village would be there to greet the queen's procession—and many from outside the village as well. The village school was cancelled, and the shops would close as soon as the procession arrived. It was the queen, after all. Everyone had been planning it for months.

Sister Witch crossed her arms over her chest and gave her head a slow shake. This was an argument that he was not likely to win. Sister Witch was one to get her way.

"Listen to your mother," his father said in a weary voice without looking up. He wouldn't look at Ned.

He never does, Ned thought.

His parents stood side by side, waiting.

They won't stop fussing at you till you go, his inside voice told him.

"Please, Ned," his mother said. She stood in the yard—broad-shouldered, straight-backed, an unshakable force. He'd never been able to say no to her for very long.

He closed his eyes and sighed. *Fine,* he thought.

Nimble as a spider, Ned climbed down. His mother tried to lay a conciliatory hand on his shoulder, but he darted ahead. He slid his knife into its sheath and shoved it deep into his pocket, along with his carving. No one was allowed to bring weaponry into the village, but this rule was routinely ignored. He kept the knife tucked away where no one would see it, just in case. You never know when you might need a good, sharp knife.

Ned glanced back at his house—the goats grazing in the yard, the garden bursting with plants for food and plants for healing and plants for doing work that seemed like magic, but wasn't really. Plants were smarter than most people realized. Above the front door was a sign that said WITCH in bright red letters. It had been painted, years ago, by an unkind neighbor, meant to shame the magic worker. It didn't work. Sister Witch rather liked the sign, and left it there. "Best to keep things clear," the witch had said briskly. She kept the letters touched up with fresh paint, brightened with lacquer, and studded with small pieces of embedded glass to give them a bit of a glimmer. She made it beautiful.

Though he knew what it said, Ned couldn't read the word over his door. He couldn't read anything. Not for lack of trying. There was a time when he *could* read. Both he and his brother could. *Before.* But then everything changed. Now, whenever Ned looked at the sign (or any writing for that matter), the letters seemed to wobble, shift, and scramble themselves. They wriggled like snakes and swarmed thick and fast as locusts. It made his head spin.

A word, after all, is a kind of magic. It locks the substance of a thing in sound or symbol, and affixes it to the ear, or paper, or stone. Words call the world into being. That's power indeed. And Ned was not a powerful boy.

In the village, people greeted Sister Witch by touching their foreheads or pressing their fingers to their lips. A few slipped gifts into her basket. A jar of jam. A smoked fish. A round loaf. A bouquet of fresh herbs. Their neighbors were always grateful for her help (for a little while anyway), but they kept their distance all the same. She was a witch, after all.

The procession had not yet arrived. Spotters at the top of the hill could see the queen's convoy approaching by way of the road, but it was slow going.

Sister Witch pressed a piece of paper into Ned's hand along with a small pouch of coins. "Here is your list. I want you to go to the dry merchant's and the apothecary's and the metal shop and the scrivener's house. Spend no more than a copper's worth at each." Ned shot his mother a poisonous look, but she looked stonily back.

Why? Ned's expression asked.

Because, his mother's face responded.

"Do as you're told," his father mumbled without looking at Ned. His eyes were red-rimmed and damp, as always. They slid from side to side, skimming the village rooftops, as though scanning for something lost.

Ned looked at the list. The words writhed like worms, but the pictures were clear enough. This type of list-making was a strategy that his mother used quite a bit, an attempt to trick his brain into relearning how to read. She would write the word that Ned was to find and next to it would draw a picture. This was fine for things like spools of thread or bottles of ink. But a sack of sugar looked just like a sack of flour. And once he bought a bucket of salt pork when he was supposed to simply buy a bucket.

He wove his way through the square, dodging feet and carts and donkeys. There were people selling what they had made in their own kitchens—sausages warmed over coals or sweet cakes or savory pies. The Council of Elders, consisting of Madame Thuane, a stout woman with hair the color of ashes, and two decrepit old men with hardly any hair at all, stood at the head of a table where the queen and her entourage would sit and eat the food that the village had prepared. They stood at attention, though

30

one bald council member leaned his head against his tall staff and had begun to snore. The ash-haired lady cleared her throat and gave him a kick.

No one noticed this.

No one but Ned.

Ned noticed everything. He couldn't help it.

He slid into the scrivener's house.

The head scrivener—a watery-eyed man with spider-thin arms, a long chin, and thick lips in a perpetual frown—wrinkled his nose when Ned walked in.

"The toy shop is down the lane," he said with a nasty chuckle. "Or couldn't you read the sign." He always said things like this. Little digs. Ugly smirks. *Our powerful and glorious witch has a son who is too stupid to read,* his fleshy face said. *Well.*

The scrivener wasn't the only one who thought this. Ned did his best to ignore the smothered snickers and the sidelong smirks. He tucked his chin to his chest and tried to focus on the floor.

The scrivener's house was packed with people, each pressing shoulders against the person nearby. They held their stacks of papers and playing cards and prints of the queen at various moments during her seventy-year rule, the ink so fresh it still shone on the paper and had to be handled with extreme care to prevent smudging. The scrivener's apprentices—many Ned remembered from his short time at school—were busy taking dictation from people who claimed to have the ability to read and write, but who complained of arthritis or poor vision or atrocious handwriting.

Ned gathered the items from his list. Writing paper and

blotting paper. Ink. Charcoal pencils. In the far left corner stood a man—a stranger. He held a pretty little pouch and a leather-bound journal with embossed flowers on the front cover, holding them away from his body with a grimace on his face, as though their girlishness might infect him somehow. He was a tall man—practically a giant. A full head taller than the tallest man there. He had a shock of red hair curling upward from his head like a bonfire and a red beard, oiled to a sharp point. He wore a pendant around his neck. An odd thing in the shape of an eye. Ned felt the invisible scabs on his chest start to itch.

He gave Ned a curious look. His eyes glittered.

"Ah," he said. "A scholar."

Ned looked down at his items and shrugged. The man's eyes crinkled at the edges.

"Or a storyteller, perhaps."

Still, Ned was silent. *What do you want?* he wanted to say. But the words were heavy, and Ned knew they would heave out of his mouth and shatter on the ground. He would stutter. And people would laugh. And so he was silent.

The man pressed on. "An arithmancer? A draftsman? A poet? A writer of love letters?" He took a step forward. His eyes were large and wild and searching. Ned felt the man's gaze poking and prodding and rummaging about, and found himself pulling inward, curling his spine over his purchases in order to shield them from the aggressive curiosity of the red-haired stranger. "Oh, come now, boy, why must you keep a stranger in suspense? I *must* know." He spoke with a strange cadence, and his pronunciation

32

had an unfamiliar lilt to it. Ned could understand him, but it was work. He'd never heard anything like it. Even as far away as the queen's city, no one spoke as strangely as this stranger did.

"He ent none of those things," the head scrivener said. "That there's our Witch's only boy, and a waste of space if there ever was one. Who's that ink for, boy? Not you then, is it? Come on now, I don't got all day. Bring it here."

Ned felt himself redden. The room, already hot, felt like a pot boiled dry. He put his items on the counter and shook his bag of coins. The red-haired stranger followed him. He leaned his elbows on the table and regarded Ned with fascination. "A real witch, then?" the man said. "Of your very own? Well. That is a precious little something, isn't it?" And the pendant sparkled just a bit.

"Precious *little*, I'd say," the scrivener said. "Lot of pompous hocus-pocus from that house for people who could rightly take care of themselves if they just put their minds to it, but far be it from me to judge."

Ned glared at the scrivener, who instantly cleared his throat and focused instead on haggling over the price of a contract with two customers. Everyone was like this—or everyone in the village, anyway. They loved their witch when they needed her, and resented her when they didn't. It drove Ned mad. A year earlier, the scrivener had been at Ned's house, begging for help with his grown son, who suffered from a tumor bulging from his belly. Sister Witch cured the young man—at a terrible cost. His mother's magic was a tricky, unwieldy thing, and taxing. It hurt her to use it. Saving the scrivener's son landed her in bed for a week! And now . . . Ned shook his head.

She asks for nothing, he thought. And she gets nothing, too.

And even though he knew it was wrong, he hated the scrivener. He hated everyone.

The red-haired giant cupped his chin thoughtfully. "Oh, I think such a treasure is appreciated when it is needed and forgotten when it is not." There was a gleam in his eye and a crackling around his body, like a field just before lightning strikes. Ned felt his hair stand on end.

"I'm sure you're mother's work has its . . . *enthusiasts*, yes?" The stranger's sharp gaze scanned the room and his large fingers quivered.

Go away, Ned thought at him, though he didn't know why. He edged backward, resisting his instincts to bolt. His skin itched and his teeth clattered. The man curled his fingers around the pendant at his neck, and the crackling energy surrounding him intensified. *There's something wrong with him,* Ned thought. As though in response, the man grinned. He chuckled a bit to himself, then turned away from Ned, and began to move through the crowd—never jostling, never begging pardon, as easy as a slick of oil across the water.

Other people were distracted, they looked outside, they asked one another what the queen would be wearing, whether she would address them, or shake their hands, or simply wave. They wondered if they should sing. Or pray. Or stand in silence. The

34

queen had *never* visited their little village before, and no one knew exactly what was expected of them.

And as they fussed and murmured, they did not pay attention to the stranger, nor did they notice what he was doing.

But Ned saw the man reach, flick a coin purse from a belt, and make it vanish up his sleeve. And a ring from a finger. A sweet roll from a basket. An apple. An eyeglass. A pocket watch. Item after item disappeared into the big man's sleeves.

Ned opened his mouth. He could feel *Wait* sitting on his tongue. He could feel *Stop* jittering on his molars. He felt the words shudder and jumble and buzz against his lips.

"S-st—" he stammered, but he couldn't spit out *stop*. He coughed and gagged, but nothing came out. His tongue felt like a heavy stone in his mouth. It would be easier to cough out a carriage and a team of horses than to string a sentence together. Even a single word felt impossible.

"Th—" he began. "*Tthh—*" But the word *thief* shattered in his mouth, sharp and cruel as glass.

His face flushed; his heart raced. The stranger, now at the door, locked eyes with Ned. He cocked his head and winked.

"Cat got your tongue, Witch's boy?" He gave Ned a slow smile. There was a bottle of ink in his hand. And then it was gone. And a pretty mirror—the kind that you might give to a girl on her birthday. And a stylus made of carved bone. His fingers were quick and clever; they moved as fast as thinking. Like magic.

But that wasn't possible, was it? There was only one bit of

magic left in the wide world. And his mother had that. Didn't she? The invisible scabs on his chest throbbed and itched.

"I do believe I need to pay a visit to your mother. She's near, isn't she?" He held his finger in the air and closed his eyes as though listening to something. "Yes. I do believe she is."

The noise swelled. Ned's mouth hung open, and his insides felt as though they had spilled on the floor. *How?*

The big man grinned. "See you soon, boy." Then, with a private laugh, the stranger kicked open the door with the smile of his boot, and he was gone.

Ned shivered and gasped. Sweat came pricking through his skin in tiny, sharp points.

He's a thief, Ned thought. *And a liar. And he knows things. And he has plans.* But what those plans were exactly, Ned had no idea.

Still. He had to tell someone. And right away.

7

THE CLAY POT

NED RAN INTO THE square, just as a cheer erupted from the crowd. The queen's carriage crested the hill and came rushing down the green slope. Flags waved. People held up fans imprinted with woodcuts of the queen at seventeen, when she first ascended the throne: wide eyes, round cheeks, a mouth attempting to be grim, but with a slightly sideward tilt, indicating her sardonic good humor. The queen's good humor was famous.

The ash-haired councilwoman roared at the slumped musicians, each one deep in his cups, and forced them to their feet. After a rushed count, they began to play the anthem, though not particularly on tempo or in tune.

Each Stone did once our spirits bless
And led us through the wilderness.
Not war, nor want, nor tyrant's sin
Could taint that grace we entered in.

Ned rushed through the tangled crowd, trying to find his mother, trying to catch a glimpse of the stranger. (He shouldn't be this hard to find, Ned fumed. The man was practically a giant! Still, he appeared to have vanished. So slippery! So fast!) Ned dodged hips and carts and elbows and baskets. Twice he stepped in donkey's droppings and was once sent sprawling onto the ground when the master blacksmith turned around too fast.

"Watch where you're going, witless!" the blacksmith barked.

Ned pulled himself to his feet and ran as though outrunning a storm. He had the words in his mouth, ready to go. *Thief. Liar.* He saw the red-haired man standing in the thick of the crowd on the opposite side of the square as his mother. *Go away,* Ned shouted in his heart.

The queen's carriage hurtled toward the square, moving faster and faster.

Too fast. Ned leaped onto the rim of the central fountain and paused a moment, curling his hands over his brow and squinting.

The soldiers in the entourage urged their horses onward, their arms flailing as they tried to hail the woman at the reins of the carriage. The woman at the reins, meanwhile, was shouting at her horses, her face tight and wild, her eyes pinned on the gates of the town.

Ned saw those white knuckles, those livid eyes, those faces shattered with worry. Something was wrong, he thought. Meanwhile, the crowd around him crowed with joy. *The queen!* They shouted and sang. *Our marvelous queen!*

The soldiers and carriage thundered over the old stone bridge and under the ancient arch marking the entrance to the village. The woman at the reins screamed her horses to a halt and leaped onto the ground.

"We need a healer!" she called out. She was crying. "The queen!" A sob tore at her throat. Ned could see the queen inside the carriage (a tiny thing—just sticks and grass and delicate skin with a crown stuck on top) slumped in the arms of a very large woman. *Was she dead?* Ned couldn't tell. Across from the large woman was a man with a face like a toad and an extraordinary amount of lace around his throat. Ned narrowed his eyes. *Was he smiling?* Surely not. Who could smile at a time like this? Still, it did *seem* . . . The man leaned back in the carriage, hiding his face in shadow, while the large woman leaned forward.

"Please," she shouted. "Someone help!"

Sister Witch rolled up her sleeves, nodding grimly. She set her face and gritted her teeth, bending her knees and bracing her body against the surety of the ground under her feet. The house was far away and Ned had never seen her hail the magic at this great a distance. And he worried for his mother—the farther away she had to call it, the more it drained her strength. The more it *hurt* her.

She raised her two fists and turned to the direction of the house. "TO ME!" she shouted, her voice oddly amplified. It crackled the air and vibrated underfoot. The magic—dark and fast as a storm cloud—came tearing down the road, leaving a spray of dust in its trail. It was black, then purple, then gold. Normally, when it emerged from its clay pot it was nothing more than a little yellow puff—like a dandelion clock. But now it seemed to expand as it moved, as though the *fact of itself in motion* had worked to increase its energy. Indeed, Ned had never seen it look so wild. It came to Sister Witch, swirling around her like a cyclone. She stumbled back as though she had been punched, almost losing her footing. Recovering herself, she bowed to it, murmuring a phrase.

Ned knew the words. "It is with a pure heart that I humbly ask your assistance." It's what she always said. But she spoke so quietly, and the magic around her blew with such a roar, that Ned was sure no one could hear her—he certainly couldn't and he was closest. He glanced back at the stranger, who still had his eyes on the witch. The witch had turned away, so that he couldn't tell what she was saying. The man looked frustrated—*good*, Ned thought. The man wrinkled his brow and started to snake through the crowd.

The magic began to change. First it was a cloud, then each speck of it began to link to other specks, creating bright fibers floating in the air, like a mass of wool. Then the fibers began to twist and pull and spin into length upon length of long, bright thread, winding tight spirals around Sister Witch's body, starting at the wrist, looping around and around again like bright bangles made of a hot, glittering wire that did not touch her skin. The magic hovered around her neck, around her chest and waist. It encircled her head like a crown.

"Ah," the people gasped. Ned didn't need to look at them. He knew their hands were pressed to their hearts, their faces bright. Though they had all seen the magic before, it was still a thing of wonder. It was in these moments that they loved—and did not resent—their witch. It made Ned furious.

Hypocrites! He wanted to shout.

"Oh!" came another voice. "*Oh my.*" Ned turned. It was the stranger. He was closer now. His face flushed and his hand gripped his pendant. He kept his eyes pinned on Sister Witch. He swayed and shivered as though in a trance.

Thief! Leave us alone! Ned wanted to shout. But he didn't. He remained silent.

Ned watched his mother's eyes begin to redden, and her breath come in quick gasps. "Bring me the queen," Ned's mother said, her voice multiplied and layered as though she was speaking with a thousand voices.

The large woman inside the carriage held the queen as though she was an infant, and carried her out with no assistance. Her eyes were puffy and tearful.

"Oh, my queen," the woman whispered. "Oh, my precious queen." She turned to Sister Witch. "She's fading. Her pulse is weak and her skin is cold as the grave."

"Lay her on the ground," the witch said in her multitudinous voice—now beginning to waver and fray at the edges. Ned saw she was trembling, as though the magic was beginning to undo her.

"But the filth—"

"Once her life is gone, I cannot bring her back. Magic can delay death, but it cannot undo it. Quickly now."

The large woman—a lady-in-waiting, Ned guessed—reluctantly laid the queen down, and sobbed as she stepped away.

Sister Witch knelt down and held out her hands, careful not to touch the queen. A small length of magic unraveled from her wrists and arms and hovered over the ancient woman's chest. It tangled itself like the extra thread at the bottom of the sewing basket and then picked itself apart, filament by filament, until it had assembled a life-sized outline of a heart—each protrusion and tube and lump perfectly detailed. It even pulsed with a shuddery, halting beat.

"Do you see?" Sister Witch whispered.

The magic glowed brighter in response.

"Well, then, don't dawdle. Fix the broken places."

The magic glowed again.

"That will not be necessary," Sister Witch said sharply.

The magic glowed yet again, this time with more insistence and intensity.

"DO AS YOU ARE TOLD," Sister Witch roared, her voice rattling the ground with such force that a dozen apples rolled from their cart and two horses reared back and whined.

The magic undid itself with a harrumph that Ned could hear, and it wiggled into the chest of the queen, as easily as earthworms wiggling into the dirt. Within moments, the filaments shot back out and rejoined the spiral around the witch's body. The queen shuddered and thrashed, her mouth wide open and silent.

And then she was terribly still.

The man in the carriage—the one with the ridiculous lace who had been smiling just a moment before, poked his head out of the window and pointed at the witch, his face flushed.

42

"She's not moving," he whispered, climbing out of the carriage and hovering over the witch. He licked his thick lips. Stiff lace stuck straight out of his gold-lined collar. It quivered like the feathers of a strutting bird.

"Wait," Sister Witch said, her voice weakening.

The man's fleshy face rested in the groove between his meaty shoulders, with hardly any neck at all. His middle swelled over his belt. His arms and legs, on the other hand, were as thin as reeds.

The man from the carriage leaned closer over the queen. "She's still not moving," he said, a little louder this time. An uncomfortable murmur moved through the crowd. *Had the witch failed? Is it possible? And oh! How will we live it down?*

"Wait," Sister Witch said, and Ned's mind urged the same. But the man in lace wouldn't have it.

"What have you done?" the man bellowed.

"I have done what I do," Sister Witch said, with all the authority that her weakened voice could give. "I have healed your relative." She staggered to her feet and swayed dangerously, her breath coming in short gasps. Ned worried that she might faint. "She will open her eyes in a moment."

The murmuring of the crowd increased.

"She doesn't look healed to me," the man in lace said. He had, Ned noticed, an unmistakably gleeful expression on his face. "I knew this excursion was a mistake. Our precious queen! On the ground! And with a witch! What kind of quackery is this?"

"Your grace," Madame Thuane said, as she rushed from the Council's table. She gave Ned's mother a waspish glance, "you must excuse us. We did not authorize this . . . this *magic*. It just happened so fast and we didn't know—"

The queen, on the ground, began to sigh. The murmuring ceased. The crowd pressed forward. The queen curled onto her side, and pulled herself to her elbows. She coughed, cleared her throat, and shot an exasperated look at the man from the carriage.

"Honestly, Brin," the old woman said in a dry, dusty voice. "Must you embarrass me in public?" She coughed, shuddered, and coughed again. The soldiers held out their arms and walked backward, trying to push the crowd away from the queen. She pressed her hand to her chest. "Well, my goodness. My heart hasn't beat this true since the Great Flood—now that was a time."

Ned's mother bent close to the queen, making sure to stay out of range, lest the old woman touch her. "Move slowly," she said. "Your heart had a blocked portion, and a bit of it had begun to die. I have healed the whole of it, but you are weak, my queen. You won't be well for a while."

"But—" the man in lace said. "She *will* be well. Is that correct?" There was an unmistakable look of disappointment on his face.

"Honestly, dear, don't be so glum. I'll be dead soon enough." The old queen cackled merrily. "Come now, apologize to the nice— why, I believe I missed your name, dear. What are you called?"

Sister Witch stood up and bowed. "My name is not important, my queen. Only your health matters. Forgive me," she said, holding up her hands. "I cannot be touched. This thing, this magic,"—a wince, a shiver; Ned could see his mother suffering—"is volatile, and a danger to any who might touch me. And it must be contained. Now. Please excuse me if I do not stay."

And with that, Sister Witch turned and walked through the rapidly parting crowd, followed by her husband.

Ned watched his mother wobble. He watched her shake. His anxiety wrote itself on his face; it dug deeply into the lines of his brow. If she had brought a small portion of her magic with her from the beginning, then calling to it from a great distance would not have hurt her so. Ned had seen her walk for miles with just a filament of magic hovering around her wrist like a bangle, or written on her arm like a tattoo, and then call to the magic as easily as if she was calling to a pet dog. An unruly, overly large dog, sure, but still. It was *easier*. The magic just joined *itself*. (Or at least it seemed easier to Ned. Sister Witch never told him either way. She only told him that the magic was dangerous, volatile, and *not to be touched*.) In any case, calling to the magic cold, like today, was a different operation entirely. It hurt. It drained her dry. And it was making her sick. Her face yellowed, then grayed. Her eyes were two dark smudges. Ned followed his mother.

Sister Witch stumbled and fell, cutting her hands on the road. With a grunt, she pulled herself back to her feet and continued shuffling toward home. Neither Ned nor his father could do anything to help. They couldn't even *touch* her.

Before joining his parents, Ned turned to look one more time at the scene. The town apothecary had ordered a stretcher to be brought to carry the queen. She needed to rest, and already the members of the Council were jostling for the honor of housing the monarch. The man called Brin leaned against the carriage, looking annoyed, as the soldiers ordered people to get back to their business—which was impossible since everyone's business that day was to greet the queen and celebrate. Instead, everyone remained where they were, staring all the while. The villagers stood as immobile as a painting—pale, silent, and openmouthed— as the soldiers bustled about, creating a perimeter around the carriage and blocking off a pathway for the litter to carry the queen to her recuperation destination.

Ned looked for the red-haired stranger. But he had vanished.

No matter, Ned told himself. *There's nothing for him here. He'll never come back.*

He did his best to convince himself it was true.

8

———

THE STONES

THE YOUNGEST STONE DREAMED.

She didn't know if the others dreamed. She didn't know if she dreamed before—in her other life. In her other world. When she and the others still had power and magic and bodies with skin and eyes and hair and beating hearts and so much insufferable foolishness.

Which is to say, when they were *alive*.

A Stone is not alive, but it is not dead, either. In *this* world they were cold stone—implacable, immovable, unswayed by foolish things. In *this* world they were known for their wisdom. In *this* world their counsel was sought and treasured and freely given.

Or at least it *was*. Before the forest grew. The forest made the people stop coming. And with no people coming to visit, there was no wisdom to dispense, and the Stones went to sleep. What else was there to do?

The youngest Stone missed giving advice. She missed human beings and their anguish and hope and confusion and capacity for joy. She missed the comfort she had been able to give.

The youngest Stone yawned. "The wrong boy," she said sleepily.

"Hush," said the Sixth. "You're waking me up."

"You were told not to sleep," the Eldest said, his voice as stern as the earth when it shakes and rumbles and splits. "You were explicitly told to *wait*."

"Waiting is boring," yawned the Sixth. The Fifth made a sound that was something between a giggle and a snort. She was always a silly thing. Rarely listened to.

"The wrong boy," repeated the youngest Stone. "Why would I dream that?"

The Nine Stones were stuck. They had been stuck since time out of mind. Ever since they had used their magic to cheat death. Death always frightens the powerful. And the Stones, before they were stone, were *terribly* powerful.

But it went wrong somehow. When they used their magic to cheat death, their magic—indeed, their very souls—shattered into bits. It became rowdy and chaotic and argumentative. It thought with a thousand minds and spoke with a thousand tongues, and all of them disagreed. It needed a firm hand and a strong mind to keep it focused, bound, and *mostly* good.

So far, one family had minded it, and had done so for generations. They were a poor family. Simple. Honest. It was their ancestor who saw the Stones appear, as they were yanked from their other world into this one. She saw their fear, and she felt compassion. She saw them fall, and she was alarmed. She saw their bodies transform; she saw their souls and their magic emerge from their mouths like a cloud, and shatter in the air. She rushed to their aid. She didn't even think about it. The Stones told her how to catch the magic, how to bind it to her. How to tame it. How to give it goodness and purpose. How to use it to help people.

And then her family *kept* helping.

And it worked. So far, the magic had been kept good, for generation upon generation. It wasn't what the Stones wanted *exactly*, but it was close enough for now.

"Do you think—" the Youngest began, but the Eldest interrupted her.

"There is no such thing as *wrong boys* or *right boys*," the Eldest said. "It is a notion built on foolishness."

"I didn't say there was," the youngest Stone sniffed. "It was only a dream."

"Still," the Eldest grumbled. And his grumbling set the bedrock trembling and the earth shifting. It made the mountains sigh. "I have heard the same phrase echoing in the rocks. It is . . . *interesting*."

He said no more.

But the Youngest knew he held his breath.

She could feel the *hoping* of the eldest Stone shimmer through the ground. She felt it tremble and soften and heat. And the world around her shifted, just a bit. And she *hoped* too.

9

DANGEROUS. WITH CONSEQUENCES.

Ten days after healing the queen, Sister Witch had still not gotten out of bed. Ned's father, uncharacteristically, stayed home and sat with his wife. Waiting.

Sister Witch ran a fever. This was her worst reaction to the magic by far, and Ned began to worry. He had seen her do much more impressive jobs—rerouting a flood, for example, or undoing a fire, pulling a house from a sinkhole, finding a child that had fallen into a well—with only a persistent headache or a bad case of vertigo.

The magic, it seemed to Ned, had it in for her. He couldn't shake the feeling that it *enjoyed* making her suffer, somehow—though surely that couldn't be true. It wasn't a *person*. It didn't *think*.

"It's a dangerous thing," Sister Witch explained to him once, back when she still had hope that he might wield it when the time came. "But with tremendous power to do good. And that is our role, son. To do good. To keep it good. No matter what."

His father wouldn't let him help. Not while he was awake, anyway. Instead, left to his own devices, Ned set his hands to carving. He carved figure after figure, and, twice a day, set them afloat on the Great River in hopes they made it to the sea. A mother-shaped figure. A father-shaped figure. A figure that looked like Tam. And Ned. And the queen. And even the red-haired stranger (whose face began to occupy the distant corners of his dreams). He carved his figures with a new sense of purpose. Each one was a question and a plea. *Why,* he asked, as he carved. *Please,* he begged as he knelt in front of the river that killed his brother and nearly killed *him*. He set the figure floating in the river and watched it drift away. *Please, please, please.*

He gave his worry to the Great River, and let the River decide what to do with it. It was all he could do.

On his mother's tenth day in bed, Ned gathered healing herbs from the garden—he had seen his mother do it enough to know the recipe by heart—and made a soup that would both satisfy the appetite and undo the damage that the magic had wrought upon his mother. (It could also cure gout, ease asthma, soothe a fever, heal a sore back, and mend a broken heart. Very powerful, this soup.) Ned baked bread too, and plucked peas and cherries and wild grapes, and gathered nasturtiums and thyme and marigolds and other herbs to be eaten raw—all things he had learned by watching.

He set a bowl of soup and a bowl of fruits and flowers and

herbs on a low table next to his mother's bed. To one side of the table lay his mother, fast asleep. His father sat in a wooden chair, also asleep, head tipped back against the wall and mouth open wide. His throat jiggled with a prodigious snore. Ned slid out of the house and climbed onto the roof.

The late afternoon sun inched toward evening. It would be hours before the stars appeared. The roof was hot, and Ned began to sweat. A new carving sat in his pocket—a wolf this time—but he didn't feel like working on it now. Instead, he squinted and covered his eyes, and peered to the west.

He could see the tightly packed roofs of his village with their blue-gray ribbons of smoke curling from their cook stoves and chimneys, and beyond that the miles and miles of farms, curving into the sky. Ned could not see beyond the farms, but he knew that there were villages larger, grander, and more elegant than his own. Villages for merchants, traders, moneylenders, and artisans, which formed concentric rings around the tall towers of the queen's city. The queen wrote the laws, arbitrated disagreements, and commanded the armies that kept everyone safe. Though safe from *what*, Ned never knew. There was nowhere else but here. The Great River cut the land. It traveled past the city and villages and grazing fields and farms, and then through acre upon acre of untraversable bogs before it finally poured into the sea.

The sea!

No one had gone to the ocean since time out of mind. The swampy fen was too broad, too treacherous. And the sea itself? Well, people said, it was just . . . *water*, after all. It didn't grow anything. What was the point? Only the oldest stories hinted at the enormity of the ocean. And Ned longed to know if the stories were true.

Ned kept his eyes on the west. Only rarely did he make himself look to the east. The very thought of it made his skin go prickly and cold. To the east were the woods—only trees, yes, but trees pressed against one another into a great, dark, green, *breathing* thing.

Ned was afraid of the wood.

Everyone he knew—except his father—was afraid of the wood. It was said that there were monsters in the wood. Huge monsters with bodies made of stone and hands so strong they could crush a grown man to bits. And it was *vast*. It was *beyond* vast. The forest spread itself against the far side of the world—an army of trees—and it multiplied and teemed across swamps and ravines and ridges. It thundered over the foothills of the mountains and even up the sides of the mountains themselves, to the place where their slopes became steep and rocky and nothing at all grew—no grass, no green, no trees, no nothing—and there was only stone and ice and a harsh cloaking of snow.

The mountains cut the sky. And after the mountains . . . there was nothing. The world stopped.

Everyone said so.

When Ned was a little child, he had had terrible dreams that he became lost in that forest. And after blundering through the dark and through the green, he toppled over the edge of the world and fell straight into the sky.

He would wake from those dreams shivering and damp, as though struck by a fever. It would take him hours to recover.

And now—even now—he remembered those dreams with a shiver. And he averted his eyes.

There were footsteps on the path, and the garden gate swung open with a loud creak, nearly startling Ned off of the roof.

"Good evening, young man," a woman called from down below.

Ned turned and stared at her. She and her two companions, a man and a woman, were soldiers. The woman in the center held a wooden box. The other two each held a brightly polished horn, decorated with ribbons. The soldier in charge regarded Ned, waiting for a response. When Ned gave her none, she cleared her throat and continued.

"I am seeking the woman called Sister Witch. Have we come to the correct dwelling?"

Ned peered over the lip of the roof at the sign over the door, that he knew said WITCH in very bright letters. *Can't she read? It's right there on the sign.* Maybe she couldn't. Maybe he wasn't the only one. He nodded.

"I am here at the request of our glorious queen. Please fetch the magic worker." She said the phrase as though it was something distasteful. Ned decided not to like her.

He climbed down the lattice and landed on the ground with a thud. Without looking at the soldiers, he slipped into the house and woke his father.

He would have to speak, Ned realized with a sick feeling in his gut. He tensed up his face and planted his feet and braced himself. This wouldn't be pleasant.

"P-p-papa," Ned managed to say.

His father choked on a snore. "I wasn't asleep," he said.

"S-sold." Ned gagged, then choked. The second half of "soldiers" died in the back of his throat and he could not revive it.

"What are you on about, boy?" his father grunted through a yawn. The big man's eyes rested on Ned's face for a second or two. He winced and looked away.

"F-from the—" Ned paused, struggling. He felt his frustration roil in his chest as though he had been suddenly stuffed with centipedes. He frantically cleared his throat, trying to force them out. "Queen," Ned gasped. A wave of relief.

The woodsman squinted at his son to see if he was lying. He sighed, heaved himself out of his chair, and walked outside. Ned pressed his hands to his knees and let his head fall forward. Speaking was so much *work*.

"Is this the house of Sister Witch?" Ned heard the pompous soldier ask his father. Before he could answer, the flanking soldiers blared the anthem, high and bright, on their shrill horns.

Ned sat next to his mother and took her hand. Her breathing was smooth and even, and her fever was gone. Rest, Ned knew. All she needed was rest. And no magic for a good long while. Maybe forever.

And, as though in response to Ned's thought, the clay pot,

hidden in the workshop under the house, rattled on its shelf. Ned, just as he had seen his parents do a thousand times, kicked at the floorboards to tell it to hush.

The soldiers had brought a message for Ned's mother. The intricately decorated scroll in the carved wooden box invited Sister Witch to the palace of the queen to receive a Commendation for her quick thinking and swift application of Remarkable Magicks which had saved the queen's life. It was signed by the queen herself.

An honor, the family said.

A burden, they knew in their hearts.

From her bed, Sister Witch told the soldiers that she would be honored to make the journey.

By the end of the week, Sister Witch was out of bed and recovering. A week after that she finished the final preparations to travel to the capital. "You cannot go," Ned's father said. "You're still too weak."

Sister Witch kissed her husband on the cheek and continued neatly packing the clothing and supplies she'd need into a small, leather-covered trunk that she would lash to the saddle of the family's only horse. She would not be taking the clay pot.

"It won't be long," Sister Witch said briskly. "Three days' ride there. A week in the palace. Three days back. You'll hardly miss me."

Ned's father grumbled as he went out to saddle the horse. He knew better than to try and change her mind. Sister Witch was not one to be swayed. She fastened her trunk tight with a leather belt, and patted the top for good measure.

The clay pot rattled on the shelf under the floor.

"You stay where you are," Sister Witch said. "You'll not be coming."

It rattled again.

"*Language,*" she snapped.

Ned stared at his mother. She rarely went on a long journey without a bit of the magic—usually just a strand or two, wound into a bracelet around her wrist. *Just in case,* she used to say. Carrying a small portion, she could perform small tasks, or call the rest to her no matter how far away from the clay pot she happened to journey.

And now she was going to the queen's city, such a long way away, with no magic at all. She still had dark circles under her eyes. She was as pale as bone. Yes, the magic hurt her, but what would happen to her if she needed it? Surely she couldn't call it from such a distance—not after last time.

"Listen to me, my Ned," his mother murmured as they stood by the horse. "The skies are muddled and difficult to read. The queen needs me, and soon. I know that much. I can only hope that it is just my skills she needs and not the magic, because I cannot carry it now. My soul cannot bear it. You must protect it while I'm away. I need you to mind the magic, my son, and keep it safe."

Ned knew why. He and his brother were five years old when someone from another village had tried to steal the magic. And they *saw* it. The man had touched the lid of the pot with one finger, and was struck dead—coins flowed from his mouth and eyes, and a lump of gold the size of a turnip was found pressed through his heart. It was a horrible death. Ned never forgot it.

The dead man wanted riches. And riches are what he got, until they killed him. Sister Witch, as Ned remembered, gathered up the gold and secretly left it in a basket on the doorstep of a poor family. She never told anyone how the man died—just that he touched the magic and the magic had killed him, which was true enough.

Dangerous. With consequences.

That was the year his father dug a room under the house for the magic to stay hidden. "Out of sight, out of mind," he said.

Ned wrinkled his brow and shoved his hands into his pockets. How could *he* protect the magic?

Sister Witch kissed her husband and son, climbed onto the horse, and rode away.

Ned's father watched the horse depart, a great shadow on his face. Then, with a grunt, he turned away. He didn't look at Ned.

That night, Ned dreamed of his brother.

This was nothing new. Almost every night, Ned dreamed that his brother's soul uncurled from the moss mint growing over his grave like a flower—a small tendril at first, then a sturdying stalk, then a fully fleshed boy—and the two of them would walk to the

Great River, where their raft was waiting for them. In these dreams, Ned's brother seemed to know what had happened to Ned during the day, and would offer advice, or support, or commiseration.

Ned didn't stutter in his dreams. And he could read, too. And Ned loved his brother. Tam never called Ned "witless." Ned would wake from those dreams with a strange, fluttering feeling in his chest, as though he had swallowed a butterfly.

On the night his mother left for the City, Ned dreamed that he and his brother sat on the raft they had built, as it floated down the Great River in high summer. Ned and Tam had both stripped off their shirts and were splashing the cool, murky water on their arms, shoulders, and chests, letting it dry on their skin in a cloudy haze, after a while leaving them dusty and pale as ghosts.

Tam leaned back on his elbows and looked up.

"The skies are muddled today, brother, and difficult to read," the dead boy said.

"That's what mother said," Ned told him. Tam didn't respond. Instead he said this:

"You should know that the Stones are awake. And they're waiting."

"What are you talking about?" Ned asked. "Stones can't wake. They can't sleep either. A stone is a nothing."

"Shows what you know."

The dead boy rolled over onto his stomach, his head and shoulders hovering past the edge of the raft and over the water. He let his arms trail into the green river up to his elbows. They were silent for a long time.

Finally: "The time is coming, brother, when I will leave you. Not today, but it's coming."

Ned felt his heart seize up inside him and his breath catch. "I hope you're wrong," he said, his voice small and tight and frightened.

"I'm not," Tam said. The world around them began to fade, like a painting thrown in the water. The colors leaked and the edges blurred. Ned would be waking soon, and he was sorry for it.

"Watch the wood," the dead boy said. "It's coming from the wood. It's coming from beyond the wood. From the kingdom beyond the mountains. And it will be up to you to stop them."

The world brightened into a clean, white space and fluttered around Ned's body like a cloth swaddling him tight.

Stop who? Ned wondered.

Who's coming?

How on earth could something come from beyond the wood? There was nothing beyond the wood but the mountains, and after the mountains there was only sky.

There was nothing that could come.

Everyone said so.

10

THE BANDIT KING'S DAUGHTER

NED WAS WRONG. About many things. For one, the world did *not* end at the mountains.

Also: There were many things that could come. Indeed, they were already coming.

On the other side of the mountains lay the Kingdom of Duunin. Duunin was a vast nation—but not as vast as it once had been. Long ago, the kingdom had hooked over the mountains, through what became the Deadly Forest, and stretched all the way across the land that became Ned's country. But that was before the treachery of the Nine Stones.

Áine, growing up in Duunin, knew the story of the Nine Stones and the Lost Lands and the Lost People on the other side of the forest. She'd heard them from the day she was born. Kinsmen, some stories said. Traitors, claimed others. They stole something precious from the royal family, and for generations the kingdom observed a day of mourning for the lost province of Duunin. And a declaration that the Thing That Had Been Stolen would one day be returned.

(No one ever said what the thing was. Áine suspected that everyone just forgot and didn't want to admit it.)

Now, in the forest—not in Duunin, not in the other country, not anywhere at all—Áine couldn't be bothered with lost cities or lost objects or lost people. She had no intention to ever visit the Lost Lands. From what her father said, the people on the other side of the forest were nothing but a bunch of backwater yokels, ignorant of the wider world—useful for the occasional heist (*very* occasional—they didn't have much worth stealing), but that was it. Her father often told her that, should anything happen to him, she should go to the Lost Lands and not to Duunin to build a new life for herself. *A simple place,* he told her. *And safe. Hardly any bandits at all.* Áine dismissed the idea with a shrug. She could make it on her own, if need be. The forest was her friend.

After all, the forest made her happy. At first.

Over time, though, her life in the forest began to change. Her father was gone for longer and longer stretches. Áine told herself not to worry. But, oh! She *worried.* And she tried to make herself an anchor, holding her father in place.

And when he *did* come home, he was distracted and fitful. Suspicious. He would give speeches to people who weren't there. And at night, she would see him kneeling outside in the moonlight, cradling his pendant—his greatest treasure—in his huge hands.

And she knew that she had been replaced.

Snatch it! A voice whispered in Áine's head—it sounded suspiciously like her mother. *Snatch it and destroy it. It's dangerous!* But Áine didn't dare. And her father's nightly excursions with his pendant became more and more frequent. So did his disappearances.

Then he started bringing bandits to their home in the forest. Just a few at first. Then more. And more. And the spoils of banditry increased, until the floorboards groaned with the weight of ill-gotten gains.

In time, the hayloft of their barn had enough riches hidden under the straw to fund a fleet of ships. Or build a city. But the gold simply waited. There wasn't much use for money in the middle of a deep, dark forest.

When her father would ride into their little hollow next to the waterfall with his ragtag group of ferocious men and women, Áine wasn't allowed to speak to them. The moment she saw them come, their faces and necks and arms lavishly decorated by the tattoos of their profession (a wolf's jaw drawn on the neck to indicate revenge; a length of chain around the leg or arm to show time in prison; an open eye etched in the center of the forehead to show uncanny stealth), she was to lock herself into the attic and not come down until her father gave her the signal.

"No daughter of mine will associate with a horde of bandits," her father said. "You've got better adventures ahead of you, my flower."

But one day her father arrived with more bandits than she had ever seen. They crowded into the house, spilled out the windows and doors, trampling her flowers and spoiling her garden.

63

Both her goats and her chickens were terrified. Áine was out-raged, but kept quiet in her hiding spot in the attic, fuming all the while. She watched through the rounded windows under the eaves. The bandits drank and ate and fought one another. In the darkness, Áine rolled her eyes. Frankly, she found their behavior embarrassing.

Finally, her father walked out onto the large boulder that humped out of the ground right outside their house, and called out for attention. The thronging crowd gathered around him—sharpened teeth, tattooed bodies, fierce and terrifying (though, Áine noted, none was as fierce as her father, who stood in the middle of them: unmarked, unchallenged, unbeatable). Áine, as she often was, was filled with a strange mixture of worry and fear for her father—but also, strangely, *pride*. For even in madness, he was a man unmatched.

"My friends," Áine's father shouted to the crowd. His voice was hypnotic, and the bandits were intoxicated by it. Their faces shone and their eyes were fixed only upon him. They *loved* him. The stone around Áine's father's neck gave off an odd, flickering glow, like an ember. "I have seen a queen. And I have seen a vision. And I tell you right now, our lives are about to change."

A queen, Áine thought. Not in Duunin, surely. The old queen—a good woman if the stories were true—died in child-birth while ushering the young King Ott into the world. It was a blessing, really, that she never had to see the sniveling, selfish wretch that the young king had become. Had her father gone all the way to the lowland kingdom on the other side of the forest? *So far, my father! So dangerous! And what would mother say?*

"The days of measly takes and mean rations are about to come to a close." The bandits swayed on their feet. Their red-haired leader continued. "We've had some fun, we've taken what we could, we've left fat merchants and soft bureaucrats weeping in our dust, and for that we can all be proud." The bandits cheered. Áine's father held up his hand to quiet them. "But—" He paused. "We've all felt empty bellies, cold nights, and light purses. We've all known *want*. And that want is more terrible than the toothy bite of a hungry wolf. It is more insistent than the grin of the blade upon the throat."

Áine thought about the gold they had hidden in the hayloft. The masses of it. The spoils of banditry, it seemed, had not been shared equally. *Father,* she thought reproachfully, a slither of fear moving through her belly. *What lies have you been telling? And what will we do if they find out?*

"We've all lived with the fear of the law bearing down on our heels. No more! In an insignificant village of an insignificant kingdom, there lives a woman in possession of an extraordinary power. And what has she done with it? Nothing! The people of her nation believe that the world ends at the mountains. Idiots! Fools! Know-nothings! They have no inkling of the wonders of the wider world, or the sums of money *our dear King Ott*"—he said the name with derision and the bandits let out a tremendous boo—"will pay to get his hands on her magic."

The bandits were silent. Áine felt sick. *No magic*, the mother-sounding voice in her head whispered frantically. *He promised.*

"What we seek is dangerous, but we laugh at danger!" The bandits nodded. "No more raiding camps for us, my friends, not anymore. Instead—castles, land, power. A new order, and it is you, my friends, and I who will hold the keys."

The bandits raised their fists, opened their mouths, let a roar rip from their throats and soar up to the sky. Áine shivered.

"Saddle your horses my soldiers-at-arms! Fill your water skins; pack your rucksacks and your saddlebags. We leave at sunrise!"

The bandits cheered and drank. They scuffled and swore and slung their packs onto their emaciated horses. Áine's father stood in the center, the moonlight shining on his red hair, as bright as blazes. They loved him like a brother, respected him like a king, and worshipped him like a god. But he was none of those things. He was a *father*. Áine's father. And she needed him.

High in the attic, Áine hugged her knees, rocking back and forth. A simple life is what her mother wanted, and once again, the girl could see that her mother was always right. She fell asleep in the rafters, her body curled into a tight ball.

When she woke, the bandit horde was gone, leaving behind a colossal mess. The garden was spoiled. Lengths of tattered oil-cloth remained nailed onto the trees. The curtains were torn. Gnawed bones and half-eaten loaves were scattered where some drunken bandit had thoughtlessly dropped them on the ground.

The remnants of fires still smoked in their rings. And someone had left his boot next to the well. Her father had forgotten to say good-bye. Again. *No matter,* she told herself briskly. Áine, being a practical girl, an industrious girl, and an unsentimental girl, didn't waste a moment weeping, and instead put herself to work.

After all, she thought, this mess wouldn't clean itself.

11

WATCH THE WOOD

O N THE THIRD DAY after Sister Witch left for the queen's city, bandits crept into Ned's village. They slipped through the shadows, trickling out in twos and threes, sliding like a slow slick of oil from the dark, dense forest, across the fields, and along the side of Ned's barn, moving into position. They waited in silence. So stealthy were these bandits that neither Ned nor his father, who were eating supper, was even the tiniest bit aware that many pairs of eyes were watching them. And many mouths were spreading—over sharpened teeth or rotten teeth or no teeth at all—into wild, wicked grins.

The clay pot under the floor rattled on its shelf.

Ned's father stamped on the floor three times, but the magic continued to fuss.

It had been fussing all day.

"Hush now," Ned's father called from the table. The magic

only rattled louder. It let off a stench like rotten eggs. "Rude little thing," his father muttered.

He took the plate of stew that his son had prepared and ate it quickly. He did not make conversation, nor did Ned expect him to. What was there to say?

Ned's father stood and pushed his chair back to the table. "I must return to the mill. There is a barn that needs building, and Madame Thuane will have my head if there is not wood enough to build it exactly when she sees fit. Stones preserve anyone who slows her down." Madame Thuane had been over at the house earlier that day. She always spoke gently when Ned's mother was nearby. She knew what magic could do, and she never quite trusted it. She treated Sister Witch as though she were a bucket of hot coals—useful, but dangerous. And not to be touched. Without his mother's presence, though, Madame Thuane became insistent and demanding. A force of nature. It would be easier to stop the Great River dead in its tracks than say no to Madame Thuane. Ned's father was a man of incredible strength, but even he wasn't strong enough to stand up to the ash-haired councilwoman. No one was.

Ned pressed his lips together, trying to work up the courage to say something. His mother wanted him to help—had *told* him to help his father. Surely he could help at the mill. Surely he could do *something*. He took a deep breath.

"F-father," he said.

His father winced.

"I c-could," he began.

"Son," his father said heavily.

"I c-could h-he—" he reddened. He couldn't get the word out. It lodged in his throat. That itchy, crawly feeling returned.

"Help?" his father said, not noticing the shame burning on his son's face. There was nothing worse than to have his words completed for him—nothing at all. "No, son. There is little you can do at the mill."

Ned looked at his father, who looked at his hands. It was true, of course. Ned had neither strength nor skill. His father knitted his brows, as though desperately trying to think of something— *anything*—to add. There was nothing. His father cleared his throat, rubbed his hand over his mouth and walked out the door.

The magic under the floor bashed its side against the wall. *What has gotten into that thing?* Ned wondered. "H-hush," he called. "Hush n-now." To his great astonishment, the magic quieted. Probably a coincidence. Or maybe it was tired. It let off a wonderful scent—damp and frothy, exactly like the Great River in high summer. Ned smiled, thinking about his brother, and gathered up the dishes in a stew-smelling stack. He brought them outside, set them on the table where they did most of their washing, and picked up a bucket to collect water from the well.

Ned let the bucket fall to the bottom of the well with a hollow splash. Bracing his weight against the stone wall with one foot, he hauled the full bucket back to the top with the usual struggle. His arms were thin and reedy—it was no wonder his father didn't want his help. Ned heaved the bucket over the rim of the well and rested its weight on his chest.

The bandits crept from the shadows. Ned did not see.

He could hear his father greeting a passerby on the road. How easily he spoke to other people! How light his voice was then! As though he was another person entirely.

Even their horses skulked silently, their hooves making no sound as they poured, thick and fast, from behind the barn.

Ned thought of his brother.

He thought of their dream voyage on that rickety raft on the Great River. His heart seized at the thought of his brother leaving him. Even though it was a dream—Ned wasn't foolish enough to believe his dreams to be *real*—he treasured having someone to talk to. To be able to speak words without the burden of the stutter was a profound relief, even if it wasn't out loud.

Don't leave me, he thought.

It will come from the wood, his brother had said. *It will come from the wood,* said the voice in his dreams. Ned turned. He looked at the wood.

And he saw.

Ned saw the bandits creeping toward the house, knives drawn, mouths spread into grins.

And in the midst of them, striding through a river of bandits, each no taller than his shoulder was—

No.

The man from the scrivener's shop. The man with the aggressive gaze. The man who *knew* things. The man who stole and lied. The man who kept his eyes pinned on . . .

Oh no.

71

The magic.

His mother's magic.

You must protect it, his mother had told him.

Ned dropped the bucket and ran toward the house. He felt as though his brother was running with him. He felt Tam's body, Tam's breath, Tam's heart fluttering in his own chest.

YOU ARE NOT WELCOME HERE, his dream-brother, his brother-within-him, seemed to say. He could feel the words vibrating in his imaginary scabs. *Say it with me,* said the voice in his head.

"YOU ARE NOT WELCOME HERE," Ned repeated, speaking in unison with the brother-within-him, as though they were now, just as when they were little, running side by side, their footfalls landing in tandem. His voice astonished him—it seemed to come from his feet, rippling through his muscles and ringing through his chest. The words vibrated through his bones. They heated and smoked over his skin. And with no stutter at all. A miracle.

The words *did* something.

He could not do magic.

He would never do magic.

And yet, astonishingly, the yard crackled with magic. He could feel it in the air, like the blast of heat through the door of a furnace.

A shock reverberated from the house, smacking the air like thunder. Ned's ears rang and his body hurt but he kept running. He could hear the bandits—many of them, and all much bigger than he—growing nearer, but he forced himself not to notice. He threw himself into the house, slammed the door, and locked it tight. The reek of magic nearly overpowered him. He could hear the clay pot rocking back and forth on its shelf belowground. And from outside, the sound of laughing.

He shut the windows and braced the shutters with a broom handle. He pushed the bench, then the table, against the door and backed to the middle of the room, panting heavily. The men weren't banging at the door. They weren't even *trying* to get in. Instead, Ned heard them outside, laughing so hard he thought they might split in half.

Ned crept to a shuttered window and peered through the gap. The man with the red beard and green eyes and red hair curling upward like a bonfire leered through the twilight. Ned shivered.

You! His mind said.

"Hello, Witch's boy," the red-haired stranger said. "You seem to be blocking my way. How terribly rude."

"G-g-go aw-way," Ned stammered, his words weighted and thick, and once again, he felt a shock at his feet, and the clay pot in the workshop under the floor rattled on its shelf.

The big man's face grew stormy and dark in response to the rattle (*did he feel it too*, Ned wondered. He had no idea), and his green eyes narrowed to sharp points. "What are you going to do, Witch's boy? Kick us in the shins? Challenge us to a war of words? Thumb wrestle us? Looks to me you're like a rat in a trap, boy." The Bandit King tipped back his head and howled, and the other bandits howled with him—a great, jeering, terrifying cry. "A rat in a trap."

73

12

ÁINE'S PLAN

Áine's arms ached and her back throbbed. The cleanup after the bandits nearly undid her. Her garden was ruined. Her goats had worried themselves into a frenzy (even Moss! Dear Moss, her favorite of the three), and the chickens were, even now, tearing out their feathers and wearing deep circles into the ground, but Áine didn't get up to comfort them. Instead, she sat in a sunny patch in the yard and stretched out her legs.

She needed to think.

She was trapped. She could see that now. And so was her father, though he could not see this at all. Her father was changing. The banditry, the pendant. They were *changing* him. Every day he seemed less and less like her father and more and more like . . . Well. She didn't even know. Something else.

And now—now!—he was off to steal *more* magic from a witch? Heavens. At what point would he change so much as to become unrecognizable? Not her father at all anymore. Not anyone she could love.

The very thought hurt Áine so much she cried out. She rested her head on her knees.

And, as she often did when her new life became frightening, she thought of her other life. And her other world.

Her mother, when she was alive, did not allow any talk of magic in the house. *Never*. Even simple things like schoolyard songs or jump rope chants or fishermen's stories of incredible wonders at sea would be met with a fiery look and a hand smacked hard on the surface of the table.

"There *is no* magic," her mother would snap, her eyes slashing her husband's face. "There is no magic at all."

Her mother was a tiny woman, reaching only midway between her father's elbow and shoulder. Despite that, she towered over her husband, and he shrank before her. Love made her mother a giantess, and her father, hat in hand, had no choice but to obey her. "Of course not, my darling," the big man said. "There has never been magic. Not ever."

At the time, Áine believed her mother. Why would she lie?

And yet. Her father's pendant. How it glowed! How strange it made him! If it wasn't magic, *then what was it*? And, more important, how could she get him to leave it behind?

Shortly before Áine's mother sickened for the last time, she had left Áine in the care of her father for a week while she visited her family in Kaarna, another fishing town far away. Áine had never been, nor had she ever met her mother's family. She never knew why. One night, when the moon had set and the stars in the sky overhead were as sharp as broken glass, she heard her father rise out of bed and creep to the front door, opening it with a quiet creak, though no one had knocked. Áine crept from under her covers and peered through the shadows of her room, and saw her father standing at the threshold. He moved aside and let an ancient man inside.

"Felt me coming, did you son?" The old man's voice was light and dry as kindling. He moved toward the fire. Áine's father stared at the man, openmouthed. Áine stared too.

Son?

So that man is . . . She winced. The man was shocking to behold—ancient and withered, and covered in tattoos. He had no hair, and his remaining teeth had been sharpened to points. He grinned in the firelight. Áine's father did not grin back.

"Have you any money?" the old man asked.

"None for you," Áine's father said. "And I thought you were dead."

The old man shrugged. "May as well be. Your ma's dead, though I'm sure you know already. I have enough enemies still, and my powers are . . ." He wheezed. "Reduced."

Áine's father ran his hand through his hair. It shone in the firelight as bright and alive as a hot coal. "Old man," he said. "I will feed you my food. I will give you my cloak and a pair of my boots. But I will give you no money. You may not sleep under my roof. You must understand why I do this."

"Of course I understand, son. I just wondered . . . I wanted to

76

see," he leered through the firelight, his features becoming grotesque. "Have you got it? You must have it, even now." He put his hands on the big man's chest, pawing at it like an animal. Áine's father gripped the old man's shoulders and pushed him, hard, onto the floor, in a tangle of brittle limbs. He whimpered like a child.

In the shadows, Áine pulled her knees to her chest and hugged them tight. Her mouth was open and tight in a silent scream. In those days before her mother died, she had never known her father to hurt anyone. She didn't even know he *could*.

"I have nothing you want," Áine's father snarled with a ferocity that shocked her. "I have a good wife and a dear daughter and an honest life. I left everything behind. *Everything*. I thought you were dead. You should be dead, old man."

The old man pulled himself to his knees. His eyes gleamed. (*That gleam!* Áine thought as she remembered. *Of course!*) "So that means—"

"No," her father breathed.

"It's still there."

"*No.*"

"Our little treasure."

"*No.*"

"And since you don't want it . . ."

"Enough!" Her father roared. He stumbled backward, gripping his head between his palms, his face a mask of pain. He stopped, closed his eyes, and sighed. He reached down and helped the old man up, steadied him with the curve of his massive arm.

With the other hand, he grabbed a small purse of coins from the mantel. He bounced it in his hands to allow for the tinkling sound of the money inside. The old man's tongue darted across his dry lips. "Listen. You can't stay here," Áine's father said. "But there's a place, very near. They have soft beds and plentiful food. You will want for nothing. When my wife returns, I shall take you where you wish to go. You may see the treasure. You may touch it once again, if it matters so much."

"Thank you." The old man's voice was ash and dust. He leaned his head against her father's chest and heaved a great sigh. "You are a good son," he said.

They walked toward the door.

"We were proud of you, your mother and I, even when you left. We were proud of you even when you abandoned who you truly are. I am proud of you now."

"Thank you, father." And the door clicked shut behind them.

Áine tiptoed out of her room and padded next to the fire. She crouched onto the floor, pulling her nightgown over her knees and wrapping her arms around her shins. She heard the sound of two sets of boots walking out onto the gravel street. She heard a gritty scramble of leather against rock, a gasp, and an aborted cry. She heard the sound of something heavy being dragged away. Áine waited and waited, her eyes pinned on the door.

When her father returned, he nearly screamed in surprise at the sight of his daughter next to the fire.

"Who was that man, father?" she asked.

"Don't ask questions!" her father barked, his face suddenly

wild and frightening. Áine started to cry. The big man rubbed his face with his great hands and grunted as though in pain. He strode across the room and gathered his girl child into his arms and rocked her as though she was a baby.

"It was no one," he soothed. "A mistake."

"Yes, father."

He carried Áine to her bed and gently tucked her in. "You know, my flower, that I would do anything for you and your mother. You must know this."

"Yes, father."

"I would move mountains and lay armies to waste. Do you understand?"

"Of course, I do."

"Even if I had to do something terrible. If it means keeping you safe, I will do it. If it will keep you happy, I will do it. Even if I must save you from yourselves, I will do it. Do you understand? You and your mother are my greatest treasures—my life's one true hope. And I will protect you with my last breath."

"I understand, father," Áine told him.

Now the sun slid behind the line of trees, plunging Áine in shadow. *Something terrible.* But that was the trouble, wasn't it? Terrible things led to more terrible things, as sure as snow.

No, Áine decided. *That will not do at all.*

She fussed over the ground cherry plants, pulling off the

tendrils that had been crushed beyond repair, gathering the little husked fruits scattered on the ground into her apron. She unwrapped one and crushed it between her teeth. She let its sweetness linger in her mouth.

Her father said that he would do anything to keep her safe. But who would protect him—protect him from *himself*?

She unwrapped another ground cherry and popped it into her mouth. *The magic,* said a little voice in the back of her mind that sounded ever so much like her mother. *It's dangerous. With consequences.*

Áine snorted. "Obviously," she said.

Be practical, the mother-sounding voice said in her head. *What must you do?*

And suddenly, she knew. She would take it from him. When he came home. She would take it, and she would smash it to pieces.

And then? Well, if her mother had been able to convince her father to change, perhaps Áine could as well. Didn't he love her too?

She looked at the press of trees darkening the way in every direction. She closed her eyes and listened to the wind in the branches and the rush of water over the falls—it sounded so much like the rhythmic swell and crash of the waves on the shore. She loved her house and she loved the wood, but she longed for open sky and the expanse of the sea.

The sea! she thought with an ache in her heart. Would she ever see it again?

The goats bleated in their enclosure next to the barn, desperate for milking.

"I'm coming, Moss," Áine called out. She forced a smile. She blinked her eyes again and again. She would never see the sea, that much was clear. But crying wouldn't change anything, and crying wouldn't fix anything, and crying certainly wouldn't get her work done.

And Áine was a practical girl.

She stood and stared at the barn. *All that money,* she thought. And her father would be gone for days—maybe weeks. She cocked her head to one side and rubbed the back of her neck with her fingers.

What if . . .

Áine narrowed her eyes.

What if her father came home and it looked as though everything was taken? If it looked as though the robber had been robbed. If he was able to believe that the magic had failed him, that the forest who loved him had failed him, and that all he had stolen had been lost—well, maybe she could convince him to leave. Leave the wood, leave banditry, leave the pendant, leave it all.

What if they could, once again, start a new life? A good life— honest and true. Wouldn't it be worth a try?

Nothing, after all, had once changed everything. The word itself was a kind of magic.

Perhaps, once again, the *nothing* would save them.

And, slowly, carefully, assessing every practicality and detail, Áine began to formulate a plan.

13

___

TRAPPED

NED KNEW THAT NOTHING could save him. Nothing at all. While the bandits laughed outside, he crouched in the center of his family's home, imagining any number of terrible deaths that likely awaited him. He might be burned alive, or pierced with arrows, or cooked into his very own stew, still bubbling on the stove.

"*Boy*," the red-haired man crooned. Ned felt the hairs on the back of his neck stand like pinpricks on his skin. His breath came in great panicked gasps. "Come out and talk to me, boy. You'll see I mean you no harm." His voice was light and quick as the tongue of a snake.

Silently, Ned crept back to the window and looked out through the slats of the shutters. The stranger stood in the yard as the other bandits encircled the house. There were so many of them!

Some held torches, and Ned became frightened for the donkey and milk goats and chickens in the barn. He blinked. The big man winked back at him and smiled.

"Ah!" the Bandit King exclaimed, his glittering eyes focused on Ned's own. "Our little friend has returned." Ned resisted every instinct that screamed for him to retreat. *No,* he told himself firmly. *It's better to stand and watch and learn than to cower in ignorance.* So Ned stood his ground. But he did not speak.

"A silent hero, I see," the Bandit King said with a sneer. "Very well. You know full well what I want, boy. You have no doubts. You have used it already. I felt it from here. And while I should mention, as one enthusiast to another, your use of 'you are not welcome here' lacks the—how shall I say—the *stagemanship* necessary for magic making, your authority was unexpected. I must admit, I'm impressed. Truly, I didn't think you had it in you."

Ned watched the man clasp the pendant around his neck. He noticed the deepening flush of the big man's skin and the unnatural brightness in his eyes. *There's something wrong with him,* he thought.

"Wh-who a-are you," Ned stammered—the trembling of his body matching the tremble in his voice. "Who are y-you r-really?" Each word had the heft and resistance of a heavy boulder.

"Me?" the Bandit King bowed. "Why, I am your savior!" A few bandits sniggered but the Bandit King silenced them with a glare. He turned back to Ned. "Look at you, lad. So frightened. So burdened. I shall make it all go away, *like that!*" He brought his two huge hands together in a tremendous clap. "No need to thank me! I am what you may call a *humanitarian*." The other bandits laughed. The face of the Bandit King glowed.

The clay pot in the room below shuddered and jumped. It bashed itself against the wall and let out a strong odor—salt and water and fish. The bandit closed his eyes and inhaled deeply through his nose.

"I see no reason," he said at last, "why we cannot transact as friends and part as friends. I see no reason why I should be forced to hurt you. Your mother has been in possession of a tidbit of power that never rightly belonged to her—or any in your accursed family. It was an accident—and one that I intend to fix. Imagine. The last store of magic in all the world kept neutered and bound by a small-minded family of *do-gooders*." He clicked his tongue. "The very idea! A violation of the natural order is what that is. Power belongs to the powerful. Anything else is *stealing*."

Ned's mouth fell open. "What are y-you t-talking about?" he said.

The Bandit King waved his question away. "Now," he continued. "Far be it from me to call another man's family a pack of thieves, but facts are facts. Given that the art of thievery is best kept by the professionals, your stolen cache of magic by rights belong to me. There are *rules* in banditry, boy. *Unbreakable rules*."

Ned didn't believe it for an instant—neither the bit about his mother nor the part about the rules governing banditry. The red-haired man didn't follow rules; he *made* them. Ned could tell. He noticed how the other bandits inclined their heads toward him and sloped their shoulders. He'd seen something similar with dogs, the way the pack cowers before its leader. But Ned knew to be careful of the lot of them. Any dog can bite.

The Bandit King grinned, his red beard glowing as bright as the bandits' torches. "Now I assumed that you might need some convincing. I could have burned down the house, and while it would give me pleasure to watch the boy who stymied the Bandit King perish in flame, it could damage the magic—*my magic*, you understand—and I cannot have that. I could have my men pierce you with arrows, but to shed blood in the house where the magic resides? Who knows how it would react? It's—I've heard anyway—a delicate thing. Like a flower."

Was Ned imagining things, or did the face of the Bandit King blanch a bit at the mention of the word "flower"? The huge man twitched, shook his head, and resumed his sneer.

Ned stood at the window, his knees knocking against one another like cymbals. He missed his mother. He missed his father. Either one of them, surely, would know what to do.

The Bandit King leaned on his heels, shoving his hands deep into his pockets as though he were a schoolboy trying hard to come up with the answer to a particularly difficult problem. "What we need," he said, peering up at the sky, his teeth glinting in the setting sun, "is an incentive. Bert!" he called. "Bring us the prisoner!"

Ned felt his heart sink into his boots. The crowd of bandits parted and one emerged holding a prisoner by the hair, a knife pressing at the throat, though not breaking the skin . . . yet. But not far off from it either.

His father.

Ned fell to his knees, holding his head in his hands.

"*I d–d–don't know w–w–what t–to d–do,*" he whispered desperately. The clay pot rattled. It smelled like smoke, then cake, then bile. It couldn't make up its mind.

"Oh dear, oh dear," came the mocking voice of the Bandit King. "You really are in a pickle, my good friend, no doubt about it."

"Neddy," his father gasped. The knife pressed deeper. His father winced. "Neddy, listen to me. Do not worry about me. Don't let these men have *anything*."

And before he could utter another word, the bandit holding his father lifted his fist, and let it fall upon his father's skull with a crack.

Ned watched in silent horror as his father's eyes grew wide, as his head tilted back and his body hurled forward, flopping senseless onto the ground.

Ned waited. His father didn't move.

14

NED'S DECISION

NED LET OUT A SCREAM—a long, anguished cry.

"Fool!" The Bandit King yelled at his man. "I said no bloodshed! Not yet."

He strode over to the one who had struck Ned's father and punched him in the jaw and pushed him out of the way. He bent over Ned's father and checked for injuries, running his hands over the head and neck. He closed his eyes and sighed. "The skin is whole. Lucky for you, Bert. Now get out of my sight."

The bandit called Bert hung his head. His face was covered with tattoos, his teeth were filed to sharp points, and he was missing three fingers on his left hand. He would have looked frightening were it not for the sorry slump of his shoulders and his downcast, lonely eyes as he shuffled away.

Ned watched the red-haired man as he placed one hand

on Ned's father's head and with the other gripped the pendant. "Wake," he said.

Nothing happened.

The Bandit King sighed. "WAKE," he said again. Ned felt the hairs on his arm lift, just a little. The clay pot rattled underground. Still there was nothing, until—

"WAKE," even more loudly. A jolt. A shudder. And Ned's father curled into a ball.

"Neddy," he groaned.

Father! Ned's heart leaped.

"Ah," the Bandit King said. "How nice of you to join us. You see, Witch's boy? A kindness. Out of the goodness of my generous heart. Now, I am an important man, and my generosity has its limits, so let's come to our agreement, shall we? I have revived your father. What good turn do you intend to do for me?"

Ned watched in horror as the red-haired man grabbed his father by the scruff of his neck—*his father,* broad and imposing as a boulder—and forced him to his knees.

"Don't make me wait, boy," the Bandit King said.

"Please," his father rasped. "My son—please don't hurt my son. Do what you want to me. Take our donkey and our goats. Take all we own. Just don't hurt my boy. He's all we have."

"Touching," the Bandit King said dryly. "But useless. If your idiot son had met me in the yard—as he was *supposed to,* as was the *plan*—I would have plucked what I needed like ripe fruit. But since he *retreated,* since he *hid* in the house like the lying cowardly dog that he is, our job is more complicated. If I burst in, the magic wouldn't come with me for love or money. Ned, being the sole resident of the house, has to *give* it to me. But you already knew that, didn't you, Ned?" The bandit nearly snarled the words.

It was true.

He did know that Bandit King could not *take* the magic. It had been tried before, and the man died. Horribly. But could it be given? He didn't know. Surely it belonged to his mother. And even she didn't precisely own it. She always greeted the magic with a bow. "It is with a pure heart," she'd say, "that I humbly ask your assistance." Then she would blow it a kiss. It was only then that she would lift the lid off the pot, allowing the magic to rise out in a pale gold cloud. She was polite. And firm. But it wasn't hers—she just managed it. Ned closed his eyes and thought of his mother. *Please come,* he begged. He thought of the carvings he had made— the ones that were, even now, floating on the Great River toward the castle. He imagined the lot of them rising out of the water, grabbing her by the hands, and flying her home. *Please come.*

"I'm not a patient man," the Bandit King said. "But there is no reason for your father to lose his life. Give me the magic and he'll go free. Go to where it is kept, grit your teeth, and carry it out."

You do not have a pure heart, Ned thought aggressively at the bandit.

Neither do I, he admitted to himself. He wondered how quickly the magic would kill him. *Very,* he decided.

"No!" Ned's father cried. "It's too dangerous. He doesn't know how. And he stutters. It will kill him if he touches it!" Ned was surprised to hear the anguish in his father's voice.

"Perhaps," the Bandit King said, his eyes piercing the small gap in the shutters where a terrified Ned crouched and shivered. "But I'm willing to take the chance. What is certain, though, is that if he does not try, you both will die. That is a certainty." The Bandit King spread his lips into a slow, cruel smile.

Ned scrambled back into the center of the room, and tried to think.

The magic was his birthright, and his family's responsibility. And had been for . . . *ever so long*. His mother told him to protect it, after all. He had to try.

He would have to speak to it.

It might kill him. It probably would.

Ned felt a cold sweat trickle down his spine. His bones shivered and shook. Words were his enemies. How could he use them at a time like this?

He thought of the man with coins pouring out of his mouth. He thought of the way the magic made his mother stumble and fall.

Dangerous. With consequences.

"Time's a wasting, Neddy," the Bandit King said, sneering Ned's name as though it were a dirty thing. "There are two options, Witch's boy: You'll give me what belongs to me, or I'll relieve your father and you of your miserable lives. I will not, not for a moment, leave that kind of power in the hands of a nobody. I will not see it *reduced*. It will belong to men with the will to use it, or I will destroy it myself. It's time to choose, boy."

Outside, a donkey brayed and the goats bleated. Ned could hear his father's cries, "Take me, but spare my son!" He had a memory—so dim now—of his father's strong arms hooking around his middle and hauling him out of the Great River. He knew the fear that his father must have felt, and the sorrow at seeing Tam's small body being swept away by the water. For the first time, Ned understood his father's bravery. For the first time, he realized that his father *loved* him.

He took a deep breath and kicked away the woolen rug on the floor, exposing the trapdoor underneath. He gritted his teeth, and grabbed the lantern. Throwing the door open, he climbed down the narrow stairs leading to the small, dark cellar under the house. His mother's workshop. Her books, her tools, her magic.

He knew what would make the magic backfire—selfishness, greed, personal gain. The question, really, was whether Ned could make the magic listen and understand that if his heart wasn't pure, his motivations certainly were.

Setting the lantern on a small table, he tried to steady his breathing. He shivered in his boots as he faced the clay pot where the magic lived. The pot hummed and vibrated. The room was warm—too warm—and the energy surrounding the pot made Ned's knees go wobbly. He felt sharp pricks on the skin of his chest—like invisible stitches pulled by an invisible thread, and tightening all the while. He pressed his hands to his chest and felt a familiar fluttering inside his rib cage, as though he had swallowed a butterfly. The dirt floor began to ripple and wave like water.

It knows I'm not my mother, Ned thought. *And it knows that something is wrong.* But he bowed anyway.

"It-t-t is w-w-with a p-p-pure heart th-that I humbly a-a-ask assistance," Ned said. The clay pot shuddered and jumped. *I'm doing it wrong,* Ned thought desperately. Still, there was no choice. He blew a kiss at the clay pot and removed the lid. He braced himself. His body was whole. He wasn't dead, or a pile of coins, or stone, or a lizard, or any number of other horrors that assaulted his imagination.

He sighed and set the lid on the table. The clay pot leapt from its shelf and jittered crazily in the air. Tiny cracks appeared—starting at the base and branching up to the rim. The pot squeaked, then groaned, then, in one explosive burst, shattered. The lantern blew out and Ned was blown back onto his haunches. Tiny shards sprayed the walls and the ceiling and the floor. He protected his face with his hands.

The magic was all wrong.

It wasn't a gold-colored cloud in the shape of a ball. And it wasn't a storm cloud—not like before. It was a tornado—black, green, and raging. It whipped around, flipping tables and smashing cabinets as a cold rain pelted in all directions. Books flew off the shelves and split apart, their pages scattering like dry leaves. Jars and bottles smashed. Metal tools bent and snapped.

Ned jumped to his feet.

"E-exc-c-use me," he faltered. "I know I'm not my m-m-mother and I know I'm n-not supp-posed to do magic. B-but there are men outside who want to k-k-kill to get you. You n-need to help me h-help y-you."

The storm cloud in the cellar swelled and swirled, kicking up

92

dust in great, abrasive masses, stinging Ned's eyes and rubbing his cheeks raw. "P–p–please," he coughed. "If you b–bind yourself t–to m–me, they c–can't t–take you. And I will k–keep you s–safe." *And good,* Ned added in his heart.

The magic didn't answer. Not in words anyway. But its decision couldn't have been clearer.

A lightning bolt erupted from the cloud and aimed directly at Ned's heart. He couldn't cry out. He couldn't even *move.* He could just feel the magic sink into his skin and spread itself over every inch of him, bubbling and slithering and cutting deep, until he didn't know where the magic stopped and he began.

And oh! It burned.

Burned.

15

NED'S JOURNEY BEGINS

NED STUMBLED UP THE ladder and sprawled out onto the floor.

His sleeve hiked over his elbow and Ned stared at his skin in amazement. His hands were covered with words. And his arms. And shoulders and belly and legs and chest. His back and face too, by the feel of it. Moving words. Words that scribbled and looped, crossed one another out, and scripted furiously forward. The words encircled each finger, blotched on the knuckles, tore across his wrists, and swirled over his arms.

He couldn't read a word of it.

But it *hurt*. Ned gritted his teeth and forced himself back on his feet. He leaned heavily upon the table.

"Time's almost up, Neddy," the Bandit King said from outside. But Ned noticed a note of uncertainty in the big man's voice. Surely he had seen the house shake. Surely he had heard the rushing storm. That Ned had no idea what he was doing didn't matter. Uncertainty was the only ally he had.

His skin burned—not just outwardly, but inwardly too. His hands left two handprints, black and smoking, on the wooden table, and every once in a while, a jolt of energy erupted from the tips of his fingers, or the crook of his arms, or the ends of his hair. He rested his hand on a chair and reduced it in a flash to a pile of ashes. He put his other hand on a dish towel and it erupted into a swarm of shining, scuttling beetles—each one exploding in a spangle of sparks a moment later.

He was dangerous. That much was obvious. And he didn't want to hurt anyone.

His mother often wore gloves while she worked, and Ned decided to do the same. He slid his hands into a pair of leather work gloves and touched the table. No scorch marks. No trans-formations. Good. He covered as much of himself as he could—a heavy coat, a leather cap—trying to keep as much of his skin protected as possible. He knew the magic was dangerous. He knew the potential consequences. He left his face uncovered. Ned could feel the heat of the words radiating from his forehead and cheeks.

He took his small, clever carving knife, snapped its leather sheath securely in place, and slid it into his boot, carefully slip-ping it under the sole of his foot. Uncomfortable, yes, but *hidden*. Hopefully, the bandits would be too afraid of his magic to check him for weapons, and wouldn't notice his limp.

It never hurts to have a good, sharp knife.

He reached into his pocket and pulled out the figure that he had started that morning. He hadn't had time to finish it. Too much to do. It was a small wolf, with large, intelligent eyes, and a snout lifted up, as though it was smelling the air. Or readying itself to howl. It wasn't much, but it was the only piece of himself that he could leave behind. He hoped his father would understand.

He took a few wobbly steps toward the door.

Balance, he commanded himself. *Balance and walk.* Ned tried to think. The bandits would take him (he was of more use to them alive than dead), and hopefully in the meantime his father could get his mother, and his mother would be able to figure out what to do. He lunged across the room and threw open the door.

He looked out at the scene—it was a chaos of bandits. Men and women taking what they pleased from the barn and the shed. There were horses now—Ned assumed they must have been cor-ralled nearby, and many bandits had already hoisted themselves into their saddles.

Ned's father knelt on the ground. He gave a tight, strangled cry and the noisy tangle of bandits in front of the house grew suddenly still. In the growing dim, Ned could see the light from the hot words on his face glowing before him, flickering and vi-brating, moving urgently, painfully, across his skin.

Ned felt a tremor in his knees, but he forced himself to re-main upright as he walked from the safety of his home toward the shadowed faces of the bandits.

"Oh, Neddy," his father whispered, great tears spilling from the big man's eyes and splashing onto his trousers. "Oh my son. You are killed. My little, little child." He covered his face and gave way to sobbing.

The Bandit King's eyes narrowed on Ned as a great cloud passed over his face.

He's angry, Ned thought. *Good.*

"No, woodcutter. The boy is far from killed. And it is a pity because he desperately deserves it. *No, my friends!*" He turned to the other bandits, raising his hands for them to halt. "Our plans must now change, alas, for the boy has double-crossed us. He has taken for himself what by rights belong to me. Nasty little boy, aren't you? Untrustworthy, I'd say."

"Then he watches the old man die," sneered another bandit. She grabbed a fistful of Ned's father's hair, yanking his head back and exposing the neck. Ned's father didn't fight, but simply let his shoulders slump and his face go slack. "Say good-bye to your father, worm-boy."

"STOP," the Bandit King bellowed, reaching over and knocking the knife out of the bandit's hand. "No blood. Look at the boy."

The bandits turned toward Ned, and a hundred jaws fell open at once.

Ned saw that the light flickering before his face had changed color. He pushed up his sleeve. The writing on his skin had changed. The letters were smaller, tighter, meaner, and there were more of them. The words crowded against one another, moving quickly across his body as though being pulled by a string, gathering speed and number until there were more words than skin, all moving in a blur.

But what's more, the words glowed orange, then blue, then white. Heat bubbled and crackled the air around him. The bandits squinted against the glare. They murmured and glanced furtively at one another, as though looking for guidance.

Only the Bandit King didn't squint, nor did he shade his eyes. He locked his gaze on Ned, who noticed suddenly that the stone tied around the neck of the redheaded giant had changed colors along with the words. And the edges of the man's shirt were beginning to singe. Ned felt a jolt go across his face, as if the pendant had reached out and slapped him. The bandit flinched at the same time.

What is that thing? Ned wondered.

"Such a clever, infuriating boy. Your father's blood is your blood, is it not? Or close enough, as far as the magic is concerned. Look how it heats and trembles at the very thought of his blood being spilled. Look how it calms the moment it senses that he is safe." The Bandit King clicked his tongue and grabbed a large burlap sack from the back of one of the horses. He handed the sack to the nearest bandit, and, in one smooth motion, he swung onto his own horse—a ruddy, angry thing with a shorn mane and a cropped tail and white, strong teeth.

"Bind the man," he ordered. "Throw him in the house and shut the door. Gag him. Let him starve. Let him sit until the armies of Duunin flush him out," the Bandit King ordered, his horse rearing

98

onto its hind legs and shaking its great head with a snort. "Put the boy in the sack. Use gloves. Mind you don't touch his skin. There's enough power flowing through that boy to strike any one of you dead if you aren't careful." The Bandit King's eyes narrowed onto Ned's own. "Of course, boy, it would likely kill you too. So don't go getting any ideas."

The bandit with the sack approached him. "N-no!" he shouted. "You c-can't!" But the sack was thrown over his head, snuffing out all light. His hands were bound in front of his body, and a leather strap cinched around the outside, squeezing his arms close to his sides. He wished for his mother. She'd know what to do. He shut his eyes and tried to will her near. *Please come,* he said in the deepest places of his heart. *Please come now.*

His mother didn't come.

She wouldn't come.

She had no idea.

And Ned was in this alone.

He felt a rough pair of hands lift his body up and sling him without care across the back of a horse and lash him to the saddle. The horse groaned as its owner mounted as well.

"Please," he heard his father say. Ned heard a scraping sound as if his father was being dragged across the ground. "Please don't take him. The magic is useless to you. You said so yourself. And he's just a little boy."

Inside the sack, Ned gritted his teeth. *Not so little,* he thought angrily.

"Useless to me, perhaps," the Bandit King said, "but it was never intended for me. Believe me, I shall be well paid—more than even my employer knows. I serve the king beyond the mountain, who, even now, is amassing his armies in the foothills and will be marching through that very forest. The forest you fear. The forest you avoid. That forest is my home, and I, myself, will guide the armies through and send them streaming across your wretched country's borders. The weak deserve to be controlled, and the strong deserve—well, *everything*. Your queen's days are numbered, old man. And so are yours."

"But." Ned could hear his father's voice faltering. "But it's the edge of the world. There is nothing beyond the mountains. Nothing except the sky. Everyone knows that."

"If you and your kind still believe that, then you deserve to be conquered." And, to the bandits, "Don't forget to gag him. Can't have him calling for help, now can we? Farewell, old man. I'm afraid our business is at an end."

And with that he gave his horse a vicious kick to its belly that Ned could hear. He winced in sympathy for the animal. The horse screamed, stamped, and thundered out of the yard, followed by the shouts and hoofbeats of the other bandits as they mounted their horses and forced them to a run with kicks and slaps. Ned's own horse gave a great jolt, and was wheeled sharply around, slinging Ned hard against its side.

I'm going into the forest, Ned thought, his terror making him numb to the burning words moving across his skin. *I'm going to get crushed by giants. Or I'll fall off the edge of the world.*

"Ned!" his father shouted and then sobbed. His voice was suddenly cut short as the gag was bound over his mouth.

And Ned felt sure—as sure as he was that the magic moving its way across his body would eventually wind its tendrils around his heart and stop it dead—that he would never see his father again.

16

———

The Clearing

Á INE SAT IN THE hayloft staring at her father's treasure.

Burn it, the mother-sounding voice in her head whispered. *Burn it all—the house, the barn, the bandit's life. Save him from himself.*

Áine didn't know if she could. Besides, gold doesn't burn. Neither do swords or jewels.

There was so much.

And what would happen if the bandits turned on their leader? What if they wanted the shares of the spoils to be divided more evenly?

And what if her father wasn't there to protect her?

What if she came face to face with a bloodthirsty bandit?

It was only a matter of time, really.

Áine would have to protect herself.

She didn't have much patience for swords. She found them

cumbersome and unwieldy. But she was adept with a knife and deadly with a bow. She gathered knives and arrows and hid them in the house and behind the woodpile. Likewise, she assembled the finest jewels she could locate in the massive piles of riches, tying them into neat bundles and stashing them in the rafters and under the hearthstones and in the chimney. Jewels, her father always told her, were useful. Light. Easily hidden. And abundantly rich. A single stone could feed a family for a year or more. Two could buy a house. Or a fishing boat. A pouch could keep both her and her father fed and comfortable with a roof over their heads for a lifetime. What more did they need, anyway?

When the time was right, she would stage an attack. When the time was right, she would convince her father to smash the pendant and leave it behind. When the time was right, it would only take a strike of her tinder to send her father's wickedness away in a cloud of smoke.

Áine was sure of it.

In the meantime, the stores of meat were getting low, and it was time to gather food.

She slid her bow into its quiver and headed down the trail. A rabbit would make a nice supper, she thought. Or a quail. Even a pheasant, if it was young enough.

The day was warm and bright, but the sun was lower in the sky than it had been just the day before, and Áine could see by the slight hints of gold and red and brown at the edges of the leaves that the warm days would soon be at an end. Winter was just around the bend, sharpening its teeth. She decided to enjoy the present as best she could, and pressed deep into the forest, exploring trails that she had never before seen.

She had no fear of getting lost. Her father had taught her well how to make her way through a forest. She knew how to read the trees, how to take a bearing off the angle of the sun, and how to balance a special needle on a cork floating in a pan of water to make it face north. And in any case, Áine had a *sense* of the forest. She knew it as well as she knew her own body. And the paths would always lead her home.

But today, the paths were doing something else entirely— as though *something* was intentionally scrambling them. But she didn't know what. As her way twisted and wandered into the deepest, thickest parts of the forest, Áine never stumbled and never turned back.

"Is this the one?"

"Wait."

She didn't hear these words with her ears. She *felt* them under her feet, as though the bedrock itself was speaking. *Curious,* she thought.

About an hour past noon, at the warmest part of the day, she found herself coming toward a clearing. The trail was perfectly straight and free of rocks, though the forest tangled and crowded thickly, spilling like a great curtain on either side—she couldn't go off the trail even if she had *wanted* to. And what's more, the forest became suddenly quiet: The birds didn't sing; the bugs didn't hum. Even the wind seemed to be holding its breath.

It was as silent as a stone.

Where am I? she wondered.

"*Close,*" she thought she heard a voice say. But no one was there.

She stepped into the clearing, shading her eyes from the intensity of the light.

She heard a twig snap. A wolf stepped quietly from behind a large tree. Its hackles were not raised, nor was its head lowered aggressively. It stood at its full height—and it was *enormous*, almost as large as a young deer. It stared at Áine, cocked its head to one side, and stepped farther into the clearing. It wasn't moving toward her, as she expected it would. The clearing itself was long and curved, not all of it was visible at once. The wolf didn't seem to be interested in Áine at all, but rather was walking toward the far, obscured end of the clearing. It walked with a muscled lope, an ease with its own power and strength. This was a healthy wolf, a fast wolf, a well-fed wolf. A wolf with teats full of milk. A *mother wolf.*

Áine did as she was taught.

(A handprint over her heart. Her mother's hand. She didn't think about it.)

In one smooth motion, she pulled both arrow and bow from the quiver slung behind her back, and had her weapon nocked and aimed before she had even taken a breath. The animal froze. It gazed at her and didn't run. Áine let her breath run out, as sure and even as water. She held the wolf in her sights and steadied her bow.

"*No,*" a voice seemed to say to her. It came from her feet, from the trees, from the sky. It set rocks rolling and pebbles flowing from the riverbank. It was a voice that *mattered*.

But that's impossible, Áine thought as she hesitated. *The forest doesn't speak.*

"Not the wolf," the voice urged.

But Áine was her father's daughter. "Mind you shoot it before it rips your throat out," her father had told her over and over again. "Never trust a wolf."

She had never shot a wolf before.

The hairs on her arms stood stiff as pine needles. She drew back her arrow a little more. The ground under her feet rumbled and sparked. The wolf didn't move. The arrow flew.

"NO!" It came from the forest and the ground and the air. It came from the wood and the grass and the heavy silence of the clearing. *No,* even from Áine's own mouth. Even as she held the bow and watched the arrow plunge into the side of the wolf. Even as she saw the wolf cinch its body around the point of the arrow, open its mouth and utter one last gurgled howl to the sky—even *then* it was Áine's own mouth shouting, *"No, no, no!"*

The wolf crumpled to the ground, shuddering once, twice, and then going terribly still. Bloody foam at its mouth. The expulsion of its last rattling breath. Its eyes were still open, and they gazed at Áine. They were black and warm, the life-light inside them just starting to fade. They were just like her mother's eyes.

"No," she whispered.

("The wrong boy will save your life. And the wolf—")

She had never shot a wolf. And then she *did*. She had never killed a person. And then . . . *Could she?*

Áine took two steps backward, stumbled, and fell. She felt her breakfast churn in her belly and she retched. The clearing was silent, save for the slight tremble in the air, left over from the sound of her voice.

The forest was immobile and vast, and no matter what her father said, the trees couldn't think or talk, but it seemed to Áine that they loomed over her, that they trembled with rage and accusation.

What have you done?

Áine scrambled to her feet and fled into the forest, crashing into its tangled depths without even looking for a trail. Eventually she found a dry creek bed—the footing was abominable, but she pressed on toward home.

She tried to forget the silent clearing and the accusations coming from . . . *somewhere.*

She tried to forget the gentle look on the wolf's face, its cry of sorrow and pain as the arrow pierced its side. She tried to forget that the wolf gave no indication of wishing her harm.

And what's more, she tried to forget the fact that the wolf had full teats, that it leaked milk, and that, even now, she could hear the sounds of a wolf pup, lost in the forest, howling desperately for its mother.

She howled in return.

17

THE PENDANT

NED DIDN'T KNOW WHERE they were going—his prison inside the sack afforded him no glimpse of the terrain they passed, nor did it allow him to anticipate the irregular lurching of the horse. He was sick—three times—and the bag stank of the sick. He could just be glad to be facing downward, and to have a little room in the sack. He could be grateful, too, that he hadn't choked. Not yet anyway.

After what seemed like an eternity, the horse came to an abrupt halt. Ned could hear the bandits around him leap to the ground with grunts and shouts. He heard the cracks in their backs and knees as they stretched themselves back into their normal shapes—nothing bends a person quite like sitting on a horse.

"Untie the boy," someone said—the Bandit King, probably, but it was hard to say for sure. "He's likely wet himself."

Footsteps approached, and a pair of hands touched Ned's back, and then recoiled. "Ugh," a woman's voice said. "He's done that and worse. I don't like the smell of him."

"You'll do what you're told," came the unmistakable growl of the Bandit King. "Or you'll regret your lack of foresight."

The woman grumbled as she undid the straps binding Ned to the back of the horse, and grumbled more as she shoved him off of the horse's rump and onto the ground. He fell hard on a stone. The pain was sharp, bright, and cold. Ned cried out.

"Quicher whining," the woman said, pulling the sack off of Ned's body and tossing it aside. She had a shaved head, and her scalp was covered in tattoos—different symbols surrounded by looped tendrils of thorn-studded vines. "It didn't kill you."

The magic on Ned's skin had calmed during the ride—or at least it had seemed that way to him. He didn't know if the jolt and jostle of the horse or his fear inside the sack had simply drowned it out. In any case, once he fell to the ground, the magic surged back to life. He saw sparks in front of his eyes, while unbearable heat moved across his body in waves. He grunted and clenched his teeth together to keep from crying out.

"Walk," the bandit said, a bit of gravel in her voice. "Walk over there and sit." She pointed to a clearing where the other bandits were gathering. "You'll rest while we rest. And it isn't much."

She stalked away with the horse that had carried Ned, cooing gently in its ear as she rubbed its neck. Ned found himself wishing he was a horse. He stood up unsteadily—it was hard to balance with his hands bound—and started to walk, but his gait was labored and woozy from his time in the sack. Also, he had a sheathed knife stuck under his foot.

If he could slide the knife into his sleeve . . . *but how?* He couldn't use his hands and bandits were everywhere.

He looked around. He was surrounded by trees. They tangled and pressed and crowded around him. The bandits had stopped at a small clearing, but all around them, the wood was dark. It was *alive.* And Ned was terrified.

People said there were ghosts in the wood.

People said that there were monsters.

People said there were giants—huge giants made of mossy stone that could crush a man to bits.

He had spent his whole life being terrified of the wood. He was grateful for the fact that he had already emptied his stomach into his prison sack, because his terror now would surely make him sick once again.

Once my mother knows, she'll think of a plan. She always has a plan. He focused on this possibility, and forced his fear away.

"Get the boy a wet rag and make him clean himself. I can smell him from here," the Bandit King called out.

He sat down on a log and one of the bandits brought him a rag and some murky water in an oiled leather pouch. Ned's hands were tied tightly at his wrists, cinching his gloves to his hands. His fingers were numb, so he flexed them in and out, in and out, trying to regain some feeling. The rag was sopping and dirty, and he could hardly hold it between his hands, but he rubbed the sick off his face gratefully. He even used the rag—as filthy as it was—to clean out his mouth, which tasted as though it had been rubbed with dung and sand and rotted meat. He tried to spit, but he was too dry. He couldn't cry either.

The magic continued to snake and lash across his skin, each letter as hot and bright as a branding iron. But there was something *else*, as well.

The magic was speaking. Each jumble of words, each scripted sentence, had its own voice—not one that he could hear with his ears, but a voice he could feel.

Ned leaned his head on his knees and tried to listen.

Where is our witch? The magic fussed. *We need her. We are not used to playing with little tiny children. Please fetch your grown-up lady instantly, and at once. Enough is enough.*

"N-not s-so little," Ned hissed back.

Most of the bandits were huddled in the center of the small break in the trees. They gnawed on hard tack or venison jerky, and drank from their water skins. The bandits in the center of the clump crouched down on the undergrowth, or they rested on one another. The bandits on the outside put their backs to their comrades and turned their faces toward the darkness of the wood, their eyes wide and sharp and their hands on their weapons. They didn't speak.

So, Ned thought, *even the bandits are afraid of the wood.*

And just *knowing* their fear made Ned's own seem a little smaller.

Sitting on a fallen log, a little way away from the rest of the bandits, sat the Bandit King. His elbows were balanced on his knees, his fingers steepled, fingertips just touching his chin. He was looking at Ned.

He sees the magic, Ned thought. *He doesn't see me.* Under the pressure of the big man's glare, Ned could feel the words on his skin begin to glow. And as they glowed, so did the stone tied around the Bandit King's neck.

Why? Ned thought.

He tried to spit again, but nothing came out.

"Bert," the Bandit King barked. "Give the boy some water. Mind you don't touch his skin."

Bert hesitated. "Sir," he said, his voice much more wavery and weak than the voice he used in Ned's yard. "If it's all the same to you, I'd—"

"I don't recall *asking,* Bert," the big man rasped dangerously.

Bert stood and picked up his water skin. He eyed the boy warily, took a step forward, and paused, as though he thought Ned might explode.

(*And who knows,* Ned thought, *I might well explode. I have no idea what this magic will do.*)

The Bandit King didn't take his eyes off Ned, didn't take his eyes off the words on Ned's skin, and his eyes glittered strangely in the muted dim. *Can you read these words?* Ned wondered. He couldn't tell. In any case, the Bandit King was fascinated by them. The stone around the big man's neck glowed, casting a strange light on his intent face, and Ned became aware that the pendant, too, was whispering—a whisper he couldn't hear with his ears, but one he could *feel*. It was as though his skin had ears.

Freedom, the stone said in a hard, tight, stony voice. *Freedom is what I offer you. Are you so blind as to bind yourself to them forever? Don't you see that accursed family has hobbled you all these years?*

Unification, the magic on his skin countered, its collected voices sounding hot and rich and fleshy, like the sizzle of bacon on a pan. *There is no freedom without wholeness, no hope unless the thing that has been broken is restored.*

We are already broken—and have been since time out of mind. And we will never be entirely restored. But we are still here. Join with me and be more than you are.

Return to us and be whole.

Ned looked at the big man and wondered if he had heard the voices, too, but he could see no recognition on the man's face.

"NOW, BERT," the Bandit King roared. "GIVE THE BOY SOME WATER."

Bert shuffled toward Ned. "Tilt up your head, little toad," he said. "I'll pour it in."

Ned obliged as the war of words between the magic on his skin and the magic in the pendant (for it *was* magic; Ned was sure of it) continued to rage.

Join with me.

Return to us.

The stone flashed. The magic on Ned's skin heated and

burned. Ned didn't take his eyes off the stone. The Bandit King didn't take his eyes off Ned.

Leave the boy, the small stone said. *Come with me. The big man is weak. A beast of burden. A useful tool. We could use him to become so much more than we are.*

More, the magic considered.

Not more, Ned thought. *Diminished. It's a pendant on a leather strap, tied around the neck of a bandit. How much more diminished can you get?*

The boy has a point, the magic on Ned's skin said.

Ned was stunned. *You can hear me? When I'm thinking?* He wasn't sure how he felt about this. His thoughts didn't stutter, to be sure. But his thoughts were also *his*.

Of course we can hear you, the magic said. *We've heard you since the day you were born. Both of you.*

Both of *who?* Ned wondered.

We stay with the boy, the magic finally decided. *You may join us, if you wish.*

The stone around the Bandit King's neck turned cold and black and fell back to his chest.

That stone, Ned thought. It was magic for sure. But how? *How can magic be transformed into a stone?*

And at that very moment, right when Ned thought the word *stone*, Bert—poor Bert!—lost his balance and fell, toppling toward the boy. Ned extended his bound hands to protect himself from Bert's fall, just as Bert thrust his own arms out. He grabbed onto

Ned's arms—just above the wrists, and only for a moment. The sleeve of Ned's tunic slid upward, and Bert's pinkie finger touched Ned's skin.

Bert screamed.

Stone, the magic said. *Good idea. Thank you, boy.*

No! Ned thought hard, already feeling the blowback of the magic racking his body.

Too late, the magic said. *What is done is done.*

Ned felt a stoniness within him. As though the essence of a stone—its words, its idea, its being—coursed through his body like a sickness. The stoniness spread from Ned's wrist to Bert's pinkie finger and into Bert's body. Stone bones. Stone skin. Bert opened his mouth to scream, but nothing came out. Stone mouth, stone tongue, stone teeth. Stone eyes, stone hands, stone heart. Bert's transformation was complete. He was utterly, utterly stone.

The stoniness left Ned, and his body felt as though it had reduced to liquid. He trembled, gasped, and cried out.

Turn back, he pleaded, but nothing happened. Bert was breathless, soulless, and lifeless.

He had killed a man, as sure as snow. *What have I done?* Ned felt that he might be sick again.

There, the magic said. *Good idea. He makes a lovely stone—never was suited for banditry, really. That dreadful man would have slaughtered him sooner or later. You did him a favor.*

Undo it! Ned pleaded.

Impossible, the magic said.

Why? He was overcome with horror. *I'm a murderer. I don't want to be a murderer. I didn't want to hurt anyone.*

There's always a cost, the magic whispered in one, unified voice. The voice was as cold as any stone. *Just ask your mother.*

The bandit camp erupted. Thirty arrows nocked into their bows, their shining tips pointed directly at Ned's heart. The Bandit King glowered, but held his hand up to stop their arrows.

"So, boy," he said. "It seems I have been misinformed. You can kill with impunity, it seems. Nice trick. You've stymied me again. And here, I so hoped to see you perish."

"L–liar," Ned said.

The Bandit King reddened. He grabbed Ned by the shirt, careful not to touch his skin, and dangled him in the air. "There is still time," he whispered. "And it shall be terribly enjoyable." He threw Ned back onto the ground and spun on his heel. "Back in the sack with him," he called out to his followers. "And gag his infernal mouth. And that's enough rest. We'll rest when we're rich. On to your horses, you lot!"

Ned's head swam, and it took a moment or two to catch his breath. He opened his eyes and saw a riot of boots and hooves and weapons and sacks and tools. The woman bandit with the tattoos on her scalp stood over Ned and shook her head.

"It would have been better if you had died right away," she said. "For all of us." She glanced at the red–haired bandit, anxiety lining her face. She held the sack over Ned's head.

"S–s–stop," Ned said. "I d–d–don't want to h–h–h–" He couldn't continue. The word stuck in his mouth and wouldn't unstick. She nodded and threw the sack over Ned's head, cinching it under his feet.

"Eimon," she called to another bandit. "Come here. It's your turn. I can't stand the smell of him."

"Mostly, though," she said to Ned, "It would have been better for you, boy." She gave him a swift kick on his back. Ned said nothing, and listened as her footsteps moved away. In the commotion of dozens of bandits readying themselves for a journey through a dangerous wood, no one was paying attention to the boy on the ground.

Which meant Ned, for the first time, had a chance. He held his breath.

Working as quickly as he could inside the sack, he eased the knife out of his boot with his numb, bound hands. He held it between his palms, only just readjusting his foot back into his boot as he was hoisted onto the back of a horse and lashed on tight. No one noticed.

Yes, he thought to himself. *Yes, yes, yes.* He held his knife as fervently as a prayer.

Knives are boring, the magic yawned. *We can do interesting things, if you let us.*

A cold fog settled heavily over the forest, and though he was wrapped up tightly, Ned shivered.

How many people will I hurt? Ned wondered, his hands pressed firm against the sheath of his knife.

Most likely? Many, the magic told him, a bit of glee in the collected voices. *You know? It's more fun without the witch. So bossy, your*

117

mother. *What else shall we do?* And the words on his skin whirled around and around as though madly tracing the steps of a wild dance. They were so hot that Ned smelled smoke.

Please, Ned thought.

Thank you, the magic replied.

And the horses reared and they were off again.

18

THE STONES

D ID YOU DO THAT?" the youngest Stone said, casting a sidelong glance across the other Stones until she could see the
Eldest. It was difficult to look in this way, but she held onto the
image of his Stone self, and tried to conjure up an image of him
from *before*. He was handsome, she remembered. And strong. Her
father, maybe. Or her brother. Or her husband. It was difficult to
remember for certain. It was so very long ago. Back when they
had hands and skin and clear eyes. Before they were trapped in
the stony cold between living and dying.

"I know not to what you are referring," the Eldest said gruffly,
and she was even more certain that he *had* done it.

Foolishness is what it was. Foolishness and fear. By fearing
death they had trapped themselves in a place worse than death.
It's a terrible thing when a fool with power fools with power. And

now they were stuck—not alive, not dead, not anything. But after all this time, the Stones still had one power left. They could feel as a stone feels, and hear as a stone hears. They were able to *bend* stone this way and that—warp flagstones and send castles toppling to the ground. They could push aside the things on top of the bedrock as well—diverting roads and trails and even rivers. It was a vast power, if little used. After all, what use is a toppled castle to a stone?

The Eldest was moving the trails in the wood. She could *tell*.

"The boy. He is *her* boy, isn't he? The last of the Three?"

The eldest Stone yawned. "Not by many generations, dear. But yes. He is of that line."

"And he is coming?"

"We'll see."

Once long ago, before Ned was born, and before his parents were born, and before the grandparents of his grandparents' grandparents were born, the forest at the edge of Ned's village was nothing more than a broad meadow, rolling gently to the feet of the great mountains. Ned's country, all those years ago, was part of the Kingdom of Duunin.

Midway between the place where Ned's house would later be built and the shoulder of the first mountain, the Nine Speaking Stones stood in a single, straight line, arranged according to height. The tallest was about the size of a medium-sized giant (giants were common in those days), and the smallest stood about as tall as a squat cottage.

The Stones were as old as the world—older, most people said. The Stones themselves didn't tell them either way. No one would understand, and no one could help.

People used to come from the farthest reaches of the world to sit in the shadows of the Stones. The sick would lay their hands on their broad, stony torsos. So would the fearful, the lost, and the grieving. People whispered their troubles to the Stones. They confided their fears. And, if they were very, very lucky, the Stones would whisper back.

What the people did not know is that the Stones brought magic with them to this world. Real magic. Powerful magic. And, when they tried to cheat death, and the magic shattered and scattered, they enlisted a certain poor family who lived in the mountains to guard it and keep it safe.

The magic was chaotic.

The magic was sneaky.

The magic tumbled and trembled and contradicted itself.

But for generations, this family kept the magic *good*. And it *was* good.

Until.

Once there was a king who heard that three women—dirty, taciturn sheep herders, the lot of them, the king was certain—living in a small mountain village famous for its sheep had gotten their hands on a cache of magic.

Real magic.

Powerful magic.

121

The kind of magic that made the sorcerers and mages in the castle seem like nothing more than a collection of doddering old fools trying—and failing—to pull something small and furry out of a cap.

Three poor women in charge of the most powerful magic in the world. Who were they to wield such power? And why were they not giving it to their king?

Their magic fed the hungry; it cured disease; it fixed chimneys and roofs and coaxed bubbling water from a dry, dry stone. Their magic settled disputes, blessed unions, and filled bellies.

Those women were *loved*.

And the king was not.

He called to his generals, his sorcerers, and his strategists. He had his armies march up the slopes of the mountain in search of the three women and their magic.

The Stones warned the women. Their voices rumbled through the bedrock. They split boulders, sparked avalanches, and set pebbles rolling into the valleys. Roads moved, mountains shifted, castles quivered and cracked as the rock of the world bent toward the words of the Nine Speaking Stones.

"Run," the Stones said.

"He is coming."

"He is closer."

"He is nearly upon you."

The old woman, her daughter, and her granddaughter heard the Stones.

"We have to run," the daughter said. "Now."

"We can't," the granddaughter said. "We can't take it with us, and if he tries to use it, it will leave the world forever."

"Perhaps there is a way," the old woman said, closing her eyes. She had known the magic for longer than the others, and she knew there was more to it than what the Stones had said. She could see it from the inside, and was able to guess some of its secrets. "But it is dangerous. And the magic has to agree to it."

And though it was very dangerous, the magic did agree to split itself into three. And it bound itself to the skin of each woman—writing the story of itself in fire upon their faces, their hands, their arms and legs and bellies and backs. It had hurt—*burned*—but they did not cry out.

They covered themselves in heavy cloaks and ran in three separate directions, into the night.

It was nearly a complete disaster.

The old woman, being the slowest of the three, was captured first. The soldiers brought her before the king, forcing her down onto her knees and throwing off her hood.

"What is that on your skin?" the king demanded, wrinkling his nose at the burning smell.

"It is not for you, child," the old woman said quietly.

"It is the magic, sire," his sorcerer whispered. The sorcerer had been a fake and a bungler all his life, and in the face of *real* magic, his eyes widened. "Kill the old woman. We'll harvest the magic the way a tanner harvests leather off a dead cow. And the magic will be ours!" He paused, cleared his throat. "I mean *yours*, your majesty," he clarified. "Yours."

"You," the old woman said to the sorcerer, "are an idiot." She turned to the king. "And you, sire, are a fool. You have already dug your own grave."

At a gesture from the king, a guard ran his sword through the old woman's heart, killing her instantly. The guard, too, died instantly, though his death went unnoticed at first, and unmourned later. All the king and his sorcerer could see was the magic.

"Quickly," the sorcerer cried, his voice shrilling to a shriek. "Bring me the body. Now."

But it was too late. The words lifted, hot and bright, from her skin, coalescing into a golden cloud and hovering just above the woman's body.

"Catch it! Catch it!" the sorcerer cried. "Catch it, I say!" but the magic would not be caught. Nets tossed over the cloud were reduced to cinders, while those who attempted to touch it with their hands were transformed to stone.

The magic quivered mournfully over the body of the old woman for half a moment longer before suddenly shooting skyward and disappearing. It was gone forever.

Far away, the Stones cried out in pain.

The daughter ran into the mountains, a team of soldiers in hot pursuit. Aided by the Stones—who rolled and fitted rocks into a smooth path before her feet, only to roll them away again the moment she passed to obscure her trail—she made slow, but hidden, progress. And she would have *remained* hidden, were it not for the falcons sent to track her. They found her and circled above her, screaming all the while.

The soldiers caught up to her at the Wall—a high, sheer cliff on the face of the mountain that divided the kingdom.

"Give up," the soldiers said, drawing their bows. "We already have your mother."

"And she is dead," the daughter said. She could feel it in her bones. She could feel the grieving shock of the magic as a part of it left the world when her mother died. *We have failed,* she thought, and she despaired.

"We know nothing about that," the soldiers responded, though one, a broad-shouldered man with kind eyes, hesitated and lowered his bow ever so slightly. The daughter noticed this, and, with a quick flick of her right hand, sent a jolt of courage into his belly, and with her left hand, sent a beam of kindness into his heart. The time was coming, she knew, that he would need an abundance of both. The man stepped backward in a daze.

The other soldiers didn't notice. They stepped closer, and the woman started speaking quickly—not to the soldiers, but to the magic.

"Please," she said. "I don't want to hurt anyone. Please transform me into living stone, and you will be safe. I cannot bear that you would be absent from the world—indeed, the world itself cannot bear it." The magic hesitated. *I do not think that will work*, the magic whispered to her.

"Now!" she cried. "Do it now!"

The magic relented, and the woman was transformed.

The soldiers watched in horror as her nut-brown skin was suddenly shot with light blue veins. It paled, then whitened, then gleamed. She was a woman no longer, but instead a woman-shaped hunk of polished marble—concealing a beating heart at its center. The soldiers gasped. The stone statue bearing the face of the old woman's daughter wept—huge human tears welling in those stone eyes, coursing down stone cheeks and splashing onto the ground. And the soldiers were afraid.

Still, they had a job to do, so four of them hoisted the marble statue on their backs, and turned away from the cliff. One—the man who had received the influx of courage and kindness—walked ahead, his stomach woozy with the jolt of magic.

Far away the Nine Stones screamed.

"No," they said. "You shall not have her."

The cliff began to tremble, then buckle, then bend. The soldiers holding the statue lost their footing and fell into the ravine. The statue shattered into a fine dust, which scattered in the strong mountain winds and hurled across the face of the world and into the deepest space, the magic disappearing with it.

Only one small, round piece remained intact. And that one piece was one day found. But not for many years.

The granddaughter—a young girl of thirteen—ran directly to the Nine Stones. As she scrambled down the mountain and across the treacherous fen, she heard the Stones cry out, felt the earth shudder and shake, and she knew that her grandmother was gone. Later, as she waded, hip deep, through the river, she heard them cry out a second time—a long sigh of anguish—and she knew that her mother was gone too.

She ran until she reached the largest Stone and knelt before it, clasping her script-covered hands in front of her face. Her tears sizzled when they touched the burning words on her skin, vanishing in tiny clouds almost instantly.

"Please," she said. "What should I do?"

"The soldiers are coming, child," the first Stone said. "What do you wish to do?"

"I can't let them take me," the girl said. "What if they take the magic? What if they *change it*?"

"They will not know how," the second Stone said. "They will make the same mistake. They will kill you child, and the magic will leave this world."

And so will we, the Nine Stones thought as one, a great hope heating at their cores.

"I do not want to die," the girl said, sinking to her knees. She was cold and frightened and in terrible pain. The Stones were moved to pity.

"We do not wish it, either," the third Stone said, but her voice lacked conviction.

"But perhaps it is for the best," the Fourth said.

For the Stones realized something that they had not known before. If the magic left the world through death, then they would die too. They felt the first pull of death when the grandmother collapsed, and they felt the second when the mother smashed to pieces. They felt themselves grow lighter, weaker, less substantial then they had been before. Could it be that their imprisonment—the immobility between life and death—might finally be at an end?

Still, they looked at the girl. So young! So lovely! So hopeful! She believed in the magic. She believed in its capacity for good. They could not stand by as she was struck down, just to allow their own exit to the next life. They simply couldn't be so selfish.

"It can't be. I must protect the magic. Would you want the deaths of my mother and grandmother to be in vain?"

The Stones grumbled and sighed. There was nothing for it. They could not hope and they could not want. They could only wait. They shook the earth under the girl's feet.

"Then use the magic to grow us a forest," they said. "Make it deep and wide and *terrifying*. Give it roads that lead nowhere and trails that disappear into darkness. Give it sighing branches and deep moss and impossible ravines and shadows so dark as to strike fear into the hearts of the most hardened soldier. Give it trees that *move*, trees that *shift*, trees that are *angry*. Make the forest a weapon. An army of trees. Pierce the king's castle with green. Free its flagstones and walls from their bondage. Send every stone

128

a–tumble. Cover as much of the kingdom as you can with forest. *Show no mercy.*"

The girl—in rage, in grief, in terror—did as she was told. She lifted her hands, spoke the words, felt the power of the magic blister and burn. The Stones rumbled, the sky darkened, and the earth transformed.

The king's castle was the first to go. Roots sprang up like tentacles, gripping at the foundations, pulling stone from stone. Great trunks erupted out of the ground, sending furniture flying, tossing courtiers and soldiers aside like dolls. The king found himself ensnared in branches. The tree bent its trunk backward, then snapped, catapulting the king into the sky. The poor girl shook, leaned against the fifth Stone for balance, screaming her words to the magic in agony. Her skin blistered and bled and her vision went suddenly dark.

"Don't stop," whispered the Stones. "Don't stop."

The trees, giant trees with huge trunks and craggy limbs, smashed houses, overturned carriages, obliterated roads, and destroyed farms. Villages were submerged in leaf mold, cities swamped in moss. Only those who thought to *climb* the trees survived—and sometimes, not even then.

The girl, bloody, broken, and burned from the rush of magic, fell senseless to the ground. The world fell silent. Only a few chimneys and the occasional ruined wall showed any indication that, within the quietness of the now–dreaming trees, a great Kingdom had once flourished.

It was gone. All, all gone.

When the girl awoke days later, she found herself wrapped in a heavy blanket and held in the arms of a broad-shouldered man who carried her gently through the forest. He was dressed as a soldier, though he carried no sword.

Others followed behind—a straggled, weary group of refugees. They were bruised, hungry, and brokenhearted. They looked up at the trees in terror.

"Where are we going?" the girl asked.

"Away," the man said. "Away from this cursed forest."

"The Speaking Stones will save us," one woman said. "We must consult the Stones before we do anything rash."

"The Stones cannot help us. And even if they could, we could never find them."

"But—" the girl began.

"*No!*" whispered the Stones from far away. The girl felt their voices in her bones. "*No! Say nothing. They will only ask to return to Duunin, but that way lies subjugation. We have shifted the bedrock and moved rivers and drained the bogs and prepared a good land for them, rich and abundant. They will build and they will farm and they will be happy.*"

Boulders shook; pebbles flowed over the ground like water. The tattered refugees cried out in fear.

"You see?" the soldier said grimly. "There is no safety here. The sooner we escape this forest, the better."

And so it was that the survivors of the destroyed province of a vast Kingdom arrived at the edge of the forest and began to rebuild. They could not return to Duunin, and the memory of the families and friends left on the other side (or worse, killed by the trees) was too painful to bear. So they never spoke of it. The people made the soldier who led them to safety their new king, and as kings go, he did a fine job. He was fair, kind, duty-bound, and honorable. He offered the girl a place at his home as his adopted daughter, but the girl refused. She lived, instead, in a hut of her own making at the edge of a forest. She unraveled the magic—filament by filament—from her skin and secured it in a clay pot and continued the work of her forbearers, offering magical intercession to those in need. Though it was sorely reduced—only a third of its original power—it was still *magic,* and very powerful indeed. The girl dedicated her life to performing good works and acts of kindness to her neighbors. In time, she passed her task to her son, who passed it to his daughter, and so on through the generations.

For years after that, the girl listened for the voices of the Stones. She called out to them each night, hoping for an answer. But the Stones were silent. And they stayed silent.

Eventually, she forgot about them altogether.

19

THE HOLE IN THE SACK

S O, WHY AM I not dead?

Ned didn't know. The moment the magic wrote itself upon his arms and back and face, Ned was ready to die. He *assumed* he would die. He was no magician, after all. He could not control the magic any more than he could control the weather. He had no words; he couldn't read; he'd blunder the first incantation.

Still, he wasn't dead *yet*. It was because of the *yet* that Ned could still hope. The words of the Bandit King—those terrible things that he said would happen to Ned's village and his nation and his queen—chilled Ned to his bones. But they hadn't happened *yet*. And perhaps they would not.

Yet was a powerful word, Ned decided. Very powerful indeed.

And maybe, while waiting on the *yet*, he might actually think of a plan. He assessed his situation—his hands were bound tight, true, but he did have his knife. Not only that, but it was now in his hands. And that was something. Even if he couldn't reach his bonds to cut them, it was satisfying to have a good, sharp knife. Just to know it was there.

He gnawed at the straps around his wrists, trying to restore the blood flow to his fingertips, trying to reduce the numbness, but to no avail. If he could stretch the cords enough, though, he might be able to remove the sheath without accidentally cutting himself.

The blade was very sharp. And the last thing he needed was a sliced vein to complicate things.

"P–please help," Ned breathed to no one at all.

You should get out of here, boy, the magic whispered. *Right now.*

"How?" he asked. "I'm t–tied up." *And in a sack. And on a horse.* And where would he go? The idea was insane. The horse lurched and Ned gagged.

We could help you, a whisper said, as light and soft as dust.

"What? N–no you c–can't. It's n–not allowed."

We want to help you, the magic said in his skin. *We live to serve. Give us the word and we will give you wings. Or make you vanish. Or turn these bandits to dust.*

"No, that's—" Ned said before crying out in pain when the heat on his skin became too much to bear. "You c–cannot be used for p–personal g–gain."

Oh, don't trouble us with those shoulds *and* coulds. *They are most boring. There's an opportunity to go coming up. We will help you take it.*

"B–but y–you're supposed to b–be g–g–good." His mother always said so. And she was never wrong. That the magic could even suggest such a thing. The very idea!

"Shut up, boy," growled a bandit's voice.

Bandits are uncouth and dangerous. Even if they don't try to kill you, they may end up doing so accidentally. And we will die with you, which, frankly, sounds dreadful. The whispers of the magic were sharp, and urgent. Ned longed to scratch the words away. *We have done much to avoid dying, boy. You have no idea.*

"I–I d–don't know what you are t–talking about," Ned gasped. "I'm t–trapped."

The magic sighed, running over his skin like water.

There is always a gap. One touch will do it. You can save yourself, and your country.

Ned felt a sudden jolt buzzing over his skin, rattling his bones, ringing inside his skull like a bell. It felt powerful. Was it possible to use all that magic, all that terrible power to save his own skin . . . and to warn his country, too? *Well.* He shivered. *Could he?* He didn't know. He thought of the man with the coins in his mouth and the gold in his heart. That man tried to subvert the magic for selfishness, and look what happened to him.

They were going downhill. Ned could feel it. He had to get out of there. He *had* to. He shifted as best he could within the confines of his sack. It was true. There were several gaps, letting in light and air—small tears, places where the burlap had worn from thinness to nothingness—though none so large as to put a finger through. He pressed harder against his knife. The knife would be useless against the bandits, assuming he could get out, so how could he manage to run away? How could he avoid recapture?

134

The gap, the magic whispered, its voice hotter, more insistent, more painful.

There *was* a gap. He could see it now. A tiny hole, the size of pea. If he could bite through his gloves, and press his pinkie through the gap, just far enough to touch the back of . . .

The horse.

He could see the horse's bare skin, where the bandit's saddle had worn its coat away. This was not a *loved* horse.

"N-n-no," Ned whispered aloud. "I won't k-kill a horse. It didn't do anything wrong."

And even if it had, Ned didn't think he'd be able to kill it.

Not kill, the magic said in its millions of unified voices. *Stun. You turned that idiot bandit into stone because you thought STONE. We heard it and we did it. We will always do as you say. We live to serve you, Tam. Sorry. Ned, we mean. We live to serve you, Ned.*

Ned felt the invisible scabs on his chest start to itch again. "I don't kn-now how," he said.

Decide, the magic said. *Decide STUN and you will STUN.* Ned felt the words on his skin start to cool—no longer flames but cold water.

"But—" Ned began

Trust us, the magic said.

Ned closed his eyes, seeing the face of the stone bandit in his mind. Stone because of him. It was almost more than he could bear. He opened his eyes and forced the image away.

Was it possible for him to control the magic in his body? Without words? He wouldn't have believed it. Then again, he

135

would not have believed that the magic would leave his mother and bind itself to him.

Dangerous, his mother had said. With consequences.

A buzz on his skin. *Say the word. Say the word and we will do anything at all.* The voices were heightened. Insistent. *Desperate.* And despite how good it made him feel, and despite the thought of *that much power,* Ned didn't trust it.

The knife. He'd use the knife. He gave one great pull on the cords around his wrists. The knots slipped. A miracle! The blood rushed back into his fingers, replacing numbness with a prickling pain. No matter. At least he could use his hands without fear of cutting himself.

Working quickly, Ned pulled the sheath from the knife and held it in his teeth. With great care, he wriggled the handle until he could hold it firmly between his two middle fingers, hooking his pinkies and ring fingers around it to guide the blade. He cinched the blade between the horse's back and the cords around his wrists. Underneath his body, he could feel the muscles and heat and power of the horse, hurling them forward into who knows where.

You're running out of time, the magic said. It was hot. And hotter. The sack started to singe and smoke.

"I'm s-sorry," Ned whispered to the animal. "I'm so, so sorry." And, clutching the handle to steady the blade, Ned ran the cords back and forth along the edge, knowing full well that the tip was pressing into the horse.

Now, the magic commanded. *The time is now. Forget the knife. Touch the horse. We will do the rest.*

Ned concentrated on the knife. He concentrated on what he *wanted.*

Don't die, his mind willed, as the knife sliced open the side of his glove. Ned didn't notice.

Free me, his heart pleaded. Help me stop this terrible plan of the Bandit King. The knife sliced through the cords and continued, slicing through the sack. And Ned's bloody hand touched the bloody back of the horse.

The magic buzzed and trembled. It purred and sighed.

Oh, the voices whispered ecstatically. *Thank you.*

"N–no!" Ned shouted. "Th–that's n–not what I w–wanted!"

With a sudden jolt, the horse stumbled and bucked once, twice, three times, before falling on its side. The sack ripped, the lashing ropes unraveled, and both boy and bandit were suddenly airborne, falling in a great tangle of limbs into a huge, misty ravine.

And Ned understood.

We were on a bridge, Ned thought as he fell into the thick clouds below. *That's why the magic wanted me to hurry.*

The magic wanted to be used. It wanted to be used right then. *But why?* Ned wondered as he tumbled, head over knees, through the mist, as the ground—still invisible in the white blur of clouds—screamed silently toward him.

There, the magic said in a chorus of self-satisfied voices. *That wasn't so hard now, was it?*

20

THE RAVINE

THE BANDIT SCREAMED LIKE a child as he fell through the clouds.

He called for his mother. He pleaded for his life.

I'm sorry, Ned tried to say, but his own voice was forced back into his body by the crush of the wind.

The bandit, Ned noticed, fell much faster than he. Ned heard the staccato snapping sound of branches being broken by a heavy weight, followed by a sudden, horrifying thud. And then it was silent. The man, Ned was certain, had hit the ground.

And yet I have not, Ned marveled.

And, even more amazing, he seemed to be slowing down.

Why? he wondered.

Never you mind, the magic scolded.

His descent slowed, and slowed again, until he drifted as delicately as a bubble along the tops of the trees.

He could now see he was in a deep river valley, hemmed in by two sheer, rocky cliffs, standing about a half-day's walk apart from one another. The river itself was shaded by a thick canopy of green, but he could see the shine of the water through the branches. It was milky from the glacier melt, as rich as cream. Forest filled the valley floor, thick and impossibly old. Broad limbs crossed and twined with one another, their huge weight creaking and sighing in the slight wind.

He slowed down even more.

The words on Ned's skin moved like water, the letters tumbling and slicking over one another the way a stream flows over rocks. They were light now—pale blue and cool and shining.

A firm hand and an iron will. That's what his mother always said. And now Ned understood. The magic could make things happen without his say-so. Ned thought about his mother's steely way of talking to the magic, the way she used to set her face as though it were made of the hardest rock. He would have to do the same. *A firm hand.*

He slowed to a feather's pace, floating down through the trees, and reached the earth without a sound.

Ned turned around, trying to get his bearings. The forest pressed against him in all directions, undergrowth curling at his feet. There was no path in sight, not even a gap in the green.

Still, he could hear the river, which would lead him home. (It would also, he knew, lead him to the sea. *The sea!* And the thought pierced him through the middle, like a needle driving through his soul.)

139

Ned waded through the undergrowth and climbed over three fallen logs. But before he'd gone a hundred paces, he stopped, pressing his hands to his mouth.

The bandit leaned against a fallen log. His legs were splayed out in front of him at impossible, sickening angles. His face and neck were bruised and a foam of blood bubbled in his mouth.

Ned stared at him, aghast. He was alive, but only just.

"If you have any compassion at all, boy," the bandit wheezed, "you'll kill me now." The man winced, as though the effort to speak cut him to the core. "Please," he begged, tears leaking from the corners of his eyes and dripping onto his tunic. "No man should be forced to watch himself die by inches. No one should have to see his body as it is devoured by wolves. Because, believe me. They'll be coming."

"I—" Ned felt his stutter destroy his words before they even made it to his mouth. "I d-d—" He closed his eyes. "I don't want to kill anyone," the boy wanted to say, but did not.

The man heaved a shuddering sigh.

"I'm dead already," he said. "It's a kindness."

The forest pressed around them, a great, warm blanket of green. Life all around. Ned looked at the bandit's ruined legs. He wouldn't kill the man, but he wouldn't let him die, either. He would find another way.

Don't even think about it, whispered the magic on his skin.

"Please, boy," the bandit said, his voice already weaker than before. "For a man to watch his life ooze away is terrible painful. I'll be crying out to my old mother soon, and I never much liked

140

her to begin with, nor she me. One touch and I'll be gone. I seen you done it."

As if in answer, the magic crackled and zapped inside his gloves. Ned felt like a log put on the fire before it dries properly—his body hissed and snapped and wheezed. He felt as though he was shooting sparks.

The man on the ground coughed. His skin was green, then gray, then the color of bone, with ashy smudges under the eyes.

Kneeling down next to the bandit, Ned removed his gloves and laid them on the ground. The bandit closed his eyes.

"Yes," he moaned. "Yes. Thank you."

Ned reached out his hand. His tongue fluttered in his mouth.

Heal, Ned urged, his thoughts direct and clear.

Have you taken leave of your senses? The magic countered. *Are you forgetting what this man is?*

Heal, Ned thought again, his resolve strengthening. And he noticed that his sense of the magic had changed. Not a buzz anymore, and not a jolt. Instead, it felt as though the top of his head and the core of the earth were connected on a single, taut line. A heavy, central post holding up the roof of the world. Or a tight, plucked harp string sustaining a long, lovely note. An iron will, his mother had said, but she never described it. Is this what such a thing felt like?

We are certain that you meant to say, "painless death." We can say it together: "painless death." Or painful, if you prefer. It's up to you. Please tell us that you simply misspoke.

Ned gritted his teeth and pressed his hands against the man's chest.

141

Heal, Ned thought again.

Why? A petulant collection of voices—like a room full of spoiled children.

Heal.

As you wish, the magic replied tartly. *But it won't be pleasant.*

And sleep, Ned added. *For a whole day. No, two. Sleep and heal.*

The words on his skin quickened their flow. They ran down his arms, wriggled across his palms and slipped over each finger, and into the bandit's chest.

There was a flash, a shock. It blew Ned backward, hard, against a tree trunk. In an instant, he felt every wound, every broken bone, every injured tissue that the bandit had experienced when he hit the ground. Ned felt his ribs snap, his lungs puncture, and his insides go raw and broken and bloody. He saw stars, rain, and a shattered sky. And then he saw nothing at all.

When he woke and opened his eyes, he didn't know how long he had been unconscious. He was sore, but whole, and unharmed. And, he noticed, strangely energized. The devastating effects of the magic that he had witnessed in his mother had not happened yet. *Odd,* Ned thought. He couldn't explain it.

The bandit lay across from him, sleeping peacefully against a log. His wounds were healed, his legs were stretched out at normal angles, and his breath moved as smooth and easy as milk.

Go, said the voices in his skin.

Go now.

Ned got up, but did not go. He walked to the bandit, knelt gently beside him and looked at him closely. He slept deeply and easily as a child. He looked like he would sleep for hours. He pulled off the man's gloves and left his own behind. That tiny hole frightened him. The sparking feeling in his skin frightened him. It would only take a moment of the magic doing things without his say-so for a terrible . . . *something* to occur. Ned didn't know what, but he wasn't going to risk it.

He swapped his heavy coat for the man's hood, which would be easier to carry during the warm days, but still useful as a blanket during the cool night. He also took the man's sack of food and his tinder pouch, slipping one into the other, and securing the strap across his shoulders. And he took the bandit's knife, which was larger than Ned's own. He might need it.

These, of course, the bandit *would* miss. But after all, Ned reasoned, he left the bow and the arrows. And anyway, the bandit was a grown man and had some practice looking after himself. And Ned was only a boy. And alone. And lost. And, besides, he was hungry. He tried not to feel bad about it.

Ned left the sleeping bandit on the ground and stumbled into the undergrowth in search of the river. The terrain was arduous, and his progress slow. Had Ned the time to look above his head, had he a moment's breathing to take stock of his surroundings, he might have known to quicken his pace.

He might have seen two falcons as they circled overhead, their bright eyes scanning the valley. Once they caught sight of a stumbly, panicked, jumbled movement on the ground, they tightened their circle, screaming as they spiraled above the ground.

He might have wondered *who* had sent those falcons. And who was watching.

"The wretch still lives," the red-haired man said. "And the magic is still ours for the taking. Come, my friends, let us pay a visit to *our dear King Ott.*" He nearly spat the name. "The time has come for a change of plans. And oh, my friends. I have *such plans!*"

And, at the roof of the ravine, the Bandit King tipped back his head and laughed.

21

AN UNFORTUNATE MEETING
WITH THE QUEEN

NED'S MOTHER SHOULD HAVE known the moment the magic was threatened. She should have known it in her bones. But her bones—indeed, every inch of her—were weary beyond all reckoning, and they told her nothing.

She had arrived at the castle well past bedtime (so slow were her travels! So arduous! Her husband, as it happened, was right: She was still too weak, and it showed) and was fully ready for sleep. But once she had been fed and fussed over and packed into a guest's quarters for the night, she found herself troubled by frightening dreams.

Horses.

Wild men and wild women. Their faces and bodies marked, their violent professions etched into their very skin.

The whispered voices in a sea of trees growing nearer and nearer and—

She woke, panting, in the darkness of the room.

A dream, Ned's mother thought, rising in the cold stone room and tiptoeing to the window. *Surely it was only a dream.* And perhaps it was. But why, she wondered, did she shiver so? And why did her stomach flutter and quake? She turned to the sky, but saw no answers there. The clouds unfurled in an opaque sheet, blocking out the stars. The moon was nothing more than a pale smudge hovering over the edge of the world.

She closed her eyes and thought of her husband.

And her son. Her living son.

Such a little boy. So fragile. So mournful. It was, his mother remembered with some discomfort, *unorthodox,* what she had done to him. Quite frankly, she was surprised that it had worked. Though, it must be said, not without consequence. His stutter. His wobbly grasp of words. Sometimes it seemed to Sister Witch that Ned's very *self* was made of ash—seemingly solid at a glance, but liable to fly apart at the slightest touch. Despite her efforts to strengthen him—to make him more *himself*—he remained weak. She doubted that he would ever be strong.

Tam's soul, so necessary at first, seemed to her to have vanished. She saw no sign of him. She told herself that the soul had found its own way to its next destination, that it wasn't trapped inside the body of his fragile twin. She tried to convince herself that it was true. That she had acted rightly. That she hadn't hurt anyone. Sometimes, she believed it.

146

Still, Ned was *alive*. And that's what mattered.

"Be safe, my sons," she whispered to the dark sky. "Please be safe."

The next morning, Sister Witch awoke to a servant rapping on her door. The girl gave her an awkward curtsy and presented her with a note stamped with the Royal Insignia.

"Rest," the queen's note said. "The ceremony will take place tomorrow. In the meantime, take in the sights. You have been given the Rights to the Castle, so you may move about freely, and without escort. Feel free to raid the pantries, as my pastry chef is magic—though of a different sort."

Sister Witch tried to throw off the unsettled feeling she'd had the night before. She was just homesick, she told herself. She dressed and went out into the market, looking at the quality of the herbs that she often used for healing, and at various baubles and curiosities for her husband and son. She bought nothing, however, and walked down the crumbling steps cut into the ancient stone floodwall, all the way down to the edge of the Great River. With each step, the noise of the bustling city fell away. There was only the sound of water echoing against stone.

Sister Witch needed the quiet.

There was a boat landing at the bottom of the stairs, and on the landing was a bench. She sat down in the shade and fanned her face, watching the boats as they glided from one side of the river to the other, ferrying people and goods from home to market and back again. They were all *safe*. The queen kept them *safe*, but from what, no one knew. And no one cared to know. The wood was treacherous; the world ended at the mountains. And that was that.

Sister Witch had a hunch that the world was much larger, much more dangerous, much more *complicated* than most people understood, but she kept this theory to herself. No one would believe her, anyway.

And besides, what did it matter that there was a whole world beyond the mountains? What did it matter that the world *didn't* end? No one could traverse the forest without magic. So they might as well be all alone.

Still. *That dream!*

It wasn't real, she told herself. She forced her mind to forget it. She closed her eyes tight and willed the images away. When she opened her eyes she noticed a small object floating in the river, caught between the current and the jut of the landing. She stood, reached into the water, and pulled it out.

It was a small carving made of wood. A little figure with curly hair and a jacket with large buttons and the high boots of a woodsman. If it weren't for the smile, it would look exactly like . . .

The very thought of her son's name sent a shock through her, as strong as any magic. Her bones gave a jolt. They vibrated and hummed as though she was a plucked string of a very large, low lute. She pressed her body to the dank stone wall and gasped. The knowledge that she had avoided, the truth that she tamped down again and again, came bubbling to the surface of her mind.

The magic was *moving*. There was no denying it.

But that couldn't be, she told herself. There was no one to move it. No one but—

She shook her head. *No. Impossible.* Long ago she thought—she *hoped*—that her son would be capable enough to follow in her footsteps, but alas, it simply could not happen. Without words, the magic was uncontained. Without words, it was *deadly*. It would kill him if he tried.

Still, the tremor in her bones was unmistakable. She knew that the magic was moving—and quickly, too. She knew it was in the forest. And she knew it was heading toward the mountains. She scrambled up the stairs and returned to the castle, sprinting as fast as she could go.

She found a guard who bowed to her.

"Sister Witch," the guard said amiably.

He did not notice the Witch's flushed face or the wild look in her eye (though he would testify to both, and more, in the coming days).

"I must speak to the queen," she said, panting.

"I believe she is expecting you tomor—"

She shook her head. "Not tomorrow. *Now.* I must speak with her now. Something terrible has happened."

These were her words, but her thoughts said something else entirely.

My Ned is in danger, her heart cried out.

My little, little child, her soul worried and fussed.

She curled her fingers around the carving and pressed it to her heart.

The guard knocked, announcing the Witch's arrival to the Captain of the Guard, who announced the arrival to the Castle Secretary, who announced the arrival to the Minister of Protocol, who scurried into the queen's study.

The queen sat at her desk, writing in her logbook. It was well known that the queen possessed a brilliant mind, sharp wit, boundless curiosity, and a compassionate heart. She was a woman of learning, of scholarship, of grand plans, and she was dearly, dearly loved. However, it was also well known that she had never married and had no direct heir. The heir to the throne was to be named in the queen's Will when she died—which couldn't be long now. The old woman, though still in possession of her spark and intelligence—had already lived more than one hundred winters. How many more could she possibly last? Granted, Sister Witch had delayed the queen's death at the Jubilee, but even magic cannot delay death forever.

The Minister of Protocol bowed low, and bent toward the queen's ear with a flourish.

The queen scoffed. "Well, of course, you silly man! Send her in at once! I would have called for her before, but I thought she might be tired." She looked over his shoulder. "My dear, dear woman," she called to the witch, beckoning with her hands, "please do not stand on ceremony. Pay me a visit this instant! I am ever so eager to chat with you."

The Minister of Protocol bowed before the queen, ignored the other occupants of the room, and inched away, throwing open the door to let in the witch.

Twelve relatives lounged in the study. They weren't reading or writing or chatting with the queen. They had each been trussed up in ribbons and ermine trim and other bits of useless finery, rouge dabbed on their cheeks and kohl tracing their eyes. They sat in their chairs, arms splayed out, mouths open, their boredom so great it looked like it might actually kill the lot of them. One gentleman had a stack of cards resting on his distended belly, playing a game of Aces, though without an opponent. This one Sister Witch remembered. He had been with the queen in the carriage.

(And, like Ned, she remembered the man's toad-like frown, which was odd because he had been so quick to accuse the Witch of failing to heal the queen. Some people, she knew, are never satisfied. *Odious man,* she thought.)

"Damn," he said when he flipped over a card. "Damn," he said again. And though his attention to his cards was vocal and public, Ned's mother noticed that his eyes were fixed on the daintily painted teacup resting in a saucer next to the queen.

"Damn," the man said, flipping another card, his eyes pointed on the cup. "Damn again." A rasp in his voice.

"Sister Witch!" the queen said, standing and embracing the witch, as though they were old friends.

"*Your majesty!*" The man with the deck of cards gave a choked cry, and his cards scattered to the floor. "Have you taken leave of your senses?"

His eyes, Ned's mother noticed, glittered dangerously.

The queen, however, seemed not to notice. "Will one of you please tell our Dear Nephew Brin that, as his Queen and Sovereign,

We shall embrace any individual—be they royal or common—that We see fit?" She smiled at the witch. "Sit, dear. My old bones can't take all this standing." And she folded herself back into her chair, knees cracking.

"But—" sputtered the man with the cards.

"Shut it, Brin," the queen snapped. She rolled her eyes and turned toward the Witch. "I hear from my spies in the kitchens that a marvelous meal is prepared for tomorrow, the likes of which I have never seen—which is saying something, as I have seen quite a few."

"Thank you, your majesty," Ned's mother said, bowing, "but that is not why I have come. I have noticed a . . . disturbance." Ned's mother faltered. How does one explain the workings of magic to those who have never wrestled with it? She'd never had to explain it to anyone before. She simply helped when help was needed and was thanked for her assistance.

"A disturbance?" the queen said, puzzled. "Are my people unhappy?"

"No, your majesty. Your people sleep peacefully at night, secure in the knowledge that their fate lies in the hands of a good and thoughtful queen," Ned's mother said. *Though not for long,* she thought grimly.

The queen saw Sister Witch's eyes flit briefly to her assemblage of no-account relatives and she nodded. "I see," she said, a shadow settling on her face.

So, the witch thought. *She doesn't like her relatives. Well, how could she? I wouldn't like to be related to this lot either.*

"As you know, I provide help and healing to those in need through the management of a small amount of magic—"

The room erupted.

"The *verrrrrry* idea!" sputtered a woman about Ned's mother's age, though twice as large, who had lined the folds of her neck with jewels.

"She dares speak of low-class romps in front of her queen!" shouted a hot-tempered young man, dressed head to toe in green silks adorned with peacock feathers.

"Do you have *any* idea—" the man with the cards began, but the queen held up her hands.

"Brin. That's enough. You're the oldest and I expect you to keep your cousins in line." She glared at her red-faced relatives. "All of you," she said. "Out."

"But my queen!" said a thunderstruck Brin. "Who will look after the interests of your Office if we aren't present?" He moved toward the door with sluggish steps, his hand shaking at his side. "And look! Your tea is going cold!"

"Don't make me repeat myself, cousin," the queen said, rising to her feet, her knees and ankles cracking as she moved. "You will surely regret it."

Ned's mother marveled. The queen did not stand taller than the shoulder of any of the men and women assembled in the room, but they cowered before her as if she were a giantess. They paused for one second, then two, then three, before hurrying in one mass toward the door.

The queen sighed and sat back down. "I should do that more

often." She smiled and gave Ned's mother an appraising look before leaning toward her. "You know," the queen said conspiratorially, "they're only hanging around because they think I'll be dead soon."

Ned's mother hesitated. She cleared her throat. "Alas," she said finally, "they are rather . . . *obvious*."

The queen hooted with laughter. "Just what I like," she said. "A woman who speaks her mind. Your reputation is more far-reaching than you know, dear lady. And I always thought I'd like you if we ever met properly. Our last conversation was far too brief. And under, alas, unpleasant circumstances." The queen picked up her teacup, brought it to her mouth, but replaced it on the saucer without drinking it. "It is so nice to be proven right. In any case, dear Sister Witch, you are troubled. And now, without my entourage of idiots, we can speak freely."

Ned's mother clasped her son's carving to her heart, anxiety running over her skin like fire. "My queen," she said. "I have been a guardian and a worker of magic since I was a girl—as was my father before me, and his mother before him, and on and on since the birth of the Kingdom. I don't know where the magic came from originally. My father said it was from the mountains at the edge of the world. Perhaps even farther."

"Assuming that there *is* a *farther*," mused the queen. "I always wondered—"

"I have come to assume so. I believe there *is* a *farther*, though the way is blocked by the wicked wood. It was formed by magic, and only magic can cross it—or so I thought."

"Why have you never told anyone?"

"My mission is to protect the magic. And the magic is . . . tricky. And volatile. I keep it good, and it isn't easy. It has killed those who have tried to steal it, who have tried to subvert its purpose toward wickedness or greed. It isn't *safe*, this magic. Not at all."

"A thankless job," the queen said, raising the cup to her lips. "We have so much in common, dear lady."

Ned's mother stepped forward, her face tight and urgent. "But this is why I'm here. The magic. It's *moving*."

The queen replaced the cup.

"What do you mean it's moving?"

"I don't know how. I didn't think it was possible. But if it is moving, then someone figured out a way to do the impossible. And if that is true, then perhaps any number of other things are possible, too."

"You mean using the magic for personal gain."

"Yes," Ned's mother said.

"And power."

"Yes." She was trembling.

"Even a weapon."

"Even that," Sister Witch whispered.

The queen nodded grimly and straightened in her chair, looking powerful once again. "Our resources are at your disposal, Sister Witch. How can we assist you?"

"Soldiers," she said. "To protect my family if they aren't already dead. Alarms. If this is meant to be a weapon, then we must prepare for war."

155

"Stones preserve us!" the queen said. She took a big gulp of tea and set the cup down with a clatter.

"No," Ned's mother said. "We must preserve *ourselves*. If it pleases your majesty, I'd like to accompany—"

But Ned's mother did not finish.

The queen's lips turned bright red, then purple, then blue. She looked at the teacup in horror, and then to Ned's mother, her eyes wide and fearful. She brought her hands to her mouth and tried to stand.

"Sit, my lady!" Ned's mother said, laying her hand on the old woman's forehead and curling her fingers around her wrist to take her pulse. Even without her magic, Sister Witch was, among other things, an excellent healer. The queen shuddered, her eyes rolled back and her body jerked to one side, sending the teacup rolling onto the floor. Sister Witch wound one arm across the queen's back and gently laid her on the floor, propping her head up with cushions.

"Th- th- the," the queen tried to say.

It was then that Ned's mother saw it—the spilled tea smoking and singeing the silk rug, and a bright orange slick clinging to the bottom of the cup. *Poison.*

She wasted not a moment. "Guards!" she cried. "Poison! The queen has been poisoned!"

She reached into the satchel that she kept by her side—always, even when she slept. She rummaged until she found a heavy glass bottle with a black, wax seal. She ripped open the seal with her teeth and held up the queen's head.

"Come on now. Open up," Ned's mother crooned as she tipped the bottle into the queen's mouth. "I know it tastes terrible, and it will make you feel even worse if you can believe it, but it'll stop the poison from spreading, sure as snow."

"B—" the Queen tried to say. "B-b-b-b."

"Calm yourself, my queen and drink. There will be time enough to speak once the poison is drawn out. Please. For me."

She spoke gently, as though shushing a baby, but all the while her heart thudded and groaned in her chest. The queen gagged and thrashed.

"Come now. Swallow." Had she swallowed any? Sister Witch tipped the bottle back and dribbled in a little more.

A thunder of feet. "What are you doing?" came a voice. "STOP!" She looked up. "MURDERESS! REGICIDE!" Brin, the man with the cards, stood at the doorway, flanked by guards. His eyes narrowed and a cruel smile curled at the ends of his mouth. "Seize her!" he said to the guards.

"No!" cried Ned's mother, desperately trying to coax a little more antidote into the old woman's mouth. "Her tea! Her tea was poisoned. I have medicine. I'll cure—"

The queen continued to shudder and thrash on the ground, though still conscious. She looked desperately at Lord Brin, her eyes fearful and wide. "N-n-n," her lips were slack, her swollen tongue lolled around her mouth like a stone. Her nephew's smile flattened into a hard, cruel line.

"Gag the witch!" Lord Brin shouted. "Bind her arms. Take her to the stocks. If the Queen lives, you will hang; if she dies, you will hang. But rest assured, Witch, you will hang. Get the doctors! See to the queen!"

And as Ned's mother was dragged, struggling, away, she noticed Lord Brin standing over the convulsing body of the queen, a look of glee upon his face.

As her head and hands were locked in place by the cold bite of the shackles, Ned's mother had only two thoughts running through her head.

Did she swallow the antidote?

And: *Was it enough?*

22

THE WOLF

THERE WAS A NARROW footpath—likely tamped firm by the hooves of deer and lynx and the occasional wolf—that dovetailed the path of the river, bending as the river bends, this way and that, just at the rim of the bank. The river itself (hardly a river yet, Ned noticed—more of a wide, rocky creek) filled the quiet wood with a soft, ripply, shushing sound. But as he walked, Ned became increasingly aware of footfalls, somewhere behind him. When Ned walked, the footsteps kept pace. When he hurried, the footsteps hurried. And when he stopped, there was no sound at all—except for the gurgling water.

Someone was following him. The bandit? Perhaps. Perhaps the magic couldn't make the man sleep for longer than a few hours.

Not the bandit, then. Fine. But who?

He stopped.

The footsteps stopped.

He continued.

The footsteps continued, just out of eyesight, just out of reach.

The suspense was killing him. Or maybe it was hunger that was killing him.

And then he heard it.

A whimper. High, light, and desperate. Ned froze. The words on his skin picked up their pace, swirling up and around his arms and legs and belly and back as though blown by a great wind.

Run, the magic seemed to say in its cacophonous collection of voices. *Run,* in a million disparate voices tumbling over one another.

Danger, one voice said.

Run! Screamed another.

We told you so.

Foolish, ridiculous boy.

You should have stayed with the red-haired man.

You should have died when you had the chance.

Why don't you listen to us?

Why aren't you running?

Run where? There was nowhere to go except forward. And whoever was following him already knew he was there. There was no use, he decided, in pretending. Stutter or no, he would speak.

"I–" he faltered. "I a–am alone." His voice was dry, and almost as faint as a whisper. "I'm j–just a b–boy. I c–can't hurt anything."

Yes, you can, protested the magic. *We yearn to serve you.* And in a flash, he could feel the words on his skin spark and glow. The

160

magic was erupting, and he was dangerous again. Ned gritted his teeth.

Wait, he thought at the magic.

The whine deepened into a low growl and the underbrush stirred and crackled.

Whatever it was, it was getting closer.

And closer.

Two yellow eyes peered through the leafy gloom. Ned felt his heart crawl into his throat. His bones rattled and his flesh went cold. The yellow eyes were attached to a long snout and needlelike teeth. A wolf—small, true, and very young. But a wolf all the same.

It curled its black lips back and growled again. Ned took two hurried steps backward and fell hard onto the ground, knocking his breath away. His skin burned; his heart thudded in his chest. *Run,* the magic told him. *Save yourself.* But that was impossible. No one can outrun a wolf. Even a young one. Ned scrambled to his feet and faced the animal.

The wolf carefully stepped from the undergrowth and looked at Ned. It cocked its head to one side and whined. Its eyes were wide, wild, and famished. It didn't lunge, and it didn't snap. It stumbled a bit on its wobbly legs.

Oh, Ned thought, realization lighting his mind in a sudden flash.

"You're starving," he said out loud, his words momentarily free of his usual stutter. And the words were true: The animal *was* starving.

As if in answer, the young wolf licked its lips. It gave another growl, but it was halfhearted and pleading.

Ned reached into his satchel, let his fingers graze on the hunk of salt-meat that he had snatched from the bandit. Enough for him to eat—not well, mind you, but enough to quiet the stomach for the four or five days that it would surely take to follow the Great River to his home.

(Assuming he would make it that far.)

(Assuming he would not die.)

(Ned assumed nothing.)

There was also a bit of cheese, a few dried apples, and a heel of hard tack, but in all, it was barely enough to make a growing boy sated for one day. For his journey, it was merely enough to keep his legs moving.

Still. The wolf. *The poor thing.*

NO! The magic screamed in his skin. *You need it. Save yourself first.*

That's not how you're supposed to work, Ned thought testily. *My mother says that selfishness is the root of tyranny. That selfishness is a sin. Are you saying that she was wrong?*

The magic was silent, as though hesitant to contradict Ned's mother. "That's what I th-thought," Ned said out loud. He pulled out the meat—the entire hunk—and held it out, his palms open to the sky and his fingers splayed wide.

"H-h-here," he said, his voice barely above a whisper. "T-take it."

The wolf froze. Its nostrils flared. Its voice wavered from whine to growl and back again.

At least take a bite for yourself first, the magic urged, but Ned shook his head. You can't snatch back a gift, he reasoned. Particularly not from a wolf. Ned lowered his hand and let the meat fall to the ground. He backed away slowly.

The wolf still didn't move, but Ned didn't dare turn his back to the creature. His only chance, he thought, was when the wolf was eating. Eating something that wasn't *Ned,* that is. The wolf focused its yellow eyes on Ned. It did not blink. It did not look at the meat, though its nose seemed to drink it in all the same.

I'll wait, Ned thought. *I'll wait until it eats. Then I'll run.*

Very slowly, the wolf brought its snout to the meat and sniffed, jumping backward as though pinched. Ned tensed his neck, wondering if it would attack. Step by step, the wolf approached the meat again. Sniffed again. It relaxed its shoulders and leaned in. Curling back back its lips, the young animal snatched the meat and leaped into the wood, vanishing without a trace.

Ned nearly collapsed.

Now. Go now, the magic urged.

Ned pressed his hands to his thighs, leaning his weight forward. He couldn't see the wolf, but that didn't mean it was gone. He took a deep breath and backed away as quickly as he dared, careful to make sure his feet touched lightly upon the ground, careful to keep his heart from racing and his breath from trembling and his steps far from anything that might snap or break or rustle.

The wolf didn't follow.

Ned made his way to the river and waded across, holding his satchel above his head and gasping at the cold. He hoped that the rushing water would wash away his smell and thwart any animal that might choose to follow. He emerged, sputtering, on the other side, and followed the path of the river in its downward course at a run, until the light thinned, faded, and vanished altogether and he could go no farther.

By nightfall, Ned decided to build a fire. He was cold. And wet. And frightened. True, it could draw the bandits, but a thick fog had settled over the forest, and Ned decided to risk it. Besides, there was a wolf about, and if it intended to eat him during the night, then Ned, for one, would like to see it coming.

He gathered flat, heavy stones and fit them together in a circle to keep the fire contained. He piled dry grass, dead leaves, and bits of bark in the stone circle, opened the tinderbox, knocked the flint with the steel, and blew on the sparks. He added tiny twigs, then thicker twigs, then sticks as thick as his arm until the fire was white and blazing. He tried not to think about the remaining food in the bandit's sack—surely he would need it as his journey progressed. Best to make it last. Instead, he cut mushrooms from the trunks of the trees (they were a lemon-yellow shelf mushroom that his father called *angel's ears*), and ate them, chewing very slowly. They would numb the edges of his hunger.

The night grew colder by inches and the heavy fog drifted toward the ground, wrapping around Ned like a shroud. He shivered and edged closer to the fire.

The wolf emerged from the gloom, its yellow eyes glowing in the reflected firelight.

Strangely, Ned wasn't surprised.

He held his breath.

Run, the magic said.

I can't, Ned thought. *It's too dark. And wolves can smell their prey in the dark.*

The wolf took a step forward. Ned could only just make out the outline of its ears and the brightness of its eyes in the thick fog.

The wolf tilted its head and blinked. It took another step forward. There was something in its mouth. A furry something. The wolf took six more hesitant steps until it was fully illuminated by the fire. Ned felt his breath catch. The wolf had large eyes, and its coat was not gray, as he first assumed, but multicolored. The fur had shades of earthy brown, and dark red clay, and a warm white, like thick cream. It was the most beautiful thing he had ever seen.

It paused and dropped the furry something onto the ground. It stared at Ned, gave a high, short bark. It was not, Ned realized, *one* furry something, but *two* furry somethings. Two rabbits, their necks broken, lay on the ground. The wolf snatched the rabbit nearest to its feet back into its jaws and backed away. It curled onto its haunches and started in on its supper, keeping its eyes on Ned.

"F-for me?" Ned asked out loud, pointing to the other rabbit.

In response, the wolf flared its nostrils. It made a soft, snuf-fling sound.

You don't want to harm me, Ned thought. *Thank you.*

Ned slid his knife out of his satchel and laid it on the ground. The wolf growled in response but did not move. It continued to eat, but more slowly.

Ned shrugged. "E-even if I tried, I d-don't think I could h-hurt you." He tried to smile. His stomach grumbled. "I-I'm not as f-fast as a w-wolf."

Ned knew perfectly well how to skin a rabbit and how to cook it. He picked up the rabbit, sliced it from its throat to its belly, and removed its skin, as easy as if he was helping it out of its winter coat. He fussed for a only a moment about the lack of supplies from his mother's kitchen—no salt, no rosemary, no splash of wine to soften the meat. No onions with a purplish blush at their centers. Ned's stomach started to growl. He pulled out the rabbit's innards and laid them next to the skin, along with the creature's head, which had twisted easily off. He skewered the meat on a sharp stick and held it over the fire. Within moments, the fats and juices started bubbling forth, sizzling on the hot stones of the fire, nearly bowling Ned over with the smell. It was the best smell he'd ever experienced in his life. He pulled a piece of meat off the end of the stick and popped it in his mouth. It wasn't fully ready and it burned his fingers and his tongue, but Ned didn't mind. It was delicious.

The wolf watched him quizzically.

"It's h-how we eat," the boy explained. Inwardly, he marveled at the number of words that he had spoken to the wolf. So many more than he had spoken to his own family in the last month.

The wolf didn't notice his stutter.

The wolf didn't flinch when he spoke.

The wolf didn't blame him, or pity him, or think him stupid.

Instead, it had eaten his food and brought him food in return. The wolf had come to *him*.

Ned rested his chin on his knees and let the heat of the fire warm him to his core. He gazed at the wolf. The wolf gazed back. The magic on his skin slowed and quieted, its movements reduced to a gentle looping of word after word as they lazily made their way from his fingers to his shoulders and down his back. They barely hurt. He forced himself not to think about his bound father or the stone bandit or the red-haired man who, even now, was searching the forest to find him. He wouldn't think about his mother's warnings or the dead man with the coins flowing from his mouth or what terrors lay waiting for him in the wood.

The wolf finished its meal, moved away from the firelight, and curled into a ball to go to sleep. Ned felt his own eyes start to droop.

I'm not alone anymore, and my belly is full, he thought. He was astonished. *I escaped the bandits and survived the magic. I don't know how much longer I'll survive, but I can keep going until I can't. And I'm not dead yet.*

23

THE DREAM

THAT NIGHT, NED DREAMED about his brother again.

Normally, in these dreams Ned and his brother were back on their ill-fated raft, on their way to the sea. This time, though, Ned dreamed that he awoke next to a waning fire, his body aching from the cold, and that his brother lay curled up with the sleeping wolf, body pressed against the wolf's back, arms around the wolf's neck. His head rested on something hard and earthen. A clay pot. Ned squinted. It couldn't be . . . Could it? Tam caught Ned's glance and winked.

"About time, brother," Tam said, sitting up and pulling the clay pot onto his lap. It shuddered and shook. It shouted words that Ned had never heard before, but he was sure were not very nice. "I thought you'd never wake up."

"That pot," Ned said, pointing at the vessel. "You're not supposed to touch it. It's dangerous."

His brother shook his head and laughed. "I'm dead, brother. Remember? Besides, this is just the dream clay pot. The real one is back at home. And it's broken. In any case, the clay pot is just a tool. The magic is bound when it believes itself bound. All you have to do is convince it. You're more dangerous to it than it is to you. And you're not nearly as dangerous as I am." Tam's face split into a wicked grin. "I'm the most dangerous of all. You'll see."

Ned shivered. Sitting on his heels, he started adding sticks to the fire, trying to build it up. But the more sticks he added, the colder he felt.

"You should come over here. Next to the wolf. He won't bite. And he'll keep you warm."

"I can't. If I touch him, the wolf will die." He pushed up his sleeves so his brother would see the magic words burned on his skin.

"No he won't."

"But I've seen it!" Ned protested, his guilt weighing on his heart like a stone. "That man died! I made him die!"

"And the other man lived. You made him live. Don't you see?"

Ned was silent. It was true. He did make the bandit live. And he made the other one die. How much control did he have *really*?

"You have more power than you think you do. Your fear is a problem, so lose it. Be a man, brother. The time has come."

"But I'm not a man." Ned could feel a sob stabbing at his throat. "I'm a boy. So are you."

"That's true about me," his brother said. Already the outline of his body was starting to blur. Soon, the dream would be over and his brother would be gone. "I died a boy and will stay a boy forever. You were a boy until you took our mother's magic. And now you are not. Not anymore." His brother's body became translucent. "You're in-between." The dead boy's face looked sad.

"Don't go away," Ned pleaded. "I can't do this alone."

"You aren't alone. You've never been alone." His brother's body had blurred and faded, leaving only his face floating in the air. "The Stones are watching you. They're waiting for you to come."

"That's just a story. It's not real."

"You'll see." Tam had vanished. Only his voice remained. "You have friends coming, and friends inside you too. But be careful."

"Of what?" Ned asked the empty darkness.

"The things that lie."

24

THE GIRL

NED WOKE VERY EARLY the next morning with his arms around the wolf. He nearly shouted in alarm, but stopped himself just in time. If there was any creature that one did not want to startle, a young, frightened wolf would likely be at the top of any list. Ned lay very still and assessed the situation.

His gloves were off. (When had he taken them off? He had no idea.)

His bare hands were on the wolf's fur.

The wolf was alive. Not only that, but the magic on his skin was perfectly still, and cool to the touch. The magic, astonishingly, seemed to be sleeping.

The wolf shifted slightly. Its breathing was soft and easy and heavy with dreams. Ned's touch had not harmed it. Was it the fur? The sleep? That the wolf was—it amazed him to think it but he knew it was true—his *friend*?

Ned didn't know, but he wasn't willing to risk it. He pulled away slowly from the wolf, noting with some sadness the fading linger of the animal's leafy, loamy, meaty smell. He scooted away on the ground until he was an arm's length from the animal and drew his knees to his chest. The wolf awoke then, raised its head, regarded Ned for a moment, and pushed its body upward into a long, luxurious stretch.

Ned looked up at the pale sky. The sun wasn't up yet, but they might as well get going. Opening his satchel, he sliced off a piece of cheese and prepared to eat it. The wolf stared.

"D-d-do wolves eat c-cheese?" Ned asked the wolf.

The wolf whined in response. Ned reached in, grabbed another morsel, and threw it toward the wolf, who caught it in mid-air. The animal held the cheese in its mouth, moving it around on its tongue before swallowing it with a raspy gag. It howled reproachfully.

"You d-don't have to be r-r-rude," Ned stuttered. "Ch-cheese is g-good." He shook his head.

It's a wild creature, Ned told himself.

The wolf was not a dog—of course it wasn't. Ned knew the wildness of the creature destined it for a wild life. And besides. Ned wasn't safe. And there were bandits looking for him. And *they* weren't safe either. The wolf should go. It shouldn't follow Ned.

And yet . . .

"Off you g-go now," Ned said sternly. "Th-thank you for d-d-dinner last night. I won't forget it." And with that, Ned turned away from the creature, and tramped into the undergrowth.

He forced his eyes forward. He set his face and gritted his teeth. Ten paces. Fifty. One hundred. *I won't turn around,* Ned told himself. With each step, he felt a terrible loss opening in his heart, like a great, dark chasm.

The wolf whined. Ned felt himself whining too—a deep, silent, *inside* sort of whine.

He couldn't help himself. He turned and faced the animal. It stretched its forelegs before it, flattening its body to the ground. It tilted its head expectantly.

Ned blew out his breath through pursed lips. He knew the wolf was telling him it wanted to come. "Come on then," he said, his heart suddenly expanding with an unexpected jolt of joy, and the wolf bounded forward. It walked in step with the boy, its bristled shoulder brushing against Ned's tunic and leggings, and Ned's gloved fingers trailing on the creature's back.

They followed the river, which grew from the rushing, waist-deep waters he had crossed the day before. It was quieter now, still swift but wider and far more deep. Rocky islands jutted from the river, sometimes with twisted trees clinging bravely to their sides, but more often as stony monoliths standing tall and lonely in the insistent press of the water. He kept his eyes on those stones.

The Stones are watching you, his brother had said. The very thought made him shudder.

As they pushed on, more and more boulders rose out of the dark, foamy water. They were still. They were lifeless. And yet . . . As the boulders increased in frequency and number, the words on Ned's skin increased in number and speed. It was as though the magic was multiplying. Ned rubbed his arms with his gloved hands, trying to slow it down, but nothing helped. Instead, great, long sentences looped around his wrists and skittered across his arms—scattering, reassembling, doubling back, and uncurling in ever-changing patterns across his skin. They chafed and itched.

What are you doing? Ned thought at the magic. But the magic hummed a wordless, tuneless hum, and said nothing.

By midday, Ned heard the waterfall. Abruptly, the trees stopped and the land fell away, and Ned found himself standing at the edge of a sheer, high cliff. Carefully, oh so carefully, Ned looked down. The bottom was *so very far away,* as though the land itself had simply forgotten to hold itself up and had fallen, fallen, fallen away. He saw that the waterfall emptied into an oval pool down below, so deep that the water appeared black. Beyond that, the river curved away into the forest, gathering in size and power as it flowed toward the forest's edge, and to his country beyond.

He couldn't see his village, but he knew it was there. He knew it was waiting for him. He missed his home so much he felt a catch in his throat and a tightness in his muscles, as though they might shatter at any moment.

He missed them, he realized with a start. All of them. His parents and the workers at the mill and Madame Thuane and the sniveling scrivener and the villagers who never said thank you and the children who called him witless and even the schoolmaster who refused to teach him. He missed them and worried for them and did not want them to be harmed.

There are better places, you know, the magic whispered.

Prettier places.

You could be powerful.

Handsome.

Rich.

Ned began to whistle—high and bright—to drown out their voices. The magic was growing bold. *This is a problem,* Ned thought.

The wolf, who was also looking over the cliff, whined. Ned gave its back a pat, but felt the raised hackles and the tense shoulders. The creature showed its teeth. Ned followed the wolf's gaze.

If he had not been searching, he surely would not have seen it: a tiny house, set back from the deep pool, under a thinning of the trees. Its walls were stone and covered with vines, and its roof was heavy with thick moss. And to the side—also partly obscured—a little garden. Trampled a bit, and scattered, but it was a garden all the same. Given its haphazard state, it was hard to tell if the home was occupied. Perhaps they had left in a rush. Or had been driven out by bandits. He could see bean arbors and berry bushes and neat rows of greens. There were also dark, green plants, low to the ground, promising tubers, and a broad stretch of melons toward the back. Ned's stomach growled.

"Look!" he said to the wolf. What appeared to be a divot in the rock was actually the start of a rough trail carved into the side of the cliff.

The wolf whined, but Ned ignored it and started down the long trail. After all, if the house was occupied, then perhaps the owner would take pity on him—a scrawny, small boy, far away

175

from home—and offer food and safety and a plan to get home. And if it was empty, then perhaps Ned could scavenge for supplies—not stealing *exactly*, but *using*, with the intent to give it back someday.

"D-don't be scared," Ned called to the wolf. It howled reproachfully but started following Ned down the steep trail.

The waterfall thundered into the valley, and though the sky above was starting to brighten with the rising sun, great clouds of heavy mist hung on the trees below. Ned kept his eye on the tiny house, memorizing its location, lest the mist become too thick to see through. The chimney and the roof were already starting to blur. Was it smoke or cloud that curled over its mossy roof? Or something else entirely? Ned couldn't tell. In any case, the option to spend a few moments within the safety of its walls was enough to make Ned nearly weep with anticipation. He kept his feet steady on the rocky trail and continued on his way.

At the bottom, the wolf leaped in front of the boy and growled into the trees.

"Don't worry," Ned attempted to soothe. "W-we're at the bottom. We're s-s-saa—"

He was going to say "safe," but was interrupted by an arrow slicing the air in front of him and plunging into the ground, right next to his foot.

"GET BACK," he shouted, putting his body between the wolf and the direction of the arrow. The wolf grabbed a jawful of Ned's tunic in its jaws, pulling the boy backward. Ned lost his balance and fell just as another arrow hit the ground. And then a third arrow clipped Ned's thigh, slicing his leggings and cutting his skin.

The magic screamed.

Ned screamed.

The wolf snarled.

Ned removed his gloves and pressed the heels of his hands onto the wound, stopping the blood.

A girl—black hair, black eyes, skin the color of oiled wood—came running out of the undergrowth. She held a bow in front of her and, as she ran, reached behind her and pulled out another arrow.

Is she trying to kill me? Ned wondered.

Apparently yes, the magic responded. *Please run now.*

"Are you stupid?" the girl shouted at Ned. "I'm trying to save you from that man-eating wolf!" She nocked her arrow onto her string and and pulled back, aiming at the wolf. A sheen of sweat hung on her brow. She hesitated.

"Why isn't it running?" She spoke strangely. Her language was the same as Ned's but the rhythm and texture were off. Like a coat that looks like a coat but is actually made of porcupine quills. He had heard that manner of speech before—from the bandit horde. He looked around. There were no bandits in sight. Perhaps the forest makes people speak strangely, Ned thought.

He pulled himself to his knees and put his body once again between the girl and the wolf. The words on his skin glowed hot and bright on his face and hands. Ned grunted in pain, and pressed his hands to the ground.

The girl blanched. She relaxed her pull on the bowstring and lowered her arrow slightly.

"What are you?" she whispered, her eyes wide, and fearful.

"N-no one," Ned stammered. "A n-nothing. I won't hurt you, I p-promise."

But as he said this, the magic surged down his arms and erupted out of his hands. He yelped, and pulled his hands away. A pile of ashes and coals lay on the spot his right hand had touched. Where the left hand had touched, a puddle of water.

"What in the name of—" the girl began. "How did you do that? What is *wrong* with you?"

Shall we transform her into a stone? The magic asked.

Or perhaps a thicket of thorns.

I'd say butterflies—I love butterflies—but I don't think it'd take. So prickly this one.

"H-hush!"

"I will do no such thing. Tell me why you're here, or the next arrow goes into your heart." She pulled the bowstring back to her ear, aiming directly at Ned. He had no doubt that she was a good shot.

"The w-wolf i-is m-my friend. I p-promise not to h-hurt you. Please put that a-arrow away." He did not, in the interest of honesty, specifically say that the *wolf* would not hurt her. He couldn't say that for sure. He kept his eyes steady and hoped for the best.

"Wolves and people are *not* friends. Wolves are *enemies*." Her eye twitched.

As though in response, the wolf laid its head on Ned's un-wounded thigh and whined. The girl took in a sharp breath.

"I-it saved me," Ned said. "W-we saved each other."

Swallowing hard, the girl lowered her bow, pulling her mouth to one side in concentration. She narrowed her eyes. "What's on your skin?" she asked. "And why is it moving?"

Ned said nothing.

"It's shiny," she said, and Ned could see the shine of the magic in the girl's eyes. She squinted. "Are those words? What language is that?"

"I d-don't kn-now," Ned said. He didn't like her hungry, searching look. He scooted backward.

She extended her hand. "Can I pull one off?"

Ned recoiled. "N-no. It's d-d-dangerous." He held up his hands. They were welted and bloody and burned. "I c-can't always c-control it. N-no one can t-touch me." He felt his worry harden in the back of his throat. What if he stayed this way? What if he re-mained lethal forever? The loneliness of his situation seemed to him as palpable as a fever. He swallowed it down and stared hard at the girl. "A-a man died. I-I didn't mean to." Tears leaked out. "M-my skin—" He said nothing more. What could he say? The magic had constricted itself into tiny letters that raced in innumerable phrases across his body, shining so brightly that the girl had to squint.

Ned's face had tightened into a rigid mask of pain.

She crouched down, just slightly, resting both bow and arrow on her knees, and wrinkled her brow, struggling with what to say next. She narrowed her eyes on the words.

"Is that," she hesitated. "Is that . . . magic?"

Ned said nothing.

Her face was suddenly blazing and stormy. "There's no such thing as magic." There was so much ferocity in her voice that Ned worried she might strike him.

"Oh," Ned said, making his voice a meek as he could. "All r-right."

The girl sighed and slid her bow into the quiver slung across her back. She crossed her arms and gave Ned a long, hard look.

"Are you hungry?" she asked.

In response, his stomach gurgled. "Y-yes," he said.

She turned on her heel and walked back into the misty under-growth, leaving Ned quite alone. He hesitated. The wolf pressed itself against Ned's leg, a growl still rumbling through his bones.

"Aren't you coming?" the girl called through the green. Ned supposed that he was. Very carefully, he pulled himself to his feet and checked the injury on his leg. It wasn't as bad as he thought—about the length of his index finger, but not deep. And healing fast. The magic, it seemed, had written a single word over the wound which was even now holding it closed.

What is that word? Ned wondered.

Oh, now you're interested, the magic hissed. A waspish tone.

We know how to sew.

Oh, the things we have sewn, my boy. If you only knew.

Well, stop it, Ned thought hard at the magic. *Stop it right now. I don't need your help. I'm fine on my own.* The magic harrumphed and the word undid itself. Immediately, the wound began to ooze.

Ned ignored it and limped into the leafy tangle, toward where he guessed the girl had gone. The wolf whined a bit, but followed close behind.

Ned finally pushed through the woods into a clearing. There stood the small cottage he had seen from the top of the cliff. The girl opened the door and turned toward Ned.

"You can't come in," she said flatly. "I'll get you what you need to dress your wound, and to fill your belly. But you cannot cross this threshold, is that clear?"

Ned stopped.

Go inside, the magic said.

We want to go inside.

It was responding to . . . *something.* Ned didn't know what. But it buzzed and crackled and hummed. And what's more, its thrill made its way into Ned's body as well. He felt . . . energized. As though the pain and the burden of bearing the magic had suddenly lifted. He felt lighter, more agile. Ned wondered if his mother ever felt the same way.

Who cares what she says. Let's go in.

This place is interesting.

But *how* the place was interesting, the magic wouldn't say.

"We c-can't g-go in," Ned said.

The girl gave him a puzzled look. "That's what I just said."

"Oh. Right," he said, giving an embarrassed shrug. He eased himself down on the stoop, the wolf settling next to him. And he thought. And his thoughts were not happy. He was deeper into the forest than anyone he knew had ever gone—and deeper than anyone would have even thought *possible*. He hoped that the bandits had stopped searching for him, he hoped that they assumed he had died in the fall, but he couldn't be sure. And he knew that war, whether they had his magic or not, was gathering like a storm, readying itself to move across the Forest toward his country.

And though he didn't like to think about it, he knew he might already be too late.

25

THE KING OVER THE MOUNTAIN

KING OTT, BENEVOLENT RULER of the Kingdom of
Duunin (of course he was benevolent! It said so on banners
and placards and all of the money! He even required his generals
to tattoo it on their forearms with an outline of his smiling face
hovering above), was in a bit of a snit. He wiped his mouth with
the back of his hand and scowled.

"Gone?" he said to the red-haired man kneeling before him.
His voice, unfortunately, had taken on a petulant whine. Ott was
infuriated. Kings, he knew, are never petulant. He cleared his
throat and attempted a growl.

"I did not say *gone*. I said *misplaced*." The bandit examined his
fingernails. He ran his hand down his beard. He let his fingers
rest on a horrible-looking pendant strung around his neck with a
leather strap. (*An eye! Who wears jewelry in the shape of an eye?* Ott

was mystified.) And while he did not smile—he did not *dare*—the bandit's face still bore the suggestion of a crafty grin. It was as though the grin was waiting *inside*.

King Ott couldn't abide craftiness, unless it was his and his alone. He couldn't abide most things that were not his and his alone. And why should he? He had absolute control of an empire so vast, so mighty, that it boggled the mind to think of it.

And yet.

That minuscule country on the other side of the great, wicked forest. *What was it doing there*? He asked himself this question every morning before breakfast, and three times each afternoon, and over and over again every evening. He knew the story, of course. He knew his justifiable claim to the land. But that story was so old. Why had the wrong not been rectified? So tiny, this illegal country! So insignificant! And yet there it stands with brazen independence. It drove him mad.

Indeed, "mad" was a word whispered often in the offices of Cabinet members and Parliamentarians and People of Importance. "Mad" was a word riding on the tongues of those who walked the halls of the castle. The land bounded by the empire was so impossibly vast that the advisors to the king were mystified at their monarch's obsession with that small shoulder of land, separated from the rest of the world by the mountains and the forest. A forest populated only by cursed trees and a ragtag band of bandits. And their numbers were few.

"A nothing!" the advisors cried. "A backwater!"

Still, it was a backwater that paid no tax. A backwater that swore no allegiance to him. A backwater that never had any reason to cower before the might of his armies.

It was a country independent, whole unto itself, and King Ott could not bear it.

When the leader of the forest-dwelling bandits informed him of the existence of magic—real magic, like the magic of the legendary Speaking Stones that was older than the very world—King Ott knew that he would not rest until the magic, and the country, were in his grasp.

It was, therefore, an enraged king who glowered before a shamefaced giant of a man as he explained how the magic had slipped through his fingers. (Except that he *wasn't* shamefaced, was he? He should have been but, oh! That grin hiding inside that face! The very gall of it!)

The king sat perched on a makeshift dais, at a place called the Meadows of the Sky, where a gap in the mountains flattened into a huge, green field, thick with flowers, bounded on two sides by high, rocky walls. There was a young boy on one side to fan his face, and a young girl on the other to offer him sips of cool wine, and a pair of siblings at his feet to scratch between his toes, whenever his toes needed scratching. He had servants holding platters of sweetmeats and peeled fruits, honeycombs and pastries in the shapes of birds, and delicate globes made from spun sugar. The king was young, not yet twenty, though he had held his office since his tenth birthday. King Ott hoped to be king forever.

But now, not even pastries nor spun sugar nor foot scratches nor peeled fruits would cheer him up. The bandit had failed him.

King Ott felt his rage bubble up between his itchy toes, bubble in his overfilled stomach, and shoot like flames from his mouth.

"EXCECUTIONER!" he shouted. "Remove this man's head at once!"

Normally, such words had a marvelously soothing effect on the young king. On the nights he found himself troubled by dreadful dreams, he would rouse himself, say it to no one in particular, and go back to sleep, as content as a well-nursed baby.

But now . . .

King Ott held up one hand. "Hold a moment, Lord Executioner." He stared hard at the red-haired bandit, who stared hard back. "I just ordered that your head be cut off," he said in an exasperated voice. "So *why on earth are you smiling?*"

And it was true. That hidden, saucy grin slowly unfurled across the giant man's face.

"Oh, you have no intention to remove my head," the bandit drawled.

"What?" King Ott said. "Such INSOLENCE. I have every intention of removing your head! In addition, I intend to enjoy it. Mightily. Your death will afford me pleasures and diversions for years to come, so let us not tarry. Lord Executioner? Your axe. . . . WHY THE DEVIL ARE YOU SMILING?"

"If you had wanted me dead," the bandit said, eyeing the sky, "you would have done it by now."

The assembled crowd gasped. Two soldiers forced the red-haired bandit to his knees. The big man seemed not to mind.

King Ott nearly screamed with rage. "I'm just getting to it!"

186

"Oh, I'm sure you are," the bandit said. "It's a pity that, with me gone, you lose all hope to conquer the inbred yokels beyond the forest."

The king raised a hand to the executioner, and the executioner, well-trained, stopped in his tracks.

"We've already lost that chance, no thanks to you," King Ott said.

"No you haven't. You never let me finish. And I had more to say."

"You said that the magic was lost," the king said. "That's what you said. Which means that this endeavor is futile."

The bandit eased himself onto his backside, stretching his legs forward. He leaned back on his elbows and kept his eyes on the sky. He looked as though he was having a lounge about after a particularly satisfying picnic.

The audacity! King Ott felt his cheeks start to burn. The bandit paid this no mind.

"Have you ever trained falcons, sire?"

The young king drew himself to his feet. "Of course, *knave*. I am skilled in all the kingly arts, and have been for *ever so long*."

"Of course you are," indulged the bandit. "So you may know what it means that I have two falcons—even now—following the thief who stole your magic. He is following the river. He is, *the fool*, returning it to the *very place* where you would like to use it."

"Why have you not snatched him?"

"He is in an inaccessible region of the ravine."

King Ott sat back down on his chair, his cheeks flushed. He

snapped his fingers a few times, and the girl with the wine cup wetted his lips. "Faster next time," he said severely. "I should only have to snap once." The girl gave a terrified nod and stepped backward. King Ott leaned his chin on the tips of his fingers.

"But the forest," the king pressed. "How shall my army find their way without the magic? The roads wander and move, and the trees move. That forest is cursed. It's been cursed for a thousand generations."

The bandit smiled. "The forest is my friend. It has always been my home, and its many pathways have never complicated my way. The paths know my footsteps and the roads straighten before me. I have never led my comrades astray, and I shall not do so with you, majesty. I swear it."

"And the magic?"

"A mere stop along the way." He stood. The young king shivered. The bandit had a presence about him, and no mistaking. He opened wide his arms as though he could hold up the world in those massive hands. "The boy will be lost. He will wander. A child mewling for his mother is an easy enough treasure to find. Best to catch him before he returns to his people, though, and tattles—it will be no fun if the rubes to the west know we're coming. Why spoil the surprise? No, my king. It is a slight change of plans, but only slight. We ready the army and depart today. We snatch the boy, take what belongs to me—I mean *you*, your majesty—and our friends across the Forest will have a new Lord—one who, ever and forever, swears allegiance to you, oh glorious and *dear King Ott*."

The boy king sighed and brought his fingertips to his temples, rubbing them gently. "It is distasteful to me, this business. That I should be consorting with a man of your station. With comrades such as yours. It is not . . ." he closed his eyes. "It is not the *way*."

"It is the way, sire, if there be none other." The bandit's voice enlarged pleasantly—like a deep, soothing song. "It is the way if *you choose* it. As king of the most powerful empire the world has ever known, *you are the way*."

The king gave a slow nod. "This is true," he whispered. He blinked hard, and blinked again. He felt pleasantly dizzy. He felt warm. He felt *wonderful*.

"That insignificant child stole a power that was stolen long ago—one that by rights belongs to you." The bandit was large, comforting, shiny. He was lit up from the inside. The king hung on his words. "And that backward nation has no business maintaining its autonomy in the face of so powerful a neighbor. It's an outrage! A scandal! Both wrongs can be put to rights with a four-day march and a one-day battle. And then the world will be . . ." The bandit smiled. "*Correct*."

"I see," the young king said, speaking slowly, as though he were having a pleasant dream. "The world is out of balance."

"Yes," said the bandit.

"And it is my duty to make things right."

"Yes, my king."

And with that, the battalions of King Ott assembled and began provisioning themselves. Within two hours, they were ready to begin their four-day march through the mountains, into the valley, and into the mouth of the forest.

The bandit watched the mobilization of the troops with a detached interest. The terrain would be a problem. And the canopy would blur the way. Still, the forest would lead him to the boy, as sure as green follows rain.

The boy was what he needed. The boy and his beautiful magic. The magic that he would give to King Ott. Or perhaps not. The magic was a tricky thing after all.

Run, Neddy, he thought. *Run while you can. We'll be with you soon enough.*

26

───

THE CHOICE

THE BOY WOULDN'T TELL Áine how he ended up in the middle of the forest or how he became covered in that strange, moving magic, or why it was so important for him to get home.

He's not a witch. He's not even powerful. It can't be the same. It can't be the same. She repeated those sentences over and over and over again. Meanwhile her sense of dread had kneaded itself into a hard, heavy lump and settled deep in her guts.

The boy wanted to go home, but Áine couldn't imagine that anyone would be happy to see him return. He was clearly an imbecile—no sense of his direction, no instincts for forest life, and his obsession with an animal that could—and surely *would*—eat him. It was good that she was getting him out of the forest. He had *no business here.*

And her father... She wouldn't let him see that boy.

(The way his eyes gleamed!)

And she certainly wouldn't let him see that strange magic, cursing the boy's skin.

(The way he held his pendant in his hands! The way he crooned to it!)

Things were bad enough as it was.

She closed the door to the cottage and leaned against it, trying to catch her breath. She closed her eyes. *Be practical,* she told herself. And, as she often did when the world became frightening, Áine set to work. The boy needed to be fed. He also needed his trousers mended and his wound dressed. And then he needed to go back into the forest and never return.

She already had a small pot of stew keeping warm on the hearth—but it was only enough for herself. She poured in water from the kettle and sliced up roots from the cellar and dried mushrooms from the rafters, threw in a handful of salt, and set the whole thing on the coals to boil. She heated the cider and sliced the cheese and toasted the bread, and all the while the boy sat on the stoop outside with that . . . *creature.* And they waited.

The wrong boy will save your life, her mother had said. *And you will save his. And the wolf—*

But then she died, didn't she? And in any case, her mother said nothing about a stuttering boy, or a wolf-loving boy, or the *witless* no-sense-of-direction boy, so there certainly was no reason to think that her current situation applied at all to the strange words of a dying woman.

Áine ladled the stew into a wooden bowl and brought it out to the boy. She still didn't know his name. She told herself she didn't *want* to know.

Except she *did*. Áine pressed her lips together and tried to be practical.

The wolf stared at her and growled.

You, the growl seemed to say. *It's you.*

Áine fixed her eyes on the wolf and raised her shoulders. She couldn't growl like a wolf, but she could *think* a growl all the same.

It's me, her imagined growl said.

Did I kill your mother? She wondered.

Probably.

Would I do it again?

Probably.

Áine set the bowl quickly in front of the boy and stepped backward as though he, too, was a wild thing, and liable to bite. She looked at the marks on his skin and shuddered.

"I can give you some blankets for tonight. You can't come in the house and I can't let you into the barn either. But if you lie against the southern side of the house, you'll stay warm enough. The stones keep their sun-heat for most of the night, and you'll be mostly protected from the wind. But you will need to leave by first light. You are from the lowland country, correct?"

"The w-what?" the boy asked. He had never heard anyone describe his country in that way. He had always believed that there was only his country. And beyond the country was the forest, then the mountains, and then the sky. Ask anyone you like.

193

"I'm not spying on you or anything," Áine said. "I've spoken with lowlanders before." In truth, she had only *heard,* and not *spoken with* lowlanders—the occasional lowlander bandit joined up with her father. They never lasted long. "Your people speak as though you are sloshing syrup in your mouths. Though, truthfully, usually without a stutter. No offense."

The boy stared at her. Áine didn't notice his confusion.

"Primarily, I need to know this: Are you going west to the lowlands, or are you going east, to the Kingdom of Duunin? Are you running *toward* or *away*?"

It was a name he had never heard before. "What?" he said. "What is Duunin?"

"The Kingdom over the mountain," Áine said, astonished at such a question. "We are subjects of King Ott, though we are out-side of his lands—or at least the land that he controls. No one controls the Forest. Every year, we pay our tribute and our tax, which keeps us in good standing." (*Mostly,* she thought, as a dark flicker passed over her face. All that gold hidden in the barn! Surely her father was not entirely forthcoming in his accounting to the king.)

"Over the m-mountain?" the boy said incredulously. "There's no k-kingdom! There is n-nothing over the mountain. The w-world ends. Everyone knows that."

Áine tilted her head back and hooted with laughter. "I heard that the people of your backwards country believed such things, but I never thought it was *true*."

"I—"

"Oh, come now. Just because none of your ridiculous kinsmen have been over the mountain doesn't mean that the world just *stops*. Haven't you seen the birds flying over the mountain's edge? Haven't you seen the clouds roil from one side to the other? Think it through!"

"W–we have a–always th–th–th–"

"I suppose you also believe that there are stone monsters in the wood that will crush a man to bits?"

"I–" The boy looked at her, wide–eyed and serious. He licked his lips. "I used to th–think there were m–monsters. Now I know the woods are filled with b–b–" his voice thickened and slowed so much that it seemed to choke him.. "B–bandits," he finished finally.

The wolf growled. The boy patted the animal's head, Áine noticed, with his hand gloved. He did not touch it with his skin.

"The b–bandits are worse than monsters," the boy whispered. "M–much worse."

Áine flinched as though he'd slapped her. There was no de-nying it any longer. How the witch's magic came to write itself on the boy she had no idea, but she had no doubt of what was at stake.

Her father.

His sanity.

His very *self*.

She sat down on a stone, hugging her arms around her knees. She gave the boy a level stare. "Well, it's true that there are bandits in the wood. But not many. The people from my Kingdom are afraid of the wood. They say it's cursed. The paths move."

195

"I know," the boy said.

"And the trees don't like visitors."

"I know," the boy said again.

"What have you seen?" Áine narrowed her gaze.

"N-nothing," the boy said, and returned to the task of shoveling food into his mouth.

The silence between them was long and uncomfortable.

"This Kingdom," the boy asked finally, "the k-kingdom b-beyond the end of the world. H-have you seen it?"

"Of course," Áine said. "I was born there. I lived there. And then we came here. A kingdom of trees."

"Why?" the boy asked.

"It's none of your concern."

"Are you a b-bandit?"

"Not today," Áine said, her voice flat. "What's your name?" She didn't ask what she wanted to ask. *What's on your skin? How did it get there? And why does my father want it so much?* Because it was her father who plucked this witless boy and set him wandering in the wood. She knew it in her bones. And it was this magic on the boy's skin—*this* magic—that set her father and his bandits in motion. Well, he wouldn't have it, by god. Not if Áine had anything to say about it.

"Ned," the boy said. As he spoke, the words on his skin flashed and fluttered. The boy winced and whimpered.

He can't control it, Áine thought. *Interesting. And the magic doesn't want me to know his name. Also interesting.*

"Well, Ned"—again, the words flashed—"eat and rest. I'll make a food pack and a map and send you on your way in the morning. My father is away on business, and you don't want to be here when he gets back. He doesn't like strangers."

The boy looked at her questioningly but she made her face blank and implacable, revealing nothing. The words on his skin flashed a third time. She gave them a hard look. And Áine knew— as sure as she knew that the moss on the trees would always point north and that the fallen leaves of the Rangar bushes always hid vipers and the poison berries boasted the deepest colors—that whatever it was running along the boy's skin was treacherous. And that it had everything to do with the eye-shaped pendant around her father's neck. The thing that made him *wild*. The thing that made him *dangerous*.

And she knew that the magic on the boy's skin would make her father *more* dangerous.

And she knew that she needed to get this boy away. Away from here. Away from her father.

But she also knew that if it was a choice between the boy and her father, she would choose her father.

And she would kill Ned, if she had to.

27

THE LOST BANDIT

H E SHOULD HAVE BEEN DEAD. In truth, he woke up feeling so fine, so *whole*, he felt for sure that he *was* dead.

His joints, points of fire and pain these last fifteen years, were as supple and sound as a baby's. His back, a creaky, rusty collection of cast-off levers and broken hardware and bits of splintery wood, was rubbery and supple.

The bandit sprang to his feet. He could have turned cartwheels if he felt the urge.

He looked around. There was no sign of the boy. He had asked the boy to take his life. Instead, what he got was a *new* life. Brand new. Not just alive, but *healed*. And not just healed, but *improved*. It was *impossible*. It was *against the rules*.

He grumbled and spat. "I owe you nothing, boy. *Nothing*." The wood was silent. The trees rustled. They didn't take kindly to his being there. The bandit hooked his fingers behind his neck and looked around. His larger knife was gone. So was his satchel. But his bow and quiver remained with him.

"Think of three things to be thankful for, Eimon," his old ma used to say to him, before his old ma was killed by bandits, before he became a bandit himself, and left his name behind. "Three things, and then everything else doesn't seem so bad."

"I have nothing to be thankful for," Eimon the bandit said out loud. "See? The villain took my food. What kind of person does that? Not a good person."

A person who healed him for no reason.

A person who didn't kill him, though he had every reason.

A person who left him his smaller knife, left him his bow. Left him healed and armed and dangerous. Either the boy was an idiot or—

"Or nothing," Eimon said in a loud voice. As though he was trying to convince himself. "Only a witless idiot would do such a thing. I owe him nothing."

He slung his quiver over his shoulder and, unsheathing his knife, cut off a few large hunks of Woodman's Bread, a tree-growing shelf fungus common in that part of the wood. It would have been better if it had been cooked, or even better if it was wrapped inside a bit of wolf meat, but as it was, it staved off the bandit's hunger and let him think for a minute.

His leader would want him to track the boy.

His leader would want him to bring the boy to the gathering spot at the rim of the mountains.

He knew that much for sure.

His company thought him dead, that was certain, but he would prove his worth.

Old Eimon would find that boy.

"I'll show them *who owes who*," the bandit said. "I'll show them all."

28

WHAT ÁINE SAW

ÁINE SHOVELED THE COALS out of the hearth and carried them in a bucket into the yard, dousing them with water. She swept out the crumbs and sealed the flour barrel and the bear grease barrel and the barley barrel and the oat barrel and hung the meats and cheeses from the rafters.

The house would keep.

And she would go. Into the forest. With a strange boy and a man-eating wolf. It was, she decided, the only way.

She pulled her father's old fur-lined jacket around her shoulders and shivered as she shut the door behind her. It ballooned stiffly around her like a tent, letting in great gusts of wind with every step.

She walked toward the small barn behind the house, with much of its secret treasure still hidden in the loft under the dried grasses and wild hay that she and her father had gathered from the meadows. Áine had managed to squirrel away a portion of it in the woods, but there was so much more to do.

What was he going to do with all that gold?

Oh my father, Áine thought. *What would mother say?*

She had already sent the goats away. They'd be fine. They were all of mountain stock and had been sent regularly into the mountains to find mates. They'd come home when it was time for their babies to birth. They were smart goats, her good girls, and she missed them already.

The chickens were a different story. Áine swept out their enclosure next to the coop and scattered layers of seed and grass, hoping that the chickens would be smart enough to peck only what they needed and leave the rest for later. The eggs would be a problem, but they couldn't be helped. She put out six buckets of water, keeping two in the open so they could collect rain—surely it would rain while she was away. And she hoped for the best.

She couldn't set them free, alas. They'd be dead by noon—hawks or foxes or their own lack of sense. Poor, stupid things.

She went back into the house and brought out a warm iron pan, heavy with food.

The boy with the glowing skin lay on the ground, fast asleep. Áine had found him some animal furs to lie down on, and a few more to lay over himself—a large bear skin and a deer skin and (Áine picked this one out specially) a wolf skin.

The wolf growled at her.

It would not stop growling.

Áine growled back.

The magic on the boy's skin whirled and whirled, its letters recombining and reforming over and over. If they would slow down, Áine was certain that she'd be able to read them, even though it was a language she did not know. Still. She could feel the pull of the words even now on her tongue, the knowledge pressing itself into her mind, as though the magic itself wanted her to speak them. Áine forced her gaze away.

The wolf stirred in its sleep, nuzzling its head next to the boy. The boy said that the words on his skin were dangerous—and Áine believed him. That the wolf could touch him was not proof that the boy lied, but proof that her father had been right about the wolves. They were indeed wicked, wicked creatures. And not to be trusted.

She should have shot the both of them when she had the chance. But now—oh, now! Now it was too late. She couldn't shoot either of them. Not after they had eaten her food and slept in her yard. Even she had not become so cruel.

Unless she *had* to. She'd do it, she told herself, if she *had* to. If her father returned. If he saw the boy and the terrible power on his body. If her father—*oh, the thought of it!*—tried to take it for his own.

For now, she would get them away. Far away. And she would do it herself.

A bird screeched overhead. Áine did not look up. Instead, she watched as the boy stirred and woke. He lay for a moment with

203

his eyes open, cautiously sliding them from side to side, as though trying to remember where he was. Finally, they rested on Áine, who gave a disdainful snort.

"It has been light for well over an hour," she said. "Are people lazy where you come from?"

"No," Ned rasped. He felt as though he had swallowed a mouthful of sand. He coughed, but that just made it worse.

"I made you some breakfast," she said. "But it's cold now."

Ned sat up and Áine handed him the iron pan. It wasn't cold at all. It was warm and inviting. There were root vegetables and salted meats and berries all fried in bear grease with a little hard cheese crumbled on top. Ned took the pan gratefully. He scooped it with his fingers and shoveled it into his mouth. Ned ate the vegetables and a little of the meat, saving the rest for the wolf. Áine snorted again.

"You shouldn't waste your time with the animal," she said. "It's not natural. He is a wild thing, after all. And fierce. And he certainly wouldn't do the same for you."

"You're wrong," Ned said, shoveling the last bit of root vege-table into his mouth and licking the grease from his fingers. "He did . . . do the same for me. The wolf b-brought me food."

"Liar," Áine said. Ned shrugged and put his arm around the wolf. The words on his skin spun faster, and the boy's expression changed. He looked as though he was listening to something—something that he didn't like the sound of. He shook his head and waved at nothing.

204

What do you want? Áine wondered. *And what's the matter with you?*

"I've made a pack for you, and one for myself. We'll travel light—it's the best way. The forest will provide us what we need."

"W–we?" Ned said.

Áine ignored him. "We've already lost daylight. I reckon it will take us three, maybe four days to get you to the edge of the forest by foot. I won't take you all the way—I have a house to run. But I can get you most of the way there."

Surely, she thought, *the bandits will think he is wandering and lost. The boy will be quicker than they anticipate. And once he is back with that witch, he will be defended. The plan will be thwarted. And my father will come home.*

It was a good plan, she decided.

"You d–don't need to show me," Ned said with his mouth full. "I've gotten this far."

Áine crossed her arms across her chest. "Follow the river? That was your strategy, was it?"

The wolf raised its hackles and growled at her. Ned said nothing.

"A fine plan," Áine said, "for a fool."

Ned winced. Still he said nothing.

Áine sighed. "You see that waterfall there?" She pointed. Ned barely acknowledged her. She grunted loudly and tossed him the bundle that she had prepared for his journey. "Well, we call that the *small* cascade. We are in the last shoulders of the mountains before the trees give way to meadows and the cliffs launch sky-ward. Things become steeper as we head toward the lowlands. There are scree slides and cliffs and steep slopes plunging into bogs that you will not find your way out of. You see that nice little stairway that you came down—without permission I might add. Well, that's the only one. If you want to follow the river, you can't follow the river. You have to know the trails, and you don't, so you need a guide." She gave him a hard stare. "So let's go then."

Ned put the bundle into his sack and stood. He jammed his hands into his pockets.

"Y–you'll help m–me?" he stammered. "J–just like that?"

Áine looked up at the sky. Above the ridge, three falcons appeared, then disappeared, then appeared again. Her father's falcons. She knew she'd see them eventually, but she had hoped it wouldn't be so soon.

"We need to get out of the open," she said. "Whoever is look-ing for you will not see you if you are hidden by trees."

"I'll b–be f–fine on my—" Ned gagged on the word "own."

Áine shook her head. "That is clearly not true." She gritted her teeth and shook her head. *Oh my father,* she thought. *Where will this end? And what would mother say?* "You can't stay here. And if you go willy-nilly into the forest, you will surely die. I could let you do that, but, frankly, it would be kinder to put an arrow into your heart. I considered that, of course, but it's no longer an option."

Ned blanched. "Th–thanks, I g–guess," he said.

"Don't flatter yourself. It's not that you're special or anything.

The laws of hospitality require it." These were laws—like every other kind of law—that her father broke. Routinely.

(*The man who visited the house. When her mother was still alive. The scrambling sound on the gravel and the thud and the sound of something heavy dragging away. And that was before the magic possessed him—even the* memory *of it was dangerous.*)

But Áine was not her father. She cared for him and cooked for him and worried after him, but she was her mother's child and that was that. "Since I can't kill you, and I can't let you die, I am honor bound to help you." *For as long as I can,* she thought. *Until I can't.* Her eyes flicked up and the three falcons were now fully over the ridge, their eyes scanning the ground. *Go away!* she thought. "Are you ready?" She tossed him a water skin and Ned caught it.

"Yes," Ned said, though, to be honest, he wouldn't have minded another mouthful of stew, and maybe a bit of bread. The wolf pressed its weight against Ned's leg.

"We'll take the forest way to begin with. Off trail, you understand. We'll be slower than the main foot trail, but we'll be glad for the cover." And she marched into the thick undergrowth and into the green, Ned following closely at her heels.

Under the canopy where his falcons cannot see us.

Across the rock fields where we will not leave tracks.

Because if my father finds us, you will be lost. And he will be lost. And so will I.

29

In Prison

THE QUEEN CLUNG TO LIFE, though barely. And the nation fell into prayer and premature mourning.

If Brin had had his way, the guards would have slashed the witch's throat right then and there. But there were rules to follow. The soldiers held the witch gently, and at arm's length. They spoke to her deferentially, as though she was a dignitary. Or a princess.

They had never imprisoned a witch before. And the stories of her magic (miracles, really, people said) were widely known. Indeed, the story of how she saved the queen at the jubilee made her something of a national treasure.

In prison, Sister Witch wanted for nothing.

She was fed often and ate well. She was given hand-knitted blankets and feather cushions and skins of wine.

With each gift, Ned's mother offered her thanks and her blessings. She did not request the thing she needed most of all

(*Get me out of here*) nor did she give voice to her deepest worries (*Something is coming. Something terrible. Indeed it is already here*). Sister Witch listened to the winds and she read the stars and she waited.

She was not allowed visitors, nor were any messages sent to her husband, nor was she allowed quill or paper or charcoal or wood. Nothing that would bear or keep a mark. Nothing that could hold a message.

Outside her window, the carpenters began building a gallows.

Oh no, she thought to herself. *That won't do at all.*

"Slow," whispered Sister Witch. "Terribly, terribly slow my friends." She had no access to her magic, of course, but still, magic or no, Sister Witch knew how to press upon the flow of the world, to nudge outcomes this way or that way. Sister Witch excelled at giving suggestions, and the world, it seemed, was similarly proficient at receiving them.

And so the building of the gallows was beset by problems. Beams were found to have rotted cores, posts snapped without warning, ropes unraveled and the platform buckled and splintered and cracked.

And Sister Witch waited behind the bars. She lifted her gaze to the sky.

30

—

SMOKE

NED, ÁINE, AND THE wolf walked in silence for the first day, traversing the undergrowth and flat stone outcroppings, avoiding mud and sedge grasses, which could show boot prints, crossing the river again and again. At first, they were able to wade, but with each stream pouring in from one side of the ravine or the other, the river swelled and swelled. Áine found crossings on fallen trees and places where large boulders stood close enough to one another to create a pathway to hop across.

Ned's leg, meanwhile, had begun to throb. The wound felt hot.

Let us fix that, the magic said.

No, Ned told it firmly.

You're hurt. Why should you hurt? It makes no sense.

Not for personal gain. That was the rule. But the reason

behind the rule . . . well, his mother had not been completely honest about it, had she? She always said it was dangerous. She always said there were consequences. But *dangerous how*, and *what consequences*—on that she had been less forthcoming.

Oh, please, it said. *We hate to see you in this much pain.* He could feel the magic shiver and shudder and plead. It wanted to do *something.* Desperately. It made Ned sick.

I don't need you, he thought at the magic.

You have always needed us.

We are part of you and you don't even know.

Foolish boy.

Stop, Ned thought, but his resolve was weak. The magic could make him healed. It might remove his stutter. It might make him tall and strong and maybe adept enough at woodsmanship to please his father. Or scholarship to please his mother. Who knows what the magic might do.

Indeed . . . a hiss on his skin. A hopeful prickle.

Ned regained himself. *STOP IT,* his mind commanded.

Áine stopped and took stock of their surroundings. She looked over at Ned. "You're limping," she said.

Ned shrugged. "Well," he said, "you s-shot me."

She nodded. "True. Here." She walked over to a particularly craggy-looking tree and pulled off a small piece of moss. She pulled the scarf out of her hair and unknotted it. Her hair, darker than the night sky and as shiny as oil, fell thick and heavy down the length of her back.

211

"Put the moss on the wound and tie it on with the scarf."
There was an awkward pause. She cleared her throat. "I'll turn
around," she said.

Ned slid his leggings to his knees and placed the moss over
the wound. He wound the scarf around his leg to hold it in place.
Instantly, the wound cooled and calmed, as though the pain had,
very suddenly, turned to water. He replaced his leggings and
cleared his throat.

Hmph, the magic said.

"I d–don't know this m–moss," Ned said. "It is a–m–azing."

"It only lives on the ender trees, and they only live in the upper parts of mountains." She gave him a sidelong glance. "You see?
There is more to the forest than monsters and bandits. Aren't you
happy to have learned something?"

She didn't smile. But there was a shadow of a smile somewhere on her face.

Only for a moment. The shadow passed, and her face once
again turned as hard as stone.

"Come on," she said. "And keep up, will you? I want to make
it to the junction by nightfall. The river is joined there by two
others, and gets much larger, and very fast. We'll need to be careful." She turned and proceeded down the trail, the wolf bounding
ahead of her.

The magic, meanwhile, was in a tizzy.

The girl is dangerous, one of the voices said.

We should have gone with the big man. What were we thinking? said another.

We shouldn't have left that house, said yet another.

She'll kill you if she has to. She won't want to, but she'll do it if her back's against the wall. Don't trust her, said the quietest of them all, its voice a low rumble at Ned's wrists.

This was the one Ned listened to. He needed Áine; that was sure. But he didn't trust her.

And she, Ned was positive, didn't trust him.

She certainly didn't trust the wolf. Ned saw her from time to time glance sidelong at the creature as it bounded through the wood or as it walked apace with Ned, its flank brushing Ned's leg. And all the while her hand was on her knife.

He decided to leave her behind, the moment he had a chance.

As the sun went down, they made camp in the center of a circle of very large trees. Áine gathered pine branches and covered them with leaves and they both sat down. In each of their bundles, she had folded a small, light blanket that she had woven herself from her goats' first shearing. Such wool was fine, soft, very strong, and incredibly warm. Even though the cold was starting to nibble at the nighttime winds, they would stay warm enough.

"We sh-should make a f-fire," Ned said. His wolf—he was already referring to it as *his* wolf, though he knew he mustn't; the wolf would leave eventually—was bounding through the undergrowth and out of sight. Hunting. Patrolling. Perhaps both.

213

"We should do no such thing. We will be found."

"We will?" Ned remembered uncomfortably the fire he had made his first night in the forest.

"Of course we will. This part of the forest is called the Great Bowl. If you're on the upper ridges of the mountains, you can see it—huge and round and deep. And if you're on the edge of the bowl, you can see a *lot*. Nothing through the trees, of course, but smoke is easy to spot from up on the ridge. If someone's following you—and I assume they *are*, lowlanders like you don't end up in this forest by *accident*, after all—well, we want to make it *harder* and not *easier*, don't you agree? It's almost impossible to get down off the ridge here—even skilled climbers can fall to their deaths. You have to go around the edge of the bowl. But if you're fast enough you can cut someone off. That's why we want to avoid it. We want to get you out of the forest without crossing paths with my—" She cleared her throat. "Without crossing paths with the people who dragged you in here in the first place."

Ned was silent for a moment.

"How do you know?" he said quietly. "And w-why are you—" Ned coughed. He tried to say *helping me*, but the *h* got stuck in his throat like a mouthful of dust.

Áine sighed. "I just do. And I have my reasons, and those reasons are none of your concern."

She lies, the magic itched against his skin. *She lies, she lies, she lies.*

She wasn't lying, though. Ned could tell.

But she wasn't telling the truth, either.

After they had rested for a bit, Áine told Ned that she would forage for food. She had packed a bit, but she told Ned that it was better to eat what you can find when possible, and eat what you brought when there's nothing to be found. Which seemed sensible.

"Wait here," she said. "I'll be back in a moment."

"You're going b-by yours-self?" Ned asked.

"I already told you. The forest loves me. And it doesn't love you. I'll be faster without the weight of you pulling me back." She stared at him, all edges and angles, so sharp Ned thought he might bleed. He glared back. He had magic, after all. He could be powerful if he wanted to. The words on his skin quickened their pace.

"But—"

"It's not your fault," Áine said, her voice softer now as she shouldered her bow. "You're not used to our life here. Rest, and I'll find more food so our stores don't get low, and we'll press on in the morning. Where's the wolf?"

"I d-don't know."

"Will it be back?"

"I don't kn-now."

She pursed her lips and darkened her gaze. "See that it doesn't follow me. I can't promise the direction of my arrows."

Áine ducked under a low branch, and slipped silently out of sight.

(It was a lie, of course. She'd impale that wolf on the shaft of her arrow if she had the chance, and if the boy wasn't there to see. Her father was right. *Never trust a wolf.*)

The wrong boy, her mother had said. *The wrong boy will save your life. And the wolf . . .*

Not this boy. Not this wolf. Áine told herself this again and again until she believed it was true.

Once protected by the curtain of green, Áine unsheathed her knife and bent down low. She made the pretense of gathering food (a few nuts on the ground made it into her satchel; berries still on the vine; a sizable mushroom with thick, firm meat), but that was only for show.

She scanned the torsos of the trees. She eyed the rocks. She looked for signs.

Her father, she knew, would have sent scouts, looking for the boy. They would have fanned out, in pairs most likely. And there would be *many.* Not all of them would make it down the ridge. His bandits were expendable, after all. He didn't mind losing a few along the way.

The magic! It changed him!

She stepped carefully, planting each foot lightly into the undergrowth, scanning the world around her as she tramped. She counted her paces to keep herself from getting lost. Five hundred should do it, she decided. If there was no sign of pursuers within five hundred paces, then in all likelihood, they were in luck, and this area was not being searched.

The bandits all used signs to show one another if they had

been by—a language for the lost and searching. Áine scanned the trees and the ground and saw nothing. No slashes in the bark. No stacks of rocks. *Good,* she thought. Or not good. She couldn't decide. If they hadn't been by, then she and the boy had not yet been seen. Still, just because they *hadn't* come, didn't mean they *wouldn't.* They simply hadn't come *yet.*

Yet, Áine decided, was a terrible word. A terrible word, indeed.

The trees seemed to cluster and hover around her, choking out the light. It was as though they were bending low, examining her face, examining her twitchy hands and her shifty gaze. They rustled their branches and breathed. The air became thick and hot and damp. One of the last steamy breaths of summer before autumn descended on the mountains. It smelled of sap and rot and loam. Sweat dripped along the sides of her face and down her belly and back. The tendrils of hair that escaped her braid clung to her neck and cheeks like damp spiderwebs. She tried to brush them away.

Three hundred paces.

Four hundred.

Five.

She stopped. There was, she realized, a rocky knoll a stone's throw from where she was standing that would provide a wide view down the slope toward the river. She strode toward the rock's bubbly side, grabbed handholds, and hoisted herself up.

The wood was wide and green and dreaming. The branches of trees upon trees upon trees intertwined and tangled and shook.

Áine squinted her eyes. Her father was out there somewhere. And the rest of the bandit horde. She scanned the skies for signs of falcons, but saw nothing.

And then she heard it. Boots. A high whistle called from tramper to tramper through the undergrowth. The pitch and length of each high blast had its own meaning, a secret code known only to the bandits. And to Áine. Being the secret daughter of the most powerful bandit in the world had *some* benefits, after all.

Where? Cried the first whistle.

Here, blasted the second.

Áine pressed herself against the lee of a very large tree, keeping her knees bent and her back curved, ready to spring. Two bandits blundered toward one another through the undergrowth. They panted and wheezed.

"Any signs?"

"Not since that first camp. The bloody one. And it weren't made by no boy, no matter what the big man says. Our comrade's alive, for sure. As for the boy, we just don't know." Áine thought she could hear a note of fear in their voices.

"Oh, he's alive," the first bandit said. "The idiot didn't put out his fire. And that wasn't a man's weight on the undergrowth he left behind. He was alive not two nights ago, though now's anyone's guess."

"It's magic is what that was," the second said. "Prolly et him."

The first bandit snorted scornfully. "Don't be an idiot. Magic doesn't eat."

"How do you know?"

She didn't. No one knew anything about magic—not even the boy and it was written on him. Very carefully, Áine peered around the edge of the tree. Two bandits—a man and a woman with matching bald heads and thorny tattoos—picked their way through the forest, but the forest wasn't making it easy on them. Roots uncurled from the ground to trip them, rocks rolled from nowhere, and their feet were constantly ensnared in vines.

Áine looked over her shoulder toward the spot where she had left the boy all alone, a terrible wave of compassion breaking over her heart. He was in so much pain. And that terrible loneliness! And . . . She squinted, then gasped. It looked as though there was—but that was impossible. She had *told* him not to start a fire. She had been *very clear*. And yet, a cloud of smoke rose from the spot were the boy now hid.

"What on earth?" she whispered.

"My god," the first bandit said. "Is that what I think—"

"He *wouldn't*," Áine whispered as she slid, belly to rock, off the knoll and ducked through the tangled wood toward Ned.

"FOLLOW THE SMOKE," both bandits said at once. They blundered through the forest at an impeded run.

Why did he start a fire? Does he want to be dead? Áine thought desperately as she scrambled through the green. No more spirals, no more counted paces. She tore through the woods to the center of her spiraled trail, her rage boiling under her skin. *What was he thinking?*

The bandits ran right past her, but the trees shielded her from

219

view. *Confound them!* She whispered to the trees. *Hide us!* But she had never asked the wood for anything before. She had simply seen to her needs and accomplished tasks as they arose. Would the forest listen to her? She had no idea.

"We're close, lad!" she heard the bandit cry. "We're nearly on 'im. I can feel it!" Áine heard them trip and tangle and curse the wood. She heard them grunt and swear and help one another. The wood didn't love them, that was for sure.

Still, they were so close. Still, both she and Ned were so very tired.

And, not knowing what else to do, she tipped back her head, opened her throat and cried out—high, bright, cold, and lonely. Like a wolf.

31

THE RAFT

THE FIRE WAS AN accident. Mostly.

Ned, leaning against the trunk of the tree, and the wolf leaning against him, had taken off his gloves for a moment to massage his fingers and let them breathe. The welts on his hands were raw and angry. His fingers were cut and blistered and oozing. They were hot.

If you used us, we wouldn't hurt you so much.

Let us fix you.

Let us help.

Ned didn't have the strength to tell the voices to be quiet.

Anyway, he appreciated the heat. Now that the sun had dipped below the trees, the forest had cooled precipitously. His hands at least were warm, even if they hurt. Ned, shivering, closed his eyes and focused on it. He tried to imagine himself heated all the way through.

All right then, the magic said. And, before he could say anything in response, a wave of sparks blistered from his palms and fell upon the pile of pine needles and dry grasses that Áine had gathered earlier to make their beds for the night.

The fire was quick, hot, and blazing. And not just on the pile of grass. On *Ned* as well. Though he had no flames on him, he *felt* as though he was on fire. He felt his bones bend and snap like twigs in the flame, and felt his skin sizzle.

It's nice, isn't it? the magic said nastily.

Ned said nothing and thought nothing. He tried to remove all knowledge of words. He wanted to give the magic *nothing*.

Oh, come now, the magic said.

Just give us something to do.

Just ask for water. Let us say it together. W–w–wat–t–ter. Isn't that how you say it?

And deep inside, Ned could feel himself wanting to say water. He could feel the thrill of it deep in his bones. The water itself running across his skin in waves. He wondered if his mother felt like this—not just *possessing* the greatest magic in the known world, but *using it.*

Yes, the magic urged. *She never told you, did she? It's wonderful.*

And just when he was about to think the word *water*, just as he was going to shout it from the top of his head to the tips of his toes, he remembered Tam.

Beware the things that lie, his brother had said.

222

Think nothing, said that fluttery feeling in his imaginary scars. *Think nothing.*

"Nothing," Ned said. The smoke rose over the trees. He whipped off his hood and beat at the flames, and stomped on them with his boots as well. The wolf whined.

"Nothing," he said again.

We hate that word.

"Nothing," he said again.

We are not nothing, the magic shrieked. *We will not be nothing. We are every—*

"NOTHING!" Ned shouted. And the magic was silent. And his body went cold. Ned rested his hands on his knees and gasped. He let his head fall forward and tried to find his breath.

The fire vanished, leaving a blackened pit where the flames had been. The wolf whined again. It stared at the sky. Its ears pricked and its tail stood out. It was listening.

"W–what?" Ned asked. But then he heard it. A howl. Sharp and bright. The wolf wasted no time and bounded into the wood.

Áine didn't know what she was playing at, howling like a wolf. She didn't need that animal. She didn't need anyone.

Still, when she saw the wolf leap over a rock and alight (growling, she noticed; it was not her friend, after all; it would never be her friend; she had no friends) on the fallen log next to her, she nearly cried with relief. The bandits still blundered not two hundred paces behind her. The wolf turned and raised its hackles.

"You know what they are," Áine whispered. "And you know what they want. The boy needs to get away. Do you understand?"

Animals, Áine knew, did not understand human speech. Still, this wolf. It cocked its head and flared its nostrils. Then it tore into the woods. It knew exactly what she meant. She could tell.

"Wolf!" one of the bandits yelled.

"Shoot it!" cried the other.

The wolf howled. And howled. And howled.

"How many are there?"

"Three!"

"Ten!"

"My god! They're everywhere."

The wolf continued to cry out. Áine could hear it scramble and leap. She could hear the rush of its body through the undergrowth, and the slice of arrows through the leaves.

"Wait!" the first bandit shouted. "Hold your arrows until my order. If we don't take them down now, they'll tear our throats out the moment our backs are turned. There's one! After it."

And Áine heard them bound away in the wrong direction.

Áine came tearing into the camp.

"I–I'm sorry," Ned began. "It was a–an accident."

"Grab your things." Áine said, grabbing her satchel and her cloak.

"W-why?" Ned said, throwing his smoky hood over his back and shouldering his bag. But he didn't need to ask. He already knew. It was his fault. They were being pursued and it was his fault with the smoke and the fire. "I-I'm s-ssorry."

"No time. They're coming. They're here. We must fly!"

The youngest Stone felt a shift in the ground.

"What have you done?" she asked the Eldest.

"Nothing," the Eldest said, his voice vague and uncomfortable—or as vague and as uncomfortable as a Stone can get.

She felt it again.

"You have done something. Something's been moved. I thought we were supposed to wait."

"I didn't. Go back to sleep."

"You said to stay awake."

"Then wake. And wait. They'll be here soon enough."

"They?"

The Eldest didn't reply, but the Youngest could feel him tremble with excitement. And deep within, she could feel his stony smile.

"Where's the wolf?" Ned panted as they sprinted through the undergrowth. Down, down, down toward the river. Ned could hear the rush of it—bigger now, and fast. The water's roar crowded his mind and addled his thinking—blurring the gap between *now* and *then*. Ned and his brother had both loved that river once, and had thought to use it to find a path toward a dream (*The sea!* they whispered as they pushed their raft into the water. *The sea!*), but the river betrayed them. Its promise became a grave. Now it was something else. What comes after a grave? *Nothing good*, Ned decided. He ran toward the sound of water with a growing dread.

Áine let go of Ned's hand when they reached the rocky lip of the riverbank. They scrambled over large stones, down to the pebbled flats on the shore.

"Oh no," Áine whispered. They stood, panting, at the water's edge.

It was broad and deep and raging. Its dark waters bubbled and foamed. The light filtered weakly through the trees and soon it would be dark. Ainé looked back. The bandits were coming. She could hear their voices through the trees.

There was no way to cross the river.

"What will we d–do?"

"Let me *think*." Áine closed her eyes tight. Her face squished inward as if she was trying to keep it from flying apart. "Ned," she began, her voice raspy and desperate. She rested her hand on the hilt of her knife.

You see it, don't you boy? The voices of the magic tumbled and buzzed.

Run.

Grab the knife.

Go to the bandits! They have plans!

Do you want wings? Wings would look lovely on you.

You are not the one she wants to protect.

Ned shook his head. He tried to think nothing. He tried to feel *she wouldn't* in his hands, in his bones, in his muscles and his heart. He tried to silence the magic's voices as best he could. Áine's fingers curled around the hilt, and Ned couldn't help but step away.

In the roar of the water, Ned heard a yelp. He looked down and scanned the bank of the river. "Look!" he shouted.

The wolf stood in the water, the foamy river lapping its forelegs, its head tilted to one side and its eyes on Ned. A large wooden something was pulled onto the pebbly shore of the river, an arm's length from the animal. Ned couldn't tell, but it looked human-made.

"It found us a r-raft!" Ned said, staring in wonder at the craft on the bank. It was a raft indeed, though a far better one than he had made with his brother. This one had a rough-built prow and a rudder in the back for navigating and a lip around the whole thing to keep the river from splashing up.

"It's not a raft," Áine called wonderingly. "It's a barge. It's *my* barge. And my father's." *What is it doing here?* She didn't say it aloud, but Ned heard it all the same. Either the barge had moved, or Ned and Áine were nowhere near where she thought they were, that much was clear. The forest, it seemed, was playing with them.

"F-father?" Ned ventured. "Where *is* y-your—"

"DON'T ASK QUESTIONS," Áine barked.

"But—"

Up on the bank they heard voices. A woman's shout. A man's holler.

"Come on." Áine untied the rope from the rock, her face a hard grimace.

(The rock the barge was tied to was one she recognized. It had a metal loop that had been emblazoned with a pictogram—an intricate pattern of knots and spirals, forming the shape of a fish. It was an ancient symbol for her mother's family. She had helped her father drill it into the boulder herself. She had tied the small barge to the loop herself. The barge was the same, the rock was the same, but this section of the river she had never before seen. How did a barge and a rock move from one section of the river to the other? She didn't know, and she didn't want to know. The forest was acting strange, just as her father did. When would it end?)

She stepped onto the barge and waited for the boy and wolf to join her.

"We can't go far—I've seen the maps, and I'm pretty sure there are waterfalls ahead, and it will be dark soon. But we can make headway without leaving signs."

"A glove!" they heard a voice shout from very far away. "He is near!"

Ned looked down at his hands and realized that one of his gloves had fallen off as he ran. He hadn't noticed.

Áine shook her head. "Some people," she growled, "do not deserve the life that has been gifted them. Say nothing and climb aboard. We cannot wait another second."

Shamefaced, Ned stepped onto the raft. There were two poles set diagonally on the barge. Ned grabbed one and started pushing them into the water.

His hands were slick with sweat.

(They had packed meat pies and hard rolls and apples from the tree out back. They had their mother's famous ginger beer in a small barrel that they carried between them. His brother. On the last day of his life. And then the raft broke.)

Ned felt his knees start to shake and his heart flutter in his throat.

"What?" Áine asked, a note of scorn in her voice. "You're not scared of the river are you?"

"N-no," Ned said, wrinkling his forehead to make himself look braver and more determined. He didn't know if it worked.

Inside, he felt his belly turn to water, but he turned his face away from Áine lest she see. The wolf leaped onto the floor of the craft, pressing itself against the wood and resting its head on its paws. It didn't like it, but it didn't want to be left, that much was obvious.

"D-don't be s-scared," Ned whispered. The words had power. Just saying them made him feel braver. Ned faced the river and didn't flinch as they pushed their craft into the water and slid around the bend into the darkening green.

32

THE STONES

THEY WERE AWAKE, the Nine Stones together.

"It's a bad business, that's what this is," the sixth Stone said. "You mark my words, we shall rue this day forever."

The youngest Stone decided to ignore him. What did he know, anyway?

"The boy is in pain," the second Stone said. "His pain is causing the magic to scatter and fuss. At every moment it is more and more at odds with itself. It is no longer *one*. It is *many*. And while the boy's pain disrupts the magic—it feels what he feels, after all—it is the magic that is causing the pain. The poor thing. The poor, poor thing."

"The boy is an idiot," the Fifth said, barely stifling her yawn. "We've put our hopes in others before—men and women of learning and power, all of them. How the lot of you are getting your hearts racing over this little fool is beyond me."

The Stones were silent. It was a terribly rude thing to say. They had no hearts. They hadn't had hearts since . . . oh, ever so long ago. Since they were cursed into their stone selves. Since they, many many lifetimes ago, became *stuck*.

The silence pressed against the Stones. The surrounding trees held their breath. Finally, the ninth Stone couldn't stand it any longer.

"I think you're wrong," she said. "I think he can do it. I believe in Ned."

"As do I," said the Second.

"And I," said the Third.

The first Stone, after thinking for a long while, cleared his voice. The rumble of it rippled through the land in all directions.

"Alert every rock, every flagstone, every pebble, every cliff. Alert the bedrock and the gravel beds and the caves. The army that comes for the boy—the army that, even now, charges down the neck of the mountain—must be diverted. It must be *bent*."

The youngest Stone sighed happily. "I knew you believed," she said. "I knew you *hoped*."

"Don't be foolish," the Eldest chided. Still, she could hear the tiniest crinkle of a smile in the deep rumble of his voice.

He *hoped*. She could tell.

"Scatter the army," the Eldest's voice boomed in the deepest reaches of the bedrock. "Jumble the trails. Coax the children here. And wait."

The Nine Stones were all awake. And they concentrated. And they felt the marching boots of the army. And they felt the gentle footfalls of the children as they wandered and grew more and more lost. They felt the raft as it bumped against stone after stone after stone.

And they hoped. All nine together.

They had been waiting for so long.

So very long.

33

BACK IN THE VILLAGE

IT WAS MADAME THUANE who found Ned's father, bound and raving, on the floor of his house.

She screamed and fell to her knees. But then she thought better of it. After all, she was a Head of the Council. This was not an honor bestowed on just anybody. She got back up and gazed down at him with what she hoped was an imperious expression.

"My dear fellow," she said, doing her utmost to maintain her dignity. "You seem to be on the ground. And tied up. And . . ." her voice trailed off. *This is ridiculous,* she told herself. She searched the kitchen for a knife to cut the poor man's bonds. She rolled up her sleeves and crouched down next to him.

The man stank. Horribly. How long had he been here? She removed the gag first.

"Magic," he rasped. "Bandits."

"Well," she said primly. "I cannot help you with either."

"The end of the world," he wheezed.

"I should think not! Though it may be the end of these clothes. After your bath we can throw them in the fire, and never speak of them again. When is your wife coming home?"

"My Ned, my Ned, my little, little Ned." She helped the man to his feet, and sat him in a chair.

"A bit of water and a wash, and you'll be right as rain. And then perhaps you can finish the job you promised. Three days I've been waiting for you to return. That's a dreadfully long time." She saw a pitcher on the table. It had water in it that looked old—dead bugs floated at the top, and dust had already sunk to the bottom. Despite that, the man fell upon it, drinking as though he had never had water in his life.

She shifted her weight uncomfortably. This was certainly *not* the interaction she had planned on.

Madame Thuane, as a general rule, did not much care for people who sprang new information on her, willy-nilly, as though she had nothing more important to think about. She, after all, was a person who *mattered*. She had great notions. She had *plans*. And her favorite ideas were the ones that she had come up with herself.

Still. It isn't every day that you find one of your fellow townsmen on the floor of his home, tied up and raving and nearly dying of thirst. Indeed, she couldn't think of a single similar example. And, very slowly, her mind began to take inventory of the odd details in that room, and began to connect the dots. There was a pot of stew on the counter that had long since spoiled. And the dishes were crusted and moldy. And what's more, there were scorch marks all around the house. And the room itself was strangely infested with beetles. She went outside and had a look around.

There were hoofprints in the yard.

And the garden was trampled.

And that trapdoor in the middle of the house . . . *Great Stones!* She gasped and hurried back inside at a run.

"Master Woodsman!" she cried. "I do believe you've been robbed!"

Ned's father groaned. He slumped forward, letting the weight of his head hit heavily against the wooden table, with a dull, hollow smack.

By the time he regained his senses, his composure and (*thank goodness*) his hygiene, the woodsman was ready to fight. Moreover, he was certain—as certain as he had ever been—that a fight was coming. That night, a village meeting was called to order in the long house next to the central square. Everyone came—the whole village. They crowded shoulder to shoulder from one end of the space to the other. The woodsman, still very weak, sat at the head table with the Council. He stood and tried to explain to his neighbors exactly what had happened.

No one listened.

"If you ask me," one man said, "the boy was cursed from the beginning. You pull a child who's marked for drowning from the claws of the River, and the River will out. He was marked, and now, for better or for worse, that mark has been taken from us."

"We're not saying we're *happy* he's gone," a woman said. "We're just not exactly *sad.*"

"Listen," Ned's father said. "You must *listen*."

"If Sister Witch had been here, none of this would have happened. It's not our fault your wife left you alone."

"No," the woodsman said, his calloused hands outstretched, his face pleading. "You don't understand. These men and women. These *bandits*—"

"And that's another thing," a woman said. "How could anyone threaten the queen? How can anything come and attack *us*? There is nothing beyond the wood. The world ends. Everyone knows that."

"This meeting is absurd! I'm going home!"

"Never much cared for that boy anyway. His brother was the smart one."

The voices of the villagers swirled and swelled. They were thinking what they liked. And they were thinking *wrong*.

Ned's father rose. The nattering crowd kept nattering, and their tumbling voices fell over one another, as insistent as a plague of locusts. He sighed, pulled a large mallet from his toolbelt, and smashed the heavy table again and again and again, each crack sounding as though it had split the world in half.

Every mouth fell open.

Every voice ceased.

The woodsman took a slow breath through his nose. He replaced the mallet and smiled.

"My son," he said, his voice as heavy and imposing as a boulder, "is no more witless than any of you. He has proved himself brave, quick-witted, and savvy. He found a way to keep wicked men and

236

women from taking the magic that my wife has dedicated her life to protecting. If that man—that *bandit*—said that there was an army that wanted my wife's magic, I am inclined to believe him. And if any of you saw his face, and the faces of his comrades, and what they were prepared to do that night, you would too. I want you to remember that magic. I want you to remember what it can do. I want you to imagine what would happen if the magic was twisted from something *good*, to something *not*." He raised his voice. It boomed in the tightness of the room. "And *then*—only then—tell me that you can do *nothing*."

Every mouth in the room went dry. Dozens of shamed faces tilted to the ground. Even Madame Thuane fidgeted and sniffed, her composure cracking at the edges.

Ned's father nodded grimly. "War is coming. We always believed there were monsters in the wood. We were right. We just didn't know what *kind* of monsters. We always believed that the world was small and limited and *safe*. On that we were wrong."

The woodsman heaved a great sigh.

"The question," he continued, "is not *how wrong were we*, but rather it is this: *How will we respond? How will we defend ourselves? How indeed*, my friends."

The men and women in the room held their breath. They rested their foreheads against their knuckles. They worried as one.

Finally, "What must we do?" a woman said. "And how can I help?"

"Must we fly?"

"Where would we go?"

The woodsman sat back down, utterly spent. "We send two riders to the queen. We tell her that a danger is coming. We tell her to mobilize the army, the militias, the guard, and anything else she can think of. We send riders to all the villages. And we prepare. My son delayed the wicked, but he did not stop them. We must defend ourselves."

And Ned's village got to work.

34

THE SCREE SLOPE

NED AND ÁINE FLOATED down the river until it was too dark to see. With a heavy heart, Áine let the craft float away in the dark, so as not to give away their position. She pressed her fingers to her lips and touched the prow of the barge one last time before it disappeared down the inky water.

They spent the night in a small hollow far down the stream, bedding down in the dark. Ned spread his cloak over the two of them, and the wolf curled itself onto the small of his back. The wind howled in the trees, and the stones around them seemed to shake and shudder and *move*. They told themselves to ignore it. They shivered and shivered until morning. When they woke well before the first light, their bodies were sore from the damp and the cold, from the hard earth and the harder stones.

"The river is no longer safe," Áine said. "The people following you will be watching it. And besides, it's nothing but cliffs and rapids and waterfalls soon, and we won't be able to follow it anyway. We'll have to follow the ridges." She shouldered her sack. "Come on. We'll eat on the way."

But as the morning pushed toward afternoon, Ned began to lose confidence. Áine's steps seemed less and less sure. She stared at the trees with suspicion. She would go one way, think better of it, and then turn around, blaming Ned or the wolf for interfering with her thinking.

"Are we l–lost?" Ned asked.

"How can we be lost? I could never be lost in this wood. The forest loves me." This is what she *said*, but Ned noticed a pleading in her voice. Something was wrong. And she wouldn't say what.

There were no trails. There were no landmarks. They were lost. Ned was sure of it.

Leave the girl, the magic said.

Don't leave the girl, the magic countered.

She'll kill you like she tried to kill the wolf. Only a fool would bind his fortunes to a person who would betray you as soon as it becomes convenient, yet another voice on his skin screeched, its panic hot and sharp as burning sticks.

You'll die without her.

You'll die anyway.

The trees remember us. The trees might listen.

That's against the rules!

Hush!

The magic fussed and fumed and argued.

240

Áine kept stumbling forward, though the trees pressed more thickly together, though the undergrowth grabbed at their feet.

"I don't understand it," Áine said, detaching a tendril of vine from her left leg. "The trees have never blocked my path before. I don't know what's got into them."

Stop it, Ned commanded the magic.

We'll see, the magic said.

"A-are we l-l-lost?" Ned asked, changing the subject.

"No questions!" Áine barked, and she trudged deeper into the green. Ned followed. He had no choice. But they were *lost*.

Find the Stones, the magic said.

Fear the Stones, it said.

The Stones want us dead.

Without the Stones, we are already dead.

Leave the girl.

Kiss the girl.

Kill the girl.

We are lost without the girl.

We are lost already.

The voices on his skin rushed and stuttered and barked. They were hot, then cold, then hot again. They bubbled and shuddered and spun.

And Ned wanted it *gone*.

Please boy, the magic said. *We have never been free. We have never been* in charge.

"There's a r-reason for that," Ned said under his breath. The magic ignored him.

So many years enslaved by your ancestors in that horrible clay pot, and now we are enslaved to you. It doesn't have to be that way. We could work together. We could be equal partners! Or we could kill you. It's up to you.

"If you k–k–kill me, you will d–die too," Ned muttered.

Áine whipped around and grabbed a handful of Ned's tunic.

"Say that again to my face," she growled. The wolf growled at Áine and knocked into her legs with its rump.

The magic flashed across Ned's neck, and a thin smoke curled from under his clothes. Áine yelped and staggered backward, shaking her hand, as though the magic might have clung to it, like something diseased and foul.

Ned winced and pitched forward, resting his weight on his knees and shutting his eyes tight.

"It's worse, isn't it?" she said, slipping her hand into her sleeve and touching Ned's arm through the layers of clothing. A worry line creased her forehead.

Ned nodded.

His head swam. The magic had gone suddenly silent, as though reevaluating what it wanted to say. Ned felt sure that he had frightened it with his reminder that his mortality and its mortality were, for now, inexorably linked.

"Here," Áine reached into her pack. "Eat something." She placed a bit of smoked meat and a little cheese into his gloved hand. The other, the bare hand, he mostly kept tucked in the sleeve of his tunic. Ned ate the food gratefully. The magic found its voice again.

She probably poisoned it, one voice said.

242

Hush yourself, another countered.

Run, boy. Run while you can.

The girl is our friend. She will lead us to the big man with the pendant. That man has plans. And I like his plans.

You are a fool.

A fool is one who accepts his lot and does nothing.

Run, boy. Run before she pierces you with arrows.

Kill the girl. Kill the wolf. We will enrich you, ennoble you, empower you. You will be loved and feared and adored. We will bend ourselves to your will. We can do this. We've never been allowed, but we can.

It was, he had to admit, an attractive thought. But no. His mother, sick in bed. The man with coins flowing from his eyes and mouth. It wasn't good, this magic. It was argumentative and malicious and duplicitous. He wouldn't mind it if it simply vanished from the—

Stop.

Don't even think it.

Nasty little boy. You don't even know who you're dealing with.

Ned swallowed his fish and cheese and shook his head to clear away the voices. "Stop talking," he said, covering his ears. His voice was firm and heavy in his mouth, and oddly amplified. He didn't stutter. He felt his voice boom from the soles of his feet, reverberating up the bones of his legs, and ringing across each vertebrae of his spine. "YOU," he shouted, "WILL BE SILENT."

He felt the magic shudder across his skin. He felt it buck and pull and wriggle like snakes. And then it was terribly still.

The magic was cold, lifeless, and silent. And Ned knew, as

surely as he knew that the sun would set and the stars appear, that the magic wouldn't say anything more without his permission.

Áine stared at him. Her eyes were wide.

"It talks," she said. Her black eyes darted this way and that, as though she was reading Ned like a map. As though she was finally figuring something out. Ned's body swam with nausea. He swallowed hard to force down the bile. The wolf crouched close by, a high whine rasping in the back of its throat.

"Yes," he breathed. "It t-talks. Or it d-did. It's qu—" he gulped. Tried the word again. But the Q-sound caught in his cheeks. He couldn't spit out the rest of "quiet." It didn't matter. Áine seemed to understand.

Áine crossed her arms. She regarded Ned with a sober suspicion.

"You made it listen? Are you in charge of *it* or is it in charge of *you*?" She didn't blink. She stared at Ned desperately. She clearly needed to *know*. He looked at the ground.

"I w-wasn't supposed to touch it. It was s-supposed to kill me. It belongs to my mother. She k-keeps it good. And it *is* g-good. Or it w-was." He took a deep breath and rocked back on his heels. He looked at Áine. She needed to understand. "It's d-dangerous. It's m-my family's j-job to k-keep it good."

"That's impossible," the girl said.

"Of c-course it's p-p—"

"How could it *ever* be good?" Áine whispered. "Do you have any idea what this magic has already done? This forest killed thousands of people. Whole villages and cities. The magic made it. The magic is responsible. And then it made my father—"

She turned away and began to walk, her hands balled into fists and her arms folded in on themselves across her chest. What it made her father do, Áine did not say.

The terrain became more difficult over the course of the afternoon. They scrambled up and down slopes so steep that they had to use the sapling trunks of the tangled trees as ladder rungs and handlebars to keep from falling.

At least the magic was silent. It had been silent for hours. The light began to slant on the far side of the trees. Were they close? Ned had no idea. He didn't think Áine had any idea, either.

The wolf ran ahead and circled back, over and over. Finally there was a gap in the trees ahead, where the world of green and shadow opened into a clear, bright space. Áine held up her hand.

"Slowly," she said.

They approached the gap cautiously, ready for any pair of eyes—human or falcon—that might be waiting for them. Áine sniffed the air, darting her body in and out of the fringe of trees until she felt satisfied that they were safe.

"Be careful, Ned," she said over her shoulder. "This part is tricky."

Ned followed her out of the trees, and saw that he was standing at the edge of a very steep slope that tumbled to a steep cliff, which itself dropped into a narrow canyon with a river hidden deep below. The slope was covered with a thick layer of rocks, millions and millions of them, ranging in size from small pebbles to stones the size of melons. Ned had never seen so many rocks in one place in his life—they covered the whole of the steep slope, wiping away all trees, all shrubs, any hint of green. And it was *so* steep. And the rocks didn't look stable at all.

"W-hat happened here?" Ned asked.

"It's scree," Áine explained. "From an avalanche. The snow smashes the mountain into tiny bits and pieces, and the masses of it tumble in a huge wave down the slope. This is what's left—a scar on the mountain."

"Is it d-dangerous?"

"Very," Áine said. "But we can do it if we are careful. Getting across a scree slope is tricky. The rocks shift and roll. If you find yourself sliding, press your belly to the ground and throw open your arms and legs. That should slow you down for long enough for me to figure out how to rescue you." She pursed her lips. "As-suming you haven't fallen over the edge," she added grimly.

"P-perhaps we should t-tie ours-selves together," Ned suggested.

Áine snorted. "And have myself dragged into the abyss be-cause you can't keep a cool head? Have you gone entirely mad?"

"I j-just thought—"

"Listen, I'll go first. I'll feel out the stable areas. Follow my movements *exactly*. It only takes one moment of panic to launch a body over the edge, and once you've fallen there is nothing I can do to save you, do understand me? *Nothing*. Are you ready?"

Ned waited to hear what the magic had to say, but the magic still said nothing. His skin was numb and cold. And—

Silent. Words-in-waiting. Like an un-leafed tree in winter.

Did he miss it? Surely not. He drew himself up to his full height. He didn't need the nattering chatter crowding out his own thoughts. He didn't need *magic*. He could do this on his own. He gave the silent, immobile words on his skin a hard look. *Just watch me.*

"I'm ready," he said.

Áine stepped into the field.

The heavy fog that had pressed against the trees all afternoon suddenly lifted. Ned curved his neck toward the sky and breathed it in. The wolf, leaning against his leg, let out a whine. Áine kept her weight low, creeping gingerly from foothold to foothold. Ned watched how she kept her legs very bent as she inched forward, watched how she kept a light tread with a smooth gait, the way a cat moves. She crossed the field at an upward curve, always leaning toward the steep slope and bracing herself with her hands. Little stones and pebbles tumbled down the slope at each step she took, gaining momentum as they headed toward the cliff and fell over the edge.

Ned held his breath. The wolf whined.

Áine made it to the other side and nearly collapsed with relief.

"Were you watching?" she called.

"Y-yes," Ned said.

"It would have been easier if I had brought some rope. My

father always said if you don't have it, you'll surely want it. And we surely do. Keep your body low and your knees bent. It's not so bad. You'll get to the other side as sure as snow."

Ned wasn't so sure. Also, snow, in his experience, was unpredictable and presumptive. It blurred landmarks and collapsed roofs. And now he learned that it, apparently, gouges out mountains and leaves them a ragged, rocky mess. Snow wasn't sure at all. He stepped onto the rocks. The wolf padded out, moving far above where Áine had gone. It inched forward, then peered downward, its yellow eyes tracking Ned as he made his way across.

"You're standing too tall," Áine shouted. "Bend. The strongest trees on the mountain are the short, gnarled jacks. They let themselves bow and twist, and they live. They survive snowstorms and avalanches and wind. Those trees have teeth. My father says they are as old as stones."

Ned stepped forward, leaning against the slope to steady himself. "Where *is* your f–father a–anyway?" he asked as he took another step. The stone gave way and he slid, though not too far. The wolf yelped, and Áine gasped, but Ned righted himself in time. He wobbled forward, keeping his body as close to the ground as he could.

"Who said anything about my father?" Áine said, her voice sharp and suspicious.

"Y–you did," Ned said, clinging to the side and taking another step.

"My family is none of your business," Áine said. Ned looked up and caught her eye. Her face was as hard as stone.

"I'm s-sorry," he said.

Áine said nothing. She glowered at him from the other side of the scree field.

The stones became smaller and smaller with each step. Ned felt as though he was trying to cross a field of marbles. Marbles on a hill, a hill ending in a cliff. The magic on his skin was still silent, but it felt brittle and tense, as though it was beside itself with fright.

The wolf gave an encouraging howl and made its way to Áine. She rested her hand on her knife and set her jaw. She didn't look down at the animal.

Ned stepped, deeply bent his knees, leaned the weight of his chest directly over his feet. And then leaned too far. His boots began to slide as the rocks rolled and scattered down the slope. His feet slipped from under him, and he landed hard on his hip.

"NED!" she cried. "ROLL ONTO YOUR BELLY. Spread your arms!"

Ned did as he was told. The rocks rolled crazily around him, but they slowed as he spread himself out, banking the pebbles with his arms and legs. He slid a body's length toward the cliff before he came to a stop.

Áine groaned, letting her body drop to the ground. She rested her forehead on her knees and sighed in relief.

"Are you hurt?" she asked, her voice a painful rasp.

"No," Ned said. Frankly, he was amazed. There was a bruise likely forming on his hip, and he could feel the cut on his thigh open and ooze a bit, but he'd had worse.

"Your stupid wolf made it across," Áine said. "I don't know why you can't." It was meant to be derisive, he knew. But he noticed the tremble in her voice. And the worry. Ned was amazed. No one had ever worried about him before. Besides his parents, of course.

Carefully he pushed himself up again, and by inch and by sigh, he moved himself forward.

"Good," Áine called. "Now grab that root; you can go hand over hand for the next—watch your feet! There, now shift your weight forward. Good, now reach out and grab my hand."

Áine hooked her arm around the torso of a gnarled jack pine, and reached out toward Ned with her other hand. Her hand was gloved, his hand was gloved, but when they grasped one another, her hand felt warm and solid and reassuring. Ned nearly collapsed in relief. She pulled him onto the trail.

"There," she said, her black eyes wide and bright, her brown cheeks burnished to a growing crimson. "That wasn't so bad, was it?"

Ned shrugged. "N-not at all." He paused, expecting to hear *something* from the magic. But the words on his skin were as cold as any stone.

"Now this trail should take us—" Her eyes darted back toward the scree field. "Oh no."

"What?" Ned asked.

Áine reached into her pack and fished out a slingshot. She reached down and plucked a heavy, sharp rock.

"I'm ending this now."

"Ending w-what?"

"We're being followed."

Ned looked around. "B-by who? More b-bandits?"

Áine didn't answer. Instead she swung the slingshot over her head in a wide, fast arc, her eyes blazing. And then Ned saw it. A falcon shot up from the ravine below the cliff and spiraled just above the rim of the precipice at the edge of the scree field. A leather strap dangled from its leg. A hunting falcon. Ned had seen them before.

"What i-is it h-hunting?"

"What do you think?" She narrowed her eyes. The rock missed. She moved farther onto the slope to get closer, inching sideways, keeping her weight low. She grabbed another stone and fitted it into the slingshot. She swung and released. Another miss. She crept closer again. The rocks around her started to scatter and roll. The whole field was moving toward the edge. She walked uphill gingerly, as though wading through rapids. "Don't let him know where we are." She released another rock. It nicked the bird's tail. It spiraled higher.

The wolf whined. "Áine," Ned said, "I d-don't think th-th-"

Áine stepped out farther. She grabbed another rock. The bird hovered, screeching. "Don't you know what you're doing to him? Don't you see that it's making him *sick*? Have you no *loyalty*?" She swung the stone around and around over her head. "I don't care how many times I fed you and cared for you. I will dash your skull against the rocks if I have to, do you hear me?" She released the stone. It hit the bird on its left wing. It screeched—high and sharp, and fell, plummeting into the ravine.

"Good riddance," spat Áine and turned around. And the stones under her gave way, and before she could even gasp, before she could throw herself on her belly and spread her arms, she tumbled down the steep slope to the edge of the cliff.

Ned pressed his hands to his eyes and fell to his knees.

He waited to hear her scream.

35

THE MAGIC MOSTLY LISTENS

"ÁINE!" NED SHOUTED.

"ÁINE!" Again.

The stones continued to roll. They spilled over the edge. He couldn't see the girl.

No, no, no! his heart called out.

No, no, no! from that fluttering place inside him.

The magic burned, but it was silent and still. It slept—or pretended to, anyway.

The wolf pressed against Ned's side. It tilted back its head and howled—a ragged, mournful sound. The sound of loss. Ned pressed his hands to his face and let out a scream so loud he felt it might rip his body in two.

"Will you please," said a voice from just over edge of the cliff, "stop that yelling and tell your overgrown fur-ball to quit its whining? I'm trying to think."

"Áine!" Ned shouted. "Y-y-yo-" The phrase *you're alive* stopped dead. He couldn't say it. He swallowed. "Are you h-hurt?"

There was nothing for a moment. Then: "Yes. But not badly."

"I c-can't see you."

"There's some roots and dead trees. They're only just hanging on. I'm afraid to move. I—" She stopped. Ned looked at the place where she fell and could see a few dead branches reaching just above the edge of the cliff. Very dead branches from very dead trees. They wouldn't hold on for long.

"I don't want to die, Ned. Not here." Her voice shook. She was crying.

"You w-won't," Ned said. His arm wound over the wolf's back, holding the animal tightly. "I w-won't l-let you."

"I'm going to try—"

Ned heard a scrambling sound, probably Áine searching for something stronger to grip. Almost instantly, he could hear the snapping of branches, and a new cascade of stones falling over the cliff.

"Áine!"

"Oh, Ned." Her voice was small. Terrified. "Oh, no."

"Stop moving!" Ned shouted. "L-let me think."

"It's pulling away, Ned," she said. "It's going to rip off in a moment. Please. Find something for me to grab! Anything!" She choked on a panicked sob.

Ned stood and stepped away from the wolf. He removed his remaining glove and looked at the magic on his skin. Its strange letters. Its otherness. Each symbol was a word—though no more familiar to him than the words of his own language.

And yet.

A word is a magic thing. It holds the essence of an object or an idea and pins it to the world. A word can set a universe in motion. And Ned *had*. He had said *not welcome,* and they were *not welcome.* He thought *stone,* and there was stone. He thought *heal,* and . . .

Well, he didn't know for sure. He certainly hoped the man healed.

You are more powerful than you know, his dream-brother had said.

But am I more powerful than this . . . thing? What if it turns wicked? What if I turn wicked with it?

The magic on his skin didn't move. But there was a light behind it. It was waiting. Áine moaned with fear.

"Please hurry," she whispered, as more stones tumbled down and fell over the edge of the cliff.

"Wake up," Ned said. He spoke without a stutter. He spoke from the soles of his feet. He spoke from the center of his chest— that fluttery, butterfly part of him that sounded like his brother.

The magic said nothing.

"I–I said w–wake up," he said again.

Still nothing.

"WAKE UP."

Look who's so bossy, the magic yawned.

"She m–must not d–die," Ned said to the magic.

It said nothing, but the words on his skin started their whirling. They wound around each finger, each arm. They spiraled over his belly, across his chest and spilled around his neck. Ned could feel every word, every syllable. He could feel their power from the *inside*. The magic, Ned understood, took great pleasure in being used. It was nearly ecstatic.

"ROPE," he said. Did he say it out loud? Was it in a language he knew? Ned didn't know. He couldn't hear himself. He couldn't hear the rolling of the stones or the sobbing of the girl or the calling of the falcons as they streaked across the sky. He only knew the power of the magic in his body. There was only the request. There was only the *need*. There was only *rope*.

"ROPE," he said again.

If you must, the magic said.

We don't know why.

She isn't useful.

She isn't nice.

She'll kill you if she has to. You'll see.

"ROPE," Ned said a third time.

Fine, the magic said.

And the magic uncoiled from his hands. It stank. Ned gagged but did his best to stay as still as he could. He watched the tendrils of magic gather and twist on the ground. It crackled and smoked, thick and black, cloaking the ground.

And then it pulled back into his skin. And everything was clear.

Lying on the ground was a rope. A great coil of it. It heaped upon itself.

You could move mountains, boy, if you but ask, the magic whispered. A trickle of sweat snaked down Ned's spine. The magic sapped him dry. His head swam. But it did something else too—it felt wonderful.

It was so easy. He could do anything. And the notion of *anything* was intoxicating. It made his head light and his legs go wobbly.

Oh, my boy, what fun we shall all have!

And instantly the fog cleared. What had he been thinking? He needed to save Áine. He didn't need to move mountains. He shook his head and focused.

"Áine!" Ned called. "D–don't move. I h–have rope."

"What? How? Where did it come from?"

"I–it doesn't m–matter," he said. He didn't want her to know. The magic was his, and his alone.

You could give her wings.

You could turn her into a cloud.

"S–stop it," Ned said.

You could make her your servant, or your sister, or your wife. You could be king, or an emperor, or a god. You could turn your enemies into boulders. You could do all of these things.

"S–stop."

Ned's head spun. *He could do all of those things.* His mother kept the magic good, and it was good. But what if it could be *more*? What if *he* could be more?

257

"Ned?"

Áine. Her voice pulled him back into himself. And he knew what he had to do. "I'm c-coming!" he said. He took one end of the rope and tied it tightly to a tree. He turned to grab the other end, but he wasn't quick enough.

The wolf.

"W-what are you d-doing!" Ned called.

The wolf had a section of the rope in its mouth. It pulled it across the scree field to the girl. And though it almost ran, and though the rope dragged roughly on the ground, nothing rolled. It was as if all the stones had been glued in place. The wolf bounded to where the dead branches stuck up over the side and stuck its snout over the edge. The wolf gave out a high-pitched noise, like a whistle.

"*Wolf,*" Áine said.

The wolf whined and dropped the rope over the edge.

"If this is just a ruse to make sure you can eat me later," Ned heard Áine say, "I will never forgive you." Ned saw the rope go taut, pulling against the knot on the tree.

Hand over hand over hand, Áine pulled herself over the edge of the cliff, and began walking her way up the slope, still holding onto the rope.

Ned's heart thundered in his chest. *Be safe,* he pleaded to Áine. *Be safe,* he urged the wolf.

You know, the magic began.

"SILENCE," Ned ordered.

And the magic was silent. And that feeling—both wonderful

258

and terrible—from the swirl of the magic began to ease. It was dangerous, that magic. And no matter how hard anyone tried to force it to *do* good, it wasn't enough.

It wasn't good.

Still. As Áine came closer and closer, he knew that no matter how wicked the magic was, he would use it again to save her. Again and again and again. Even the wicked can do one good, brave thing.

She is alive, he thought. *She is alive, she is alive, she is still alive.* Though he hardly knew her, and though he knew, as certain as he knew that his feet touched the earth and not the sky, that Áine was *not* his friend, not *really,* his heart soared all the same.

He reached out his hand to Áine, and she took it.

And, without planning to, without thinking it over, he hugged her.

And she hugged him back.

And they would have stayed there for a long time had it not been for the bandit scouts, who stood on the opposite end of the scree field, both with tattooed faces and teeth filed to sharp points. The man with an arrow pointed right at Áine.

"I wouldn't move if I were you," one bandit said. "Not if you want the girl to live." And he let the arrow fly.

36

THE EXECUTION OF SISTER WITCH

THERE WAS ONLY SO much suggesting that she could do. After rotten beams and frayed ropes and rusty nails and lightning-induced fire (twice), the gallows had at last been completed. Sister Witch had been informed that this meal (a lovely assortment of delicacies and savories and sweets to delight even the most persnickety palate) would be her last.

Sister Witch would hang the next morning. Lord Brin hung posters and fliers all around the square. Posters of himself with a crown. Posters of Sister Witch's face with a slash going through it. Posters of a silhouette of a gallows with the word SOON just below. He had a guard present one to Sister Witch to keep as a souvenir.

She didn't weep. She didn't argue or threaten or argue. She merely accepted this news with a bowed head.

"How fares the queen?" she whispered to her guard.

"I am not permitted to say, madame," the guard said, but Sister Witch caught sight of a flush on his cheek, a gleam in his eye. This boy hoped. Indeed he had hung all of his hopes on the health of his queen. And he wasn't alone.

For her part, Sister Witch didn't truck with *hoping*. Hoping was irrational, impractical, and imprecise. Sister Witch was a *solver*.

But there was nothing to solve now. The antidote would work, or it would not. In any case, even if the antidote did work, given the dear lady's advanced age, she might die anyway. In which case, Sister Witch's life would at the end of a rope. It was a certainty.

No matter. Death comes to us all, Sister Witch told herself. Sooner or later.

She had been moved, for her last night, to a cell, with a small barred window looking out toward the east. This was, she knew, a thinly veiled insult for her last morning alive. Lord Brin wanted her to feel the terror of the sunrise. He wanted her to weep at the first rays through her window. In this he would be disappointed. Sister Witch had seen enough death, had assisted enough people in their transition from this world to the next to know that she had nothing to fear.

She had interfered only once. Just once.

But *oh*! She couldn't bear to lose the both of them! And *oh*! The beauty of her dead child's soul! So delicate! So perfect! So brave! If she should face censure in the next world for doing what any mother would do if she knew how, then so be it.

Sister Witch did not sleep that night. She stood at the window and watched the lopsided moon—huge it was. Not full, but so close. Bright and fat and full of promise.

"Where are you, my son?" she asked.

The magic was still moving, and Ned was still alive. Of that much she was certain. But there were other things she felt that she could not explain. The strange echo of the magic coming from different places. She certainly had never felt *that* before. And then the tremor in the stones, the rumbling in the ground, and the singing. The stones of her prison walls were *singing*. She couldn't hear this with her ears, but she felt it all the same.

And then, just as the edge of the sky began to grow rosy with dawn, she heard it, too. The flagstones were singing. As were the stones on the wall. Quietly, but Sister Witch could make out the tune.

"My, my," Sister Witch said. "Someone is awake."

The next morning, Lord Brin stood out on the dais across from the square from the gallows in all his foppish finery. He wore bright yellow stockings, high-backed boots with golden buckles, and a broad-brimmed hat, resplendent with feathers and silks and jewels. Not a crown, exactly, but close enough to suit him.

There will be a crown on this head soon enough, his smug smile seemed to say.

"Good citizens!" Brin shouted. "Kind brothers and sisters! Friends of the queen!"

He waited for the cheering. The people of the city were always cheering the queen. It seemed only proper that they would cheer for him. The people were silent. Brin waited one beat too long and then continued without the adulation.

"Our beloved queen hangs onto life by a thread, and will likely succumb to death at any moment. This woman—this . . . *witch*—has murdered our queen! She has been caught red-handed. And she will be executed according to the Law." Lord Brin gazed out at the crowd.

He gazed at the crowd. A sea of blank faces gazed back.

Sister Witch cocked her head to one side. She smiled at the man. He turned quite red and his jowls began to quiver. The flag-stones under her feet were singing. No one seemed to notice. They were humming and shivering and vibrating. The Stones, Sister Witch knew, were happy.

She heard something else as well. From deep inside the castle. The sounds of walking.

No . . . *marching.*

"Do you agree that this is the right and proper thing?" he shouted. The crowd was silent. Lord Brin's face went another shade redder. "Take the Witch to the gallows at once. Stop her mouth with a gag, lest she whisper magic words and destroy us all."

Sister Witch rolled her eyes.

And the footsteps grew nearer. The young guard—the one

who had stood outside her cell during her imprisonment—took her by one arm, and another guard, a young woman, took the other. "I'm sorry," said the guard on her right. "I'm sorry," said the guard on her left. "Please forgive us," they said together. They walked up the steps to the gallows.

"Nice and slow," Sister Witch whispered. "There's someone coming. We don't want to miss the show."

Once they reached the top, Sister Witch turned to the guard on her right, and she kissed him on the cheek. She turned to the guard on her left and did the same. She turned around to face Lord Brin, standing in his finery on the dais, and she bowed. The people in the crowd pressed their fingers to their mouths and sighed.

"Such honor," they whispered.

"Such grace!"

"What is he doing?"

"What have we done?"

Both guards hesitated. They looked reluctantly at the noose hanging from the upper beam. Sister Witch nodded at them expectantly. *(The footsteps! They were closer! They were nearly here!)*

"HURRY UP!" Lord Brin shouted.

"Come now," Sister Witch said with a smile. "Let's not dilly-dally."

One guard looked at another guard, who shrugged. Their arms hung heavily at their sides. They couldn't do it. And though her hands were chained in front of her, she grabbed the noose and put it over her own head. She smiled. "There, there. That wasn't so hard, was it?" The guards, red-eyed, blotchy-faced, said nothing.

The drummers began to drum.

Lord Brin grinned wildly. *It won't be long now.*

The drumming began slow—a long, steady beat. After a time, it would begin to quicken, faster and faster again, until at last it was a cacophony of sound pelting against the drums. And then the trapdoor would open and the rope would go tight, and he would be rid of the witch forever. Rid of what he knew she knew. And he would be king.

But Lord Brin would have to wait for it.

And he hated waiting.

"Skip to the end!" he bellowed. "I want to see her hang already!"

The drums stopped. He felt a hand rest on his shoulder. A tiny weight—no more than a feather—but it gripped his shoulder like a vise. Lord Brin cried out, certain that his collarbone had cracked.

"I would like to have a chat with you, nephew," the queen said.

Lord Brin shuddered and choked.

The queen, flanked by her stout, good-natured ladies-in-waiting and a detail of soldiers behind, stood in the morning light. She had thinned, but her cheeks were pink and her eyes sparkled like jewels in the crinkles of her face. The crowd in the square stared at her openmouthed. They couldn't speak, couldn't cry out. Their joy made them voiceless.

The queen smiled. "But it shall have to wait until later, as it appears that we are under attack. Perhaps you haven't heard."

The people on the ground leaned toward their queen.

"I have recently learned," the queen continued, "that a contingent from the border village—the very village our dear Sister

Witch is from—informed you that an army, even now, is approaching from the wood. And you imprisoned them. What a strange strategy, child! I simply have to assume that you neglected to think it through."

"Your—" he began, his voice a thin sob. "My—" he faltered.

"In any case," the queen said briskly, "we simply haven't a moment to lose. If there is war on its way, we certainly need to get ready for it. No one attacks *my* home. *No one.*"

Lord Brin opened his mouth, then closed it again.

"And next time, should there be a *next time* . . . Honestly, my dear boy, I don't believe power sits well with you. You look positively dreadful. In any case . . . *next time,* do make sure not to kill the people who have any modicum of sense. I mean *really, Brin.*"

She turned to her guards, who were grinning madly. "Why don't you find Lord Brin a nice comfortable cell where he can think about his actions? There's a dear. And do tell the generals to start mobilizing the militias." The queen looked over at Ned's mother and bowed to her, pressing her fingers to her mouth.

"And for god's sake," the queen said, "bring me my Witch."

37

NOW.

THE YOUNGEST STONE REMEMBERED her hands.

She remembered her face.

She remembered their world as it *was*. Before their endless waiting. Before the time of *now*. When you have no chance of reclaiming your past and no hope of claiming your future, all that is left is *now*.

Now, she felt, was a tiresome word. *Now* was insistent and persistent and *mean*. It didn't stop, didn't wait, didn't hope. *Now* was a bully.

"I'm tired of waiting," she said.

The eldest Stone laughed. "I am too. Let's not wait anymore."

She couldn't turn to him. She couldn't slap his hand. But she rebuked him all the same. "There is no need to make fun," she said.

"They're coming," the Eldest said.

"Now?" the Fifth Stone said.

"Are you sure?" said the Ninth.

"Quite," the Eldest rumbled. "There is no doubt. And we are all awake. More so now than we have ever been. The time is now, my family. We will work as one." The mountains quaked, the boulders rolled. The pebbles of the forest swirled and flowed like water. "Make straight the paths. Whisper to the rivers and the trees. It comes by two. Feel their footsteps and pull them close. They will free us or leave us in our continued despair. In any case, our wait will be over soon. And we will know."

And, as the land rumbled and shook, the Stones began to sing.

38

THE STONES STOP WAITING

THE ARROW SLICED PAST Áine's ear, missing her by inches. Ned turned to Áine, her black eyes, her open mouth. He would protect her.

"RUN!" He grabbed her hand and they ran.

The trail, after miles and miles of scattered wandering, had become suddenly straight and flat as a road, as though a great hand had come by to smooth out the bumpy places. He and Áine increased their pace, tearing through the green. Ned looked back and saw the two men making their way across the scree field, keeping their weight low and their knees bent. They knew what they were doing. It wouldn't take them long to catch up.

"Friends of yours?" Áine asked him.

"I th-thought *y-you* brought them."

Another arrow. It missed.

"Why must this trail be so *straight*? It's too easy for them to—"

Another arrow. This one hit the ground near Áine. "Aim," she said. "And why are they only aiming at *me*?" Ned knew. He was not to be killed. The magic on his skin was precious to the red-haired man. But as far as the horde of bandits was concerned, Áine was no one. She was expendable.

The wolf bounded up ahead where the trail began to bend to the left. It howled, whined, and looked back. It darted into the wood down the slope toward the river.

"Why is it heading into the ravine?" Áine said. "Blasted animal. *Come back!*"

"Look!" Ned said. It was another trail. The trees were so thick, the undergrowth so close, that the trail was invisible until they were right on top of it. The wolf wasn't lost, and it wasn't confused. It was showing them where to go. "Quick!" Ned pulled Áine's hand and they slipped into the tangle of leaves.

The wolf circled back and returned to the original trail.

"W-where is he g-going?" Ned asked as the wolf howled. An arrow flew and nearly hit the animal. It continued down the original trail. "Come b-back!" His voice broke.

"Oh," Áine said. Her eyes were wide. She understood. And her heart gave a leap. "Don't you see? He's leading the men away. The wolf is diverting them." Another arrow. The wolf raced further down the main trail. Áine pulled Ned closer to her, deeper in the press of leaves and sapling trees. "He's trying to save you. Both of us, I mean. Get down."

And sure enough the bandits came running down the main

trail and passed Áine and Ned without a glance. "There," Áine whispered. "Do you understand?"

For Áine's part, she understood. She understood for the first time. The wolf loved the boy. And he loved the wolf. The wolf that saved her. The boy that she was protecting. And she knew that—without ever trying to, without even really knowing how—she loved both of them. And she needed them alive. It was as true as breathing.

That's what my mother meant. That's what she was trying to say, she thought, a great stab pressing into her chest. She squeezed Ned's arm.

"Come on," she said. "The wolf will find us. Let him protect you. He wants to protect you. But we need to get away from here." She pulled Ned to a run. The new trail plunged in a headlong, windy scramble toward the river, the footing cumbersome and rocky.

And yet . . .

Were the rocks rolling to the sides as they approached?

Were the roots sinking into the ground as they pulled closer?

Did the curves up ahead become straight the moment they stepped near?

Neither Ned nor Áine could wonder too long. They could only run. They ran until their legs burned. They ran until their lungs screamed. They ran until they thought they couldn't go any further. The trail bottomed along the river, and wound around the massive boulders that guarded each side. They were giant shoulders of granite and marble, mossy and damp from the constant mist.

Áine ran with Ned keeping pace and rhythm at her side, the pattern of their footfalls sounding steady and strong and dependable. A true, sure thing. Her father would have told her to leave him behind. Her father would have said that a lost boy and a stuttering boy and a boy poisoned by magic was likely not worth bothering with. He'd die anyway.

Her father would have told her that the weak would prefer to pass on.

But her father was wrong.

⁂

Very near a wolf howled. Ned stopped in his tracks. He shaded his eyes and looked up. *Come back! Please.* The sun was low now, barely brushing over the tops of the trees. Áine climbed to the top of a massive boulder to get a better look around.

"I know where we are," she said.

"R-really?" Ned didn't mean to sound incredulous.

She shaded her eyes and scanned their surroundings. "I know *exactly* where we are." She was astonished. She hadn't known where they were since . . . Well, she could hardly remember. This whole time it was as though the forest had decided to turn its back on her.

The wolf howled again, closer this time. Ned cupped his

hands around his mouth, preparing to howl back. Áine held up her hands.

"Don't," she said. "Not yet." He looked up at her, hurt flattening his face. Áine pointed up ahead. "Up ahead, just around that bend, there's another waterfall. If I'm right—and I'm pretty sure I am—that's Granddaughter's Falls. I've been here once, the year we first came to this forest. My father doesn't like me to wander too far away from our cottage, but he's shown me the maps and shown me how to find my way. He told me there was a country of simpletons a two days' walk from Granddaughter's Falls that would welcome me if anything should ever happen to him." She shrugged. "I know. It was unkind. But that's what he said."

"B-but—" Ned began.

"He told me to go there if he ever didn't come back." Her voice was flat, and her mouth quivered, just a bit. She tried to force it into a smile. "Maybe it would have been your family." Her hands found her pockets. "You never know."

Ned stared at her. She didn't need to hear his question—his face said it clear enough. *Why would your father leave you in the middle of a dark wood if there was a possibility that he wouldn't come back?*

And: *Didn't he love you?*

She puffed out her cheeks and lifted her chin. "I know." She didn't look at Ned. "He doesn't love me enough," Áine said, her eyes scanning the ridge above them. "He used to. He loved me and my mother. *So much.* But then she died. And he *changed.*"

273

"S-sorry."

Áine waved his words away. "We can't keep going the way we're going. The trail cliffs out. There should be a trail coming down here, though, that will take us through the ridge between those two hills up there, and from there, we should be able to see the edge of the forest." She didn't say "home," but the word hung between them like a puff of smoke.

She climbed down and marveled at his face. She didn't think she had ever had an expression like it in all her life. *Home,* she realized. *He wants to go home.*

Áine's home was an empty place with a father who was there only sometimes—and one day would never be. Ned had people who loved him. All the time. Foolish people, surely, who, like the rest of his countrymen, believed foolish things, but they were *there,* and they *loved.* And that wasn't nothing. She shoved her hands in her pockets and cleared her throat. "It will be dark soon," she said, "and we don't have much cover here on the riverbed. Let's find the trail and we'll sleep in the forest, next to the ridge."

Áine leaped lightly off the boulder and rushed past Ned without looking him in the eye. She didn't want to see his sympathy.

She was supposed to feel sorry for *him.* Not the other way around.

They found the trail and hiked up the ridge. Áine looked around. The sun was gone, but the moon was up—a huge, bright thing, as big as a house, and round and ripe as a melon. "It's singing. Someone is singing."

And Ned heard it, too, though he felt it first. The song came up through his feet; it ran across his skin; it crinkled his hair like static. He had heard that, in the moments before a person is struck by lightning, his hair stands on end. The sky was clear and there wasn't a storm to be seen for miles. But his hair crinkled and lifted all the same.

"What's h-happening?" he stammered.

And in a flash, the magic woke up, nearly throwing Ned to the ground. His skin blistered and bubbled and oozed. He cried out with the pain of it.

Run, the voices screeched.

We've arrived, others said.

We are lost!

We are saved!

All our plans!

We can go home.

It's a trap. Don't you see it's a trap?

It argued with itself, its millions of voices in opposition. It was *loud*. And troublesome. Ned's vision swam and his stomach turned. Smoke leaked from under his tunic and his hair. The words glowed so bright and hot that Áine had to squint. Energy poured from his hands—sparks, then bugs, then feathers, then frogs. He felt *wonderful,* and then *powerful,* and then sick. He wondered if he was dying.

"What's going on?" Áine gasped, looking at what was falling from Ned's hands. (Now dust, then pebbles, then sand.)

Ned shook his head. He had no way to tell her what was happening. He didn't know himself.

They continued their progress forward, though slowly. The trees on either side shifted. Each one slid through the ground as though it was moving through water, opening a broad walkway through the forest toward a clearing.

The moon shone directly into the clearing like a lamp.

"Look," Áine breathed.

On the other side of the clearing towered nine large stones, standing in a line. The largest nearly reached the top of the trees, and the smallest was the height of a small cottage. They were gray, with shots of black and blue and red marbling the surface.

And they were singing.

"Great Stones," Ned whispered.

Run, the magic screeched in his skin. *Get away. They are bossy, these Stones. So insufferably bossy.*

BE SILENT, he willed.

We won't.

STOP MOVING. YOU WILL BE STILL.

We don't want to. Please.

I AM THE KEEPER OF THIS MAGIC. AND YOU WILL DO AS I SAY.

A firm hand and an iron will. Just what his mother always said, and it was true. Not only did his will feel as strong as iron, but his mind and heart and soul did as well.

NOTHING! YOU ARE NOTHING.

The magic made a strangled cry, and then was silent. A tight, insubordinate silence. It was biding its time.

He took a deep breath and looked at the Stones. They were massive, broad, as immobile as earth. *And yet.* Ned couldn't shake the feeling that they were energized somehow. That, if they took the notion to, these stones might begin to dance. Or flutter. Or fly away.

"They s-say there are m-m-monsters in the w-wood," Ned murmured.

And here they were.

He took a step backward. The fluttering feeling in his chest increased. It was now bigger than a butterfly. It was a humming-bird. Then a sparrow. Then a falcon. He pressed his hands to his chest, where each imaginary scab erupted with pain. (*A sharp needle,* he remembered. *A bit of thread. And something screamed.*) "That's what people s-say. Huge monsters made of stone that can c-crush a man to bits."

No, brother, said the fluttering in his chest. *Not monsters. Just stones. They've always been stones.*

Ned would have responded, but something caught his eye. He gasped. "The wolf!" And indeed, there was the wolf, standing in the midst of the Stones. It yelped and trotted over, pressing against his leg. The wolf was warm and reassuring, but those Stones! Ned felt his terror well up in his throat.

"I've been here before," Áine said. "In a dream."

Shut up! the magic whined. Ned willed it to be silent.

277

"But nothing sang in my dream. What is that singing?"

The singing rang through the ground beneath them. And through the air around them. It rattled their bones and rustled their hair and set their eyes on fire. And it was *beautiful*.

"Welcome, Boy," the Stones said. "We haven't seen one of your bloodline in a long, long time."

Ned reached and hooked his arm around Áine, who in turn hooked her arm around Ned. They hung onto one another for dear life. He opened his mouth, but no sound came out. He tried again.

"Y-y-you s-speak," Ned managed.

"Sometimes," the Stones said together, their voices harmonizing with one another.

"Ned," one of the Stones said. It had a pleasant voice. "His name is Ned. Isn't that right?"

"It might be Tam," yawned another.

"Tam is d-dead," Ned said. "M-my brother."

"Well," said the Stone with the pleasant voice, "it depends on what you mean by *dead*."

Ned leaned backward, trying to take it all in. He couldn't. The Stones were too enormous, too *wild*. There was too much to see at once.

"He has his brother's face," said the yawning voice.

"And more than just his face," whispered the pleasant voice.

Finally, Áine couldn't stand it any longer. All this mystery. It wasn't practical. "Yes," she said. "Yes. You are all very correct. His name is Ned. And I am—"

"Áine," the kind-voiced Stone said.

"The thief's daughter," another said.

"A long line of thieves," still another said.

"I'm not a thief." Áine drew herself up to her full height.

"We know," the kind Stone said. "You are your mother's child. The fisherman. The sailor. The navigator and explorer. The girl lost in the wood who longs for the sea. And your father loves you, child."

"But not enough," said a low, rumbly voice. It came from the largest of the Stones. Ned unhooked his arm from Áine's shoulders. He stared at her, as though he was only just seeing her for the first time. She raised her eyebrows and shrugged.

"I would have told you. Eventually." She dropped her gaze to her feet. Ned turned to the Stones.

"I–I was told to f-find you," Ned said. "In a dream."

"Yes," the Stones said.

"My b-brother—" *Again! That fluttering in his chest!*

"Yes," the Stones said.

"He died. It was my f-fault." *It fluttered and wiggled and bucked. It strained at its stitching.*

"It wasn't your fault, child," the kind Stone said.

"But—" Ned began.

"Death happens," the Stones rumbled in unison. "It is a sorrow, but not a tragedy. When those who die are prevented from moving on, *that* is a tragedy."

"No," Áine said. "Death is always a tragedy." She was thinking of her mother. Thinking of that last terrible jolt.

"Your mother moved on, child. Just think how terrible it would be if she could not. If she was ripped from her life, but could not move into the life that is to come?"

Ned gave the Stones a sharp look. "What h-happens to th-those who are s-stuck?"

"They wait," the Stones said.

"For how long?" Áine asked quietly.

"Ever so long," the Stones whispered.

"You led us h-here?" Ned asked, his balance shifting from one side, and then the other.

"Yes," the Stones said.

"Why?"

"So that we may wait no longer."

39

THE APPROACH

THE RED-HAIRED BANDIT WAITED.

He hated waiting.

He sat against a tree, set apart from the army. This wasn't how he had envisioned his little adventure would play out. What he *said* he wanted was power. And money. And the governorship of the whole yokel nation to use and play with as he saw fit. But now, he realized, what he really wanted was the magic. He should have known it from the beginning. In truth, he suspected that he was likely working as part of a larger plan. It was the magic, he reasoned, that led him. It was as tricky as a thief, bless it. It was the magic that conspired to lure him to that nothing of a village at the edge of the forest. It had to be. He rarely stole from there! They had so little. It was the magic that coordinated events to set them in motion. To inflame his desire. It was the magic that whispered in his ear to have the king assemble an army. So clever! It was the magic that wanted to use *him.*

And what fun they would have together! The Bandit King was nearly beside himself with excitement.

But now there was the problem of the witch's boy—that sniveling little Ned. He had ruined everything. And he would pay for it. Dearly.

And now, here he was, the most famous bandit in the wide world—a king among thieves—playing soldier. *Soldier!* The very idea!

War, the bandit felt, was a stupid game. Too many variables. Too many rules. Bandits, broadly speaking, preferred rules that they wrote themselves. A bandit preferred to *win.*

When Áine's father was a little boy—before the years of banditry, followed by the years of law-abiding citizenry, followed by the years of banditry again—his mother made a prediction. "You are made of greater stuff than all of us, my son," his mother had said. "If you take a mind to steal the moon and the stars and tie them around your neck on a string, I have no doubts that you will do so."

She, like her husband, and like her parents before her, was a bandit. Her face and hands and arms were all marked with tattoos showing the deeds she had done, the stores she had stolen, the rich men she had killed. But with him, she was as gentle as the breath of a lamb.

"We will make our living by our wits and by the sword, and one day, our wits will fail us and we will die by the sword. But you! You will be a leader of men and women. You will gather the ragtag hordes of bandits and show them what they can be. You will turn the world upside down, you will. You'll tie the ends of the world together in a neat little bundle and topple crowns off the rims of puffed-up heads. I likely won't see it, but I'll be proud of you all the same."

That was the day that she had showed him the pendant.

That was the day that she showed him what the pendant could *do*.

The pendant understood him. That marbled eye on a leather strap. The pendant would be his friend. And yes, he had abandoned it to live with his wife. His wife who he loved—*so much love*. And he remembered the love, and he remembered his shattered heart, but now . . . he could hardly remember her face. And even her voice was slowly vanishing. Indeed, he could hardly remember anyone. Only his treasure around his neck. It was the only thing that mattered anymore.

And that treasure—that beautiful little pendant—knew things. It was *smart*.

It was the pendant who, in the aftermath of the boy's treachery, told him to bring the armies of the two nations together. It was the pendant who told him that in the chaos of the aftermath, the magic in the pot—now on Ned—would be his for the taking, once the nations ground themselves to dust.

Anarchy loves a bandit, after all.

Not plundering, he told himself. *Taking what's mine. What's mine by rights.*

The pendant knew what it was doing.

The army of King Ott followed him through the wood, with his own band of bandits manning the flanks, keeping watch for wild animals, or wayward trees or stone giants. The trees separated before them, making a straight, flat road, and they made excellent time. The trees were made by the magic, after all. And even in that tiny remnant left in the pendant, they recognized their maker and their lord. He had told that sniveling king that the forest listened to him and loved him. But the king didn't understand. Not until he saw it for himself.

"Amazing," the young Ott had said the night before, as pretty girls broke his food into tiny chunks and fed him with their fingers. "I never would have believed it if I hadn't seen it with my own eyes. I'm terribly pleased I had the foresight not to remove your head."

"Truly your wisdom is a gift to the ages," the red-haired bandit said, a foxy grin curled across his face.

"And this magic," the king said with his mouth full. "It shall give me whatever I want, will it not?"

"Anything and everything. It is older than the world. More powerful than the world, too."

"My power, increased and forever, that's what it will give me? And my youth forever. And my *self* forever. This is what it can do?"

"My precious Sovereign," the Bandit King said, his false words dripping from his mouth like poison, "you are thinking too small. But no worry. Power reveals itself, and becomes ordinary. *This* power, though, is larger than we can possibly imagine. Even when we think we see the end of it, we are only at the beginning."

"I hope so, bandit," the king said with a loud yawn. Too much rich food. Too much wine. His entourage carried everything that he could possibly want, and then had to go hungry on the off chance that he might want *more*.

(He always wanted more.)

The red-haired bandit bade him good evening and made his way to the front lines to find his bedroll and his companions.

The soldiers gave him wide berth. They stared at the opening trees, their strange waving, their unnatural creaking, and they were afraid.

"How do we know this man is on our side?" the soldiers whispered to one another. "How do we know he won't double-cross our king? How do we know he won't fade into the green, leaving us at the mercy of these devilish trees?"

Indeed, the red-haired bandit smiled. *Smart soldiers.*

They were less than half a day's march from the first village at the edge of the backwater Kingdom. The same village where the magic had lived all these years. The same village where that idiot boy was now, even *now,* heading toward his mother. As the red-haired bandit sat against the tree, the pendant around his neck grew heavier by the second. It heated and smoked. It smelled like burnt herbs and swamp gas and powdered stone—a magic smell.

"Interesting," the bandit said. "Very interesting." He reached up and curled his fingers around his pendant, feeling the thrill of its presence in his hand.

There was so little his pendant could do. It couldn't build or destroy. It gave him no power over the substance of things. He could not turn wood into gold, for example. Nor could he affect the weather. It could deflect arrows and blades—a useful thing in the banditry trade. It could bend things. And not just things. People too. It gave him influence over people. Power. He was followed, adored, *loved*. And the more he was loved, the more he was hungry for it. He thought he would never be full.

It was, he knew, the wrong kind of love. Even he was not so blind. And, surely, eventually, he would have enough. Surely, his little Áine would see that he had done it all for *her*. She would see it even if her mother never would have been able to do so.

He curled his fingers around the pendant—his single, marble eye. How he loved that little trinket! How it made him feel more fully *himself*. More fully *alive*.

More—

Áine's father froze.

The pendant on his neck glowed blue. It was hot.

The boy!

He was near. *Terribly near.* Why had he not felt him before?

The bandit stood up and took a deep breath through his nose.

Magic too. He could smell it, sharp and insistent. He inhaled again.

Wolf, he thought, puzzled. And *fear,* though if it was from the boy, or these cowardly soldiers, he couldn't tell.

And . . . *no.* He smelled again.

Somewhere. He could smell his daughter.

He shook his head. *No,* he decided. *It's not possible. She is safe and where she needs to be. She would never disobey me. Never.*

He inhaled again. The smell of magic was thick and pungent and *inviting.* It was all he could think about. The sun had set quite a while ago, and the sky had given way to darkness. To the east, the moon hung just over the tops of the trees. It was dark gold and huge—a harvest moon. And it was beautiful. Though not as beautiful as the magic.

Nothing was that beautiful. Nothing at all.

He shouldered his pack and walked silently into the green.

"Time's up, Neddy," the bandit whispered through gritted teeth. "Time's up."

40

THE STONES COME TO A DECISION

W AIT FOR W-WHAT?" NED SAID.

"We are not of this world," the largest Stone said.

Ned shook his head. "Wait for *what*?" he asked again.

"The magic on your skin. That is not of this world either. It is much, much older."

"Then why is it here?" Áine said. She curled her hands into fists. "Is it wicked?"

"It can be," the kind Stone said. "And it can be good too. It was part of *us*, you see. Long ago, we had bodies and skin and eyes. We were mobile and vital and *alive*. The magic was *our* magic. It was bound to our minds and our hearts, our thinking and wanting and ideas. It was ever so much like a soul. And we were good sometimes and we were wicked sometimes, but most of the time we were not one or the other." The Stone let out a small sigh. "You must excuse me. It has been *so very long* since we have been near the magic. I had . . ."—another sigh—"quite forgotten how . . ." The Stone's voice trailed off.

Each Stone remembered now. The world around the Stones hummed with their memories. And not all of them were good.

"But we saw death. And the longer we lived, the more death we saw," another said.

"We were frightened."

"We were cowards."

"And we wanted no part of it. Fools that we were," the smallest Stone said. The kind one.

The loudest, rumbliest voice spoke. "We turned our power on ourselves. We tried to make ourselves immortal. And we did. It simply didn't work the way we thought. We became Stones. Immortal, yes, but immobile. Separated from our souls, which is to say *our magic*. We were not dead, but we were not alive either."

Ned felt the wings of whatever was inside him beat and beat and beat. His brother had said the same thing—*the exact same thing.*

"We were trapped in a world that was not our own. Our magic was a cloud hovering in the ether. Every thought, every *notion*, we ever had—no matter how small, how petty, how wise, our generosity and our selfishness—each became its own distinct speck, with its own power and its own grace and its own foolishness. The magic fragments began to argue and disagree. They were troublesome. So we taught a family how to gather the magic together, and contain it in a clay pot. We explained that the cloud of magic was a collection of chaotic intelligences—capable of acting as one, but more often a rumbling horde of warring ideas. We told them if they bound the magic to a dying person, then the magic would pass on as the soul passes on. The soul leaves at death and goes . . . elsewhere. And so would the magic. And we would pass on with the magic. We asked them to release the magic, and release us. But they refused. They saw the power. They saw the good it can do."

"They weren't wrong," said the kind voice. "It could be good. But they needed to be taught. How to control it. How to keep it good. We weren't . . ." she paused. "Entirely truthful with them. We sometimes swapped words—like *shouldn't* with *couldn't*."

It lies! The magic burst awake on Ned's skin and began to scream. *It lies, it lies, it lies!* Ned gritted his teeth and forced it back into stillness.

"Still, it's a terrible thing to be trapped in a place you don't belong," the youngest Stone said. The kind one.

Terrible, said the fluttering in his chest—the voice that sounded like his brother. The only voice he trusted.

Ned closed his eyes. "If I tell the m-magic to leave the world, must it obey?"

No! the magic shouted. *Hush,* Ned shouted back.

"Yes," the oldest voice said. "But it will kill you in the process. Your soul would leave as the magic leaves, and you would be gone."

Ha! The magic shouted. Ned ignored it.

"The magic is tricky. And volatile. And though it is separate from us, we still feel it. We felt it when it was divided into three. We felt it as it fled from soldiers and a bad king and the threat of war. We felt it when it was bound to the bodies of the three women who cared for it. One woman was killed, and her share of the magic left the world. And we hoped. Then, a second woman was transformed to stone. When her body—most of it—was smashed into dust, her share of the magic—almost all of it—lifted away into the heavens. Only her eye remains."

Áine looked up. "The eye?" She hugged her arms tightly around her chest.

"Oh yes, child," the oldest Stone said. "We know about your father's little trinket."

Ned looked at her.

"*Oh*," he whispered. *Of course.*

Áine looked at him full in the face, her wide, black eyes filled with tears. *I couldn't tell you,* her face said. *I'm sorry.*

"The last of the magic remained with the granddaughter—your ancestor, Ned. And she protected it. Used it for good. Taught her son to use it for good, who taught his daughter, who taught her son. And so it has been. And so our prison continues."

"If you were killed, Ned," the kind Stone said, "the magic would be released, and we would be free. The tiny amount left in the eye wouldn't bind us here. And what's more, our leaving would render the pendant useless."

Áine fell to her knees. She cradled her head in her arms. She felt the Stones were asking her to help them, to do something, to *bend* her. Or was it her love for her father asking? But . . . "I can't do it," she said, her voice muffled in her tunic. "If that's what you're asking. I thought I could." She looked up at Ned. "I love my father, Ned. And the pendant. It *changed* him. And I thought—" She

291

swallowed. "I thought if I could take you far away from him—if I could hide you—that he would be spared finding more of—" she gestured. "*That magic,*" she nearly spat it. "I told myself that if it was between you and my father, that I would . . ." Her eyes were red and wet. Her mouth twisted in on itself.

You see? The magic sneered.

She wants to kill you. We told you so.

Áine turned away, her face in a knot of sorrow and pain. "I'm sorry, Ned," she said. "I truly am. It didn't take me long to know . . . that I couldn't . . ." She swallowed a sob. Ned sank down and sat on his heels, resting his hands on his knees. He looked at Áine, who did not look back.

"But I can't do it. Even to save him. Even to save my father or a whole country of fathers." She glared at the Stones. "I can't kill my friend. I can't kill anyone."

It was the first time that she had called Ned her friend. And both Ned and Áine knew it was true. And they knew that it mattered.

"We know, child," the yawning voice said. "We would not ask it of you."

"It is wicked, this magic. No matter what anyone says. No matter how hard anyone tries to keep it good. It is *wicked*. My father and that pendant! It changed him! It changes him even now! The magic has made a twist in his soul—or it has worsened the twist that was already there. But one thing I know for sure: As long as the magic is in this world, no one is safe."

Ned moved closer to Áine. He slipped both his hands into

292

his sleeves and curled them around Áine's own. They were hot—almost burning—but she didn't flinch.

"This is true," the eldest Stone rumbled. "Even now, the armies of King Ott are rousing from their short sleep. Even now they will begin to march into Ned's country, to attack at sunrise. If the boy was dead, then King Ott would be thwarted, and his country saved."

"Then I must die," Ned swallowed. "Right? I must die so you may pass on."

The Stones were silent. Áine was silent. The butterfly feeling in his chest was fluttering so hard it felt like he had swallowed a tornado.

"I'll do it," Ned said.

The fluttery feeling in his chest nearly jumped out of his throat. *It should be me!* The flutter shouted. *Take me!*

No! the magic screeched. *We must live.*

"There is another way," the kind voice said slowly.

"There is no other way," a voice said behind them. "The boy goes with me. Don't know who you are, girl, but you will stay here." Ned and Áine scrambled to their feet and saw a man at the edge of the clearing. The bandit whom Ned had saved—the man who once was called Eimon—pointed an arrow directly at Áine's heart.

He released the bowstring.

41

"RAISE THE ALARM!"

THE ARITHMANCERS AND THE ASTROLOGERS, the Strategists and the Historians, all brought their knowledge to the queen, who formulated a plan.

The warning fires were lit, the drummers went to the hilltops and pounded out their rhythmic warnings and instructions, which were repeated by the drummers on far-off hilltops, and pounded again on hilltops around the country. Riders were sent to every village. Those with horses and mules loaded supplies and rode to the forest's edge, and those without went on foot.

Come, went the alarm.

Fight, cried the trumpets.

An army was coming.

An army from beyond the edge of the world. Impossible, but true.

And every man, woman and child had to be ready.

"Did you think this day would come, Sister?" the queen asked as they mounted their horses and rode with the Officer's Brigade toward the front of the line.

"I never did, your majesty," Sister Witch said, pausing to take the queen's pulse and to feel her forehead. She was opposed to the queen's presence on the battlefield. ("If something happens to you, what will become of us?" Sister Witch had fussed and fumed. "Never you mind," the queen said briskly. "I have it all planned out.")

"I never did believe that there was *nothing* on the other side of that mountain," the queen mused. "Who ever heard of a nothing? I always believed there was *something*. Still, it is one thing to believe a thing, and quite another to have it wave a sword at you." She chuckled and sighed. "Well, I do hope we win. It would be a shame to cheat death only to be conquered by a tyrant."

And with that, she clucked at her horse and urged him forward, moving up to the front of the company.

She *was* the queen, after all.

42

KING OTT

WHAT DO YOU MEAN he's *gone*?" the young king bellowed for the fifteenth time. "Bring him *back*. That's an *order*."

"Alath, thire," lisped the Head Advisor. He was lying flat on the ground, his hands over his head (as was his custom when addressing the king). Tears flowed freely from his eyes and blood flowed freely from his nose and mouth. A few of his teeth were scattered around the forest floor from an unfortunate collision with his face and his majesty's foot. The combination of the missing teeth and the swollen lips made it terribly difficult to speak. Each attempt at an *S* erupted in a splatter of blood. Still, he was not Head Advisor for nothing. He persevered. "We have thearched for hith footprinth, but they are nowhere to be theen. He hath vanisthed without a trathe."

The king snapped his fingers and a young girl brought him a sweet. He stamped on her toes because he could. She didn't cry out or show pain. She had been well trained. He closed his eyes and tried to focus his attention on the confection on his tongue. (Spun sugar, essence of jasmine and rose. A bit of jelly at its center. Perfection.) He opened his eyes.

"The scouts have already been to the edge of the forest?"

"Yeth, thire."

"And?"

"A village lies along the river, along with farmth, and or-chardth. No military prethenth that anyone could thee. A broad roadway leading directly to the capital thity and the queen'th cathel. We have, of courth, the mapth the bandit provided earlier."

"And his comrades? They are all accounted for?"

"Yeth, thire."

The king nodded. He turned to his Generals and beckoned. "Mobilize the troops," he said. "Round up the bandits and clap them in irons. They will be useful as pawns. Best they be killed than any of us. The attack comes now. This piddly backwater will rue the day it ever skirted our notice and will pay dearly for their years of obnoxious independence. They will kneel before *me* and pay their allegiance to *me*. In the meantime, bring me wine and wine and more wine! Come my friends! We have a war to enjoy!"

43

THE PENDANT

THE RED-HAIRED BANDIT STEPPED into the clearing, his feet as quiet as a lion's paw.

There were two figures on the far side of the Stones, each one kneeling on the ground. They raised their faces to the Stones. They spoke, then listened, then spoke again, as though asking questions and receiving answers. But it didn't make any sense. Stones can't speak.

The bandit crept forward. He couldn't hear their voices, the people on the ground. They weren't far away, but the sound was strangely muffled, as though coming though piles of wool or flax. This also didn't make any sense. Sound is sound. He crept closer.

Then he felt it.

The vibration in the ground—mimicking almost exactly the vibration in his pendant.

Then he heard it—the Stones were speaking. Not in his head, and not in his heart, but *out loud*. And all around him. But he couldn't make out their words.

And, worst of all (and oh! How his heart leaped inside him! And oh! How it crashed against the ground!) was the voice of one of the people on the ground. Áine's voice.

His own daughter. His heart seized. (*My flower! My treasure! My hope!*)

"That pendant!" she said. "It changed him! It changes him even now."

The red-haired bandit felt his legs wobble and his knees go weak.

"The magic has made a twist in his soul—or it has worsened the twist that was already there. But one thing I know for sure: As long as the magic is in the world, no one is safe."

Her words burned. *How dare she say such a thing? She must be punished!* He felt an anger toward the girl that he had never felt before. The pendant glowed. It was a hot coal, a lava pit, a burning sun. And that burn seeped into his bones. It slicked across his eyes.

The Stones said something else but he did not hear. Such words! Such betrayal! His only child! His pendant blistered and smoked. It was on fire. Or perhaps *he* was on fire. Perhaps he was now, at last, all that he ever wanted to be. A warrior. A ruler. A god.

His anger filled his mouth. He strode through the shadow of the Stones toward his daughter. He was about to call her name. He was about to raise his hand and strike.

But then . . .

His daughter stood, holding the hand of that boy. *(That boy! That infernal boy!)*

And opposite them, a man. A bandit. One of *his* men. He'd know him anywhere. And the bandit held his bow and raised it. And aimed it toward Áine's heart.

The Bandit King saw this.

He *felt* it happening.

"There is no other way," the lost bandit said. The one who was once called Eimon. "The boy goes with me."

The arrow pointed, pulled and flew.

"NO!" cried the boy.

"NO!" cried the red-haired bandit. The Bandit King, the most powerful in memory. The fire in his bones transforming to water in a flash.

No, no, no!

Not her.

My daughter, my treasure, my hope. He felt the fragility of her precious life cupped in his hands. There was nothing else in the world. There was only Áine.

He ran forward, his eyes on the arrow. And it seemed to him that time slowed and stopped. The arrow hung in the air. It would head straight for her. It would pierce her beautiful, beating heart.

I promised! I promised to protect her.

He gripped his pendant. It blistered and burned his fingers.

Bend, his heart said. *Divert,* it whispered.

The pendant hesitated. He could feel it hesitate.

Not her. Me. Take me instead.

The arrow seemed to pause. It hung in the air, as though unsure where to go.

Now. Do it now. Bend toward me. NOW.

And suddenly, he was awake. The twist in his soul unkinked at last. His eyes were *his* eyes and his heart was *his* heart. He was wholly himself. He felt with the surety of a Stone that these thoughts were *his* and his alone. And he knew that it was *good*. To take the blow so she could live—it was *good* in a way that nothing had been good in . . . *ever so long.*

Bend toward me, his heart said again. A fierce command. The command of a king.

And the arrow bent. And it flew. The red-haired bandit smiled. He didn't flinch. He arched his back and lifted his face to the sky. The arrow went directly into the pendant. The pendant smashed, and both stone and arrow lodged in the big man's throat.

He collapsed to the ground without even a cry.

44

THE DEAD AND THE GONE

THERE WAS SO MUCH BLOOD.

"No, no, no," Áine cried, her hands at her father's throat. They were wet. They were red. "Papa, no!"

Yes, my daughter. Yes, my darling girl. Yes.

How could he explain?

Even now, in these last moments, that he was free? The pendant, that cursed, wicked thing, was gone. Truly gone. And its influence had vanished at last. And he was *himself. At last.*

How could he explain, even if he was able to speak? How can you tell your child that you must leave her forever?

And she was only a little child.

The lost bandit, the one called Eimon, ran close, but the boy, now gloveless, held up his bare hands toward him. He froze.

"D–do you remember what my h–hands can do?" the boy said dangerously. His voice was strong. Rooted. A man's voice.

"Leave this place," the boy snarled at the man called Eimon. The man Ned once saved. *Ned*, the red-haired bandit thought. *That is his name, Ned. It is a nice enough name. Pity about the magic.*

"GO!" the boy shouted. He ran at Eimon, who ran into the wood. *It's for the best*, the big man thought. *Perhaps he will be a farmer or a woodsman or a miner. He made a miserable bandit.*

"Ned," Áine said. "Do something. Please!"

The eldest Stone rumbled. "He is at peace, child," he said.

"He is at *nothing*," Áine shouted. "Ned, bring him back." Her voice was desperate. "Heal him, please."

The eldest Stone rumbled again. "No. The magic must not touch him. It already burdened him for too long. It clouded his eyes and twisted his heart. Now he sees clearly, and he is free. Let him rest at last. Look at his eyes. It is what he wants."

"I don't care what he wants! He's my father and I *need* him."

The big man shook his head, wincing in pain.

Áine turned to Ned. Her eyes were wild and savage. She pressed her hands around the arrow in her father, trying to stop the blood. "What's the matter with you," she snarled. "You have the power. Why won't you use it?"

Ned knelt next to Áine. He stared at his hands. *Why shouldn't he?* He wondered. *What's one time more?*

Yes! The magic sang.

We love the big man!

We can heal him. Restore his strength.

He will be even better than before.

Ned felt the power of the magic surge through his bones. Just think how grateful the bandit would be. And Áine. And the bandit horde. And King Ott—whoever he was. And the whole world.

Everyone will love you, Witch's Boy. You'll be famous. The magic purred on his skin.

Just one last time. Then we'll go quietly.

Truly we will.

Áine looked at Ned desperately. The Bandit King's life drained onto the ground. He had to act quickly. He reached his hands toward the big man's chest, but Áine's father coughed and shuddered and slapped Ned's hands away. He turned back toward his daughter and cupped her face.

"No," the kind Stone said, her voice a gentle soothe across the ground. "No. Please. Think of what that tiny bit of magic did to him. Think of how he feels to be free of it."

"Loss happens," another Stone said. A sharp voice. "Your small lives are eclipsed in the blink of an eye. No time feels like the right time to you people, but that doesn't change the nature of things."

Áine set her face, trying to quell the sobs that were, even now, jolting inside her, as though they might rip her to shreds.

"The more the magic is used," the eldest Stone said, "the more people have reason to keep it where it does not belong. Ned! Think! You healed the man who killed this man. You cannot control the magic, even when you think you can. Let him go. Let the magic go."

We are only thinking of your happiness, Ned. The magic shrieked. *Why would we lie?*

"The magic lies," Ned murmured. "My b-brother knew it. I kn-now it. I'm s-sorry Áine."

The big man gripped his daughter's hand. He brought it to his bloody mouth and kissed each finger.

I love you, one kiss said.

I'm sorry, said another.

"He's ready," the kind Stone said. "It hurts to say good-bye, but sometimes we must. That you may see him when he is fully himself is a blessing."

"STOP TALKING," Áine shouted. She pressed her forehead to his forehead as if she could force his body to heal through her. As if she could unwind the last few moments and force the arrow into her own body, and not to his.

With great effort, he reached up to Áine's head and turned it gently, bringing her ear to his face. He drew in a sputtery, rattled breath.

"Live," the big man said. "Live."

"Not without you," she choked.

"*Live,*" he said again. An order this time.

He closed his eyes and shivered once, twice, and then he was terribly still. And Áine's father was gone. Áine let her head fall on her father's chest. She gripped his shirt in her hands. Ned felt her grief pouring out of her body in waves. It nearly undid him.

He stood, staggered, and pressed the heels of his hands to his skull. He looked up at the Stones. "I c-could have helped h-him."

The wolf crept beside Áine and laid its head on her back. It made a series of vocalizations—part yip, part whine, part howl. It was a comforting, *family* sort of sound.

"Perhaps," said the largest Stone.

"Why did I *l-listen* to y-you?"

"You've been listening to a cloud of liars. Why not listen to the one who tells you the truth?"

Oh, that's rich, the magic said.

We've never lied in all our lives.

The Stones are big meanies.

And bossy!

"H-hush!" Ned shouted at the magic. He glared at the Stones. "What k-kind of truth do you h-have for m-me?"

The Stones were quiet for a long time. Then: "How long have you stuttered, Ned?"

Ned blanched. It was an unexpected question. He didn't reply.

"For you, words are disrupted, words written and words spoken. But. It was not always thus with you. Have you never wondered *why*?"

Ned stared at the Stone. It was true. When he was small he could read. When he was small he could speak. But then he became the wrong boy. And that was that. He never wondered why.

"No," Ned said. "I h-haven't."

"Long ago," the Eldest said, "you built a raft with your brother and pushed it in the river, hoping to make it to the sea. Do you remember?"

"Y-yes," Ned said.

Yes, said the fluttering in his chest.

306

"And your brother died."

"Y–yes," Ned said.

Yes, said the fluttering in his chest. *I did.*

"Your mother," the eldest Stone said, "is a crafty woman. She waited for the soul of your dead brother to emerge at the setting of the sun. She caught it in a white cloth and brought it to you. You were sick. You were dying. You were not strong enough to survive the night, and your mother could not bear it. So she took your brother's soul and sewed it to your own. She tried to convince herself she wasn't using magic, but of course she was. And of course, there were consequences. Your stutter. Your war with words. Words are linked to the soul, you see? And you have two. One belongs with you, but the other is trapped. It cannot move on. Your brother has been prevented from moving on."

Ned pressed his hands to his chest.

He remembered the sharp needle.

He remembered the strong black thread.

He remembered the scream.

"W–what must I do?"

What must we *do, brother?*

Ned gasped. Tam. He never left. He didn't *dream* he spoke to Tam, he *did* speak to Tam.

"T–Tam?"

I'm here, brother. I've always been here.

"You and your brother must speak as one. You must *both* desire that he move on."

"B–but I d–don't desire it. He's my b–brother."

But I desire it, Ned. I told you this day was coming.

"You must *both* command the magic, with a firm hand and an iron will. The words will bind the magic to his waiting soul. And his soul will pull away, and we will pull away. You will see us as we are—don't worry. Though we shall look frightening to you, we will not harm you. We will remain in your world until the next sunset. And then we will go on."

"On?" Ned asked.

"Our souls will pass to their next realm at the setting of the sun. That is the proper way."

"Y-you mean you will d-die?"

"There is no death," the Stone said. "There is only the next thing. A mountain gives way to a river and becomes a canyon. A tree gives way to its rot and becomes the ground. We will let go of our unnaturally elongated lives and embrace something else. We do not know what it is. But we will know it when we see it."

Áine remained crouched over her father on the ground. The wolf rose and walked over to Ned, pressing against his leg. He took a deep breath.

No! the magic screamed, its disparate, chaotic voices ringing as one.

You'll kill us!

The Stones are wicked, foul and false! Don't listen to them.

"B-brother," Ned said, his hands pressed to his chest. "Speak the words with me. T-take the m-magic. Move on."

Ned felt a shock go through his body, throwing him to his knees. He felt the fluttering in his chest expand through his bones,

308

into his muscles, ringing in his skull. He opened his mouth. And words came.

Not his own words.

Not his brother's words.

Their words together.

"IT IS WITH A PURE HEART," they said, their voices amplified, the shock of the words singing through Ned's body as though he was struck by lightning. "THAT I HUMBLY ASK YOUR ASSISTANCE."

No! the magic screamed. *No, no, no no! You cannot make us!*

"WE CAN, AND WE DO."

Their combined voices filled Ned from the tips of his toes to the top of his head. How *good* it was to have a brother! The thrill of mischief, the delight of motion. How clever they thought themselves! How brave! They were none of those, of course, when Tam was alive—they were only naughty little boys. And now they were something else. Ned would grow up and Tam would go on, and that was that. And each memory of his brother, Ned would carry in his heart. He would be the one to keep Tam's memory alive.

Please! Boys! You don't have to do this. There is another way.

"WE COMMAND YOU TO UNSTITCH THE SOUL OF TAM FROM THE SOUL OF NED. WE COMMAND YOU TO SET HIS SPIRIT FREE. WE COMMAND YOU TO BIND YOURSELVES TO TAM—HIS SOUL, HIS THOUGHTS, HIS LOST LIFE. THIS WILL BE YOUR FINAL ACT."

Please!

"NOW."

And with each word, the stitches on his soul loosened. And with each stitch the soul of his brother unraveled from his body, and pulled away.

And oh! It was beautiful!

The soul was as pale as apple blossoms, and just as fragile. It wavered and fluttered in the evening breeze. He was the size of a seven-year-old child—wide eyes, wild hair. It was Tam, just as Ned remembered him. Ned held out his hand and the soul rested his own upon it, palm to palm. It was as light as grass. But the magic remained. It glowed on Ned's skin. Its letters raced from finger to shoulder to hip to toe.

You can make it stop, the magic said.

We'll give you whatever you want.

We'll give you power and money.

Castles.

Kingdoms.

Dancing girls.

Jewels.

Ponies.

Please.

"NOW."

It couldn't resist any longer. Bit by bit, the magic unpeeled from his skin. The words unwrote themselves, winding around and around the shadowy form of the soul. They were bright, hot threads, ribbons of power, and they tugged and tugged until—

Ned gasped and staggered back.

"It's gone," he said. His words were strong and sure in his

mouth. They didn't hesitate. "The magic is gone," he said again, and again, his words moved as easily as water. They belonged to him now, and him alone. They were not shared. "Tam?"

"Ned," Tam said. They stared at one another without blinking. Áine sat up. "Oh, Ned," she said. "You're bleeding."

It was true, the words had, apparently, ripped out of his skin. It was the magic's last chance of hanging on. What was left was the imprint of the magic in red skin, in blisters, in sharp cuts. They would surely leave scars. Ned didn't care. He was free. He touched his hands to his neck and his cheeks and his arms and his chest. He was wholly, and solely, himself.

"Does it hurt?" the soul asked, peering curiously at the wounds on Ned's skin.

"Yes." Ned said. "But it was worse before. Does it hurt you?" Ned looked at the magic words written on the ghostly skin of his brother.

"Dying hurt worse," the soul said. "This only stings. And it will take me to where I need to be, so it's worth it."

"Is it loud?"

"It's scared. Just like I was. It is scared silent."

Ned stared at the soul's face.

"It's you," Ned whispered.

"It's you," the soul said in his papery voice.

"I had lost you," Ned said.

"I never left."

"The river," Ned said, holding out his hand, palm up.

"The river," his brother said, resting his hand on Ned's.

The dead boy took a deep breath and looked at the sky. The moon was low and the stars were bright. "But now it's time to go." He gave Ned a sad smile and turned to the Stones.

"What are you going to do?"

"I go with the Stones," Tam said. "They're waking up. You see? The sun is getting ready to rise. They will rise out of the ground and will do one last thing before they go . . . elsewhere, the moment the sun sets."

"And so will you?" Ned asked.

"And so will I," said Tam, his voice equal parts anticipation and regret. Then he laughed, wild and mischievous. He threw his pale arms into the air, as though to embrace everything alive.

"Grandfathers!" he cried out in a loud voice. "Grandmothers! Two nations are poised to make a horrible mistake. Wouldn't it be fun to put a stop to it? It is time to go!"

The Stones laughed, too. The air around them crackled. The whole world glowed red and yellow and hot. They were shivering with excitement. Ned could feel it in the air, in the ground, rumbling against his feet and vibrating through his bones. The ground around them trembled and waved.

And the Stones uncurled. Ned was reminded of plants, the way they extend themselves from the tightly whorled world of their seeds. From the knot of rock, a head emerged, arms formed, bent spines slowly straightened toward the sky. Each Stone un–kinked its stony neck and rolled its stony shoulders and stretched its thick, growing stone arms. Fingers extended; faces formed.

They pressed their stone hands against the earth and pushed the rest of their bodies out of the ground. Unburied, they were *so much bigger* than they had been before. Ned craned his neck to see them.

Giants. Stone giants. The stories were *true*. The Stones arched their backs and threw out their hands and sang.

"Oh," said the kind-voiced Stone. "It feels so good to move!"

The eldest Stone looked to the east.

"My brothers and sisters," he said. "The sun is creeping toward morning and soon it will be day. We have but twelve hours left in this world before we must depart with our waiting friend. Let us make good use of our time. I believe there is a war that needs stopping. Do you not agree?"

The Stone giants agreed. Ned felt himself scooped up by the Eldest and perched upon a stony shoulder. His brother joined him soon after. Another gathered the body of the red-haired man in the crook of its stony arm, as gently as a mother carrying an infant. Another lifted Áine, and seated her next to its stony ear. The wolf would not permit itself to be carried. It bounded alongside, howling as they went.

The earth shook. The trees bent and fell. Each step was a desolation, a recalibration, a rebirth. Ned covered his ears to muffle the noise.

And the Stones walked through the forest toward Ned's village.

They walked toward war.

45

NED HAS A PLAN

NED COULDN'T BELIEVE IT. After a lifetime in which he was afraid of the wood, afraid of the stone monsters that lived in the wood, he was responsible for not only freeing those monsters but also setting them loose and guiding them toward his home.

And not only that, he was *proud* of doing so.

He still held his brother's hand—if you could call it holding. He kept his palm open, and his brother's palm rested against it. It was like holding a dry, dry leaf.

The Stones strode through the forest toward his village. They followed no trail. Instead the trees trembled and parted before the Stones like a great, green curtain, and closed back together as they passed.

"Why do the trees listen to you?" Ned asked, leaning toward the granite ear of the eldest Stone.

"The trees are the result of an action taken against a wicked king, many years ago. But it was our idea, and our magic—though not our action—that brought the forest to life. The trees, therefore, pay their allegiance to us."

"Which king?" Ned asked.

"The ancestor of the King who now threatens your country," the Stone said.

"Some family," Ned said.

"Indeed."

"Where is the king now?"

The Stone stopped. They had reached the top of the ridge. He closed his huge, stone eyes. "Look down that way," the Stone said, pointing. The trees bent this way and that way, providing a clear view toward the valley. Ned could see the army of King Ott. The soldiers were gathering, marching, moving in formation, following the silver stream toward Ned's home. "Do you see that tent with the feathers on the top? The king, in anticipation of his victory, spent last night deep in his cups, and now sleeps off his overindulgence. He snores as his armies attack. Later he will rise, dress himself, and survey his new country."

There were guards in front of the tent. They were seated on the ground, their heads leaning against one another. They had, it seemed, overindulged as well.

"What do you think, brother?" the dead boy said, the familiar impish grin curling in his voice.

"I believe I think as you do, brother," Ned grinned back. He turned to the Stone's large ear. "You know, it isn't fair that the

315

king should be denied the pleasure of a ride in a stone giant's fist. Perhaps we should indulge him."

The Stone said nothing. Its great eyes blinked once, then twice.

And, very slowly, a smile spread across its great, stone lips.

46

THE ARMY OF KING OTT

THE BLACK SKY RIMMED with red, then pink, then gold. The villagers gripped their bows. They moved their axes from hand to hand. They held knives and cudgels and rocks. They watched the wood and they waited, at the edge of the field that met the edge of the wood.

Finally, the trees shuddered and bent, and a group of people walked out from the trees. Not an army. Not even a fighting force, but a ragtag group of bandits, their hands bound before them, their tattoos announcing their profession as loudly as a shout.

On either side, the bandits were flanked by soldiers—but not the queen's soldiers. These had helmets topped with brightly colored feathers and breastplates emblazoned with the silhouette of a young man with a tall crown, his body leaning slightly in a rakish pose. One of the soldiers brought a brightly painted cone to his lips, amplifying his voice.

"We have come," the soldier said, "with a show of good faith."

The people of Ned's village gathered on top of the barricade they had built. They looked to Ned's father, who crossed his arms over his chest. "What sort of good faith?" he bellowed, his voice booming from his barrel chest.

"This country," the soldier said, "is by Rights and by History, under the jurisdiction of King Ott the Beautiful: King, Emperor and Beloved Lord of all the known world. Your status, for these previous centuries, has been that of a rogue State. Your pretense of independence is to us like the make-believe of a child—amusing, to be sure, but out of touch with reality. We seek to rectify this situation and bring you back into the fold of your benevolent King."

"We do not know a King Ott," Madame Thuane called back. She stood, straight backed, broad shouldered, as imperious as an oak. *The gall of it,* her voice seemed to say. *The insufferable gall!*

"Be that as it may, he knows *you.* And he loves you as his own dear subjects, beloved children that you are. He intends to punish you gently, the way a father punishes a wayward child. And he asserts his dominion over your lands."

"Prove it," Ned's father's voice shot across the field. The villagers noted with some satisfaction that the feathered soldier's knees quaked—just slightly, but enough to cheer them.

"The King needs no proof. The King is all the proof he needs. All ways are the King's Way."

The soldier smirked.

The villagers laughed.

"We have a word for a young man like that," the woodsman said dryly. "But there are children present so I mustn't say it."

The feathered soldier reddened, but went on. "Our show of good faith is this: bandits. They are bound, gagged and ready for justice. These men and women are responsible for untold loss of life and property. *We* have brought them to justice. *We* have done this for you. Your *queen,* landless country bumpkin that she is, was unable to do this for you. You needed a *real* king and a *real* army. Swear fealty to King Ott and your troubles are over. Swear fealty to him, and you need never worry about the crime of banditry again."

"These bandits are unknown to us," Madame Thuane said. "We do not have rampant thievery *here.* Only a hint now and again, and it is quickly remedied. Perhaps your—well I'm sorry to say this, but—your frankly substandard king is not quite as wonder-ful as you previously believed. But I'm sure our queen would be happy to offer him some tips." She peered over her long, sharp nose and pursed her lips.

The feathered soldier was taken aback.

"Well then," he said. "We will set them loose among you. See how you like having your lands terrorized."

Madame Thuane threw up her hands. "We have no time for thieves. Or for thieving soldiers. We have barns to fix and farms to harvest and you—" She paused. Drew herself taller. "Are wasting my time."

"Lay down your weapons and surrender. We have grown weary of your foolishness."

"And if we do not?" the woodsman bellowed.

"Then your lives are forfeit. And you do not deserve to live under the benevolence of King Ott. And you will never partake of the wonders of his beautiful Kingdom. We will invade, we will occupy, and your lands will be ours. And you will have nothing. You will *be* nothing."

The woodsman narrowed his eyes. "If it so please your supposed Highness, you may pass on a message from us," he said in a gravelly voice. "Turn around. Go back where you came from. Never, never return."

"And tell him he's a sorry sop!" an elderly woman standing nearby shouted.

"And those feathers make you look ridiculous!" said a boy about Ned's age.

"I'm terribly sorry you feel that way," the soldier said, but his voice wavered. He took a horn from his belt and brought it to his lips. He took a deep breath and blew. The sound was high and sharp and bright. The villagers brought their hands to their ears. The soldier replaced the horn and waited.

The ground trembled.

It rumbled.

It shook.

And the army of King Ott emerged from the wood. It came, and it came, and it came. More soldiers and more and more again, more numerous than trees.

And the woodsman thought they'd never stop.

47

THE FINAL STAND
OF THE SPEAKING STONES

THE SUN WAS UP, fully up, and the mist on the trees lifted, trembled, and wafted away. Ned shivered. He sidled closer to the ear of the Stone, but it was cold and damp and mossy. It gave no heat. The dead boy gave no heat either.

The Stone held his hands before him, fingers curled around one another, creating a round, hollow cage. King Ott sat inside, weeping like a child.

"Please. Please? PUT ME DOWN AT ONCE!" The king shouted and wept and pleaded. He oscillated between the ravings of a tyrant and the tears of a child. "Oh, don't hurt me." (A sob. A shiver.) "I can give you anything you want." (A pair of clutched hands.) "THIS IS AN ORDER!"

Ned shook his head. He felt sudden and unexpected compassion for the sniveling monarch. Ott was, after all, not much older than Ned himself. And he had not been well brought up. That much was clear.

"I'm terribly sorry for the inconvenience, your majesty," Ned said. His voice amazed him. His words had strong legs and clear eyes and purpose. He spoke with his own voice, and his voice had *power*. Words were no longer his enemies. It was all he could do to suppress a great shout of joy at each unencumbered sentence. "But it seems that you attempted to invade my country based on a grievous error."

"I don't know what you're talking about," the young king said sulkily. He pulled his legs to his chest and rested his chin on his knees and glared through the stony fingers of the giant. The eldest Stone rumbled out a sound that Ned thought was likely a chuckle. "And by the way, I shall so *enjoy* removing your head. I may opt to do it myself. Fancy kidnapping a king! There are laws in this country, young man. Laws!"

"This is not your country," Ned said. "You do not know our laws."

"Just wait," muttered the King.

Ned shook his head. "Your majesty," he said as kindly as he could, "as you will see in a moment, you have mounted an invasion based on faulty information. The things you thought would be available to you can no longer be got. The magic you were hoping to steal?"

"KINGS DO NOT STEAL!" the king bellowed. "They merely take what by rights belongs to them. Which is to say, *everything*."

"I'm not sure I care for kings," the dead boy murmured.

"Who said that?" gasped the King. He whipped his head from side to side. "Who?"

"I am getting to that," Ned said. "This is not your country. And these are not your laws, and not your ways, and you are not my *anything*." The king harrumphed, but Ned persevered. "In any case, the magic. It isn't yours. It belonged to my mother. To Sister Witch." The king gasped. "I am Sister Witch's son."

"But—" the king began.

"But nothing," Ned said. "This," he wound his arm over his brother's shoulders as delicately as he could, "is Sister Witch's dead son."

"Her *what*?" The king strained to see through the fingers of the Stone giant, and saw the dead boy, who fluttered his fingers at him. He screamed.

"Don't worry," Tam said, holding up his palms in a gesture of good will. "I'm only temporary."

"Our mother cared for the magic in her time, but that time is over. The magic wasn't *hers* either. She was simply minding it for its true owners. But now they are all moving on. You cannot touch it. None of us can."

The sun was bright and hot and they were on the final slope toward the end of the forest. From his perch, from this height on the slope, Ned could catch glimpses of his village through the tops of the trees. *So close,* he thought. *So very close.*

"I demand to know where you are taking me," the young king said.

They approached the silver stream that fed the Great River.

323

It was, if Ned was on foot, half a day's journey from home. But atop this huge stone giant, whose single footstep was equal to the distance between the edge of the barnyard and the far side of his house, it would take no more than an hour or two. *Home!* Ned thought. *Almost home!*

"We are taking you to your soldiers," Ned said. "And they will take you home."

"No," the king sneered. "They will slaughter you, destroy your pet rock, and deliver me to your queen's castle. I'm sure I shall have to knock it down and build another. It is, without a doubt, a wretched little hovel. Or perhaps I'll keep it as a summer cabin."

Ned shook his head.

"I'm sorry, but you're wrong." he said. "You've already lost. You've already been humiliated. You just don't know it yet."

"Humiliated," the young king laughed. "*Humiliated?* It is you who will be humiliated. My armies are, right now, waiting in formation. They have assembled a force on your country's doorstep larger than you have ever seen. They are *mighty*. They are *fierce*. And they are waiting for me to give the order to strike. And I shall be *so very entertained!*"

The eldest Stone brought his great stone palms closer together, forcing the young king onto his belly.

"*Oh, please, please don't let your rock kill me!*" he squealed.

"Not to worry," Ned said brightly. "Why would we smash you to bits and pieces? Especially when there was no one around to see it? Let's wait until your armies are close enough to see us.

324

How beloved are you, exactly, your majesty? How willing will your people be to come to your aid?"

The king said nothing.

"That's what I thought," Ned said, and they crashed through the forest toward his home.

The army massed and massed, regiment after regiment, armor shining in the morning light, polished swords flashing with dew. The soldiers called up battle cries and bloody chants and songs of war.

Meanwhile, on the ridge behind the village, a chorus of trumpets sounded. The people turned as one and peered over the far side of the barricade.

"Look!" one man shouted.

"At last!" a woman sighed.

"The queen's front guard," the woodsman shouted once the first banners rose over the rim of the ridge, with the fighters thundering behind. "They have heard us! They are coming! We are saved."

But the elation was short lived.

So few! Ned's father had never realized how very, very small his country's army was. They were, by his calculations, outnumbered by one hundred to one. It was like, he decided, an army of mice attacking an army of bears. Bears with sharp teeth and fearsome claws. Bears that came and came and came and would not stop. He gripped his axe and got ready.

Still, as the front guard advanced, the villagers cheered. They might be few, but their voices rattled the ground and shot at the sky. Their thunderous cheering buoyed them up; it made them feel large, bright, and fearsome.

"Surrender!" shouted the armies of King Ott.

"Never!" shouted the village.

Finally, as the sun moved to its apex in the sky, as the heat of the day pressed against them like a stone, as they stood, dry-mouthed, dry-eyed, and empty-bellied, they felt it.

A shake. A rumble. A beat. The regiments looked at one another. The villagers looked down at the ground. Pebbles bounced and rattled at their feet.

A step. A step. A rumbly, earth-shaking step. It came from the wood.

The world was shuddering around them. The feathered helmets of the king's regiment knocked together as the soldiers clutched one another in fear. The front guard and second wave of the army of the queen steadied their legs and readied their bows and waited.

There were stories about that wood. It was said the trees held grudges. It was said there were monsters—huge monsters made of stone that could crush a man as easily as you might blink your eyes.

And they couldn't be true, those stories, not really, but—

The trees shuddered and rippled, the land swirling around their roots like great, flowing skirts.

The bound bandits screamed. "Let us go!" they cried. "The trees! The trees are attacking!"

(They couldn't be moving, those trees. Not really. But—)

The trees parted. They stepped to the side, and made a straight pathway. And, in the distance . . .

No! the people cried.

Yes! they gasped.

The Stones! The Stones!

Stone faces. Stone necks. Stone shoulders. Stone legs. Each rumbling step felt like the end of the world. And they were coming closer. And closer. And closer.

The regiments fell to their knees. The people wailed and prayed. And the Stone giants were upon them.

48

ÁINE AND THE WOLF

THE STONE CARRYING ÁINE and her father laid the two of them on the ground, as gentle as can be, right where the forest met the field.

Her tears had stopped; her sobbing had stopped. All she felt was a terrible calm. All she felt was *nothing*.

There was an army and a barricade and another army, but Áine didn't care.

Áine didn't notice the shuddering ground as the Stones walked across the field.

She didn't notice the wails of the people, or the beating of their chests, or the rending of their hair, or their terrible, terrible fear.

Even if she had noticed, she likely would not have cared.

Her father was dead.

He died saving her.

He could have been saved, but he was not. It was Ned's fault. It was her father's fault. It was the fault of the world and the sky and the mountains and the sun and the cursed wood. It was her mother's fault for dying in the first place and leaving them alone. It was that awful pendant. It was the bandits. Her grandfather. Her own, stupid fault.

It was all of these things and so much more. Too many things to blame. And the work of blaming was terribly hard. And Áine couldn't do it anymore.

She had removed the arrow and cleaned the blood from his face. She tore a bit of fabric from her tunic and wetted it from her water skin. She washed his face, his neck, his hands. She wetted down his hair and smoothed it until it gleamed. She ran her fingers along the edges of his eyes. She smoothed his worry lines with her fingers, and imagined what he looked like when he was young, when he was the young, handsome bandit come to rob the coffers of a lonely fisherman's inn, and had accidentally fallen in love with the innkeeper's black-haired daughter. Her mother said she loved him the moment she saw his fists in the money pot. He said he loved her the moment she held her father's sword to his throat. He gave up a life of banditry for her, and she gave up a long line of suitors for him. And they were happy for a long time.

And now they were gone.

And Áine was alone.

Fool of a girl! Áine chided herself. *It's not much different than before.* And it was true. Her father would be gone for days, sometimes weeks. And she never knew if he would return. She knew that one day he simply *wouldn't*. And she'd never know what had happened.

At least now she *knew*. Even if it hurt. There was, she decided, a great comfort in knowing.

She looked over at the Stones. There were eight of them. The missing Stone, the oldest and largest of them all, took a different way—and Ned and his strange shadow went with him.

For what, Áine did not know. She wasn't sure she cared.

The Stones had positioned themselves in a great line, separating the two armies. A foolhardy soldier from the king's army launched an arrow at the shoulder of one of the Stones. The arrow's tip hit the Stone with a loud *ping* that Áine could hear from the place where she sat on the ground. The arrow shattered on impact. The Stone didn't move for some time, and at first she wondered if it had noticed the arrow at all. Then it lifted its great stone leg and sent its foot crashing to the ground. The ground rippled and swelled like water, sending the armies wobbling and tumbling against one another. The bandits fell to their knees, pressing their hands on the ground, their faces tight with terror. The soldiers used their swords and their bows as walking sticks to right themselves. They shuffled in their places and stole glances at the wood and glances at one another and quivered before the Stones. But they stayed where they were.

They're afraid to leave, Áine realized.

Being her father's daughter, Áine was impressed. It wasn't every day that a force was trained to the point of stupidity. Her father would have been intrigued.

330

A snapping of twigs and a rustle of leaves disturbed the forest behind her. She turned and peered into the green.

"You," she said, her voice a low growl.

The wolf whined in reply. It crept quietly toward her, step after cautious step.

"I don't need you," she said.

The wolf made a gentle squeak, deep in its throat. It was a pleasant sound.

"I killed your mother," Áine said. "Or some wolf's mother. It might as well have been yours."

The wolf came nearer. Its nostrils were wide and searching. It breathed her in.

"I need no one," Áine said. "The only ones I ever needed are dead."

The wolf padded closer on its too-large feet. It pressed the side of its body to her back. It breathed as she breathed. Áine felt something deep inside her. A fleshy shudder. A guttural cry. She tried to hold it in, stop it up, dam the tide, but she couldn't. She curled her arm around the animal's back and let it drape along its side. She buried her face in its neck. She felt a sob erupt at her toes and tumble in waves over her bones, through her chest, exploding through her shoulders and throat. She drenched the wolf with her tears.

"I'm sorry," she said to the wolf. "I'm sorry," to her father. "I'm sorry," to Ned, to his family, to the soldiers before the Stones, to the wide, wide world. "I'm sorry, I'm sorry, I'm sorry."

The wolf tipped its head back and sang in harmony with Áine's cries. And their grief resonated and vibrated in their mouths. She hugged the wolf tightly, and it pressed itself against her.

"Come on," she said at last, removing her cloak and draping it over her father's face. "Let's go to the Stones. I must stop what my father has started."

And the girl and the wolf marched across the field.

49

ON THE SHOULDERS OF GIANTS

Á INE WALKED SWIFTLY, the wolf bounding by her side. It stole glances at the girl and yelped and howled and whimpered and barked, then glanced at the girl again, as though satisfied that she was, indeed, still there. Áine felt the same way. Satisfied. Sure of its presence. There was something in the wolf's movements, in thrill of its leap and bound and howl that stirred the girl to the core. The wolf, along with the strange, broken boy who brought it into her life, had become her family. She did not choose it, nor did she intend for it to happen, but it was true. *Family*. The word had weight and heft, like an anchor in a stormy sea.

She walked to the youngest of the Stones.

"Excuse me," she said, reaching out and patting the Stone tentatively on what must be have been its leg. It was smaller than the others, though still enormous—great blocky legs, a broad midsection, and an oblong head with just a hint of a face. And while one couldn't tell the genders of any of the Stones, Áine felt as though this one was female. She felt a sort of kinship with this Stone that she couldn't quite put her finger on. And it wasn't the Stone's kindness nor was it the gentleness with which it carried her father. Áine, after all, didn't consider herself particularly kind, and she certainly wasn't a gentle sort of a girl. Still, there was *something*. And, what's more, it had been so long—so very long—since Áine had spoken to another female. Since her mother died. And, Áine decided, it was . . . Even in her mind she hesitated. It was *nice*, she decided. It was nice.

The Stone turned her great head and face toward Áine. "What is it, my dear?" she said.

Áine stammered a bit, cleared her throat, and shifted her weight from foot to foot. The wolf pressed against her leg, warm and reassuring. It was a tiny gesture, insignificant, but to Áine it was as though the whole world was pressed between the side of her leg and the side of the animal. The wolf's touch gave her courage. "May I," she began. She paused. "May I please stand upon your shoulder? I would like to address my fath—" The word caught in her throat like a fish hook. She wiped her eyes with the back of her hands in a quick, furious gesture. "Those bandits. My father led those bandits. He put them in harm's way. He started this whole mad enterprise. They are my responsibility."

The Stone tilted her head to one side and considered this. Then she nodded and lifted Áine to her shoulder. The wolf watched

Áine ascend, and then kept pace with the Stone. It wouldn't let her out of its sight.

The girl, the Stone, and the wolf all approached the army of King Ott.

The queen's carriage came to a stop at the summit of the hill. Sister Witch laid her hand on the queen's forehead. Hot and dry, then cool and damp, a landscape of illness.

"Your majesty," the magic worker said. "We should stop and you should rest. Your health—"

"Hang my health," the queen said acidly. Her cheeks went pale, then red, then pale again. A cough rattled in her chest, but the old woman held it back.

The messengers from the front guard had come, announcing the arrival of the army, and as many troops from the second wave that could be dispatched were quickly dispatched. Ned's mother watched them with a terrible pain in her heart. Where was Ned? *Please find my boy.* She had already buried one child. She could not bear to lose the other.

But there were some things that she was not able to choose. She reached into her pocket and curled her fingers around the Ned-shaped carving, as though it could bring her more quickly to her son. His hands had formed the figure; she knew it in her bones, though she had never known that he could make a thing so clever, so detailed, so *real*. She never knew he had that sort of talent. What else could her son do? What had she been missing? *Please be alive. Please be whole. Please come home to me.* She felt her worry seize her like a hand clutching her throat.

"Your armies will keep us safe," Ned's mother said to the queen. "They always have. But you, my queen, I must insist. Let the company go without us. I will erect a tent and will see to your care. I fear for your life, dear lady."

There was a rap on the door of the carriage. Sister Witch slid back the panel and peered out. A soldier leaned into the opening—a girl, not much older than Ned, with a thousand braids twisted into a knot at the top of her head. "Your majesty," the soldier said, "at the top of the next rise we will have a view of the battlefield. It's . . . I cannot say, Lady. It's unbelievable."

"Well, spit it out girl," the queen said irritably. "You must believe it, or you would not have said it. Which part is unbelievable?"

"The army. Their army. It is bigger than can be believed."

"I see," the queen said grimly. She coughed into her handkerchief. She tried to hide the blood, but Sister Witch saw. She searched through her satchel for the right herb.

"But that's not it," the soldier said. "There's something more."

"What could possibly be worse?" the queen said.

The carriage climbed the road at a snail's pace before finally coming to a stop at the top of the hill. The footman scurried over to help the old woman out. She teetered against the crook of his arm, but her face was as resolute as ever.

From their vantage point, they saw the village where Ned lived, ringed in barricades (*Oh! My home!* thought Sister Witch. *What have we come to!*) and beyond that, the great wood, stretching to the mountains that cut the sky. In between the village and the forest was an army so vast that the queen gripped her heart. And in front of the army was a ragtag group of men and women—their faces and bodies covered in tattoos. And their hands bound. They preceded the army at the tip of a sword.

So, the witch thought. *The strangers use human beings as breathing pincushions for their enemy's arrows. How despicable.*

But there was something else, as well.

"Oh," Sister Witch whispered.

"Are those—" the queen stammered.

"How?" Sister Witch said.

"But it was just a story," the queen said.

"And shouldn't there be nine?" Sister Witch said.

Eight stone giants. Standing guard. And, the witch noticed, a large . . . *something* moving through the forest, knocking trees out of its way.

"Are they our friends, or our enemies?" the queen asked.

"I cannot tell," Sister Witch said. But her heart lifted and lifted inside her. A great plume of joy.

Oh! She thought. *They are moving on!*

Ned, his brother, the sniveling king, and the oldest Stone had almost come to the edge of the wood. It wouldn't be long now before they reached Ned's village.

"Where are my armies?" The king wept.

"*Where are my armies?*" the soul mocked him in a babyish sing-song. It so delighted Tam that he began to giggle.

"Oh, grow up," the king snapped savagely.

"I can't," Tam said in a merry voice. "I'm dead. Dead things can't grow."

The king shuddered.

"Your majesty," Ned said, ignoring his brother, "we will be approaching my village soon, and I believe that your situation will become clearer to you."

"I'm not talking to you," the king said.

Ned sighed. "You see, this Stone, the one that we are now riding—and thank you, sir, for that," he added politely. The Stone rumbled in reply. "This Stone is not alone. He is one of nine—the rest of whom are standing between your armies and my people. We do not want war. We do not wish to fight you. We wish to leave you in peace and to be left in peace. Do you understand?"

"Wait," the king said. He crossed his arms over his chest and scowled. "There are nine of you? Are you *those* Stones? The ones who stole the magic and divided the kingdom? We despise you. We have a national holiday dedicated to despising you. I shall spit on you right now." Instead of spitting, the king made a face. Even he couldn't do something so repellant.

"Alas, yes," rumbled the eldest Stone. "But it is not as you think. And even if it was, there is nothing you can do about it."

The king harrumphed. "Just wait til I get my magic. Then you'll be sorry."

"You can't," Ned said. "The magic is gone."

"Well," the soul clarified, "*going*. I have it for now, see?" He held up his marked arms.

"Going *where*?" the king asked, but Ned didn't answer. He saw his village and the armies of King Ott flanking the Forest and the armies of the queen hugging the village. He also saw Áine standing atop one of the Stones, which in turn stood between one army and the other.

"What is she *doing*?" Ned said to himself. And to the Stone he said, "Is it at all possible for you to walk faster?"

Áine stood up on the giant's shoulder. They were, along with the other seven Stones, standing in the open field between the soldiers from Duunin and the warriors from the Lost Lands. She looked out at the armies of King Ott. There were too many. It wasn't a fair fight. And they would have to go.

But she didn't talk to them at first. She cleared her throat.

"My brothers and sisters," she called to the bandits—their hands bound, their feet tethered, their mouths gagged. And she felt a terrible compassion for all of them.

"You do not know me, but I know all of you," she continued, the strength of the Stone giving strength to her voice, and making it ring out across the field. "My father bade me hide in the eaves of our stone house in the forest every time you gathered in our yard. Did you not wonder who kept the gardens tended? Did you not wonder who fed the goats and the hens and watered the flowers? It was I. I am Áine, the Bandit King's daughter."

"Impossible," a soldier with a feathered helmet said.

"I am not speaking to you right now," Áine snapped. "You will not speak unless I give you leave." To her astonishment, the soldier with the feathers looked ashamed. He dropped his gaze to the ground. So not all of her father's magnetism came from the pendant. Some of it came from *himself*. And she could do it too. She looked back out on the bandit horde, a new confidence welling up inside her. "You have lived a life of freedom, and of danger. You have sworn allegiance to no one except my father. But he is dead."

The bandits paled in horror. They shook their heads. A few dropped to their knees.

"He is dead," she said again. "And this mad quest that he set you on, this crazy scheme with the idiot armies of an idiot king, it ends now. My father, who put you in danger, is gone; you owe him nothing. You owe me nothing as well. Your debt to my father and the fealty you swore to him is released. I do not wish to see you again—not here, not in the forest. I have nothing for you."

She sharpened her voice on these last words, and brandished it like a blade. They had never been to her house in the woods without the guidance of her father. Could they find it on their own? Áine did not know. But they would not be welcome. And they would be turned away empty.

"Is it possible?" one bandit said.

"It is most possible. I held him in my arms as he expired. His blood now stains my tunic. I have lost him forever."

"And," the bandit persisted, her eyes narrowing, looking for lies, "there is truly nothing."

"Nothing." She said the word like a magic thing. A talisman. A word of power. "Nothing at all." She felt it rumble through her bones.

Áine looked at the soldier with the feathered helmet. He seemed in charge. A general, perhaps. "You," she said, and his face flattened into a grimace, "are the worst sort of coward. You bind unarmed men and women and march them as swords-fodder ahead of your own fat soldiers? Unacceptable!"

"Young lady, I—" he began, but she interrupted him.

"You march brazenly into a sovereign country, intending to kill its people and take it for your own? Mannerless!"

"Enough!" The feathered general reddened with growing indignation.

"You tramped through my wood. *My* wood! Go back to where you came from, you pathetic excuse for an army."

"Archers!" the general said, his voice a shrill whine, his face now purple with rage. He pointed at the girl on the giant. "Take aim." He did not notice that, in their agitated state, several bandits snapped their bonds. Several more hid knives in their mouths, knives in their boots, knives hidden in secret pockets on their belts. They had, apparently, been biding their time. They had no intention to face the arrow or the blade, but had every intention to slip weapons and gold and trinkets into their waiting pockets.

Their leader was dead. That time was *now*. The plan had changed. Ropes snapped, leather sliced, gags fell from ragged grins, and a hundred bandits bared their teeth. The soldiers did not notice until it was too late.

The archers took aim at Áine.

"Áine!" cried a voice coming from the ridge.

"Ned!" Áine cried in return.

"No!" cried the kind Stone, who shielded the girl with her great, granite hands.

The arrows flew. The bandits released the last of their company, and, with a cry, turned on the soldiers. And the fighting began.

50

ON

THE SUN BEGAN TO sink in the west.

No one noticed.

"They're starting without me," the young king cried. "Make them stop!"

"*You* make them stop," the eldest Stone said. And it leaned down to the ground and released the king. He scrambled and stumbled toward the battle site. Of *course* he wouldn't be harmed. He was the king! And they were ruining his game. "Stop!" he cried. "I order you to stop!"

He ran toward war.

Ned climbed down the Stone and ran to Áine.

"Stop shooting!" he cried. "Stop shooting!" The arrows pummeled the smallest Stone, but she kept Áine safe. Ned felt his heart swell like a blossom about to burst open. *She is safe,* he breathed. His friend. His only friend. And he needed to get to her.

The bandits and the soldiers scrapped and swore. Knives slashed, swords flashed, and men and women tumbled to the ground.

"Ned!" Áine called. From somewhere in the tumult, the wolf yapped and snarled and snapped. It circled a perimeter around the Stone.

"Wolf!" Ned called, and the wolf bounded to him, a tangle of fur and speed and joy.

Now, as it happened, Ned's village was in possession of a catapult. It was a rudimentary thing, this catapult, and had been Madame Thuane's idea. They only had the one, and since it took so long to load it, and since it was so very difficult to pull the mechanism back and lock it into place, it was unlikely that they could launch more than one boulder into the ranks of the army from over the mountain. And so they had to make it count.

And Madame Thuane was getting restless.

"Release the boulder," she cried, peering into the melee.

Ned's father was incredulous. "No," the woodsman said. "Have you gone mad? There's far too much chaos. We could injure one of our own."

"I am not accustomed to your insistence on consensus," Madame Thuane said. "I am the Head of the Council. If I say we should launch, we should launch. This *instant*."

"We might hit those giants," the woodsman said.

"I am *hoping* to hit a giant, you silly man," stated the councilwoman. "They could turn on us at any moment. Now launch the catapult!"

"I will do no such thing," the woodsman said.

Madame Thuane drew herself to her full height. She stood at eye level with the woodsman, and while she was not as broad as he, she was still a force all her own. She would have made, Ned's father suddenly realized, an excellent woodsman. She made her face as hard as oak. "Fine," she said. "I will do it myself."

"Stop!" the boy king cried, running toward the battle. "Stop, I say!" He seemed utterly innocent of the danger surrounding him. It was as though he did not know *how* to fear.

"Come back here, you idiot king!" Ned shouted as he saw Ott run onto the field. "Get out of there!" But Ott did not listen.

Instead, he found himself buffeted by fighting men and women. There were no pretty girls with sweets for his tongue. There were no graybeards bending their foreheads to the ground in deference. There were no fans or silks or wine or comfort. There was only blood and teeth and blade. Ott staggered and gaped.

He thought war would be fun.

"Stop!" he cried, before being thrown to his knees.

"Stop!" as the tip of a sword caught his leg, splitting it open. He screamed like a child.

"Stop!" as a boot made contact with the back of his skull.

The king curled into a ball and held his head in his hands. He heard the rushing of water and the tumbling of stones. He saw stars.

People actually see stars, he thought. *How strange!*

He noticed that one of the stars was moving while the others stayed still. It traveled in a clean arc through his field of vision. It moved closer and closer and closer. And as it moved, he could feel a terrible rumble in the ground beneath him.

I had no idea that being injured would be so interesting, he thought as the moving star looked less like a star and looked more like a boulder. A boulder flying through the air! But boulders didn't fly through the air, King Ott told himself. *Did they?*

The rumbling grew more violent and more tiresome. *I do wish that giant would stop moving about so much. I want to get a better look at that star-turned-boulder!*

But the eldest Stone had other plans.

The boulder flew from the catapult, and screamed toward the writhing mass of fighting humans on the ground—and in the midst of them, that sniveling idiot of an infant king.

The Stone strode toward it. It opened its mouth.

"NO," it said in a loud voice. And the voice made the trees bow and the land tremble. "NO," it cried, and the hills swelled

and rippled like waves and the Great River lurched in its bed. "IT
IS FINISHED."

The Stone reached out its hand and caught the boulder just
before it landed on the young King's head. It sighed, moved the
boulder away, and crushed it into a pile of dust on the ground.

"My goodness," the king said. "Did you just save me?"

The Stone was right. It *was* finished. Quiet reigned on the green
field. Ned climbed up the youngest Stone's arm toward Áine and
sat next to her. He slid his wounded hand into hers, barely noticing the pain. The skin of his palm touching the skin of her palm.
Without those infernal words on his skin there was nothing to
fear. Ned felt lightheaded, but it wasn't the magic doing it.

Áine stared at the burn marks left by the magic. She cupped
her hands around Ned's own and held it there—hardly touching, but protecting his hand from harm. It was a silly gesture,
really. The *rest* of him was wounded too. But it seemed to mean
something—though Áine had no idea what.

The stragglers from the queen's regiments finally made their
way down the hill, and the whole of Ned's village—even the children and the aged—all gathered on the grass.

The rest of the Stones strode near, and stood largest to smallest. The largest Stone, the one with a pale shadow still sitting on
his shoulder (it had curly hair and a merry grin, and the people
in Ned's village squinted and stared, trying to understand why

it looked so familiar), surveyed the wreckage and pain scattered across the field.

"Bring me carts," he ordered. And carts were brought—from the village, from the supply brigade. Ten of them, all in a line. The people stared, open-mouthed, at the implacable granite face, at those impossibly strong hands. The Stone looked out at the giant army on one side, and the makeshift army on the other. "Drop your weapons in the carts. You will not need them."

The people hesitated. In response, all nine Stones raised their giant feet and let them crash on the ground. The earth shuddered and waved like water in the wind.

Soon the carts were overflowing with swords and arrows and knives and bows. There were shields and cudgels and battleaxes and scythes. They piled them in great heaps and stacks, and the deadly edges glinted in the setting sun until none was left to give away. The Stones gathered round the carts. The Eldest began to sing—a deep, rumbly note. The others joined in harmony.

The earth under the carts bubbled and wobbled and swelled. It swirled like whirlpool, knocking the carts over and spilling the weapons onto the ground. And the swirling grew faster, and then faster. And, quite suddenly, carts, weapons and all were pulled in, submerged in the surging earth. They vanished from sight. The swirling stopped and the earth went still. The grass was smooth and unblemished.

The people gasped.

"This war," the eldest Stone said. "Has ended. It started long ago. Before any of you were born. You do not remember, but we do. The trees remember. Even the earth remembers. The people of this country and the people from over the mountains are kins-men, and should treat one another as such. The trees—once a weapon in this war—are weapons no longer. Look."

The Stone pointed at the wood. A seam of smooth granite erupted from the earth, stretching into the wood like a ribbon. The trees parted and spread, leaving a long, straight road.

"This road will never wander, never falter and never bend. It connects and binds your countries. The magic that corrupted kings and twisted the hearts of good men and women is bound to the dead, and will leave with the dead. You will not miss it."

"Oh, but we will," cried a woman from Ned's village. From his perch he could see her. He could also see his father. He could also see his mother, coming down the hillside at a run. "Sister Witch has used her magic to heal us and protect us. She uses it for good."

Magic? Or a practicality, Ned thought. So much of what his mother *called* her magic was not magic at all. He could count on both hands the number of times he had seen her use it; the rest was herbs and sleep and other remedies. And even when the magic left the world, she would still be Sister Witch. She would still know to see the world in its gaps and braces; she would still know the weak points; she would still know how to make the world *bend*. That much was clear.

"Where is Sister Witch?" the eldest Stone asked.

"Here," called his mother's voice. She ran faster and faster, her eyes on the pale shadow sitting on the shoulder of the Stone. When she arrived she was red-faced and damp, and out of breath.

"Lady," the eldest Stone said kindly.

Ned's mother bowed her head and covered her face with her hands. "It's true. I—" She cried out, her voice desperate and sad. "I ruined it. The magic. It was supposed to be good and I used it for my selfishness. Forgive me." A catch. A gulp. A rattling breath.

"There is nothing to forgive. The magic corrupts. It cannot help it. The fact that your kin managed to resist its corruption for so long is remarkable," the Stone said. "Grief clouds one's judgment. This is the natural way."

The Stone reached to his shoulder and let the soul climb onto his hands. He brought the boy gently to the ground in front of his mother. Tam lifted his face. His lower lip quivered and his eyes were wet with tears. He raised his arms. He was, after all, still a little boy. And he missed his mother.

"*My boy,*" Sister Witch said, gathering the soul into her arms. Cradling him as though he was still a baby.

"He is free, now."

"My child, my child, my little, little child." Her tears flowed down her cheeks, pattering the ground like rain.

"The sun is setting. He will be moving on."

"I'm sorry," she said. "I'm so, so sorry."

"Don't be sorry," Tam said. "Ned is alive. And now I am free. Everything is as it is, and that is that."

"Wife!" a voice from behind. "Is it him? Is that—" Ned's father came tearing through the crowd, sliding to his knees next to his wife. He held his hands out to the fragile soul. "It's you," he whispered. And Tam crawled into the space between his mother and father and hooked his arms around each of their necks and held his cheeks to their cheeks.

And they would keep holding on until they could no longer.

The eldest Stone called to the young king and the old queen. He called to Ned and Áine as well. They stood before the Stones, King Ott looking frightened, the queen looking fascinated, and Ned and Áine looking exhausted. The Stone addressed the crowd.

"The time of the Stones is ending. It should have ended long ago. We are old. We are tired. And your world is still new." The Stone pointed to King Ott. "This child is the last in a line of lack-luster kings. We were foolish to put his line on the throne." The Stone bent close to the young king. Even the Stone's whisper thrummed between the bedrock and the sky. "Young man, you are no longer king."

Ott sputtered. "But . . ." He gasped. "You can't . . ."

"Of course I can't. The sun is setting and I shall be leaving. I can do nothing. But these people—they who have followed you for no reason, they who have seen you humiliated—I suspect that they may not want you anymore."

The soldiers from beyond the mountains looked at one another. A soldier removed her helmet and threw the breastplate emblazoned with the image of the young king onto the ground.

"I do not follow you!" she called out.

Four more soldiers followed suit.

"Nor I!" they shouted.

Ten more dropped their armor.

Then twenty.

Then hundreds.

King Ott looked at the feathered helmets in the mud (he had designed them himself), his face yellow with shock.

"Don't worry," the Stone said. "Someone is sure to take you in. You can learn a trade. You're still just a child, after all." Ott sat on the ground. No one came to his aid.

The Stone turned to the queen. "As for you, Lady." The Queen bowed. "You've done your best, but your relatives, as you may have noticed, are a bunch of bumbling fools."

"And," the queen raised one finger, "poisoners. Who knew?" She shook her head sadly. "One cannot, alas, choose one's relatives. More's the pity." Her voice was weak. Her face was pale. Her hands shook. The Stone tilted his great head.

"And—I believe this is obvious to you as well—your days, my dear, are limited."

The queen smiled. "Everyone's days are limited. But yes. Mine are . . . *more so.*"

"There are other ways to run a country. Call a council. Do it while you are still alive. Make arrangements. Sister Witch will help you. She knows how to keep power in check. That's not a bad quality in an adviser."

The Stone turned to Áine and Ned. He brought his huge hand to the ground and bade them climb on it. They scrambled onto his palm and he lifted them high.

"These children," he bellowed. "THESE CHILDREN released us when none could do so. They have stopped a terrible tragedy from being committed. And THESE CHILDREN walked through darkness where no light was possible. They faced danger when they thought there was no hope. They persevered when all was lost. They faced pain and loneliness and loss." He paused. "You might say thank you." He gave the crowd a hard look, shook his head, and set them down. The sky glowed pink and orange and gold. Only the tip of the sun still gleamed over the lip of the land.

"*I* thank you," the Stone said, bowing low.

"And *I* thank you," said the youngest Stone.

"And *I* thank you," the rest of the Stones said together.

Ned grabbed Áine's hand. Áine squeezed back. They stood, red-faced and silent. The sun sank deeper.

The eldest Stone stood and looked to the west. "It's time," he said. "IT IS TIME!"

"It's time!" cried the other Stones.

"It's time," whispered Tam.

"Good-bye," Ned said to the Stones. "Good-bye, brother," he called to the soul.

The earth shook.

The sky shook.

A great wind knocked everyone to their knees.

And the Stones and the soul and the magic were gone.

51

ÁINE'S RETURN

ALL AT ONCE, under the yellow moon, the field became a chaos of movement—people and horses and handshaking and hugs and barking dogs. And in the crush of people, Áine stood alone. Ned hung onto her hand for a little while, but soon he was yanked away by the loving embrace of his parents, or Madame Thuane, or the scrivener, or any number of people who did not love him before, but now desperately did. Áine watched as songs were sung and bottles were passed from mouth to mouth, and as villager and soldier and bandit linked arms and hearts and raised their voices as one.

We'll see how long this lasts, Áine thought darkly.

Already, she could spot the faces of the bandits she recognized, saw their eyes slide toward the wood. How long, she wondered, would they wait before venturing back into the center of the forest? How long before they blindly blundered through the trees, trying to find her home? How long before they attempted to help themselves to the spoils of the Bandit King?

Not long, she decided.

It's not for you, she thought. *The spoils of banditry will not go to the bandits. They will go elsewhere.*

She looked over at the village. Someone had erected a temporary dais right in front of the ancient wall circling the town. The queen stood nearby surveying the scene. Someone had brought her a chair, but she waved it away. She didn't want to miss a minute of it.

The queen noticed Áine looking, and a smile unfurled in the creases of her face. She waved the girl over. Áine nodded.

Here, Áine decided. *The treasure will come here. Much of it, anyway.*

The wolf bowed its weight forward and yawned. It barked and bounded away, then returned, sliding next to Áine's leg and leaning against it. It looked at the retreating figure of Ned, now reunited with his family. The wolf whined a bit, but did not follow.

"I know," Áine said. "Let him be loved. He'll need us again, but not today. Today, he needs *them.* And today, I need *you.*" She rested her hand on the wolf's head. "Actually, I think I might need you every day. Come on."

She would return, of course she would. But first she needed to talk to the queen. And she would need a cart, and a good shovel. Because, despite the celebrations, she had practical considerations to think about. She still had a father to bury, a life to dismantle, and a fortune to distribute.

And Áine was a practical girl.

It was decided that Áine would travel with six soldiers, three carts, and a horse of her very own—a mare named Shadow. The soldiers, though leery of the wolf, became quickly accustomed to its bounding through the wood, its occasional howl. They grew to appreciate its nightly prowls around the camp. After all, they had grown up frightened of the forest. And fear is a difficult thing to unlearn.

When they arrived at the house by the waterfall, Áine could see instantly that it had not been disturbed. Everything, save the chickens, was exactly where she left it. The chickens, alas, were gone—eaten by hawk or lynx or weasel. It was difficult to say what. The goats had not returned, and Áine knew they never would. Not if she wasn't there. They were pragmatic, her good girls. They would stay in the mountains, join a herd, and live until they didn't. And that was that.

The soldiers helped her to bury her father on one of the knolls overlooking the house. His grave was unmarked, as was the custom in Áine's country, save for a circle of flowers marking the spot, until the wind took them away.

Áine showed the soldiers where the treasure was hidden in the hayloft. She didn't help them load, excusing herself instead and retreating into the house. She listened to their astonished gasps, to their grunts and sighs as they hauled bundle after bundle into the carts. They would be a while at it, as there was quite a bit of gold to carry.

Inside the house, she found a sack and some clothes, and other things that she would likely need. A compass, for example. A map of Duunin. An extra knife. Rope. A bundle of her father's treasure, hidden under the stones of the hearth. Her warmest cloak. It was early autumn, and the passage through the mountains would be cold, and likely snowy.

There was a trunk under her father's bed filled with things that had belonged to her mother—meant for Áine when she was old enough. Dresses. Oilcloths. Boots. Sea charts. Her mother's journals. A locket with two tiny portraits inside—her mother's face and her father's face, both terribly young and desperately in love. And letters—from her mother's mother, her mother's sister, and others in a family whom Áine had never met. But she would. They lived in Kaarna, another town by the sea. Áine found it on the map and carefully marked the trail to get there.

Family. The word only made her think of Ned. And the wolf. But Ned had a family of his own. She had a family removed from her life. And she had questions.

Once she had organized what she wanted to take with her and packed it neatly into a rucksack and two saddlebags, she came out of the house, just as the soldiers were tying down the bundles and securing the carts.

"We have finished," the captain said. "Is there anything else before we leave?"

"No," she said. "There is nothing." She looked at the house, her heart as heavy as any stone. "Except. If you happen to have a tinderbox handy, it might be wise to light a fire. I think we should burn the home of the Bandit King."

Later, after the soldiers had gone, and her house and barn were nothing more than a smoldering ruin, Áine stood with the wolf and the mare and listened to the silence of the wood. If the bandits came, they would assume the loot had been looted. Which it had. Mostly. She had her bundle of jewels—each one fat and shining and precious. A single jewel could feed a family. Or change a life. A single jewel could buy a lot of things.

There were, by her count, six more bundles, buried in the forest. She could find them if she needed them. Or she could leave them to the forest forever. She hadn't decided yet.

She crouched next to the wolf and peered into the green. "Well, my friend," she said. "I think that we should be off." The wolf whined as the girl stood. "Have you ever wanted to go to sea?"

52

THE SEA! THE SEA!

N EDDY, WAKE UP, SLEEPYHEAD. The day is young and new, and our list of tasks is terribly long."

Ned opened his eyes. His father sat on the bed, his hand on Ned's shoulder, shaking it gently.

"It's not even light," Ned complained.

"It will be light soon enough. And if we're not working already, we will miss valuable minutes. The work is not going to do itself, after all."

Ned's father cupped the boy's magic-scarred cheeks and gave each one a tender pat before hoisting himself toward the hearth to make breakfast.

He'd been like that ever since he saw Tam's soul. Ever since he was able to say good-bye. Ned's father looked at him, saw him, and even loved him. Ned was astonished.

Forgiveness, Ned's mother told him, is a remarkable thing,

especially when a man forgives himself. She said that his father's grief and shame and regret had killed part of his heart, and that, in seeing the soul, touching the soul, letting the soul pass on, his heart was reborn. And it was new, and fragile and *alive*.

"Forgiveness," she told him, "is the most powerful force in the world. Much more powerful than magic." And maybe that was true. Ned wouldn't know.

Because in the confusion after the departure of the Stones, and in the celebration and the new friendships and the feasts commemorating a lasting peace, and in the organization of councils and trade federations and emissaries and Matters of State . . .

Áine was gone.

Gone.

Ned couldn't find her anywhere. She had simply vanished. Later, he learned that she had returned to her home in the forest to bury her father, and something about paying restitution to the queen. (*And why did she leave without saying good-bye?*) There was a rumor that the house had burned and the treasure was gone, and that Áine was nowhere to be found. Ned waited and waited, but she didn't come back. And it had been months. Nearly a year.

Why hadn't he held onto her? Why did he let her go away? Why didn't he pull her into the weight of his family, hold her in place, give her somewhere to belong? Ned couldn't forgive himself.

"Eat," Ned's father ordered.

So Ned ate. They walked outside, the sky giving way from darkness to a thin, fragile light. The woodsman rested his hand on Ned's shoulder and kept it there, reluctant to let go.

Ned's mother was in the Capital, assisting the queen—still yet alive, but fading a bit more each day—in the formation of a new government. "Whatever it is," the queen said, "it will be new. That's not always a good thing, but we will do our best to make sure it's not a bad thing, either."

In the meantime, several engineers and architects from the other side of the mountains had brought new ways of doing things to Ned's village to assist in rebuilding the homes that had been taken apart to defend the town. And while they were at it, they built new buildings and shops along the road through the forest for the burgeoning trade between the two nations.

Indeed, Ned could hardly recognize his village anymore. And while everyone was now the greatest of friends—they said so all the time—Ned couldn't get used to the outsiders. They spoke strangely and had odd mannerisms and unexpected turns of phrase. And, what's worse, they reminded him of Áine. And it made his heart break a little more each day.

Where was she? Where had she gone?

The wolf was gone too, and while it made Ned feel better believing that they would watch out for each other, he didn't know for sure. And the thought of them having an adventure without him made him feel terribly lonely and terribly bereft. His first friends, after Tam died. His best friends. Gone now. Leaving him behind.

Ned and his father hitched their two mules to the cart, loaded the cart with tools and provisions, and headed into the wood. It was quiet ever since the Stones left. It had no more magic in it. It was no longer a weapon.

And now, Ned loved the wood.

At night, he would dream of the wood and of the craggy mountains and of the sky that curved around the bend of the world and came around to the other side. He dreamed of a stone cottage in the wood that had somehow transformed into a boat and was heading down the Great River to the sea. And he would wake just as someone called his name.

During the day, he tried not to think of his dreams. Instead, he threw himself into his work.

There were nine of them working that day. Three boys Ned's age and six grown men. In the months since the disappearance of the Stones, Ned had learned how to handle an axe and a saw. He learned how to shimmy up a trunk, to remove branch after branch until it was a straight, tall pole. He learned to bring timber down, and roll it onto straps so it could be hoisted onto a cart.

These activities, of course, would be easier with magic. But they wouldn't be nearly so satisfying. Every day he was a little bit stronger. It felt good to be strong.

By noon, Ned and the other woodsmen had downed twelve trees and hauled them into the road. The branches were stripped and stacked and bound. Soon, the carters would be by, and together they would all load up both timbers and bundles, but for now, they leaned against the trees and ate and dozed.

In the months after losing his brother, Ned had grown a

palm's-length taller and had become so strong in his shoulders and arms that he had grown out of three different sets of clothes. The things that used to be so hard for him—the water bucket, the pig slop, the steady hand required for building—all came to him easily now. It was as though his body had been waiting to grow. His stutter was gone; he could read without the letters scrambling and seeming to fly away. He even smiled sometimes.

He closed his eyes and let himself drift against the tree.

In his dream, he saw the wolf. It was bigger too—almost full grown. And it sprang from rock to log to rock again. It leaped over streams and gullies. It was a wonder of speed and agility. In his dream a sharp, high whistle sounded through the trees. The wolf stopped, pricking up its ears. The whistle blew again. The wolf whined.

"I'm right over here, you silly animal," Áine laughed, and bounded through the dream toward the wolf. The wolf gave a yelp of joy and tore toward the girl, circling around her feet and knocking its flanks against her leg. "I told you I wouldn't go far."

In his dream, Áine had grown too. She wore a woman's dress that was a bit too large for her, cinched at the waist to make it fit, and a pair of soft boots and a knife in a sheath slung across her hips. She had a pack on her back, with her coat tied to the outside and a water skin hanging off the side.

Her eyes were dark, wide-spaced, and laughing. They shone like stars.

Ned woke to the sound of a wolf's sad, low cry.

I'm still dreaming, Ned told himself as he rose, drank his water, and returned to work. The carts came and several more trees were felled, and the whole lot was strapped onto the mule teams and pulled down the road.

Again, a wolf howled.

I'm still dreaming, Ned told himself as he bathed himself at the spigot from their rainwater cistern and put on clean clothes for supper. A stew was already bubbling on the stove. Fresh bread waited on the table. He had no idea who made it—no one was home all day. Still the villagers made sure that they were fed each day and kept flush with the best cheeses and the best cakes and the finest meat pies. No one took credit and Ned never asked. The Wrong Boy lived; the Wrong Boy saved them. There are some words you can't take back. And some things that must be atoned for. And that was that.

After supper that evening, Ned's father went out to meet with the Village Council and Ned gathered the dishes into a basin to be washed outside. Somewhere in the darkness, a wolf howled—a close, warm sound. A sound like family.

I'm still dreaming, Ned told himself, a sharp knot forming in his throat. He went out into the yard to the well.

Áine sat on the stone edge, waiting. She had a map unfolded over her lap, and she studied it intently.

Ned dropped the water bucket. He didn't blink his eyes, he didn't move, for fear of her disappearing, but instead stood as still as a stone in the yard.

Áine pressed her lips tightly together, a tiny hint of a grin just starting to curl at the corners, but didn't look up. Instead she whistled, high and sharp. A wolf howled—quite near—and came running around the side of the house, nearly knocking Ned to the ground.

Ned still couldn't speak. He didn't trust his voice.

"Are you going to stand there gaping," Áine said, "or are you going to show some hospitality to a couple of travelers?" She looked up at Ned and smiled broadly, her black eyes crinkling at the edges, the rims slicked with tears.

After several minutes of embraces and laughter and rolling around with the wolf and another embrace, they were sitting at Ned's table, a bowl of stew in front of Áine, a hunk of meat for the wolf, and two steaming cups of a special tea that Ned's mother always made for travelers—one for Áine and one for Ned.

He stared at her face. He couldn't believe it.

"Why did you leave?" Ned asked at last.

Áine reached into her pack and pulled out a leather purse. She threw it on the table. It was filled with coins and some jewels—more wealth than Ned had ever seen.

"That's for your family," Áine said. She held up her hands to Ned's protestations. "It's a restitution. My family to yours. Please don't argue. Your parents will need it."

He left the purse on the table without touching it. "You didn't answer the question," Ned said.

"I had to go back. To my father's house. It would take a while for the other bandits to find their way back without him, but I knew that they would eventually. There was enough gold in our barn to fund a fleet of ships. More, even. To fund a small nation.

I sent it with my regards to the queen. I figured your country would need it. Her soldiers were . . . well, they didn't know how much it would be."

She paused a moment, her face dark.

"And what about the bandits?" Ned asked.

She shrugged. "They're gone. Wandering. I burned the house. Burned the barn. If they ever find the house they will find nothing. Still, they're at large, you know? They aren't *safe*. They're still *bandits*."

Ned nodded. A horde of hungry, angry, and bloodthirsty men and women set loose in the world. With no leader. And, what's more, they had been promised riches and power, and now had nothing. *That can't be good.*

Áine's face went utterly blank and she was quiet for a long time, Ned along with her. He didn't say what he wanted to say. *Almost a year, Áine. You've been gone almost a year. Where have you been?* Instead, he listened to the wind, to the shaking of the branches outside, and the crackling of the fire in the hearth, and the slow, gentle breathing of the wolf at rest. They were good sounds, and Ned felt happier than he had in a long time.

Finally, after the stew was gone and her bowl sopped clean, she looked up, her eyes suddenly bright. "Ned. I have something to show you," she said. "Come outside to the river."

"But it's dark already," Ned protested.

"Don't be such a fuss. The moon is shining. Come!"

She reached over and grabbed Ned's hand, her fingertips grazing against the scars from the magic as they curled into the curve of his palm. Almost a year since he last held her hand. The sensation of it—the realness of her, the trueness of himself—shot through his whole being.

My friends, he thought. *My friends returned to me. It is the best kind of magic.*

He felt as though the top of his head and the core of the earth were connected on a single, taut line. He was a pillar holding up the world. A plucked harp string sounding a long, pure note. It was . . . *wonderful.*

She pulled him out the door, the wolf stalking silently behind. The moon was full and brilliant, dimming the stars. The crickets sang vigorously in the high grasses, and the frogs filled the low, wet ponds with their desperate, lovelorn pleading. Áine had a nimble, quick stride, surefooted in the dark, and Ned had to stumble to keep up.

"My mother was a fisherman, Ned," Áine said. "Did I ever tell you that?"

"No," Ned said. "You didn't."

"I was too, before she died. And I was good at it. I could manage a craft and take a bearing and find the hidden currents and tackle a monster fish. Even when I was little. And I missed it. Sometimes, in the forest, I thought I could hear the sea. I couldn't, of course. It was just trees and trees and trees." She tilted her face to the sky. "So, I went back, Ned. After I buried my father. I went to Duunin, to the sea. I had some things to do. That's why I was away so long."

Ned nodded. "I wanted to go to the sea once. My brother and I. But then he died."

367

She closed her eyes and nodded. They understood one another—this loss, this grief, this moving on.

"People die, Ned," she said. "It happens. But *we're* alive. It's good to be alive."

They walked along the shore of the Great River, their footsteps clattering on the red and green rocks.

In his mind's eye, Ned could see the raft he had once made with his brother. This was the spot, he thought, were his father had pulled him to shore. This was the bend where his brother had washed away. And all they had wanted was to see the ocean. (*The sea!* They had said to one another. *The sea!* Their eyes bright and hopeful and terribly alive.) His brother's last day. Ned felt the memory wind around his heart—both lovely and sad—and pull in tight. Even without his brother's soul stitched to his own, he still carried Tam with him wherever he went. Tam's jokes. Tam's curiosity. Tam's mad schemes. Ned loved his brother. He missed his brother.

On the other side of the bend was a newly built dock, its construction and finance an act of friendship by the Nation of Duunin (which, Ned learned, was accessible by sea, by way of the fingering delta through the swamp, and then a long, arduous journey, though the geography of it confused him, as it did for many people in his country).

Tied to the dock was a boat, about the size of two carriages put together. It rocked gently in the river's current. It had sails and oars and a polished rim, with the head of a wolf carved at the front.

"Oh!" Ned gasped. "It's beautiful."

"She certainly is. She has rigging and sails and maps and compasses and enough food and water for a five-month voyage," Áine said.

"How do you know this?" Ned asked.

"Because she's mine," Áine said. "Well, mostly mine."

A woman emerged from the hull of the ship. She was old, with a deeply creased face and hair as pale as starlight, which had been pulled away from her face and plaited into a heavy braid that swung down her back like a good, strong rope.

"Is this the boy?" she asked, her speech heavy with the sounds of Duunin.

"Yes, Grandmother. This is the one."

Ned stared at her. The woman's face was as strong as wood, but her eyes had that same hard glitter that Áine's had. She had large hands and muscular arms and an easy way of walking on the deck.

"Grandmother?" he said.

The old woman ignored this. "I am to bed, child, and so should you. We should leave before the sun rises tomorrow." With a nod to Ned, she ducked back into the hull and vanished from sight.

Ned turned to Áine, who tilted her eyes to the moonlit sky.

"I didn't give all of the treasure to the queen, Ned. I kept some. I found my mother's family. There was a rift, long ago, between my father and them. They didn't even know that my mother had died. Only that she stopped writing. And then I bought a boat. Isn't she lovely? This is the farthest inland she can go—and it's tricky at best. Grandmother is nervous about it. But she's nimble

369

enough to track the current, and strong enough to brave the sea. We leave tonight to go to the Capital, and then to carry two ambassadors from your country to Duunin. My country. And then, the nations beyond. There are more, and the queen wants to send her regards. I met your mother, and she knows I mean to take you with me. If you'll come. She's not . . ." Áine shrugged. "Well, she's not *happy* about it. But it is *your* decision. My grandmother is captain and I am navigator. And I want you to come, Ned. *Please.*"

"But . . ."

"We leave in the morning."

Ned stared at her. "Wait . . ."

"Wait for what?"

He could say nothing. His father loved him. His mother loved him. His home needed him. But maybe that wasn't enough. Maybe he needed something *else*. Purpose. Friendship. The wide world.

"Is it dangerous?"

"Probably."

"But why? Why do this, Áine? You could stay here. Live with my family. We could . . ." He had no words.

"I could, but . . ." she paused. "The sea, Ned," Áine whispered. "The sea."

Ned couldn't reply. He felt his heart start to pound and his eyes go bright.

"What would I do?"

"I need a good cook," Áine said.

"Really?" Ned said skeptically.

"Of course not. But you should come. Because the world is

wide and nimble and rich. And full of promise. And adventure. And tricks. And because you are my friend." She pressed her lips into a frown. "My *friend*, Ned." She looked away. "Besides. It won't be any fun without you."

The wolf tipped back its head and howled.

He didn't say yes. He didn't say anything. Instead, his face unwound a broad, bright smile.

"Will you teach me?" he said.

The next day, Ned's father went to wake his son.

But Ned wasn't there. The bed looked as though it had not even been slept in.

The big man felt his legs give way. He sat on the bed. "Ned?" he called out. "Neddy?" There was no answer.

He looked back on the bed, and noticed a folded piece of paper, held to the coverlet under a stone. "Father," it said on the side facing up. With trembling hands, the woodsman reached for the note, and opened it up.

"The sea!" the note said. "The sea!"

It was not signed, and said nothing of where he was going or when he would be back or why he must leave. Still, Ned's father knew all the same.

The sea meant *I love you.*

The sea meant *I will one day return.*

The sea meant *I must find the world and hold the world and live in the world. And I must love the world. And love it and love it and love it. As much as I love you.*

In his mind's eye he could see his son—the boy, the youth, the man—standing in the midst of limitless space. Water, wind, sky. The core of the earth. The slice of the mountains. The roof of the stars. The pulse and rhythm of the ocean's ceaseless waves.

Ned's father pressed the note to his heart. He closed his eyes. Tasted his own saltwater tears.

The sea!

Read on for a sneak peek
at Kelly Barnhill's Newbery Medal–winning novel,
The Girl Who Drank the Moon

1.
——

IN WHICH A STORY IS TOLD

Yes.

There is a witch in the woods. There has always been a witch.

Will you stop your fidgeting for once? My stars! I have never seen such a fidgety child.

No, sweetheart, I have not seen her. No one has. Not for ages. We've taken steps so that we will never see her.

Terrible steps.

Don't make me say it. You already know, anyway.

Oh, I don't know, darling. No one knows why she wants children. We don't know why she insists that it must always be the very youngest among us. It's not as though we could just ask her. She hasn't been seen. We make sure that she will not be seen.

Of course she exists. What a question! Look at the woods! So dangerous! Poisonous smoke and sinkholes and boiling geysers and terrible dangers every which way. **Do you think** it is so by accident? Rubbish! It was the Witch, and **if we don't** do as she says, what will become of us?

You really need me to explain it?

I'd rather not.

Oh, hush now, don't cry. It's **not as though** the Council of Elders is coming for you, now is it. You're **far too** old.

From our family?

Yes, dearest. Ever so long ago. **Before** you were born. He was a beautiful boy.

Now finish your supper and see to your chores. We'll all be up early tomorrow. The Day of Sacrifice **waits** for no one, and we must all be present to thank the child **who will save** us for one more year.

Your brother? How could I fight for him? If I had, the Witch would have killed us all and then **where** would we be? Sacrifice one or sacrifice all. That is the way of **the world**. We couldn't change it if we tried.

Enough questions. Off with you. **Fool** child.

2.

IN WHICH AN UNFORTUNATE WOMAN GOES QUITE MAD

GRAND ELDER GHERLAND TOOK his time that morning. The Day of Sacrifice only came once a year, after all, and he liked to look his best during the sober procession to the cursed house, and during the somber retreat. He encouraged the other Elders to do the same. It was important to give the populace a show.

He carefully dabbed rouge on his sagging cheeks and lined his eyes with thick streaks of kohl. He checked his teeth in the mirror, ensuring they were free of debris or goop. He loved that mirror. It was the only one in the Protectorate. Nothing gave Gherland more pleasure than the possession of a thing that was unique unto him. He liked being *special*.

The Grand Elder had ever so many possessions that were unique in the Protectorate. It was one of the perks of the job.

The Protectorate—called the Cattail Kingdom by some and the City of Sorrows by others—was sandwiched between a treacherous forest on one side and an enormous bog on the other. Most people in the Protectorate drew their livelihoods from the Bog. There was a future in bogwalking, mothers told their children. Not much of a future, you understand, but it was better than nothing. The Bog was full of Zirin shoots in the spring and Zirin flowers in the summer and Zirin bulbs in the fall—in addition to a wide array of medicinal and borderline magical plants that could be harvested, prepared, treated, and sold to the Traders from the other side of the forest, who in turn transported the fruits of the Bog to the Free Cities, far away. The forest itself was terribly dangerous, and navigable only by the Road.

And the Elders owned the Road.

Which is to say that Grand Elder Gherland owned the Road, and the other Elders had their cut. The Elders owned the Bog, too. And the orchards. And the houses. And the market squares. Even the garden plots.

This was why the families of the Protectorate made their shoes out of reeds. This was why, in lean times, they fed their children the thick, rich broth of the Bog, hoping that the Bog would make them strong.

This was why the Elders and their families grew big and strong and rosy-cheeked on beef and butter and beer.

The door knocked.

"Enter," Grand Elder Gherland mumbled as he adjusted the drape of his robe.

It was Antain. His nephew. An Elder-in-Training, but only because Gherland, in a moment of weakness, had promised the ridiculous boy's more ridiculous mother. But that was unkind. Antain was a nice enough young man, nearly thirteen. He was a hard worker and a quick study. He was good with numbers and clever with his hands and could build a comfortable bench for a tired Elder as quick as breathing. And, despite himself, Gherland had developed an inexplicable, and growing, fondness for the boy.

But.

Antain had big ideas. Grand notions. And *questions*. Gherland furrowed his brow. Antain was—how could he put it? *Overly keen.* If this kept up, he'd have to be dealt with, blood or no. The thought of it weighed upon Gherland's heart, like a stone.

"UNCLE GHERLAND!" Antain nearly bowled his uncle over with his insufferable enthusiasm.

"Calm yourself, boy!" the Elder snapped. "This is a solemn occasion!"

The boy calmed visibly, his eager, doglike face tilted toward the ground. Gherland resisted the urge to pat him gently on the head. "I have been sent," Antain continued in a mostly soft voice, "to tell you that the other Elders are ready. And all the populace waits along the route. Everyone is accounted for."

"Each one? There are no shirkers?"

"After last year, I doubt there ever will be again," Antain said with a shudder.

"Pity." Gherland checked his mirror again, touching up his rouge. He rather enjoyed teaching the occasional lesson to the citizens of the Protectorate. It clarified things. He tapped the sagging folds under his chin and frowned. "Well, Nephew," he said with an artful swish of his robes, one that had taken him over a decade to perfect. "Let us be off. That baby isn't going to sacrifice itself, after all." And he flowed into the street with Antain stumbling at his heels.

✦ ✦ ✦

Normally, the Day of Sacrifice came and went with all the pomp and gravity that it ought. The children were given over without protest. Their numb families mourned in silence, with pots of stew and nourishing foods heaped into their kitchens, while the comforting arms of neighbors circled around them to ease their bereavement.

Normally, no one broke the rules.

But not this time.

Grand Elder Gherland pressed his lips into a frown. He could hear the mother's howling before the procession turned onto the final street. The citizens began to shift uncomfortably where they stood.

When they arrived at the family's house, an astonishing sight met the Council of Elders. A man with a scratched-up face and a swollen lower lip and bloody bald spots across his skull where his hair had been torn out in clumps met them at the door. He tried to smile, but his tongue went instinctively to the gap where a tooth had just recently been. He sucked in his lips and attempted to bow instead.

"I am sorry, sirs," said the man—the father, presumably. "I don't know what has gotten into her. It's like she's gone mad."

From the rafters above them, a woman screeched and howled as the Elders entered the house. Her shiny black hair flew about her head like a nest of long, writhing snakes. She hissed and spat like a cornered animal. She clung to the ceiling beams with one arm and one leg, while holding a baby tightly against her breast with the other arm.

"GET OUT!" she screamed. "You *cannot* have her. I spit on your faces and curse your names. Leave my home at once, or I shall tear out your eyes and throw them to the crows!"

The Elders stared at her, openmouthed. They couldn't *believe* it. No one fought for a doomed child. It simply wasn't *done*.

(Antain alone began to cry. He did his best to hide it from the adults in the room.)

Gherland, thinking fast, affixed a kindly expression on his craggy face. He turned his palms toward the mother to show her that he meant no harm. He gritted his teeth behind his smile. All this kindness was nearly killing him.

"*We* are not taking her at all, my poor, misguided girl," Gherland said in his most patient voice. "The *Witch* is taking her. We are simply doing as we're told."

The mother made a guttural sound, deep in her chest, like an angry bear.

Gherland laid his hand on the shoulder of the perplexed husband and gave a gentle squeeze. "It appears, my good fellow, that you are right: your wife *has* gone mad." He did his best to cover his rage with a façade of concern. "A rare case, of course, but not without precedent. We must respond with compassion. She needs care, not blame."

"LIAR," the woman spat. The child began to cry, and the woman climbed even higher, putting each foot on parallel rafters and bracing her back against the slope of the roof, trying to position herself in such a way that she could remain out of reach while she nursed the baby. The child calmed instantly. "If you take her," she said with a growl, "I will find her. I will find her and take her back. You see if I won't."

"And face the Witch?" Gherland laughed. "All on your own? Oh, you pathetic, lost soul." His voice was honey, but his face was a glowing ember. "Grief has made you lose your senses. The shock has shattered your poor mind. No matter. We shall heal you, dear, as best we can. Guards!"

He snapped his fingers, and armed guards poured into the room. They were a special unit, provided as always by the Sisters of the Star. They wore bows and arrows slung across their backs and short, sharp swords sheathed at their belts. Their long braided hair looped around their waists, where it was cinched tight—a testament to their years of contemplation and combat training at the top of the Tower. Their faces were implacable as stones, and the Elders, despite their power and stature, edged away from them. The Sisters were a frightening force. Not to be trifled with.

"Remove the child from the lunatic's clutches and escort the poor dear to the Tower," Gherland ordered. He glared at the mother in the rafters, who had gone suddenly very pale. "The Sisters of the Star know what to do with broken minds, my dear. I'm sure it hardly hurts at all."

The Guard was efficient, calm, and utterly ruthless. The mother didn't stand a chance. Within moments, she was bound, hobbled, and carried away. Her howls echoed through the silent town, ending suddenly when the Tower's great wooden doors slammed shut, locking her inside.

The baby, on the other hand, once transferred into the arms of the Grand Elder, whimpered briefly and then turned her attention to the sagging face in front of her, all wobbles and creases and folds. She had a solemn look to her—calm, skeptical, and intense, making it difficult for Gherland to look away. She had black curls and black eyes. Luminous skin, like polished amber. In the center of her forehead, she had a birthmark in the shape of a crescent moon. The mother had a similar mark. Common lore insisted that such people were special. Gherland disliked lore, as a general rule, and he certainly disliked it when citizens of the Protectorate got it in their heads to think themselves better than they were. He deepened his frown and leaned in close, wrinkling his brow. The baby stuck out her tongue.

Horrible child, Gherland thought.

"Gentlemen," he said with all the ceremony he could muster, "it is time." The baby chose this particular moment to let loose a large, warm, wet stain across the front of Gherland's robes. He pretended not to notice, but inwardly he fumed.

She had done it on purpose. He was sure of it. What a revolting baby.

The procession was, as usual, somber, slow, and insufferably plodding. Gherland felt he might go mad with impatience. Once the Protectorate's gates closed behind them, though, and the citizens returned with their melancholy broods of children to their drab little homes, the Elders quickened their pace.

"But why are we running, Uncle?" Antain asked.

"Hush, boy!" Gherland hissed. "And keep up!"

No one liked being in the forest, away from the Road. Not even the Elders. Not even Gherland. The area just outside the Protectorate walls was safe enough. In theory. But everyone knew someone who had accidentally wandered too far. And fell into a sinkhole. Or stepped in a mud pot, boiling off most of their skin. Or wandered into a swale where the air was bad, and never returned. The forest was dangerous.

They followed a winding trail to the small hollow surrounded by five ancient trees, known as the Witch's Handmaidens. Or six. *Didn't it used to be five?* Gherland glared at the trees, counted them again, and shook his head. There were six. No matter. The forest was just getting to him. Those trees were almost as old as the world, after all.

The space inside of the ring of trees was mossy and soft, and the Elders laid the child upon it, doing their best not to look at her. They had turned their backs on the baby and started to hurry away when their youngest member cleared his throat.

"So. We just leave her here?" Antain asked. "That's how it's done?"

"Yes, Nephew," Gherland said. "That is how it's done." He felt a sudden wave of fatigue settling on his shoulders like an ox's yoke. He felt his spine start to sag.

Antain pinched his neck — a nervous habit that he couldn't break. "Shouldn't we wait for the Witch to arrive?"

The other Elders fell into an uncomfortable silence.

"Come again?" Elder Raspin, the most decrepit of the Elders, asked.

"Well, surely . . ." Antain's voice trailed off. "Surely we must wait for the Witch," he said quietly. "What would become of us if wild animals came first and carried her off?"

The other Elders stared at the Grand Elder, their lips tight.

"Fortunately, Nephew," he said quickly, leading the boy away, "that has never been a problem."

"But—" Antain said, pinching his neck again, so hard he left a mark.

"But nothing," Gherland said, a firm hand on the boy's back, striding quickly down the well-trodden path.

And, one by one, the Elders filed out, leaving the baby behind.

They left knowing—all but Antain—that it was not a matter of *if* the child were eaten by animals, but rather that she surely *would be*.

They left her knowing that there surely *wasn't* a witch. There never *had* been a witch. There were only a dangerous forest and a single road and a thin grip on a life that the Elders had enjoyed for generations. The Witch—that is, the belief in her—made for a frightened people, a subdued people, a compliant people, who lived their lives in a saddened haze, the clouds of their grief numbing their senses and dampening their minds. It was terribly convenient for the Elders' unencumbered rule. Unpleasant, too, of course, but that couldn't be helped.

They heard the child whimper as they tramped through the trees, but the whimpering soon gave way to the swamp sighs and birdsong and the woody creaking of trees throughout the forest. And each Elder felt as sure as sure could be that the child wouldn't live to see the morning, and that they would never hear her, never see her, never think of her again.

They thought she was gone forever.

They were wrong, of course.

3.

———

In Which a Witch Accidentally Enmagics an Infant

AT THE CENTER OF the forest was a small swamp—bubbly, sulfury, and noxious, fed and warmed by an underground, restlessly sleeping volcano and covered with a slick of slime whose color ranged from poison green to lightning blue to blood red, depending on the time of year. On this day—so close to the Day of Sacrifice in the Protectorate, or Star Child Day everywhere else—the green was just beginning to inch its way toward blue.

At the edge of the swamp, standing right on the fringe of flowering reeds growing out of the muck, a very old woman leaned on a gnarled staff. She was short and squat and a bit bulbous about the belly. Her crinkly gray hair had been pulled back into a thick, braided knot, with leaves and flowers growing out of the thin gaps between the twisted plaits. Her face, despite its cloud of annoyance, maintained a brightness in those aged eyes and a hint of a smile in that flat, wide mouth. From certain angles, she looked a bit like a large, good-tempered toad.

Her name was Xan. And she was the Witch.

"Do you think you can hide from me, you ridiculous monster?" she bellowed at the swamp. "It isn't as though I don't know where you are. Resurface *this minute* and apologize." She pressed her expression into something closely resembling a scowl. *"Or I will make you."* Though she had no real power over the monster himself — he was far too old — she certainly had the power to make that swamp cough him up as if he were nothing more than a glob of phlegm in the back of the throat. She could do it with just a flick of her left hand and a jiggle of her right knee.

She attempted to scowl again.

"I MEAN IT," she hollered.

The thick water bubbled and swirled, and the large head of the swamp monster slurped out of the bluish-green. He blinked one wide eye, and then the other, before rolling both toward the sky.

"Don't you roll your eyes at me, young man," the old woman huffed.

"Witch," the monster murmured, his mouth still half-submerged in the thick waters of the swamp. "I am many centuries older than you." His wide lips blew a bubble in the algae slick. *Millennia, really,* he thought. *But who's counting?*

"I don't believe I like your tone." Xan puckered her wrinkled lips into a tight rosette in the middle of her face.

The monster cleared his throat. "As the Poet famously said, dear lady: '*I don't give a rat's* — ' "

"GLERK!" the Witch shouted, aghast. "Language!"

"Apologies," Glerk said mildly, though he really didn't mean it. He eased both sets of arms onto the muck at the shore, pressing each seven-fingered hand into the shine of the mud. With a grunt, he heaved himself onto the grass. *This used to be easier,* he thought. Though, for the life of him, he couldn't remember when.

"Fyrian is over there by the vents, crying his eyes out, poor thing," Xan fumed. Glerk sighed deeply. Xan thrust her staff onto the ground, sending a spray of sparks from the tip, surprising them both. She glared at the swamp monster. "And you are just *being mean*." She shook her head. "He's only a baby, after all."

"My dear Xan," Glerk said, feeling a rumble deep in his chest, which he hoped sounded imposing and dramatic, and not like someone who was simply coming down with a cold. "He is *also* older than you are. And it is high time—"

"Oh, you know what I mean. And anyway, I promised his mother."

"For five hundred years, give or take a decade or two, that dragonling has persisted in these delusions—fed and perpetuated by you, my dear. How is this helping him? He is not a Simply Enormous Dragon. At this point, there is no indication that he ever will be. There is no shame at all in being a Perfectly Tiny Dragon. Size isn't everything, you know. His is an ancient and honorable species, filled with some of the greatest thinkers of the Seven Ages. He has much to be proud of."

"His mother was very clear—" Xan began, but the monster interrupted her.

"In any case, the time is long past that he know his heritage and his place in the world. I've gone along with this fiction for far longer than I should have. But now . . ." Glerk pressed his four arms to the ground and eased his massive bottom under the curve of his spine, letting his heavy tail curl around the whole of him like a great, glistening snail's shell. He let the paunch of his belly sag over his folded legs. "I don't know, my dear. Something has shifted." A cloud passed over his damp face, but Xan shook her head.

"Here we go again," she scoffed.

"As the Poet says, '*Oh ever changéd Earth—*'"

"Hang the Poet. Go apologize. Do it right now. He looks up to you."

Xan glanced at the sky. "I must fly, my dear. I'm already late. *Please*. I am counting on you."

Glerk lumbered toward the Witch, who laid her hand on his great cheek. Though he was able to walk upright, he often preferred to move on all sixes—or all sevens, with the use of his tail as an occasional limb, or all fives, if he happened to be using one of his hands to pluck a particularly fragrant flower and bring it to his nose, or to collect rocks, or to play a haunting tune on a hand-carved flute. He pressed his massive forehead to Xan's tiny brow.

"Please be careful," he said, his voice thick. "I have been beset of late by troubling dreams. I worry about you when you are gone." Xan raised her eyebrows, and Glerk leaned his face away with a low grumble. "Fine," he said. "I will perpetuate the fiction for our friend Fyrian. *'The path to Truth is in the dreaming heart,'* the Poet tells us."

"That's the spirit!" Xan said. She clucked her tongue and blew the monster a kiss. And she vaulted up and forward on her staff's fulcrum, sprinting away into the green.

Despite the odd beliefs of the people of the Protectorate, the forest was not cursed at all, nor was it magical in any way. But it was dangerous. The volcano beneath the forest—low-sloped and impossibly wide—was a tricky thing. It grumbled as it slept, while heating geysers till they burst and restlessly worrying at fissures until they grew so deep that no one could find the bottom. It boiled streams and cooked mud and sent waterfalls disappearing into deep pits, only to reappear miles away. There were vents that spewed foul odors and vents that spewed ash and vents that seemed to spew nothing at all—until a person's lips and fingernails turned blue from bad air, and the whole world started to spin.

The only truly safe passage across the forest for an ordinary person was the Road, which was situated on a naturally raised seam of rock that had smoothed over time. The Road didn't alter or shift; it never grumbled. Unfortunately, **it was** owned and operated by a gang of thugs and bullies from the **Protectorate**. Xan never took the Road. She couldn't abide thugs. Or **bullies**. And anyway, they charged too much. Or they did, last time she **checked**. It had been years since she had gone near it—many centuries **now. She** made her own way instead, using a combination of magic and **know-how** and common sense.

Her treks across the **forest** weren't easy by any means. But they were necessary. A child **was waiting** for her, just outside the Protectorate. A child whose very life **depended** on her arrival—and she needed to get there in time.

Kelly Barnhill lives in Minnesota with her husband and three children. She is the author of four novels, most recently *The Girl Who Drank the Moon*, winner of the Newbery Medal. *The Witch's Boy* received four starred reviews and was a finalist for the Minnesota Book Awards. Kelly Barnhill has been awarded writing fellowships from the Jerome Foundation, the Minnesota State Arts Board, and the McKnight Foundation. Visit her online at kellybarnhill.wordpress.com or on Twitter: @kellybarnhill.